Robert m
high s of
newspapei and radio jobs. He took a career break from
journalism to complete a degree in politics and philosophy,
then spent more than twenty years in London working for
Independent Radio News, ITN and the BBC. Robert and
his wife and young sons now live in Melbourne.

Tropic of Death is Robert's second novel; his first, *The
Shadow Maker*, was published in 2007.

TROPIC OF DEATH

ROBERT SIMS

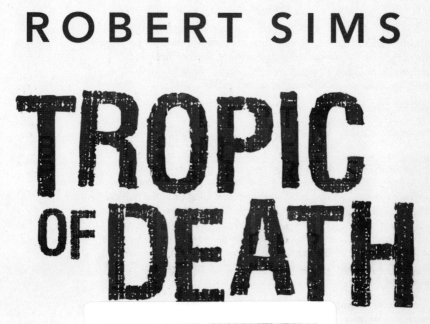

TROPIC OF DEATH

ARENA
ALLEN&UNWIN

First published in 2009

Arena Books, an imprint of
Allen & Unwin
83 Alexander Street
Crows Nest NSW 2065
Australia
Phone: (61 2) 8425 0100
Fax: (61 2) 9906 2218
Email: info@allenandunwin.com
Web: www.allenandunwin.com

Cataloguing-in-Publication details are available
from the National Library of Australia
www.librariesaustralia.nla.gov.au

ISBN 978 1 74175 671 5

Set in 12/15 pt Adobe Garamond Pro by Bookhouse, Sydney
Printed and bound in Australia by Griffin Press

10 9 8 7 6 5 4 3 2 1

'And this also . . . has been one of the dark places of the earth.'

Joseph Conrad

1

The little girl stood back and admired her sandcastle. It sat there, a shapeless blob, on the wide wet flank of the estuary. Seagulls were wheeling and cawing overhead. A breeze ruffled the waves in the distance. The sludge from drains traced the rim of a sandbank a few yards away from her. Over on the far shore, the concrete bulk of grain silos loomed against the sky and dirty-looking smoke drifted from factory chimneys.

The day had an unsettled mood, something shrill in the air and, among the parrots fighting over fast-food scraps, a hint of tainted innocence. But the child didn't sense it, not even in the distant boom of artillery rumbling over the mudflats from the testing range beyond. She'd made her mark and her soul was content. She bent down and topped her castle with a flag made from a piece of tissue. It fluttered in defiance of the tide that would sweep her small work of art into oblivion.

Her mother sat on a promenade seat. She smoked and stared with empty eyes into the middle distance where a tourist launch headed out towards the Great Barrier Reef. Its wake rippled among the mangrove thickets of a nearby inlet. The girl waved but the mother didn't notice, so she drifted off to look for shells. She passed a bait digger who stooped beside his pail, slopping mud with his spade. He watched her darkly. She said hello, but he just nodded in response. She wandered over to a clump of seaweed and squatted and tugged at a slimy strand. It dislodged something strange in the mud. She gazed in fascination. Then she went back to the bait digger. He paused and looked at her with irritation, and she smiled at him.

'There's a man in the mud,' she said.

He didn't say anything, just stared at her through cold eyes.

'There is,' she insisted. 'A man in the mud. Come and see.'

He leant on his spade and watched her plod back to the seaweed and point at something.

'Come and see.'

He sighed and jabbed in his spade so it stood upright, and then he squelched across to her. She was pointing triumphantly.

'See! I told you!'

At first he just saw a muddy lump and a crab scuttling away. Then he saw the shape of the severed head. The skin was death-white. Parts of the face had been eaten away. The little girl was still pointing excitedly as the bait digger began to vomit. She looked at him with disappointment.

2

'Still with us, Van Hassel?'

The greeting, from DSS Wayne Strickland, was meant to be ironic. It drew an indulgent smile from Detective Sergeant Marita Van Hassel as she brushed past him into the squad room.

'Till I get my ticket of leave,' she replied.

'Ticket to ride is more like it,' said Strickland. 'And an easy ride at that.'

'Does that mean you want to keep me in the squad?'

'Huh.' Strickland smoothed back his thinning hair. 'Do I look like I'm in your fan club?'

The banter contained the usual mock hostility but Rita knew it reflected something deeper. It wasn't so much dislike as a clash of styles. While Strickland was her immediate boss, he was also her opposite in a number of ways. Like many of her male colleagues he was old school – uncompromising, pragmatic and committed to traditional methods of policing. An astute detective, he was also hard-faced and middle-aged, a man suspicious of innovations such as behavioural analysis and psychological profiles. Rita specialised in these areas after doing the necessary fieldwork and academic study. In Strickland's eyes that made her an intellectual, as well as a perfect example of the feminising trend within the Victoria Police. When she'd been selected to become a profiler he'd called her overindulged and over-promoted – a fair-haired favourite of reformers who were bent on re-marketing the force.

The barb had been prompted by her photo in *Police Life* magazine. Rita liked the shot. It captured something of how she saw herself – a woman with an independent mind, a trim figure and the ability to succeed. There she stood between the pillars of Melbourne's police headquarters, arms folded, head turned sideways to the camera, staring directly into the lens. The pose, in a white linen blazer and trousers, was almost symbolic. With her gaze of concentration and short blonde hair blown back, it showed off her best features – the blue of her eyes, the curve of her cheekbones, the serious expression of her mouth. Her friends told her it was the portrait of an alpha female, but Strickland dismissed it as image manipulation. He said it made her look like a warrior in a pantsuit – part detective, part Visigothic princess. The comment had made her laugh. There was an element of truth in it, not least because of her northern European ancestry.

That had been the low point in their working relationship. Since then he'd mellowed. He also conceded she got results. That's because she was diligent and assertive, much like Strickland himself. But unlike him, her ambitions were far from realised. At thirty years old, she was convinced her finest achievements lay ahead of her.

'One thing I'll admit,' said Strickland. 'Things won't be the same without you.' He laid on a gritty smile. 'I've actually got used to you being a pain in the arse.'

Despite her breezy manner, Rita was losing patience with the delay over her future role. In the past month she'd officially completed her profiling course, processed a backlog of case files and generally cleared the decks ahead of her next appointment. But the senior commanders at police headquarters were yet to decide where to assign her. They were having trouble finding an appropriate slot for a fully qualified criminal profiler, something of a rare and exotic breed among rank and file officers. Until they made up their minds she remained in limbo, a semi-detached member of the Sexual Crimes Squad, feeling professionally unsatisfied and at a loose end.

With a sigh of frustration she sat down at her desk, dumped her bag next to the keyboard and logged on. The inbox had collected a dozen new emails, mostly routine messages and junk mail, but one item stood out. Titled *Man in the Mud*, it had two attachments.

Rita clicked on the email and read the covering note: *Please look at the attachments then phone me.*

It had been sent by an officer she didn't know, a DS Steve Jarrett based at Whitley police station in Queensland. Already intrigued, Rita opened the first attachment. It contained a copy of a clipping from the local newspaper, the *Whitley Times*:

WHO IS THE MURDERED 'MAN IN THE MUD'?
By Nikki Dwyer
A week after the discovery of a severed head on the northern end of Whitley Beach, police admit they are no nearer to identifying the victim.

A DNA check and searches of dental records have failed to produce any results.

Officers have also been circulating a computerised image, reconstructing the decomposed face, but so far no one has come forward to put a name to it. The victim is described as a male Caucasian in his 20s or 30s, with shoulder-length black hair.

The investigation was launched after the gruesome find by four-year-old Jennifer Griffiths, who dislodged the head while playing on the mudflats of the estuary. She impressed local police and journalists with her composure, describing the grisly object as simply 'the man in the mud'.

A post-mortem examination showed the unknown homicide victim had been shot through the top of the skull.

Since the initial discovery, more pieces of the dismembered body have floated ashore. Last Friday a handless forearm washed up south of the town and two days ago another macabre find was made by a man walking his pet labrador near the dunes. To the owner's horror, the dog retrieved a boot containing a foot.

The officer in charge of the investigation, Detective Sergeant Steve Jarrett, said yesterday it seemed obvious that the body was dumped at sea by someone who failed to take account of local currents.

'It's a case of waiting to see what else the tide brings in,' he said.

When she'd finished reading the article Rita opened the second attachment, a computer-generated image of the victim. The face meant nothing to her. While the crime presented an interesting challenge, she couldn't see what it had to do with her. Nevertheless, she phoned the number provided and asked for DS Jarrett.

'Is that Van Hassel?' drawled a male voice.

'It is,' she answered. 'Are you Jarrett?'

'Yeah,' he said. 'G'day.'

'G'day to you too, Jarrett. You get this morning's prize for the most ghoulish email. Any more body parts float your way?'

'No more human joints of meat,' he said. 'Though I did get a false alarm about a torso under the pier. It turned out to be a side of pork wearing a Kakadu T-shirt.'

Rita laughed. 'Sounds like the deep north has its own brand of humour. Okay, so I've caught up with the local news about your corpseless head, but what's it got to do with me?'

'That's what I was hoping you could tell me.'

'What do you mean?'

'I was wondering what connections you have up here.'

'Around Whitley?' asked Rita, puzzled. 'None that I know of. What makes you think I have?'

'A boot containing your name and a size-eight foot lopped off at the ankle.'

'I hope this isn't a piss-take.'

'I know it sounds weird,' admitted Jarrett with a dry chuckle, 'but I'm just trying to make sense of it. That's why I sent the newspaper article with the background before I spoke to you.'

'If you're talking about the boot in the report, how could my name possibly be inside it?'

'When the crime lab boys in Brisbane extracted the foot they found a soggy beer coaster with four words written on it: *Van Hassel Sex Crimes*.'

'You're sure about this?' said Rita. 'It's not some sort of mix-up?'

'I've got the lab's digital photos on the screen in front of me,' answered Jarrett. 'I've done a database check – I even Googled the words – and you're the only one it can refer to.'

'I believe you,' she said. 'Though I'm less than thrilled that my name was under a severed foot.'

'Yeah, it's all a bit gross. Welcome to my horror show.'

'Describe the beer coaster to me,' she said.

'A square cardboard mat with the Four X label on it. Could've come from any of the dozens of bars we've got around here. This is backpacker central. The words were written on the back with a ballpoint pen, so they survived a soaking.'

'And what about the foot?'

'Chopped off post-mortem with something like a heavy meat cleaver, and still wearing a white Nike sock. The DNA matches the other body parts, so it's the same victim.'

'Well, no pun intended, but I'm stumped,' she told him. 'Got any theories?'

'I toyed with the idea that a psycho might've deliberately planted evidence but I've ruled that out. The body parts weren't meant to be found. Whoever dumped them miscalculated, and the tide did the rest. So that leaves me with one working theory, for what it's worth.'

'Let's hear it.'

'I think our victim might have heard, or overheard, something about you while he was in a bar up here. So as not to forget, he picked up the nearest thing to hand – a beer coaster – wrote down your name and squad, and concealed the information in his boot because he was worried it might be discovered on him. Before he could contact you, he was murdered, dismembered and dumped at sea. What do you reckon?'

'Could be.'

'Of course, that leaves me with the burning question: what's your connection up here?'

'I can't think of any,' she sighed. 'But I'll check back through the files.'

'Thanks. At the moment this case is going nowhere. The man in the mud is starting to haunt me.'

'Anything else I can do?'

'Just one thing. You can say hello to a colleague of yours, Detective Sergeant Erin Webster.'

'You know Erin?'

'Yeah, she's uh . . .' He paused. 'She's a friend of mine.'

'Mine too.' His hesitation made Rita curious. 'How do you know her?'

'We worked a case together a few years back when I was still stationed in Sydney. A Victorian rapist was on the loose. Erin was sent up as liaison.'

'I see.' Rita thought she caught a hint of irony, but she just said, 'I'll pass on your greetings.'

'Thanks.'

'No problem.'

As she hung up Rita was intrigued, not so much by the decapitated head but by Jarrett's association with Erin. This was her closest friend inside the force, someone to confide in, a woman to share secrets with. But there'd never been any mention of Jarrett. Why? She got up and crossed the squad room to where Erin was working at her desk.

As Rita approached she observed her friend more closely than usual. She was poring over a document, highlighter in hand, a frown of concentration on her freckled face. Typically, there was a restless energy about her as she shifted in her chair; the sign of someone who'd rather be out in the field than pushing paperwork. It was in her background. With her soft hazel eyes, shapely figure and copper-coloured hair pulled back loosely, she had the looks of a country girl from the Wimmera. That was her appeal, along with her provocative smile and a crude sense of humour that had men chasing her even though she was married with a three-year-old son.

But while the marriage was rocky, the only suggestions of infidelity surrounded the husband, a uniformed inspector who insisted on remaining one of the boys. Erin's days of playing around were supposed to have ended with her wedding vows, or so she'd said, but Rita had her doubts. There was a perennial friskiness about her friend that needed to be satisfied. The more Rita thought about it, the more convinced she was that Erin was not only capable of jumping into bed outside a marital relationship that was part workplace, part battlefield, she was also slick enough to conceal it from her husband, her colleagues and her friends.

Rita stopped in front of her desk, hands on hips. 'So what have you been getting up to?'

Erin looked up. 'Well, right now I'm going through the transcript of a public masturbator's trial from 1978. The old scuzzbag's reoffended.' She threw down the highlighter. 'What about you? Got the nod yet?'

'No.' Rita pulled up a chair and sat. 'Any day now, or so I'm told. But they'd better pull their fingers out or I might choose another career.'

'What do you mean?'

'I've been offered the chance to do a PhD. The workload's horrendous but it's tempting. I'm doing little more than twiddling my thumbs at the moment.'

'You wouldn't chuck in your career here?'

'Maybe. An academic post's an option.'

'But you'd be wasted among a bunch of eggheads.'

'They might appreciate me more.'

'Well *I* appreciate you. And I need you here.' Erin sighed. 'You're the only one I can really talk to.'

'Well, while we're on the subject of talking,' said Rita, 'what's this about a liaison with Steve Jarrett?'

'Shit.' Erin glanced around nervously. 'What've you heard?'

'So it's true, you tart. And you've never breathed a word of it. Is it still going on?'

'Not here!' insisted Erin in a harsh whisper.

She got up and led Rita to the tiled interior of the women's toilets, checking the cubicles to make sure they were alone before turning abruptly.

'What's been said?' she asked.

'Nothing I know of,' Rita answered. 'It's just informed guesswork on my part.'

'Based on what?'

'Your track record, for a start. Your prenuptial conquests.' Rita was still amused. 'Plus, I've just got off the phone with Jarrett. He asked me to say hello.'

'Oh, for fuck's sake! Men never know when to keep their mouths shut.' Erin shook her head. 'Why the call?'

'A case he's got in Queensland. My name's come up.'

'And he decided to drop mine in passing, silly bugger.' She relaxed a little. 'Thank God it was you on the line.'

'So, what's the story with you two?'

'Good beer and good timing.'

'Come on. Spit it out.'

Erin laughed. 'You don't realise how fitting that is.'

'Knowing you, I've got a rough idea.'

'That's how it started. On attachment in the Sydney suburbs. Going off-duty with women from the station. Getting pissed at Marrickville RSL. And the question comes up in conversation: spit or swallow?'

'As it does.'

'By the time Jarrett joined us I was legless. He helped me out of the club. I thanked him with a blowjob in the car park.'

'And this was after you got married?'

'Yeah, but in the middle of a bust-up and before Tristan was born.'

'What about since?'

'There've been a few opportunities. And I haven't wasted them.' Erin leant against the row of basins, her back to the washroom mirror. 'But, fingers crossed, you're the only one who's found out.'

'And it'll stay that way.'

Erin jumped forward and gave Rita a hug. 'That's why you can't quit. There's no one else around here I could trust with that.'

'What about Jarrett? You trust him?'

'I need to remind him what discretion means. But, yeah, he's okay.'

'So, what's he like?'

'A bit of a charmer but, underneath, a decent bloke. Good detective too. The laidback type. Thorough without being macho.' Erin pushed aside an auburn curl that had come adrift. 'Not a bad fuck either.'

3

Rachel Macarthur believed that a woman's ultimate act of nurture was to protect the planet. It was a sacred duty handed down from the time of earth-mother worship at the dawn of humanity, and just as imperative today in the battle to save the environment. With that thought in mind she prepared to declare war on the military establishment of the western world.

Rachel faxed off the last of the press releases, swallowed what was left in her coffee mug and listened to the wet static of the rain spitting against the window. She was waiting for midnight. Around her, the walls of her campaign office were hung with images of ecological disasters. There were posters and leaflets from past protests, and photos of eco-warriors being manhandled by police. Some victories. Some lost causes. There was also a noticeboard devoted to announcements from the Anti-War Coalition, for which Rachel was the local organiser.

Her mind was on the conflict to come as she gazed through the window over the southern outskirts of the town. Beyond the rooftops were the chimneys of the old sugar mill and the line of the docks. Beyond them, somewhere in the darkness on the far side of the estuary, lay the Whitley Sands military research base. She had evidence that the base was polluting the environment with radiation, and tomorrow's mass protest would bring it to the public's attention. It was her personal crusade, and she'd gathered enough material to call for an official inquiry. Once that started, there would be a growing clamour to shut the place down. It would be a sweet victory to see Whitley Sands returned to nature.

She looked at her watch and punched a number into her phone but got the 'unavailable' message. Freddy had his mobile switched off. She wanted to know why he was ignoring her again. As a computer hacker he couldn't be bettered, but as a lover he was unreliable. The two hours she'd spent in the pub were a waste of time. He hadn't shown up. She sighed, tapped her fingers on the desk and went on waiting for midnight.

Dead on twelve the office phone rang. She picked it up. The caller gave no name but she recognised the voice from before. He'd promised photocopies of classified documents.

'You've got them?' she asked.

'Yes.'

'When can I have them?'

'Ten minutes, if you can get down to the docks.'

'I'll be there. Where do we meet?'

'The Diamond. You know it?'

'Of course I do. How will I recognise you?'

'Don't worry about that. Just come alone.'

He hung up.

She took a deep breath and phoned for a taxi.

The beam of the taxi's headlights swept into the narrow lane that led down to the docks. A dark figure was caught momentarily in the glare. It flitted into the shadows of a doorway. The cab driver yanked on his handbrake and peered uneasily down the curve of the black cobblestones to the flickering neon at the bottom of the slope – *The Rough Diamond Club*.

'This is as far as I go,' he said warily. 'It's a dead end down there and I've been caught before at this time of night. Cost me all my takings and a night in casualty.'

Rachel was also gazing down the alleyway.

'You were mugged?'

'Yeah, down by the club. And I'm not the only cabbie. We call it Apache Canyon,' he said humourlessly. 'Sure you want to go down there?'

'I've arranged to meet someone.'

As she got out, the driver gave her a dubious look. When she'd paid the fare, the taxi reversed quickly back around the corner, plunging the lane into semi-darkness.

It didn't bother Rachel. She was about to get hold of hard evidence on excessive radiation levels around the base. She felt excited. The night was shifting around her and the wind was gusting. It had blown away the earlier drizzle, but rolls of thunder were approaching. Lightning flickered at the edges of storm clouds sliding over the town from the Coral Sea. Waves were crashing against the rocks at the harbour entrance.

Rachel shoved her hands into her coat pockets and began walking down the alley towards the neon sign. Her footsteps on the cobbles echoed from the brick walls of boarded-up chandlers' shops. She was more than halfway down the alley when someone stepped out from a darkened doorway behind her, clasped a hand firmly over her mouth and fired a nail gun at the base of her skull. It was so quick, and Rachel so unprepared, that she didn't realise immediately what had happened. The thick metal nail ripped down through her body, severing her windpipe and jugular vein before lodging in her ribcage. Her legs crumpled under her as she fell face first into the gutter. Her fingers were sticky with hot blood as she grabbed at her throat and gasped silently for help. The scrape of shoes against the cobbles was in her ears as someone turned behind her, but she was already losing consciousness. It left her just a moment to fix her eyes on the grubby setting of her death. Just time enough to watch the dark stream of her blood flowing down the gutter towards the fading neon sign.

4

Six men sat around a conference table on level six of the Whitley Sands research base, unaware of the deteriorating weather outside. They were in a windowless room more than fifty metres underground. The carpeting, leather chairs and landscapes hanging on the concrete walls did little to dispel the atmosphere of a bunker. The room was sealed and shielded from electronic surveillance so the men could talk freely. No one could eavesdrop, no minutes would be taken and no record of the meeting would ever exist, yet its tentacles stretched beyond national boundaries as far as Washington and London. Officially these men comprised the International Risk Assessment Committee that convened on an irregular basis, but their true role was far more clandestine, with responsibilities in the field of security and intelligence. They formed a covert decision-making cell in the global network conducting the war on terror.

At the head of the table sat the director-general of the base, Lieutenant Colonel Willis Baxter.

'I wouldn't have called you here if it wasn't urgent,' he said. 'But we face an immediate threat.'

The man to his right leant forward and asked, 'From inside or outside?' His name was Rex Horsley, his accent English home counties.

'Both,' was the reply. 'We've intercepted part of a technical report sent to the anti-war movement in the town. It contains classified figures on radiation emissions. We've traced the source to level four.'

'Have you identified the leak?'

'Not yet, but we're narrowing the list of suspects.'

'Surely timing is critical,' said the Englishman. 'You're only hours away from a mass protest at your gates. This whole issue could blow up in your face.'

'I'm well aware of that,' said the director-general, 'which is why I've called you here in the middle of the night. That's what this meeting is about. I want agreement on our immediate strategy.'

An American, Rhett Molloy, spoke next. 'I hope I don't have to stress that any breach of security is unacceptable. There's too much at stake here.'

'Thanks for stating the obvious,' said the man sitting opposite. He was Roy Maddox, the base security director.

'Let me make myself clear,' said Molloy, an edge to his voice beneath the smooth West Coast intonation. 'When I say *unacceptable*, I mean there can be no risk of secrecy being compromised. None whatsoever. There are no excuses. Failure won't be tolerated.'

'Don't doubt for a moment we're prepared to do what's necessary to defend the project,' said Baxter.

'Defence is not enough. You have to be proactive in eliminating any threats. Even after the event, they must be traced and silenced. If there's any hesitation over this, let me assure you, by one agency or another, absolute secrecy will be enforced.'

'We've already taken steps to limit the damage,' said the security director. 'And we're in the process of putting spoilers in place.'

'Fine, but half-measures won't be enough. Let's not forget why we're here. This is no ordinary piece of military real estate. This research establishment will produce a crucial weapon for the global coalition against terrorism.' Molloy spoke with such conviction it sent a chill through the room. 'We are representatives of an alliance at war. Extreme measures are justified.'

5

The club bouncer came outside to give his eardrums a rest and found himself confronted by a wall of rain and a skyful of pyrotechnics. The storm was at its height, but the noise of the thunder was a relief after the teeth-jarring feedback from the amplifiers. He stood in the doorway of the club and watched a cascade of water churn past the bottom step.

When he'd finished his cigarette he flicked it into the puddle spreading under the entrance canopy. The butt bobbed and drifted with the slow eddy of the current. As he watched it he noticed a trickle of red swirling through the water. It aroused his curiosity. The longer he gazed at the red stain in the puddle, the thicker it got. Looks like blood, he thought.

He peered up the slope through the rain. At first he couldn't see anything. Then a lightning flash revealed a dark hump in the gutter. Might not be anything. Just a rubbish bag kicked down the alley by larrikins. They were doing it all the time. But the stain kept coming and he got a bad feeling about it.

He went back inside the club, then emerged again and, hoisting a striped umbrella over his head, stepped out into the pouring rain. Nearly halfway up the alley he stopped beside the crumpled shape in the gutter. The darkness and the splash of water all around made it difficult to be sure of what he'd found. But when he prodded it with his shoe he caught his breath. He was bending over for a closer look when another flash came – and left him standing bolt upright. The twisted shape of the dead body seemed to leap out at him from the gutter.

The bouncer hurried back to the club. Just one minute later he was back out again, this time with the manager. The two men stood under the umbrella with the rain soaking their shoes and trousers, while the manager shone a torch on the slumped figure and swore under his breath. Parts of the body were missing. There was no head. Where the neck should be there was a raw gaping wound still leaking blood. Part of the spine was protruding. The hands had also been cut off.

When Detective Sergeant Steve Jarrett arrived police had already taped off the alley and a photographer was taking close-ups of the body in the glare of arc lights. A uniformed constable was helping to keep the rain off by holding one of the supports of the overhead plastic sheeting. The duty doctor sat in a police incident van nearby. He was writing in his notebook that he'd pronounced life extinct in the homicide victim. Scene-of-crime officers were examining the narrow surroundings.

Jarrett got out of his car, turned up the collar of his jacket and walked around the parked patrol vehicles. Then he stepped over the tape and jogged down the alley. The downpour had eased to a steady shower. The lightning and thunder had receded down the coast. A faint glimmer of first light appeared beneath the rim of the clouds in the east.

Inside the club officers were questioning the customers. The music and drinking had stopped, all the lights were on, no one was allowed to leave and the mood was getting ugly. Jarrett was greeted with catcalls, jeers and feral eyes. A detective constable came over to him.

'E-freaks,' he said. 'They want to go on raving till dawn.'

Jarrett shook his head sombrely. 'I called the pathologist before I left. He should be here in about ten minutes.' He looked around. 'What have we got so far?'

'A headless woman,' said the constable. 'No purse, no ID on her. No weapon at the scene. No hands either.'

Jarrett gave him a heavy look. 'Just what we need – another anonymous victim with missing body parts.'

6

The turnout for the protest was better than expected despite the fierce midday sun and tropical humidity. More than a thousand demonstrators were marching along the road bordering defence department land towards the gates of the Whitley Sands research base. Rachel Macarthur had organised it well. There was a good media contingent – radio journalists, local newspaper reporters, photographers, a TV crew – and a low-profile police presence. But where was Rachel herself? Her fellow organisers had decided not to wait for her. They started the march on schedule and hoped she'd arrive in time for the sit-down demo and rallying speeches in front of the gates.

The chanting and placard-waving intensified as the marchers converged on the base entrance. The police called for backup as groups of protesters sat down, blocking the road, while others began massing at the gates and pressing against them, urged on by an activist with a megaphone. That's when the chains and bolt-cutters suddenly appeared. Anti-war militants and eco-warriors in the crowd weren't content to listen to speeches. Already they were cutting holes in the perimeter fence. Others were chaining themselves to the gates. From within the base, squads of military police came charging towards the breaches in the fence, ready to tackle the intruders. Placards were being hurled. It was on the verge of turning into a riot when the violence was cut short by a piercing scream.

Everyone stopped. Police. Protesters. Even the cameras swung around to where the scream had come from on the far side of the road. All they could see at first was a woman on her knees, sobbing, her knuckles clutched against her mouth, her face staring upwards at a pylon that stood directly opposite the gates. As they followed the direction of her gaze there was a collective gasp. On a spike projecting from the metal leg of the pylon was a severed head. A woman's head. Her dead eyes were staring at the base.

7

Freddy Hopper sat in the airless heat of the police interrogation room, perspiring freely and feeling in need of serious narcotics. It was two hours since his dead girlfriend's head had been retrieved from where it had been skewered on an electricity pylon. His relationship with Rachel Macarthur was at times volatile, they'd rowed in public and his jail-time for creating the Edge of Chaos virus had given him a bad reputation and bad friends. More than once he'd stormed out of their rented house and taken a prolonged break from her disapproval. But Freddy resented being a suspect in Rachel's murder. His emotions shuffled between anger and grief as Detective Sergeant Jarrett questioned him, recording his answers on an interview tape.

'So you can't think of anyone who'd want to hurt Rachel?' asked Jarrett.

'No one specifically,' answered Freddy, 'apart from the police, the government and the research base.'

'Why are you sweating so much, Freddy?'

'Because it's bloody hot in here.'

'You're wriggling like a lizard in a tin, so I know you're lying about something.'

'I didn't touch Rachel,' he insisted. 'I didn't even see her last night. I couldn't have. Just ask the monks.'

'An officer is on the phone to them now,' said Jarrett. 'But tell me, for the record, what you were doing?'

'I got a call from St Cedd's yesterday afternoon.'

'What time?'

'About four. The monastery's computers had crashed, the website was offline, their programs were corrupted and they wanted me to come to their rescue.'

'Why you?' asked Jarrett.

'Because I helped set up their system.'

Jarrett couldn't help laughing. 'The holy brothers got a depraved hacker like you to put them on the net? That's priceless.'

'One of them was an altar boy at our church when we were kids,' retorted Freddy.

'What time did you go there?'

'I drove up straightaway to catch the tide. I must've crossed the causeway to the island by five but it took hours of work to get them up and running again. A virus had attacked their software.'

'One of yours?'

'When are you all going to get off my back?' snapped Freddy. 'I developed the virus as a test program. Its release was an accident. One day you'll all realise your mistake.'

'Careful, Freddy. That sounds like a threat.'

They were interrupted by a detective constable knocking and entering the room.

'The monks confirm Freddy's story,' the officer said. 'He arrived late afternoon, fixed their website and was caught on the island by the high tide. They put him up for the night in one of their monastic cells, would you believe?' The officer gave a grunt of admiration. 'I think that's what you call a perfect alibi.'

Freddy stood up. 'Can I go now?'

'Okay.' Jarrett nodded. 'But I know you're lying about something – and I'll find out what.'

'Whatever.'

Freddy blew out a sigh of relief as he walked out of the police station and crossed the street. He was relieved to be away from the stifling interview room and out from under the penetrating gaze of the detective sergeant.

As he dodged between pavement cafe tables in the shade of palm trees, Freddy pulled out his mobile phone and fired off a text to someone with special connections. It was a dealer who claimed he could get his hands on a military code-breaker, something

Freddy was in the market for. With that sort of technology at his disposal, beating the Whitley Sands firewall became a real possibility. He was determined now to pull off a revenge mission against the research base. In the meantime, he planned a free fall into forgetfulness.

8

Rita was sitting in the squad room doing nothing in particular when Detective Inspector Jack Loftus called her into his office. She hoped it meant a decision had finally been made about her new role as a criminal profiler. She found Loftus watering the potted fern by his window.

'Make yourself comfortable,' he told her.

She sat down and watched him remove a dying frond then check the moisture around the plant's roots, before placing his china watering can on a shelf beside a framed photo of his grandchildren. His meditative ritual over, the head of Sex Crimes glanced at the clouds accumulating over the city skyline, sat down behind his desk and looked at her squarely.

'The good news is they've created a new position for you, complete with a new title and a higher pay grade,' he said.

'Thank God, at last!' said Rita with relief. 'I was starting to doubt it would ever happen.'

'You'll be appointed the force's Special Police Investigative Resources Officer.'

'That's a mouthful.'

'Yes,' Loftus agreed. 'Not my choice, by the way.'

'And it spells SPIRO,' she observed. 'Bit of a dubious honour. Which bureaucratic genius came up with that? No, let me guess. Nash.'

'As a matter of fact it *was* Superintendent Nash.'

'That figures,' said Rita. 'Does a big new office come with the title?'

'Sadly, no. Nor will your new post come under the umbrella of the Intelligence Data Centre or the Behavioural Analysis Unit. Essentially, you'll be on your own.'

'Is that the bad news?'

'Partly. And it means you'll no longer have a desk in the squad room. There was even a suggestion of shifting you to another building in the city.'

'Nash again,' she said. 'He'd like to sideline me, Jack.'

'Well, I've forestalled him. The room you use for research is now our Criminal Profiling Archive. So you stay where you are. Nash isn't the only one who can play with formalities,' Loftus added with a rueful smile. 'The announcement of your new appointment will be made tomorrow and you'll start in the job six weeks from now.'

Rita couldn't help smiling broadly. 'I can't believe it's really happening. All the hard work and study was worth it.'

'You can be proud of what you've achieved. You've broken new ground at a difficult time for the force.'

'I have, haven't I?' But as she relaxed she noticed he was frowning. 'Do I detect a note of caution?'

'You know as well as I do what's going on around us – "the battle within". We're on shifting ground between reform and resistance to change.'

'And I know which side I'm on.'

'Exactly.' Loftus rubbed his chin thoughtfully. 'It's just as well you're staying where I can keep an eye on you.'

'You're worried I'm going to tread on people's toes.'

'Sometimes you need reminding about which battles to fight. And because I'm the one who set you on your present career path, I have a responsibility to watch your back.'

'Relax,' she laughed. 'I know what I'm facing.'

'Are you sure? Much of the foot-dragging over your appointment was because of concern about how to deploy you. After all, you're one of a kind now – *sui generis*.'

'Now *that* worries me, you quoting Latin. I can almost smell the incense.'

'Very funny. What I'm saying is you face a potential pitfall. In a way you'll be your own boss, with access to all the crime squads, but in another sense you'll be a floating specialist, moving from one section to another.'

'I take your point,' she agreed. 'I could end up being nomadic in an organisation structured around entrenched territorial loyalties. That's the cops for you. It's a risk I'm prepared to take. As a woman in a male stronghold I'm used to being cold-shouldered.'

'As long as you're aware of it.'

'Of course I am. You know what the men in Homicide call what I do? *White woman's magic!* That's what I'm up against. Most cops are still old school. Anti-academic. Maybe I should go for broke. I've got the chance to do a PhD in psychology.'

'I don't think that's the right move. Anyway, there's a better alternative in the pipeline. I've been on the phone to Quantico. The FBI is prepared to give you further training, with a six-month attachment next year.'

'Now that's great news, though I'm not sure my boyfriend would agree.'

'So you and Byron Huxley are still going strong?' asked Loftus.

'We are,' she answered with a smile. 'And tonight we're marking a milestone – a year ago today I moved in with him, symbolically at least.'

'Really?' he said, distinctly unimpressed. 'I thought you were still flat-sharing with your Ecuadorian friend.'

'I'm based at Lola's during the week. Commuting from South Yarra's a lot easier than the Dandenongs. But I stay at Byron's place on weekends.'

'I hesitate to ask, but what was the symbolic aspect of moving in with him?'

'My books and CD collection. When I unpacked them at Olinda he saw it as a definitive gesture. It certainly would be for him.'

'Is that so? Sounds like you're both a bit light on emotional commitment. How are you marking this milestone?'

'A champagne dinner at the Windsor,' she said as she stood up to go. 'And now there's a double reason to celebrate.'

•

Rita walked back to the squad room exhilarated at the prospect of her new post. It would release her from routine work and give her the freedom to pursue an independent course. Despite Loftus's misgivings about office politics, she resolved to tackle any obstacles with her usual single-minded approach. As she sat down at her computer screen, she was distracted by a new email from Queensland. Detective Sergeant Steve Jarrett wanted her to contact him again, but this time there were no attachments. It was a week since the story of the head on the pylon had been the focus of national media coverage, and Rita wondered if something fresh had emerged.

She picked up the phone and called him. 'Hi, Jarrett. I hope you're not about to hit the news again.'

'So do I,' he answered. 'Thanks for getting back to me, Van Hassel – I've been waiting for your call.'

'Any progress with the local crime wave?'

'Not that you'd notice. I've had the boys from Homicide here to hold my hand. A bunch of hotshots telling me how it is. But they packed up and went back to the big city yesterday, none the wiser.'

'Any suspects?' Rita asked.

'No suspects. No leads. No apparent motive. Nothing to tell me why people keep losing their heads around here.'

'But the count still stands at two?'

'So far.'

'That sounds ominous.'

'We've got some sort of wacko on the loose,' Jarrett said with a sigh. 'What I'm about to tell you hasn't been made public, and it won't be. It's about the way the two victims were killed.'

'Both shot in the head?'

'Shot, yes, but not with a bullet. The "man in the mud" had a hole in the top of his skull and a trajectory wound through what was left of his brain. The second victim, Rachel Macarthur, had an identical hole in her skull. This time, though, the pathologist found what caused it. There was a nail wedged in her ribs. It means they were both shot at very close range with a nail gun.'

'Now that is interesting,' said Rita. 'But why are you telling me this?'

'Because your name is linked to the case. Because it looks like I've got a serial killer in my backyard. And because I've found out you're a criminal profiler – and we haven't got one of those up here.'

'All right, I'm listening.'

'I want my regional commander to put in a formal request for you to come up and help with the investigation. That's only if it's okay with you, of course, and if you haven't got too much on your plate already.'

'As it happens, I've got sod-all on my plate.'

'Queensland Police would pay for your travel, accommodation and modest expenses,' said Jarrett. 'And you'd get to experience our tropical beach resort.'

'That sounds like a sales pitch.'

'You have to admit it's tempting.'

'I'll have to check with my boss,' Rita replied. 'But your timing's good.'

'That's what all the girls say.'

Rita spent the next hour sorting through files, books and magazines in her small, glass-panelled office. It was like a minor ritual of adjustment as she prepared for her future role.

'Congratulations,' said Erin, pushing open the door. 'You've got the nod at last.'

'That was quick,' replied Rita. 'It's not supposed to be announced till tomorrow.'

'What do you expect? This is a building full of detectives. Soon as I heard I guessed you'd be lying low in your cubbyhole.'

'Cubbyhole, excuse me!' Rita stretched back in her swivel chair, gesturing at the over-stacked bookcases, grey metal filing cabinets and cluttered pin boards. 'From now on this is officially the Criminal Profiling Archive.'

'And just a few years ago it was a storeroom.' Erin laughed. 'Anyway, there's something else I need to talk to you about – or *someone* else.'

'Who?'

'Steve Jarrett.' She perched her backside on the edge of Rita's desk. 'He just phoned me. Says you're going up to Whitley.'

'That's right, on Tuesday. Jack's okayed the secondment. What did Jarrett want?'

'He wanted to know if he could confide in you.'

'About your relationship?'

'Of course not!' Erin gave Rita an affectionate slap on the knee. 'He knows you know. That's enough.'

'Then what?'

'The case up there – the one you're going to work on. It's causing problems he hasn't dealt with before. Political problems. He's being given a hard time.'

'And he's nervous?'

'Well, he's not shitting himself exactly. But he's definitely worried. So he wanted to know if he ought to fill you in.'

'What'd you say?'

'I told him to be completely open because you'd find out anyway. I said you're like a fucking mind-reader at times.'

'Thanks. You got any other input?'

'Yeah. If it gets heavy up there, I want you to call me. Even if it's just to talk things over.'

'Okay. Is that all?'

'No. One other thing.' Erin gave her a sleazy smile. 'When you see Jarrett you can say hello for me.'

With nothing to keep her at work, Rita left the office early and made her way to the Fast Forward Science Convention being staged at the Docklands exhibition centre. The vast site was crowded with corporate displays from around the world, staffed by hyperactive sales people busy doing marketing pitches. The week-long convention had also attracted entertainment multi-nationals, with several halls devoted to computer games, sci-fi movies and tech toys. Streams of people moved through strobe and laser-lit sideshows with avid looks on their faces. The whole place projected a mood of overstimulation.

Rita joined a queue of undergraduates and cyber-geeks filing into the main auditorium, which was filling up with people waiting for the guest speaker to arrive. Already a buzz of expectation could be felt in the hall. His reputation as an orator matched his growing fame as an apostle of cybernetics, and his young admirers had flocked from around the city.

Rita was sliding into a seat at the rear as applause broke out. Professor Byron Huxley was strolling in, looking more like a sportsman than an academic in his polo shirt and chinos. He acknowledged the welcome with a nod, and Rita smiled to herself, proud of the man who'd been her lover and companion for the past year.

During that time she'd seen his influence spread beyond the boundaries of academic life and scientific journals, with appearances on TV and even in the glossy pages of a women's magazine. His youthful good looks and easy smile made him a natural pin-up, something Rita had mixed feelings about, although Huxley seemed oblivious to the distractions of glamour. His focus remained firmly scientific, even when he was playing the role of populariser, something which had drawn fire from critics within the university establishment. The disapproval didn't bother Huxley, who saw it as validating his unorthodox approach. His breakthroughs in research, along with the international recognition he was gaining, were defence enough. Besides, he was strongly committed to making science accessible to the general public.

He stepped up to the rostrum, opened his laptop and waited for the hubbub to subside. Then he spoke in a loud clear voice.

'*Cogito ergo sum.*' He was met with puzzled expressions. 'I can see from the blank faces that Latin's a dead language to most of you, so let me translate: *I think, therefore I am.*'

His words brought a hush to the hall. He let the silence linger, adding its edge, before he went on.

'Human intelligence is a remarkable thing. Infinite yet organic. A source of genius, and corruption. It is consciousness floating in a biological soup, a sublime mechanism of thought housed in wet membrane and irrigated by a throbbing river of blood.'

Huxley gripped the sides of the lectern as he gazed at the audience.

'Imagine, by contrast, a smooth crystalline intelligence. Instead of relying on fluid secretions and soft tissue, it inhabits a cool silicon universe of thought. A mind that is serene, undisturbed by the tyranny of glands and hormones. It is free of the dark cesspits of the unconscious for it perceives everything throughout. An awareness that has no focus because it is total consciousness. An intelligence that is all-knowing.'

A photographer fired off some shots, the flashes adding to the strangely electric atmosphere.

'More than three hundred and fifty years ago,' Huxley continued, 'French scientist, mathematician and rationalist René Descartes founded modern scientific method. He also gave us the quote I used a moment ago. We owe so much to the discoveries of such people of genius, resulting in where we find ourselves today. Here and now, in the opening decade of the twenty-first century, we are moving across the threshold of a radical change in which human beings will merge with their technology. We are, in a sense, on the brink of the post-human era, extending our mental capabilities with what we plug into our skulls.

'Let me list some of the innovations . . . Neural implants will allow connections from people's heads directly into computers. Swarms of nanorobotic machines will be injected into the circulatory system to help us reverse-engineer the human brain by exploring the maze of blood vessels and monitoring all electrical activities. Scanning techniques will reveal the intricacies of the neuro-biological structure within the brain, including synaptic connections and neurotransmitter clusters. Molecular robots will be able to reprogram the dynamics of cognitive processing to heighten perception, expand mental faculties and interface with virtual reality.

'At the same time, neuromorphic engineering will analyse how individual neurons, circuits and architectures compute information, store knowledge and adjust to evolutionary change. This will enable the design of artificial neural configurations based on the principles of biological nervous systems. Self-organising and genetic algorithms will assimilate patterns of information in a way that corresponds to human learning. New architectures using nanotech circuits constructed of atoms, quantum processing and advanced neural computing will allow us to re-create the entire framework of the brain, including the structure of memory. Finally, we could scan someone's head and download the replicated "mind program" into a computer.'

Rita felt a tingling down her spine as she watched him. It was a side to Huxley she'd witnessed on only a few occasions: the charismatic teacher determined to spread enlightenment. For the next half-hour she listened to him expanding on his theme, detailing the future scientific breakthroughs he'd listed, convincing his audience that a new cybernetic order was already emerging. Then he looked at the implications.

'So where does the science of intelligence lead? Let me put it this way. What's the possibility of me, Byron Huxley, downloading my consciousness into a computer? Sound absurd? Then think about this. Molecular biology looks at information as the essential code expressed by our bodies. So the challenge is to decode the brain's information-processing methods. With the devices I've just mentioned, it becomes possible for Byron, as a personality construct, to be programmed into a computer that stores my identity. This is the triumph of pattern over physical life. The being that unfolds within the machine will appear to have the same character and memories as the Byron standing before you now. And when this Byron is pushing up daisies and no longer exists in his organic brain, the machine Byron will endure. Post-human indeed! As long as the pattern exists in cyberspace, Byron has acquired a type of immortality.

'Perhaps no scientific reconstruction can produce human awareness, but computers could become sentient in a new way. Which begs the question: when do you assume something has a will of its own? It's not possible to *objectively* gauge a *subjective* presence – there's a logical contradiction in the terms. And how do you tell the difference between something that's really conscious and one that appears to be conscious? The Byron in the machine can be very persuasive, insisting emphatically that he's the genuine individual. He'll say to you: *I spent my infant years being dragged around hippie hotspots by my parents, was schooled in Melbourne, went to Cambridge, studied science, underwent scanning and regained consciousness here in the computer. The process of downloading identity is amazing!* You can try arguing, but in the end you'll go along with what he says. Byron will get pissed off if you don't.'

Huxley waited for the laughter to subside before wrapping up his address.

'In our world today, three dynamic forces are converging: the expansion of cyberspace, the refinement of virtual reality and the science of intelligence. The result will be a new wonderland as deceptive and paradoxical as anything Alice encountered. And like Alice's experiences down the rabbit hole and through the looking-glass, the inhabitants of this wonderland will not necessarily be friendly. While many of us here anticipate what's coming with a subversive glee, let's not forget that its power to liberate is matched by its power to control. The future will be just as menacing as the past, especially when the digital dark arts are applied by political, military and corporate oppressors. I'll just leave you with that Cartesian doubt in mind.'

As the wave of applause died away and the audience began to rise from the rows of seats and disperse, dozens of admirers milled around the podium, crowding in on the guest lecturer as he closed his laptop and slid it back into its case.

'It's early days yet, of course,' Huxley was saying to them. 'But the new revolution will transform our lives. It's inevitable.'

A barrage of questions came back at him from the press of bright young faces. He was hemmed in and would be stuck there for a while, so Rita decided to leave him to it. Anyway, she needed to shower, do her hair and make-up, then dress for this evening's anniversary celebration. That's when she'd have him all to herself.

9

'I wonder where we'll be a year from now,' pondered Huxley.

Although his words were meant to be reflective, Rita detected something equivocal in his smile.

'Does that mean you doubt we'll still be together?' she asked.

'Oh,' he said, taken aback. 'I wasn't assuming one way or the other.'

He was trying to be tactful, but it was the wrong answer.

She sighed. 'It's about emotions, not assumptions.'

He realised his mistake. 'Sorry. I missed my cue, didn't I?'

'You certainly did,' she replied, and flicked an ice cube at him. It bounced off the lapel of his jacket and he tugged at his shirt collar sheepishly.

Their anniversary celebration was getting off to a hesitant start. As a prelude to revisiting a Victorian suite at the Windsor, scene of their first night of passion, they were sitting in the genteel interior of the hotel's dining room. Candles flickered on the table. A bottle of champagne glistened in an ice bucket. Murmured conversations came from nearby diners, accompanied by a piano tinkling through melodies from the 1950s. The sedate setting was meant to lend a romantic tone to the evening, but perhaps it was a little too sedate. Rita felt restless and Huxley seemed preoccupied.

'Our relationship isn't based on dependency, is it?' he asked suddenly.

The question took her by surprise.

'No, it's based on love. And mutual trust,' she added with a surge of alarm. What was he about to tell her – that he was seeing another woman? 'Neither of us has a dependent personality. Why do you ask?'

'I've got some news,' he answered. 'And it affects our relationship.'

Rita felt her mouth go dry. She picked up her glass and swallowed a mouthful of champagne. 'Tell me.'

'I've been offered a post overseas. Visiting professor, Cambridge University.'

A wave of relief washed over her. 'That's wonderful news! When do you go?'

'At the end of this semester. I'll be there for the English academic year.'

'A year away.' Her relief was tinged with regret. 'Wow.'

'I know,' said Huxley, bowing his head. 'It's quite a break. I can't expect you to join me over there. Not with your own career taking off at last. But I'll certainly miss you.'

She reached across the table and put a hand on his. 'I'll miss you too. But that means it's easier for me to make a decision. I'm in line for an attachment in Virginia. Now I can say yes. So at least we'll be in the same hemisphere.'

'On opposite sides of the Atlantic,' he observed. 'Not very intimate.'

'But with access to cheap flights,' Rita pointed out. 'Think of the anticipation!' She gave him a teasing smile. It complemented what she was wearing – a low-cut black cocktail dress, tight on her curves, and black high heels.

'Maybe we should treat tonight as a last desperate fling,' she said. 'Before your fan base goes international.'

'You're the only fan I notice,' said Huxley. 'Especially when you wear a dress like that.'

'What, my little black number?'

'Yes, with all its revealing calculus.' He raised his glass. 'Happy anniversary.'

Rita echoed the toast, then said, 'There's another reason to make the most of tonight. I'm flying up to Queensland on Tuesday and I could be gone a few weeks.'

'Why?'

'The murders in Whitley. The local police want me to help. It'll be my first case as an official profiler.'

'Now that's interesting,' said Huxley. 'I could've ended up working there. They tried to headhunt me for the Whitley Sands research base a couple of years ago.'

'Who's they?'

'The defence department, with a lot of money on the table. Very tempting. And not just for the financial package. The speech I gave today – about the application of artificial intelligence and so on – scientists there are already doing it.'

'So why didn't you accept?' asked Rita.

'The idea of having military masters. It bothered me. It worried me even more after I phoned a former colleague who's working there.'

'Who?'

'Konrad Steinberg, a physicist – an expert in electromagnetism. He advised me to forget the money, the job wasn't worth it and I shouldn't touch it with a barge pole. That's all I needed to know.'

Rita was beginning to wonder if Huxley was her mysterious link to Whitley, although she couldn't see how.

'What makes him so negative about the place?' she asked.

'For a start, the research isn't science-driven. According to Steinberg it's all geared to fast-tracking new technology for use in the war on terror, so they're cutting corners when it comes to procedures and safeguards.'

'Do you know what sort of technology they're developing?'

'Steinberg was too nervous to say – national security and all that – but I've got a rough idea from what he let slip and from questions put to me by the departmental headhunters. I think they've come up with some sort of integrated surveillance system and the data feed is so massive they need advanced AI computing to process it. That's my informed guess, anyway.'

'You said "for a start",' she reminded him. 'What else doesn't he like?'

'The security. Apparently the base is patrolled by a specially recruited bunch of military police. Steinberg says they act like fascist thugs who treat the researchers as if they're inmates. It's a huge establishment with several thousand scientists employed there.'

'Do you know any of the others?'

'A few, but I haven't kept in touch. One of them – Audrey Zillman – is among the leading experts in the science of intelligence. I was on her course at Cambridge. It shows you how serious the base is about using AI, and twitchy with it. Steinberg phoned me a few months ago – back around New Year – to pick my brains about data encryption.'

'Did you ask him why?'

'Of course. He was compiling a confidential report and didn't want anyone at Whitley Sands to access it. Steinberg said the protesters were making valid points about the environmental threat and things inside the base were getting worse. It all seems a bit nasty.'

'Yes,' agreed Rita. 'So much for the tourist brochures. Whitley sounds less and less like a tropical paradise.'

10

On level six, the International Risk Assessment Committee reconvened inside the concrete walls of the conference room.

'I'd like to say we're on top of events, with a crisis averted,' the director-general, Willis Baxter, began. 'But it's obvious we're facing a new set of problems, though the threat posed by the protesters appears to have subsided.'

'Have you identified the leak?' asked the Englishman, Horsley.

'We have a handful of suspects,' answered Roy Maddox, the security director. 'We've been watching their work patterns closely and monitoring their behaviour off base.'

The American, Molloy, cleared his throat. 'Whoever it is must be dealt with uncompromisingly.'

'Noted,' said Maddox.

'You'll be aware of a new headache imposed on us by Canberra,' continued Baxter. 'I'm under instructions to set up a panel to review security and report back to the minister. The constitution of the panel is largely up to me, though there'll be senior public servants present as observers. I'm inclined to make it as broad as possible – invite the local police and emergency services – and give all those on the panel only level-one clearance. Canberra's intentions may or may not be commendable, but I'm determined there'll be no interference in what is already a rigorously policed operation.'

'I concur,' nodded Molloy. 'The more you turn it into a talking shop, the less intrusive it will be.'

'I trust the Panopticon Project won't be up for discussion,' said Horsley.

'Absolutely not,' Baxter assured him. 'Its content and purpose will remain top secret and out of bounds.'

'Good. We must keep it that way.'

'As for the panel's agenda, I've been told there are four areas of concern. In practical terms we're already on top of three: the anti-war protest, publicity control and internal protocols. The fourth, in my opinion, doesn't fall within my remit, which is why you're here. I've been informed there is now a credible threat of a terrorist presence.'

The director-general sat back and cast his eyes around the others at the table.

Molloy responded first.

'Two days ago, CIA eavesdroppers at Langley intercepted a burst of electronic traffic in the Middle East referring specifically to Whitley Sands,' he said. 'It's clear that terrorist overlords are targeting the base. We have the protesters to thank for drawing their attention to it. Ominously, one of the decoded messages refers to a "fixer".'

Baxter frowned. 'What's that mean?'

'Like a lot of raw intel it's open to interpretation, but Langley believes it's a specific reference to a man. It's thought he's on his way here.'

'So who is he?'

'He has any number of identities,' answered the American, opening a folder in front of him. 'But we think the Fixer is one Omar Amini, the product of a militant family in Tehran. It's that Iranian connection again. He's a specialist operative at the disposal of the global extremist network. Amini works undercover doing advance preparation for an attack – planning, recon, making contacts, exploiting locals. It's a key role ahead of a terrorist cell being activated and deployed. He's well educated – Omar and his brothers went to the Sorbonne – so that makes him westernised and adaptable, hard to spot. It's that old Aryan blood of Persia. The one picture we have of him is from his student ID when he was attending the Sorbonne under the name Mounir Al Sahar. It's twenty years old and of little use. He's a computer expert, fluent in several languages, including French and English, and a combat-trained member of the elite Quds Force, the foreign operations branch of Iran's Revolutionary Guard Corps, which runs Tehran's covert activities.'

'And if this man arrives on our doorstep,' put in Baxter, 'we can't afford to be distracted by internal housekeeping.'

'Exactly. But, of course, there can be no mention of the Fixer at the security review. The attempt to identify and locate him is strictly classified. And that's the major problem we face. With his ability to blend in, he could be right under our noses and we wouldn't spot him.'

'That's more likely than you realise,' added Horsley, opening an A4 envelope and distributing photocopies around the table. 'Langley will have to backdate its timeline. This was sent to me a few hours ago at the consulate. A hard copy of a fax has been retrieved by soldiers in Peshawar after a fire-fight near the Afghan border. It's a map of Whitley Sands and its surroundings.'

'Well that confirms the threat,' said Maddox.

'It's worse than that,' continued Horsley. 'The fax was dated three months ago.'

They lapsed into silence until Molloy uttered what was on all their minds.

'We have to assume the Fixer's already here and well entrenched. That means an attack is imminent.'

11

On the flight from Melbourne Rita studied the case files that Jarrett had emailed, including witness statements, transcripts of interviews, pathologist reports and crime scene photos. As she scrolled through them on her laptop a disturbing possibility occurred to her. It didn't originate with any of the material compiled by the police investigation but was prompted by Dr Konrad Steinberg's misgivings about the research base.

According to the files, Homicide detectives could find no motive for either of the murders. That was understandable in the case of 'the man in the mud', who still hadn't been identified. Rita examined the pathologist's findings again but nothing leapt out at her, though the list of trace elements lifted from the hair and body parts seemed strangely eclectic: sand, seaweed, fragments of shell and coral, glass, nicotine, motor oil, engine grease, cement powder, tar, rope fibre, hessian, tissue paper and effluent. It was an inventory of what the decapitated head had come into contact with, what it had been carried in and wherever it had been rolling around at the mercy of the tides. But with no points of reference, other than the sea, it was hardly enlightening. The identity of the man in the mud – with Rita's name in his boot – and the reason for his murder remained an annoying mystery.

But the nail-gunner's second murder victim was another matter. The detectives had returned to Brisbane assuming Rachel Macarthur had been stalked and lured to her death by a psychopath with a sick agenda. His point in placing her head opposite the base gates, they reasoned, was to taunt police and protesters alike, at the same time ensuring his handiwork gained maximum publicity. It was a workable theory but Rita had her doubts.

What worried her was Steinberg's suggestion that the protesters were right about damage to the environment. In that context the killing of Rachel, the local leader of the protest movement, could have a specific motive. If this was the case, the location of the decapitated head was more than a taunt, it was meant to send some sort of message. It also implied that the base itself was central to the case. Of course, it was mere conjecture at this stage. Rita didn't have enough information to justify a suspicion either way. As a profiler she needed to examine the crime scenes and start doing her own background work, but she'd already decided that Steinberg would be among those she would approach.

Another would be Rachel's boyfriend, Freddy Hopper. Members of the protest movement had told Detective Sergeant Jarrett that Rachel had a secret pipeline to information inside the base, but they had no idea who or what this conduit was, and she'd refused to enlighten them. Maybe Freddy knew. As Rita reread the transcript of his police interview she began to suspect, like Jarrett, that Rachel's lover was hiding something.

When the pilot announced they'd be landing in twenty minutes, Rita packed away the laptop and looked out the window as the airliner headed out over the South Pacific Ocean in a wide arc, altering course to make the approach to Whitley airport. Far below, hundreds of islands, reefs and islets dotted the tropical blue water, its glistening surface creased here and there by the wakes of yachts and powerboats.

As the jet descended, the ragged line of the coast came back into view, indented with bays and rocky headlands, creeks and mangrove swamps. Up ahead the residential sprawl of the town could be seen, dissected by the lazy curves of a river. Its weaving course ended in a broad estuary that spilled into the sea beyond the breakwaters of a man-made harbour where half a dozen cargo ships were docked. The place had the look of a busy port. Its flat storage area was studded with tanks, silos, fuel depots and sugar sheds, linked by a crisscross of rail yards crawling with freight trains. The loading pier of a coal terminal jutted out into the water.

There was another industrial cluster around the airport, and past the urban limits, where the cane plantations gave way to sand dunes, rose the concrete shapes of the Whitley Sands research base. Further along the coast, covering more than four thousand square kilometres of rugged hinterland, stretched the Whitley Bay Military Reserve. Among a variety of defence functions, it was used for infantry training, artillery testing and joint exercises by the armed forces of Australia, the United States and Pacific Ocean allies. Other activities were cloaked in official secrecy. On a distant plateau of the rainforest Rita could see weird white spheres, like giant golf balls. They housed American satellite tracking installations, more reminders that the region had elements of a dark presence linked to the tactics of international warfare. But as if to dispel the impression that the town was anything other than hospitable, directly below there were glimpses of a marina, an amusement park, a foreshore lined with palm trees and a beach scattered with the oiled bodies of sunbathers, while out to sea windsurfers skimmed the waves.

The plane landed with a thud and came to a halt on an apron of tarmac beside a tin-roofed terminal. When the passenger door opened a gust of heat came through. As Rita walked down the steps the ferocity of the sun seemed to swallow her like the blast from a furnace. The humidity, too, was intense, making her realise she was overdressed. And that was only the first adjustment she had to make. After the wintry setting of her departure thousands of kilometres south of here, she now had to switch her mental and cultural geography as well. She'd never been this far north in Australia before, and she'd already been warned to expect a more casual, more cavalier approach to everything. She was deep in the tropics now, and somehow it felt like foreign territory.

And yet she felt a strange familiarity, like a flashback. It brought an unwelcome reminder of early childhood in the tropics – a cool, spacious home in Jakarta, cane furniture on the landing, rotating blades of overhead fans, a pet lizard on the ceiling and a father who abandoned her in his obsession for a Javanese girl. It came back with painful clarity: her mother and sister in tears and the tightness in her chest, like a dead hand gripping her heart. With a shudder, she pushed the memories aside and went in search of her luggage, then a taxi.

•

The four-star Whitsunday Hotel, built on a bluff above a strip of beach, had the look of a smart holiday venue aimed at young professionals. Reception was in an air-conditioned glass atrium with ferns, a fish pond and an indoor waterfall. An activities desk catered for everything from sailing to scuba-diving on the reef and a range of adrenalin sports. To one side was a piano bar where men in tropical shirts drank cocktails decorated with little umbrellas. On the other was a dance floor with a poster advertising a singles night. The man at reception gave Rita a smile of approval. She was clearly part of the target market.

A porter showed the way to her room on the fifth floor, wheeling her suitcase, cabin bag and laptop case on a trolley. Once alone in her room, she opened the sliding glass door to the balcony and stepped out to take in her surroundings.

As she leant on the railing the brilliance of the colours made her squint – the crimson riot of bougainvillea in the hotel gardens, the opalescent blue of the water, sparks of sunlight glinting on the waves. A flotilla of yachts bobbed at their moorings and out in the deep channel a US aircraft carrier rode at anchor, its huge grey bulk the one anomaly in the vivid light.

After freshening up in the shower she went through her luggage and decided the most sensible option was smart casual, pulling on a cool linen top, denim skirt and deck shoes. Then she phoned Jarrett.

'I've checked into the hotel,' she told him. 'I can drop in on you now if you're clear.'

'Stay where you are, I'll come to you,' he said. 'It gives me the excuse for an afternoon beer in the shade.'

'Where will we meet?'

'Grab a table in the rotunda by the pool. I'll see you in ten minutes.'

The rotunda, as Jarrett called it, was a bamboo shelter with whitewashed pillars and wrought-iron furniture. It stood on the edge of the bluff beyond the hotel swimming pool. Rita had it to herself as she sipped a lime and soda, observing some of her fellow guests sunbathing. Half a dozen women, mostly young, mostly slim, glistened like bronze nymphs in deckchairs. Brief bikinis were *de rigueur*, along with designer shades, designer bags and glossy nail polish. A waiter fetched the women iced drinks as they sprawled indolently or flipped through the pages of magazines, waiting for time to pass, conserving their energy for the night.

A man was heading towards her across the slope of lawn. She assumed it was Jarrett. He was weaving through the display of female torsos as sure-footed as a mountain goat, a chilled bottle of Mexican lager in his hand and a testosterone grin on his face. In his tropical shirt, canvas shorts and sunglasses he looked right at home, less like a cop than a poolside Lothario. Rita could see at a glance he had more than police work on his mind.

'G'day, Van Hassel,' he said, extending his free hand as he sat down.

She reached over and shook it. His grip was firm. 'Hi, Jarrett. Nice to meet you at last.'

'You too.'

As he made himself comfortable he looked her up and down, a casual appraisal, neither blatant nor furtive, the instinctive habit of a man at ease with women. It was obvious why. Jarrett was wickedly handsome with an equally wicked smile, the sort of man who got around women's defences effortlessly. Little wonder Erin had jumped on him.

'The camera wasn't lying,' he said.

'Ah.' Rita nodded. 'You've been browsing.'

'Amazing what you find on the web. My favourite shot was the purple bikini.'

'That's an episode I'd rather forget. My ex sold private photos to a tabloid.'

'Unwelcome exposure, huh? Your ex is obviously a louse.'

'He is.'

'Any man who betrays a woman's trust deserves to be hung out to dry.'

'He does and he was. But that's history, and so is he.'

'Okay, I won't ask.'

'Good.' She put down her drink. 'But you're not getting off so lightly.'

'Oh. Erin.'

'She asked me to say hello, by the way.'

'Huh. Returning the favour. I copped an earful over that.'

'Can you blame her?'

'I didn't mean to give anything away,' said Jarrett. 'I thought I was just being sociable.'

'Think again. It doesn't take much to set off a wave of gossip and her marriage is under enough pressure already. She doesn't need any additional stress.'

He looked suitably sheepish. 'Point taken.'

But Rita wasn't finished yet. 'So, tell me. Your relationship with her – how do you see it? I'm asking as her friend.'

'Well, for a start, it's not a *relationship*. It's a bit of fun on the side. That goes for both of us, and our paths haven't crossed since September last year. I get the impression I'm occasional light relief from heavy-going at home.'

'And you're happy to do the relieving.'

'You disapprove?'

'No. As long as Erin doesn't get hurt. She's not as tough as she thinks.'

'That goes for all of us,' he said with a rueful smile. 'But you've got my word. She won't get hurt by me. Now, what about you? Do we have an understanding? If I give you the full picture of where I'm at, can I trust it won't go any further?'

'I can keep a secret.'

'Yeah, I guess you can.' Jarrett took a swig of beer and sighed, a serious expression replacing the smile. 'Let's talk shop. First of all, thanks for agreeing to come up here.'

'No problem.'

'I wish I could say the same.' He frowned. 'But the truth is, I'm feeling more out on a limb every day. I'm being pressured in a way I haven't been before. The murders have made people panicky, especially what happened to Rachel Macarthur. It's changed the town. There's a bad vibe and at times I'm on the receiving end of it.'

'Can you be a bit more specific?'

'Let me put it this way,' said Jarrett, cradling his bottle. 'I'm an easygoing sort of bloke. I like where I am at the moment.

I put life before ambition. I run an investigation branch with a handful of detective constables in a beach resort, where uniform does the donkey work and my station commander is a master of inertia. By the way, that's also between you and me.'

'Obviously.'

'That said, I still pride myself on being professional, even if our biggest cases are usually car theft, shoplifting and the occasional flasher. There's the odd backpacker making trouble, and I keep my eye on a couple of hoods who've moved up from the Gold Coast, but so far they're behaving themselves. It's all manageable, straightforward police work, the stats look good on my personnel file and I have a friendly relationship with the local authorities. Or at least I did have.'

'A change of mood's understandable,' said Rita. 'Two violent deaths, both inexplicable at the moment, will naturally bring a sense of crisis to a community. And you seem to be doing what's necessary. I've looked at the case files you sent. Very thorough.'

'Maybe, but I've hit a wall. In fact, I hit it the moment the first head rolled up on the sand. I've gone through every bit of evidence available, every detail, and it tells me precisely nothing about who's behind these crimes.' Jarrett gave a grunt. 'That's not what I'm talking about though. There's something else going on.'

He was more downbeat than Rita expected. It was beginning to worry her.

'Look,' she said. 'I'm here to help with the investigation in whatever way I can, at your request. I'm doing it on the basis that I'm working directly with you. If I do come up with anything you get it first, no one else.'

'That would be good.'

'Fine. Then get it off your chest. Tell me exactly what's bugging you.'

Jarrett put down his bottle and looked out to sea, as if deciding how frank to be with her. 'I feel remote,' he said at last. 'For the first time in my career I get the feeling I'm isolated – professionally, I mean. It's as if various officials around me are positioning themselves for a shit-storm that's blowing in and they won't even lend me an umbrella.'

'Which officials?' Rita asked.

'Town councillors, for a start. They're wetting themselves over negative publicity. They've got a one-track mind: the tourist dollar. My name's come up in committee. They're questioning whether I'm up to the job. I thought these guys were mates of mine.' Jarrett tilted his head awkwardly. 'Then there's the media. The local hacks are jumping up and down for new information and when I don't have it they get personal about it. This is after the Homicide Squad came and went, leaving more questions but no answers. On top of that I've had the regional brass on the phone expecting me to track down the killer with no manpower. It's like a memo's gone out announcing I'm available for target practice.'

Rita gave him a sympathetic slap on the shoulder. 'I hate to say it, mate, but the things you describe are typical social responses.'

'Maybe I'm not describing them well enough.'

'You're facing a barrage of angst – communal, institutional – at a level of intensity you haven't experienced before. Like the crimes themselves. Such savagery not only scares us, it threatens our sense of humanity. It reminds us we're only partly civilised – that our species has merely repackaged its instincts. Psychologically, it tells us we're still wading through a primeval swamp.'

'Thanks for the reassurance. Do I hear the profiler talking?'

'Get used to it, Jarrett. That's what I've got to offer – behavioural psychology. That's what a profiler does, if you haven't heard.'

'But you're also a cop.'

'You think that makes me a bit schizoid?' She sipped her drink with a shrug. 'Like your town, in fact.'

'The town? Last time I looked, pre-murders, it was uncomplicated. And, on the whole, peaceful.'

'Then look again. This place has the trappings of peace *and* war. There's more here than a beach, a port and a bunch of houses.'

'You mean the military?'

'They've got a big presence. I could see it from the air – artillery range, research base, war games reserve. And up in the high country a satellite tracking facility. You've got it on all sides.

In the taxi from the airport I saw army trucks in convoy and GIs in the street. Right now, I'm looking at a massive warship.'

Jarrett followed her gaze to the US aircraft carrier, its deck bristling with jet fighters. The vessel rose above the ruffled blue of the channel like a floating metal fort, dwarfing the spread of yachts bobbing in the foreground.

'I suppose we've got used to it. I don't even notice it anymore. What are you getting at?' he asked.

'The bad vibe you were going on about – you didn't mention defence officials. And there's no record of interviews with them. Surely that's an oversight.'

'Funny you should bring that up,' he grimaced. 'I wanted to interview the military police about Rachel's head on a pylon at their front gate, to find out if they'd noticed anything or had any relevant CCTV footage. So I called the security director, an aggressive bastard called Maddox. He told me no way. I said they might have witnessed something. He insisted they hadn't. When I tried to push it he told me to get lost, in those exact words.'

'Now *that* reaction *is* interesting,' said Rita. 'So far I haven't heard a good thing about the Whitley Sands base. Did you take it further?'

'I told my station commander, Inspector Derek Bryce. He went off, made a phone call, came back and told me to drop it. Bryce has clammed up on me ever since.' Jarrett sagged back, watching a powerboat cut a line of foam through the water in the middle distance. 'Ever get the feeling you're out of the loop?'

'Try being a woman detective. No matter what you do, no matter how tough you are, you're never one of the boys.'

'Bryce isn't a fan of women cops or profilers. He's a traditionalist. He thinks seconding you is a waste of money. Luckily the super disagrees and has underwritten the cost.' Jarrett gave a sly smile. 'Bryce told me *forensic psychology* is an oxymoron, whatever that is.'

'White woman's magic,' muttered Rita. 'Anyway, so much for your town being peaceful. It's also been a flashpoint for violence more than once.'

'You're right, of course. Pitched battles between protesters and the military. And now there's a new headache. Land rights activists have joined in. There's a long-running dispute about Whitley Sands and a chunk of the military reserve being tribal land. A native title claim is going through the courts but Rachel's murder has heightened media coverage so the environmentalists and anti-war brigade have got the public backing of the Indigenous lobby. And I'm piggy in the middle. To the peaceniks and eco-warriors I'm an establishment lackey. As for the defence department, I might as well be a leper.'

'The security director you mentioned,' said Rita, 'does he run the military police unit at the base?'

'Yes. Captain Roy Maddox.'

'What's he like?'

'Smart, tough, hard as nails. Ex-commando. He was with Special Forces till his truck got blown out from under him in Afghanistan. No time for civilians, cops included.'

'Who's in overall charge at Whitley Sands?'

'The director-general's another piece of work – Lieutenant Colonel Willis Baxter,' snorted Jarrett. 'One of those formal army types programmed to see human beings as cannon fodder. No sense of humour. Just gives you a dead-fish stare.'

Rita went silent, sipping her lime and soda absent-mindedly and gazing towards the horizon.

'What is it?' asked Jarrett. 'Does everything I've told you just sound paranoid?'

She finished her drink and put down the glass. 'Sounding paranoid and *being* paranoid are two different things. What if your feelings are right?' She turned to him. 'The *bad vibe* you sense – what if there's more to it than the murders? What if they're having an impact in a broader scenario than a police investigation? Which, of course, begs another question: what are we missing?'

'I wouldn't know where to start.'

'The only place we can at this stage: with the offender,' said Rita.

'But we know nothing about him.'

'No, that's not true. His identity's unknown but the Homicide detectives have already started building a profile of him. According to them, he's a serial killer with a personal agenda yet to be determined. They see him as a sociopath, a stalker who likes to get up close and personal for his kill. Hence the nail gun, which is an odd choice of weapon. It probably needs to be pressed against his victims' skulls to be fired. The fact that he's used it twice shows it's not opportunistic. It's part of his signature, along with dismemberment.'

'But I need to know where he comes from, what he looks like.'

'He's a big, strong man – someone powerful enough to use an unwieldy weapon effectively and tall enough to fire it at a downward angle through Rachel's body. He's also organised. He plans his attack carefully, equipping himself with what's necessary to carry it out and tidy up – nail gun, some sort of meat cleaver, a sack or bag for the severed head and hands. That shows he's socially competent – an intelligent man who fits in with his surroundings. He also gets a buzz out of taunting the public – the way he displayed Rachel's head. That makes him very manipulative and contemptuous of people in general. Homicide are convinced he'll strike again, and when he does they'll be back on your doorstep.'

'So you agree with their analysis?'

'Essentially, yes. But the context of the research base bothers me. It seems to me they've ignored it – possibly because, like you, they've been told to. And that's not good police work. That's political.' She looked at him pensively. 'By the way, do you know a research scientist called Dr Konrad Steinberg?'

'No.'

'What about Professor Audrey Zillman?'

Jarrett shook his head. 'Never heard of her. Not surprising though. The only contact I've had with people from the base is official meetings on local security or civic receptions. And that's more than enough. As for trying to question any of the civilian workers there, forget it. They're included in the *get lost* advice.'

'Well, that might have to change. But first things first. I need to start mapping out everything you've got so far.'

'You can do that at the station. I'll take you there now,' said Jarrett. 'There's more in the files than I emailed. A lot of useless paperwork in my opinion, but you're free to go through it. I've assigned you an office and a car, a Falcon. Steel blue. It's got a couple of dents and a few k on the clock but a souped-up engine under the bonnet.'

'Steel blue?'

'Yeah, it'll match your eyes.' He grinned. 'I'm told profilers need peace and quiet to concentrate so I've sorted out some office space where you won't be disturbed. Part of the old watch-house.'

'Not in the cells, I hope.'

'Nah,' chuckled Jarrett. 'More like an antique bondage chamber.'

12

The drive to the police station took them along the coast road towards the heart of the town. Jarrett travelled at a leisurely pace, an arm resting on the wheel as he pointed out significant landmarks.

'Rafferty's.' He gestured at an Irish theme bar. 'Always good for a few arrests. The kids can't cope with the Guinness.'

As the road curved down to the seafront they cruised past caravan parks and a marina. A couple of hundred yachts drifted at moorings that fanned out from boat ramps and a clubhouse with wooden decking.

'The sailing club,' said Jarrett. 'Our social centre.'

'You a member?'

'Damn right. Perfect for catching boats, beers and blondes – ah, if you know what I mean.'

'I do.'

'It's also the place for live entertainment.' He nodded at a marquee on the club's lawns opposite an outdoor stage rigged with microphones and banks of speakers. 'Great venue for rock concerts.'

'Like who?'

'The best was a Billy Thorpe gig, complete with thunderstorm.'

'Sounds risky.'

'It was. He broke off, saying he was in danger of having his arse nailed to the stage by lightning. But when it stopped he came back on and played till midnight.'

'When was that?'

'About a year before he died. What a voice – "Over the Rainbow" – blew the audience away.'

They passed a beachside development with a lagoon for toddlers then an open-air market on a grassy stretch of foreshore, customers ambling among stalls and hibiscus bushes. Beyond that the road branched towards the harbour alongside a row of burger and fried chicken outlets, an amusement park, a bowling alley, games arcades and cheap-looking bars. Among the potential customers, knots of US sailors strolled along under a range of neon signs. An ice-cream parlour was doing a busy trade with the Americans.

'The rough side of town,' muttered Jarrett. 'Rachel Macarthur was murdered down one of the alleys.'

At a junction by the pier he turned away from the sea and headed into the shopping precinct, marked by a line of palm trees towering above shopfronts, coffee bars and pubs.

'The main street,' said Jarrett. 'The council's tarting it up with tiled pavements and outdoor cafes, but we still get the hoons at night.'

As the traffic slowed, Rita watched a lazy stream of pedestrians moving around food stalls and beer umbrellas. The universal dress code seemed to be T-shirts, shorts and sandals, with women in straw hats and boys in baseball caps. The avenue of palms ended where the street sloped up a hill through petrol stations, supermarkets and a clutch of backpacker hostels. The police station stood at a crossroads bordering the residential area. From there lines of houses stretched into the distance where steep wooded gullies and the peaks of the rainforest hemmed in the outlying neighbourhoods.

'Here we are,' said Jarrett, pulling over.

The original part of the building was a two-storey structure made of local stone.

'The watch-house,' said Jarrett with a smile as they got out. 'Nineteenth century. Probably haunted.'

'Too bad I'm just a profiler,' said Rita. 'And not an exorcist.'

The modern offices and cells were housed in a brick addition.

Jarrett took her through the main entrance, past rooms crowded with desks and filing cabinets, introducing her to uniformed officers as they went. In the office of his crime investigation branch she met two of his detective constables. They were young, tanned and impressed by both her appearance and what she represented.

'I've always wanted to see profiling in action,' said one of them as he shook her hand. 'Assessing the criminal mind. All that weird insight stuff.'

'I appreciate your enthusiasm,' said Rita, 'but it's not voodoo.'

'Will you give us some tips?' asked the other. 'Show us the basics?'

'Shut up,' Jarrett told them. 'You're like a pair of spaniels.'

As he ushered her out along a corridor to the room that would be her office, she couldn't help laughing.

It didn't take Rita long to settle into her new workplace, even though it felt more like a time-warped gallery than an office. While day-to-day police work was conducted in the modern block, the old watch-house was used mostly for storage and administrative purposes. The sandstone building retained much of its nineteenth-century fabric along with a faint musty odour. With its high ceilings, plaster cornices and creaking wooden staircase, the structure evoked echoes of a bygone age. No wonder people felt it was haunted, thought Rita.

The ground floor housed a community relations bureau, an accounts unit and a records section extending to the Victorian cells at the rear, now crammed with filing cabinets. The first floor was used as a repository for spare equipment and a store for logbooks and registers from the distant past. There was also a colonial-era exhibit room, the area assigned to Rita for as long as she required it. Because of its heritage value the watch-house had been listed by the National Trust and the local historical society maintained the exhibit room as a small museum, library and occasional lecture venue. As well as attracting academic interest it was good PR for the police, although Jarrett had declared it off-limits to history buffs for the duration of Rita's stay.

She approved of the choice. It suited her needs, providing both plenty of space to spread out case material and a quiet setting to think in. Even the antique fixtures, the source of Jarrett's bondage chamber reference, were somehow conducive to a profiling mind-set. As she paced around the room, psyching herself up for the investigation, she observed her new surroundings with a mixture of amusement and curiosity.

The three internal walls were lined with glass cases displaying artefacts and documents preserved from the days of imperial rule. The items included batons, caps, holsters and pouches, together with reward posters for the capture of bushrangers and newspaper articles about the frontier war between white settlers and Aborigines. Wall mountings above the cases held rows of leg irons, chains and handcuffs alongside a collection of swords and pistols. A series of tinted lithographs hung from a picture rail, while a heavy oil painting was suspended from the chimney-breast in the corner. The gilt-framed canvas, dark with age and dated 1870, depicted a dozen men, white and black, armed with carbines. It was titled *The Hunting Party*. There was something intimidating about the group's pose and as Rita peered at it she found the image distinctly sinister. Below it the fireplace was virtually in mint condition, with an iron filigree surround and glazed tiles. She wondered how much it had actually been used in the past hundred years.

The external wall was dominated by bookcases on either side of a double-sash window. The shelves were filled with leather-bound volumes. The view outside, which a century ago would have looked down the hill over the town to the sea, was completely obscured by a backpacker hostel, its peeling paintwork and rusting fire escapes looming over an alley. The laneway below was cluttered with rubbish bins and parked cars. A patchwork of graffiti and posters littered the hostel's lower wall.

From the window's base came the wheeze and rattle of an air-conditioning unit, one of the few modern accessories in the room. Others were a computer desk, swivel chair, a seminar table where Rita laid out the case notes and a whiteboard to which she blu-tacked photos of the victims. As she stood in front of them, trying to draw some insight into the killer's mind, she began to see something contrived among the graphic images. The crime signature was plain to see: death by nail gun followed by decapitation. But one series of shots was more compelling than the rest. Rachel Macarthur's head on a spike, placed there for maximum attention, appeared to be an emphatic statement as much as a psychotic gesture. So what exactly was the killer's message, and why did the impaled head seem oddly recognisable? The notion bothered her, though she couldn't quite grasp an association.

With a sigh Rita strolled back to the display cases, gazing distractedly at the collection of vintage handbills and broadsheets. As she stood there, arms folded, her eyes fell on a front page from 1867. It carried a report on justice meted out to a bushranger under the headline: HOMICIDAL OUTLAW EXECUTED. Somehow it was apposite. And then it clicked. The killing of Rachel Macarthur bore the hallmarks of an execution. Even the positioning of the head, transfixed and elevated for public show, reflected the traditional fate reserved for traitors.

Such a possibility was consistent with a political theme or motive for the murder. It would make the setting – the confrontation between protesters and defence officials – extremely relevant. More ominously, it could also explain why such a line of inquiry was obstructed by officers at Whitley Sands. And there was something else. Rita was privy to additional information that justified investigating the research base – the warning delivered to Byron by Konrad Steinberg. If Dr Steinberg was right about 'fascist thugs' in charge of security, the implication was deeply disturbing. It gave Rachel's death a clear context and made identifying the first anonymous victim, the man in the mud, even more imperative.

The next move was obvious. Rita strode over to her desk, picked up her mobile and called the number Byron had given her.

It was answered with a curt, 'Yes?'

'Dr Steinberg?' Rita asked.

'Who's this?'

'My name's Rita Van Hassel,' she replied. 'Detective Sergeant Van Hassel. I'm a criminal profiler with the Victoria Police but I've been seconded to Whitley for the investigation into the beheadings.'

'How did you get my number?' he demanded.

'From Professor Byron Huxley.'

'Byron?'

'He and I are –' she searched for the appropriate words – 'very close. We've been together for some time now. Before I came up here he repeated your comments about the research base.'

'That's regrettable,' said Steinberg. 'When did you arrive in Whitley?'

'Today.'

'Then I've got some advice for you. Make your excuses and go. Leave as soon as you can.'

'Why?'

'Because of what I told Byron – it's worse than I thought.'

'Even so, I've got a job to do, questions to ask.'

'Well, don't believe anything you hear from the military and don't trust the local police. They're all in it together.'

'The police? With all due respect, that sounds extreme.'

'So is the war on terror and its contempt for the law. You're investigating the results.'

'If I understand you correctly,' she said slowly, 'you're talking about two murders.'

'There's a prevailing force here that's extremely dangerous.'

'Can you be more specific?'

'Not over the phone, no.'

'Fine. Let's meet.'

'That's unwise – for both of us.'

'Dr Steinberg, I intend to talk to you and I'd rather do it discreetly.'

'In other words, with or without my cooperation.' He sighed. 'Are you at Whitley Sands right now?'

'Yes, but I'll be in town mid afternoon. Dental appointment.'

'Nothing serious, I hope.'

'Minor repair work, since you ask. I lost a gold filling. The appointment's at three thirty. I can meet you at three.'

'Tell me where.'

'It'll have to be somewhere noisy and public. Surveillance here is total.' He paused for a moment. 'There's a pub, the Steamboat, in the centre of town. Find a table near the brass bell. If you're not there I'll wait no more than ten minutes.'

'How will I recognise you?'

'Check my website. And you?'

'Okay: I'm thirty, medium height, fair hair, blue eyes.' That sounded too much like a police description so she added, 'And for what it's worth, Byron calls me his blonde Nederlander.'

'Lucky Byron.'

'I'll be wearing a white top and denim skirt.'

'Now it's essential,' said Steinberg, 'that you tell your colleagues nothing about me. I can't overemphasise the risk. Remember what I said.'

'Yes, I get the message. Don't trust the military or the local cops.'

As she ended the call a voice came from behind her.

'That sounds seditious.'

She turned abruptly to find herself being observed by a senior police officer in uniform. He was standing in the open doorway, an equivocal smile on his face.

'So you're the profiler,' he said, walking into the room and closing the door behind him with a proprietary flick. 'I'm the man in charge of the "local cops", Inspector Derek Bryce. Who were you speaking to?'

Rita had to think quickly, wondering just how much Bryce had overheard.

'Someone my partner wanted me to look up, a local academic,' she responded with a half-truth, deciding to respect Steinberg's request for secrecy. 'You can ignore my comments – I'm just humouring them both.'

'Your partner's name is Byron?'

'Yes. He's a computer scientist. And I won't let any social calls distract me from the investigation, which from a profiling point of view is intriguing. Though I must admit this room has distracted me a bit.'

Her swift change of subject seemed to have worked.

'I hope it's suitable for you,' said Bryce.

'It's excellent,' she said. 'And I've got much more space here than in my office in Melbourne.'

'Good,' said Bryce, moving forward and shaking her hand at last. 'I'm glad we've got you on deck, Van Hassel. Any light you can shed will be welcome.'

'Thank you, sir.'

She wasn't sure if Steinberg's warning had alerted her to an undertone in Bryce's manner, or if she was simply imagining it. But there was something that made her wary. Bryce was broad-faced and smooth-skinned with wavy hair and an expression that was hard to read. While a smile played around his lips, there was something less friendly in his eyes.

'Has Jarrett told you anything about the history of the old watch-house?' he asked.

'Not really, other than that people think it's haunted.'

'I don't mean to spook you,' Bryce went on, strolling across to peer at the crime photos she'd arranged, 'but it's supposed to be this very room, in fact.'

'So who's the ghost?'

'A predecessor of ours,' he said with a low chuckle. 'A law officer with an unenviable reputation – Sergeant Kenneth Logan. He was in charge of half a dozen mounted and foot troopers here about a hundred and forty years ago. This room was his office.'

Rita glanced around with renewed interest.

'Why unenviable?' she asked.

'It's all here. Have a browse when you've got time to kill,' answered Bryce. 'Reports, documents, even Sergeant Logan's journal. Fascinating stuff. Of course it's easy to condemn him now, but I've often wondered how I would have acted in his circumstances.'

'What circumstances?'

'The "war on savages".' Bryce moved across to the seminar table, scanning the case material she'd placed in neat rows. 'You may not know much about the early history of Queensland – a lot of people don't. It was written in blood.'

'You're referring to the time of the first white settlers.'

'Yes, and the violence in the nineteenth century was worse here than in any other state.' Bryce turned to her, arms folded. 'The Indigenous people resisted what they saw as an invasion of their land by perpetrating the occasional massacre. The colonists responded on a scale that we'd now consider genocide. Around two thousand whites were killed in the frontier wars and at least ten thousand Aborigines.'

'And Sergeant Logan's role?'

'After a dozen Europeans were killed upriver, the big landowner here, Squatter Brodie, demanded mass reprisals. Under his leadership, Sergeant Logan helped organise and inflict indiscriminate killings. And over here,' continued Bryce, moving across the room, 'you can see both men in their pose of retribution, accompanied by their armed henchmen.' Rita followed him to where he was pointing at the oil painting above the fireplace. 'The bearded man in the centre is Squatter Josiah Brodie, the man to his right is Sergeant Logan.'

'So the hunting party hunted people?' said Rita.

'Exactly. And they killed as many as three hundred members of one tribe – men, women and children – all in the name of civilisation.'

'What happened to Logan?'

'He was eventually ambushed while riding back alone from a homestead. He was bashed, tied up and left to die on an ants' nest. But there was no comeuppance for Squatter Brodie. He prospered and established a family dynasty. Mind you, his descendants weren't keen on the painting. Brodie had commissioned it at the height of the war on savages, but his heirs were happy to bequeath it for display here.'

The history lesson gave Rita an insight into Bryce's personality. He seemed to relish both the sound of his own voice and the gruesome details he related.

'I'd be interested to hear your take on it,' said Bryce.

'In terms of forensic psychology?'

'No, on the position of Sergeant Logan and whether you'd be sympathetic at all with his response.'

'Somehow I doubt it.'

'Think about it. You're responsible for enforcing the law in an outpost of empire. It's a remote region seen as a frontline in the battle between civilised values and barbarism. People under your protection – the families of white settlers – are slaughtered by what are seen as bestial primitives for doing nothing more than peacefully cultivating the land.'

'Hardly the way the Aborigines would see it.'

'Of course not. From their perspective, the Europeans were a cruel occupying force with alien customs that were anathema to their own. If you look at it that way, acts of terror are justified. You commit murder as a form of resistance, the more horrific, the better. You'll do anything to repel invaders from your tribal land and sacred earth. Viewed objectively you have a clash of cultures, not to mention religions. In effect, one side launches a holy war while the other wages a war on terror. Sound familiar?'

Rita wasn't sure how to answer. The point he was making seemed too pertinent to be a coincidence. Was Bryce testing her? Had he overheard enough to make him suspicious and was he indeed involved in an official cover-up? Or was Steinberg's paranoia catching, causing her to misinterpret Bryce's loquacious welcome? To find out she needed to do some probing of her own.

'From what I hear about this town,' she said, 'the war on terror is pretty close to home.'

Bryce sniffed and strolled over to the window, casting his gaze down into the grubby alley.

'And what does that mean?'

'The war games in the military reserve. I saw the US carrier offshore and the sailors in the town so I checked the web,' she explained. 'Twelve thousand American troops on manoeuvres with Australian soldiers ahead of deployment to Iraq and Afghanistan. That's a heavy presence. A reminder of global conflict on your doorstep.'

'To be honest,' said Bryce, 'I try not to think about it. And as long as the GIs behave on leave, I don't have to.'

'And what about the Whitley Sands research base?'

'What about it?'

'Do you have a hands-off policy there too?'

'Ah, surprise, surprise.' Bryce turned to her with a sour smile. 'Jarrett has been grumbling to you.'

'You don't think he's got a point?' Rita queried. 'From my initial assessment it's clear that people on the base could provide material help to the investigation.'

'I'll repeat to you what I told him,' said Bryce, straightening up. 'The base and its personnel are none of our business. It's a highly sensitive establishment run jointly by the government of the United States and the Commonwealth of Australia. Whoever and whatever are deployed there fall under national security restrictions. In other words, we have to consider it out of bounds.'

'Like foreign territory.'

'Exactly. All the military land south of the town, including the war games reserve and the research base, comes under the jurisdiction of the defence department.'

'A modern occupation force.'

'That's how the land rights activists see it, not to mention the greens and the anti-war demonstrators. But these issues don't fall within your remit as a criminal profiler.' Bryce tapped the display of crime photos. 'We've got a serial killer on the loose. That's the issue to focus on. That's why you're here, Van Hassel. I don't want you getting sidetracked by peripheral controversies. Understood?'

'Yes, sir.'

'Good. I'll let you get on with it.' Bryce opened the door to leave. 'Though I must admit I'm a bit mystified as to what profilers actually do.'

'We think a lot, sir.'

Bryce looked at her askance, as if not sure whether that was a good or bad thing, nodding dubiously as he went out.

He was right to worry because what Rita was thinking was the very opposite of his advice. She was now even more convinced that what went on behind the gates of Whitley Sands was worthy of scrutiny.

13

At quarter to three Rita walked into the saloon bar of the Steamboat, an old-fashioned pub decorated with a jumble of maritime antiques. The brass bell that Steinberg had mentioned was mounted on an end wall between sepia photos of paddle-steamers. An assortment of lanterns, anchors and ensigns continued the theme throughout. A TV tuned to the Discovery Channel prattled above the bar. Rita ordered a lime and soda and sat at a table near the ship's bell to wait.

The pub was busy but not crowded, with a scattering of tourists, kids thumping away at slot machines, and a handful of regulars, by the look of them, leaning on the mahogany counter and putting the world to rights. At a corner table American sailors were drinking bottled beer. It had a relaxed feel and nobody bothered her.

Rita had done as Steinberg suggested, checking his website and finding a photo of a balding middle-aged man who looked like the archetypal scientist – dome-headed with a studious face and dark eyes behind black-rimmed glasses, and a hint of scepticism in his smile. At precisely three o'clock he walked in and looked directly at her. A tall man with shoulders slightly stooped, he was easily recognisable from the website image but, on this occasion, he wore no trace of a smile. In his checked shirt and cream trousers there was almost an air of formality about him, given the surroundings. After a cautious glance around he approached.

'Dr Steinberg,' said Rita.

He sat down, his hostility undisguised. He gave her a look as heavy as a lead cudgel.

'I don't appreciate coercion,' he said in a low voice. 'The only reason I'm here at all is because you're Byron's friend.'

'Well, thanks for coming.'

'You gave me little choice. Hardly the way to treat the friend of a friend.'

'In that case I apologise. I didn't mean to be officious.'

He dismissed that with a grunt. 'How is he anyway?'

'Popular,' she answered. 'A bit too popular, sometimes.'

'Still tweaking the faculty's nose? Still preaching hi-tech revolution?'

'His big theme is machine intelligence, if that's what you mean,' she replied. 'But his nose-tweaking will be at Cambridge next semester. He's landed a post as visiting professor.'

'Hmm.' Steinberg nodded sadly, as if revisiting a source of regret. 'He's always been smart, young Huxley. One of my brightest students, then he overtook me. He was destined for success.'

Rita studied his expression. 'And what about you? You don't seem too happy with where destiny's brought you.'

'*Here?* Of course not. But you already know that.'

'Yet many of your fellow academics would be envious – of a defence research salary, if nothing else.'

'The money's generous because it purchases your soul. The discoveries here have nothing to do with enlightening humanity. Quite the opposite. Working here negates the reason I became a scientist.'

'Why don't you leave?'

'Timing, my dear. Timing. And endurance.'

'At least you've got a pleasant location to endure.'

'Ha!' There was no humour in his strangled laugh. 'You may think you've arrived on an idyllic stretch of the Queensland coast, but you haven't. You've entered no-man's land.'

'You're talking about a tropical beach resort.'

'No. I'm talking about a tropic of death.'

'I assume you're speaking metaphorically.'

'Not at all. Look . . .' Steinberg hesitated, then went on. 'I don't want any friend of Byron to find themselves in harm's way. But if you stay here and conduct your investigation with anything like integrity, that's exactly what will happen. You'll be treated as a hostile.'

'By whom?'

'The real authorities here.'

'Dr Steinberg,' Rita said. 'I'm having trouble making sense of what you're trying to tell me.'

'Think East Berlin in the seventies. Think Stasi.'

'I find that hard to imagine.'

'Not for me. Members of my family had to suffer it, and the parallel here is unnerving.'

'When you say *here*, you mean the base?'

'A closed institution with a reach far beyond the perimeter fence,' he answered. '*Here* is wherever it wants to be. Unlike the Stasi, our guardians have access to the full range of twenty-first-century technology.'

'The comparison, I've got to say, seems a bit Orwellian.'

'The comparison is valid and if you stay long enough you'll see why. There's a line I keep thinking of: "death skulking in the air, in the water, in the bush."'

'What's that from?' she asked.

'Conrad's *Heart of Darkness*.'

Rita couldn't decide if the physicist was giving her a genuine warning, or if being embedded in a military research establishment had made him more than a little paranoid. Either way, she needed evidence.

'What do you know about the murders?' she asked.

'I have no direct knowledge. Sorry to disappoint you.'

'But you know something.'

'There's no doubt the death of Rachel Macarthur served a purpose. Ergo, so did that of the first victim. The purpose was to silence them.'

'You don't believe they're victims of a serial killer?'

'No. That flies in the face of probability. And logic.'

'Logic?'

'Yes, Miss Nederlander.' Steinberg clasped his hands together in something of a professorial pose. 'Ever heard of Ockham's razor?'

'Isn't that some medieval concept?'

'It's a scientific principle: the simplest explanation to fit the facts is most likely the correct one. A random lunatic on the loose is a superfluous entity and an all too convenient misdirection.'

'Hmm.' Rita still needed convincing. 'Silence them about what?'

'The environmental threat posed by the base.' He glanced sideways before continuing. 'I know for a fact the protest movement was right about radiation pollution. That's what I mean by a tropic of death.'

'Electromagnetic radiation?'

'Precisely.'

'Byron says you've compiled a report.'

'Then Byron's been talking out of school. Please don't mention it to anyone.'

'Can I see it?'

'It's on a disk.'

'Is that yes or no?'

'Let me think about it.' Steinberg looked at his watch. 'I've got to go.'

As he pushed back his chair Rita placed her hand on his.

'Dr Steinberg. When will you think about it?'

'You're very persistent.' He sighed. 'I'm going straight home from the dentist. That's when I'll consider producing an edited version for you. I'll call your mobile. Five o'clock on the dot. Satisfied?'

'Thank you.'

'Don't thank me. If we're discovered it will put both our lives in jeopardy.'

Rita drove back to the police station and touched base with Jarrett. He had nothing new to tell her and she wasn't about to inform him of her visit to the Steamboat. She left him with a glum look on his face and made her way into the old watch-house, climbing the stairs to her makeshift office. There was little to do other than wait and think, the computer screen in front of her, the archaeology of crime propped around her.

She did a series of online searches, calling up background pieces on the protest movement, the research base, the war on terror, but her mind was distracted by doubts about Steinberg and his conspiracy theory. He was convinced of its truth. That was obvious. Just as obvious was his bitterness and resentment. Had it warped his judgement? It was very easy for a deeply disgruntled man to blame a hostile force for his plight, much as Jarrett felt that fellow citizens were turning against him. Somehow there seemed to be an overlap, though that wasn't enough to turn the investigation on its head. She needed more to go on than Jarrett's anxiety and Ockham's razor. She needed something tangible. Perhaps Steinberg's secret report could provide it.

Five o'clock came and went with no call on her mobile. Steinberg had been definite about when he'd phone her but by ten past five he still hadn't rung. She gave him another five minutes. Still nothing, so she called his mobile. It was switched off. That didn't surprise her. His failure to contact her had an ominous feel. Something must have gone wrong. There was no point in hanging around.

Trying his number again, with the same result, she walked briskly to the police car park where she'd left the Falcon. The weather was changing. A wild wind had blown in a low ceiling of cloud. She got in the car and pulled a local street directory from the glove box. According to the address Byron had supplied, Steinberg lived south of the town at a place called Leith Ferry, which was little more than a dot on the map. She decided to pay him a visit, whether he liked it or not.

14

Rain was sweeping in off the sea as Rita drove south from the estuary along a road skirting defence department property. She passed the research base, a barracks and an artillery range behind tall wire fences studded with warning notices: COMMONWEALTH OF AUSTRALIA – AUTHORISED PERSONNEL ONLY. On the other side of the road cane fields stretched into the distance, their dense mass of stems threshing around in the wind. After a few kilometres the fields receded inland, giving way to soggy ground and the upper reaches of tidal inlets, while to her left was the fringe of the vast military reserve.

There was no sign of activity, war exercises or otherwise, as she followed the road through an empty landscape. The place had an end-of-the-world feel to it, nothing but muddy creeks and mangrove swamps. Remote sugar sheds lay low on the land. Solitary trees stood bent and stunted, deformed by the coastal winds. The isolation obviously suited the government. The flatness and inaccessibility made security easy.

Beyond the mangroves was open scrubland and the first sign of habitation, a weatherboard shack set back from the road, but as Rita drove by she noticed the windows were boarded up. She passed overgrown field gates, a disused barn and broken fences bordering what might once have been sheep pasture, and as the road curved around a stand of ironbarks it led to a wooden bridge over a swollen river tributary. As the car's wheels thumped over the planks, lamp posts and powerlines came into view, then rows of houses, several dozen of them. This was Leith Ferry.

The main street was deserted. Rain fell against an almost eerie quiet as Rita drove past silent houses behind uniform picket fences. The style of the homes, decorated with geometric motifs and leadlight windows, dated them to the 1920s or 30s, yet they were in immaculate condition. There was something anomalous about the scene, an almost regimented neatness, with no shops to be seen, no services of any kind, just accommodation. Even a small stone church had been converted into apartments. A board beside it that once would have held parish notices was printed with a list of directions to military installations. That explained it. What had been a rural community decades ago was now in the hands of the government, leased and maintained as living quarters for staff employed at defence facilities. Leith Ferry, which no longer possessed a farming population, a church or a ferry, was now effectively a civilian barracks.

Rita found the turn-off she needed at the top end of the main street. It led her down a dead-end lane with no other houses around. When she got to Steinberg's home she pulled over, her senses alert, a hollow feeling in her stomach.

She sat in her car with the engine off and spots of rain whipping against the windscreen. She was parked in a dreary landscape beside a remote weatherboard cottage. The white wooden structure looked forlorn as dusk closed in. It was a lonely, windswept spot – a dispiriting view of fields returning to wilderness, with just a few spindly trees around, while in the distance rose the inhospitable slopes of the ranges. Far away, along a high ridge, the giant white spheres of the US satellite tracking station loomed under the grey cloud cover. Some hint of what Steinberg had said, his suggestion of a presence alien to Australia, was starting to ring true. She didn't like the mood of the place.

The gate was open and a car was parked in the driveway, but something wasn't right. Then she noticed not a single light was visible inside the house. Almost instinctively she reached for her bag and took out a pocket torch.

She got out and walked through the rain to the front porch. She pressed the doorbell but couldn't hear a sound. The circuit seemed to be dead. She knocked loudly several times. Still no response. Her sense of unease was growing. She leant her weight against the door. Locked solidly. She tried peering through the front windows but they were curtained. She could see nothing. Then she went around the back. The kitchen door was also locked, but a rear window was slightly open. She caught a smell of electrical burning. Now she was certain something was wrong.

Rita slid her hand inside, opened the window wide and hoisted herself over the sill. She found herself standing in a bathroom with patterned tiles. She listened. A heavy stillness filled the house. Then she walked quietly from the bathroom along a carpeted passageway towards the front of the house. It led into a hall with a sideboard, a mirror, an old-fashioned umbrella stand and open doorways right and left. The tang of electrical burning in the air grew stronger, along with a much nastier smell. It came from the door on the right. Rita stepped quietly through it.

Steinberg was lying on the floor, his body contorted in a motionless convulsion. Rita breathed out slowly and reached for the light switch. She flicked it. Nothing happened. Lights fused. That explained the smells — both of them. Burnt circuits and burnt flesh. She got out her torch and shone it on the body. It was beside the open door to an inner room — a computer den. She moved closer and squatted down. The features were those of the man she'd spoken with just a few hours ago but now they bore the warped rictus of a face in shock. The skin on his hand was scorched and blistered. She raised the torch beam till it rested on a security keypad. Its metal buttons were buckled and blackened. So that's how it had happened. Just as he'd punched in his personal access code the door of his computer den clicked open and a lethal surge of electricity shot through his body.

It looked like a freak accident. None of the wiring was exposed. There were no marks she could see in the torchlight to indicate the keypad had been rigged to electrocute him. But as her hand rested on the polished floor she felt something on her fingertips, a light powdering of fresh sawdust. That made it professional. And it changed the whole complexion of the case she'd been seconded to investigate. Rita had wanted evidence to justify Steinberg's paranoia about the research base and its military authorities. Now she had more than she needed but at the cost of his life. She hung her head as a pang of remorse shook her.

It was also all the more urgent that she get hold of the disk with Steinberg's report on it. She stood up with a sigh, stepped over his body and went into the computer room. The terminal on his desk was dead with the disk drive left open and empty. As she directed the torchlight around the interior the beam fell on rows of disks, a bookcase, a TV stand and an antique dresser, its shelves filled with DVDs, mostly recordings of opera. Steinberg must have played them in the background while working at his keyboard. Framed university qualifications, including his doctorate, were hung around the room, along with posters for *Tosca*, *La Traviata* and *Parsifal*. Everything appeared to be neat and systematic. But where to start?

Rita went through the carefully labelled disks that filled a rack on one of the walls. Hundreds of them. They all referred to technical and scientific topics. If Steinberg's report was among them she had no way of knowing. Next she checked the desk drawers and dresser cabinets, again without luck. She didn't expect him to have left a copy of it lying around the house, but she searched it anyway. She found nothing of interest – just the tidy, comfortable home of someone who liked classical music, European literature and solitude. She sat wearily on the sofa in his sitting room and sighed. Whatever revelation Steinberg had worked on, he'd taken it with him. There wasn't much more she could do here.

She had just pulled out her mobile to call the police emergency line when the front door burst open, shattered off its hinges, figures lunging towards her. Armed men in camouflage clothing were shouting, 'Get down on the floor! Flat on the floor! Now!'

Red points from laser sights flashed across her eyes and danced on her chest.

She didn't hesitate.

She did as she was told but shouted back at them, 'I'm a police officer!'

She was told to shut up.

As Rita lay face down on the floorboards her arms were wrenched behind her back and her legs were kicked apart.

'Okay,' said a man's voice. 'Cuff her.'

•

Rita loathed them even before they manhandled her into the back of an army truck and strip-searched her. She'd encountered their type before on a hostile environments course: thick-necked regimental bullies with buzz-saw haircuts who delighted in intimidating women. Making sexual threats was part of their nature, reinforced by group psychology. She knew enough not to show an emotional reaction to the mistreatment. That would only encourage them. She also guessed they were some of the 'fascist thugs' Steinberg had referred to. If so there was an added danger. It was possible they were operating outside the law, and for all she knew they were directly involved in his murder. She had no way of knowing what agenda they were following.

But she refused to let them unnerve her. Though she stood there naked, she was plainly unimpressed with their aggression.

'Just let me know when you're finished,' she said.

They told her to get dressed then handcuffed her again.

'There's no need for this,' she insisted. 'You've got my ID.'

'We don't know it's genuine,' came the answer.

'Why would you think that?'

'Security protocols. We're on alert for a terrorist cell.'

'And I'm a suspect?'

'You could have fake ID.'

'It's not. Call Whitley police station.'

'Forget it. Either way you'll have a lot of explaining to do back at base. In the meantime, shut up.'

There was no point arguing and she had no choice but to comply. Their directive was clearly to treat her as a potential hostile until ordered otherwise. As well as barking commands, restraining and searching her, they'd seized her shoulder bag, mobile phone and car keys. Her personal details had been scanned on a battlefield laptop and relayed ahead to whoever would conduct the interrogation. While her predicament seemed bizarre, it was also entirely consistent with the oppressive use of force that Steinberg had warned her about.

They put Rita in the back of a jeep. The rain had blown over leaving the air clear but damp. No one spoke to her as a small convoy of military vehicles, with her Falcon being driven at the rear, followed the road back towards the town, the headlights sweeping along a tangle of mangroves at the edge of swamps now engulfed in blackness. The silence suited her. It gave her time to think out a plausible version of events.

She'd guessed where they were heading long before they arrived at the entrance to the research base. The gates opened, the barriers lifted and they drove through the grounds to the back of the main complex then through another set of gates into a security compound. Still handcuffed, she was escorted into a low concrete building with all the charm of a prison block and along a corridor to a bare interrogation room. Only then were the cuffs removed. She was told to sit down and wait. There was a table with chairs on either side of it, video cameras high up in the corners of the room, and a two-way mirror on the end wall. Rita pulled out a chair, sat down and found herself agreeing with another of Steinberg's observations. As a state security facility, the Stasi would have approved.

They made her wait for half an hour. At one stage she got up and tried the door. It was locked. She paced around the room for a while then sat down again, sure she was being watched. At last the door was flung open by a man in a short-sleeved army shirt. He was in his forties with streaked blond hair, thin, sharp features and a slight limp. There was scar tissue on the side of his face from what could have been a shrapnel wound. His manner was brisk and combative as he slapped a file on the table, leant on the back of the chair opposite and stood over her.

'Okay, your police background checks out,' he said. 'I've spoken to Bryce who says you've been seconded here to profile the murders. Which is all well and good. But answer one question. What the fuck were you doing in Steinberg's place?'

Rita pushed back her chair. 'You know who I am,' she replied. 'So who are you?'

'Security director of Whitley Sands, Captain Roy Maddox. And I don't tolerate backchat.'

'But you tolerate thuggish behaviour by your squad,' she retorted.

'They follow protocols.'

'We'll see about that when I file a report on them.'

'There'll be no report,' he snapped. 'And I'm yet to be convinced I should even release you.'

'You've got no grounds to hold me.'

'Don't be naive.' Maddox pulled out the chair and sat down, facing her squarely. 'All this falls under the umbrella of national security – the base, staff quarters, Steinberg's home, anything deemed relevant. Even Steinberg's death remains classified until we decide otherwise. So answer the question.'

'I could have explained back at the house if I'd been allowed to.'

'Explain it now.'

'Fine. But it has nothing to do with national security or even police business. It was a social call. I was looking up a friend on behalf of my partner.'

'Some social call. You break into a man's house and we find you there with his dead body. You didn't even phone it in.'

'That's what I was trying to do when your men came busting in like storm-troopers.'

'It doesn't explain why you broke in.'

'I was hoping to meet him in town and he'd promised to call me back by five,' answered Rita. 'When he failed to call and didn't answer his phone I drove to his house. His car was there, but no lights were on, the place was silent, I got no response to my knocking and there was a smell of electrical burning. I sensed something was wrong. I got in through an open window.'

'This partner of yours,' said Maddox, taking out a gold pen and opening the file. 'Name?'

'Byron Huxley,' she sighed.

'What's his connection to Steinberg?' asked Maddox, writing in the file.

'Byron's a professor in computer science at Monash University. Dr Steinberg was his friend and colleague there for a number of years. They've kept in touch. They have views in common.'

'God save us from the chattering classes,' said Maddox, putting down his pen. 'Now, I know you examined the body and searched the house,' he added, watching her closely. 'Why?'

'Why do you think?'

Maddox thumped the table with his fist. 'Answer the damn question! Right now you're about one lippy comment away from getting on my shit list.'

'I'd assumed I was already on it,' she replied, then leant forward in what could have been a conciliatory gesture. 'Look, Captain Maddox, put yourself in my position. I was planning to meet someone. He didn't get back to me. I called at his house. There was something wrong. I got inside and found him dead. From that point on I acted professionally – not as an uninvited guest but as a police detective. Of course I examined the body and checked through the house. For all I knew it was a crime scene. But before I called it in I wanted to see if there was anything suspicious.'

'And was there?' Maddox asked, a little too promptly.

Rita realised the question was a trap. If she answered the wrong way she would set herself up as a target, so she had no hesitation in lying to his face. 'There was no sign that any intruder had been inside. Nothing appeared to be out of place. So what I was about to report, when your men raided the place, was that Dr Steinberg was the victim of a freak accident.'

Maddox's eyes scanned her silently before he sat back.

'A freak and tragic accident is what it looks like at this stage,' he said flatly. 'Although your presence has added a confusing dimension.'

'As a matter of interest,' asked Rita, 'why did your men hit the place when they did?'

'You triggered the raid,' he answered. 'You have no idea the level of surveillance we have to maintain in this area.'

'Because of an alert for a terrorist cell?'

'Where did you hear that?'

'In one of your trucks after I was strip-searched and handcuffed as a terrorist suspect.'

Maddox picked up his pen again and tapped the file distractedly.

'You might see your treatment as an overreaction,' he said, 'but under the circumstances, it's not.'

'What circumstances?'

He paused as if wrestling with how much to tell her, before relenting.

'The information is not for public consumption, but the local authorities are about to be briefed, so you might as well hear it now. We have reason to believe a group of four men, suspected of being members of a militant cell, are plotting a terrorist act against the base. They vanished from where they were under observation in Sydney's western suburbs. The latest intelligence points to them being in the vicinity of Whitley Sands. Because of the heightened alert, we're informing the police, council and emergency services and asking for extra vigilance.'

'What's the link with Whitley?'

'Don't bother to ask, you don't have the clearance,' was his curt reply. 'So let's stick to what happened tonight. You might be telling the truth, but you're not off the hook. You're now subject to restrictions pertaining to the security and intelligence agencies, and your full cooperation is required.'

'My cooperation?'

'Yes.'

'Why?'

'Time to get real, Van Hassel. In crude terms, I've already got you for unlawful entry, failing to report a death and obstructing a federal investigation. So you'll do what you're told.'

'Or what? I'll be prosecuted?'

'We both know it won't come to that. But I can put an end to your career with one phone call. Understood?'

'Yes.'

'Good. And if you want to leave here tonight, there's a procedure to follow.'

'What procedure?'

'You'll have your photo, prints and DNA taken, you'll sign the witness report on Steinberg's death that we're drafting, along with official secrets forms and consent agreements undertaking never to disclose you were at his home. You'll also be given a reference number for our files and any subsequent exigencies of the service.'

'Exigencies?' The word almost stuck in Rita's throat. 'That sounds like an excuse for dragooning me into things outside the law.'

'I don't care what it sounds like. In formal terms, you'll be inducted as an associate officer of the Whitley Sands security force.'

'And if I refuse?'

'You won't leave here.' Maddox put his pen away, collected the file and stood up. Before walking out he paused to add, 'And you'd kiss your future goodbye.'

That final threat seemed to have more than one meaning. It hung in the air as he shut the door behind him.

Rita did as she was told, of course, complying with the ID requirements, signing the declarations and filling in what amounted to a formal registration under the terms of the security and intelligence services. It was like sealing a diabolical pact, acknowledging surrender to an invisible and remorseless authority. The amount of documentation reminded her of a property transaction, which in a sense it was, something akin to mortgaging her professional independence. What the hell, she thought. I can live with it.

Once she'd been processed out, her bag and mobile phone were handed back to her and the blue Falcon was driven to the entrance of the security block. She was handed the keys and told to get in. As she slid behind the wheel she was given a final warning to keep her mouth shut and was then escorted by jeep out of the compound and off the base. When the barrier and gates closed behind her, and she was alone at last, she gunned the engine and roared off towards the town. She couldn't get away fast enough.

Although the experience of the past few hours had been both chilling and humiliating, she took more than one positive from it. She now knew first hand what sort of force Steinberg had been referring to, and she accepted he was justified in likening it to a corps of state-sanctioned hoods. There was also the deception she'd pulled on Maddox. As far as Rita could tell he was satisfied that she'd discovered nothing of consequence. But that thin residue of sawdust had told her everything. Steinberg had been a witness to the truth and had paid with his life.

15

It was coming up to midnight as Rita sat cross-legged in front of the webcam, her laptop propped on the hotel bed, a Scotch over crushed ice within reach. It was her third and it was having the required effect. So was the chocolate. Four discarded wrappers from the mini-bar supply of confectionery lay on the bedside cabinet. Her mobile phone lay in pieces around her, dismantled in her check for bugs. The curtains were open on the night sky, now clear and bristling with stars, the television was playing quietly in the background, tuned to MTV, and from her open balcony door came the sound of waves surging against the foot of the bluff.

She was wearing the green satin pyjamas Byron had bought her, while his face filled the laptop screen and his reassuring voice, coming from the speaker, was helping to soothe away her residual stress.

'So what do you think of the new webcam?' he asked.

'It's fine,' she said.

'Fine? It's faster, with no blips and video-quality resolution.'

'Okay, if you say so. All the better to see you with, my dear. Though your movements are a bit jerky.'

'It's a webcam, not a TV camera,' he laughed, but he seemed to notice her expression. 'Are you okay?' he asked.

'Just tired.'

'Is anything wrong?'

'The day was full-on.' Rita gave him a weak smile. 'I miss you.'

'Look,' frowned Huxley, 'I hope they're not going to keep you up there too long.'

'The investigation's already complicated.'

'I could fly up in a couple of weeks. I could even claim it as an academic junket – call it research and drop in on old Steinberg.'

Rita didn't say anything.

'I don't suppose you've had time to make contact with him,' Huxley went on.

She just shook her head in answer.

'Well, if you get the chance . . .' He looked at her carefully across the live link. 'And if you happen to bump into Audrey Zillman, give her my best.'

'Sure.' She sighed, reaching for her drink.

'You seem down.'

'So cheer me up.'

'That would be easier,' he complained, 'without a couple of thousand k and a web-link between us.'

'Why?'

'Because I'd start with a kiss.'

'Where?'

'The sensitive part of your neck.'

'Then what?'

'Your ears.'

'You know that tickles.'

'From there I'd work my way down.'

'All right, enough.' She laughed.

He gave her an affectionate look. 'I found the pasta and the note you left. I miss you too.'

'Now that's what I wanted to hear.' She swallowed another mouthful of Scotch. 'Tell me about your day.'

'It was great,' he told her, 'until it was ruined by incompetence!'

Rita was mystified by both the comment and his sudden vehemence. 'Byron, what are you talking about?'

'The faculty football match! Bloody umpires!'

'Oh,' she groaned. 'Football.'

'I was constantly infringed without getting a free kick while my opponent couldn't be touched!' he exclaimed. 'We lost by a goal. In other words, the result was decided by bad umpiring. You rely on those applying the rules to have decent judgement and consistency. But if they're morons the result is a travesty!'

'For God's sake,' said Rita. 'It's just a game.'

'You don't understand. Most women don't. They can't see the level of commitment men bring to football. It's a metaphor for life: passion, courage, striving together to achieve success.'

'Yes, yes. I can see it's a ritual of male bonding.'

'Just the sort of remark I'd expect from someone who's female and a psychologist. You're missing the point. Football is a healthy way of channelling physical and social energy.'

'It's tribal.'

'Damn it, Rita,' he said crossly. 'Sometimes you refuse to see there are higher ideals.'

'Maybe that's because I'm a woman,' she said, bemused. 'Though it seems your ideals have trouble surviving the umpires.'

'Of course they do! That's what I'm saying. Like so many things in life, when you have arseholes making bad decisions a worthy endeavour is reduced to absurdity. Chaos theory reigns supreme!'

'Well, I'll agree with one point,' she conceded. 'I'll never understand why football makes you so irrational. It's definitely a male thing. But if we can get away from noble savages chasing a leather ball, what else have you been up to?'

'Oh, just plodding through the tail end of the semester. Two seminars and a departmental meeting over wine, cheese and backbiting that gave me a headache for the drive home.'

'Sounds like hell.'

'Academic bitching! No wonder there's a brain drain to the defence industries.'

'You really thought about it, didn't you? Making the jump.'

'Yes. No more campus politics and a lot more money. Very tempting, as long as you don't feel you're selling out.'

'Who are you talking about?'

'Steinberg, of course. Maybe Audrey too. Somehow I can't visualise her as a defence scientist. She was a brilliant performer at university. Inspiring.'

'Was she now?'

'I'm talking about her sense of vision.'

'I'm sure you are.'

'That's why she was headhunted by NATO. I only studied a year under her at Cambridge.'

'Sounds delightful. How old is she?'

'That was ten years ago, so she'd be thirty-nine.'

'That means when you were twenty-one she was twenty-nine. No wonder she was inspiring.' Rita watched him watching her on the screen. 'I must definitely look her up.'

'Why?'

'For a start I'd like to meet one of your ex-lovers.' She paused to let him fidget. 'And you're right about the quality of the webcam picture. I can see you blushing.'

Huxley wasn't sure how to react. 'I thought we'd agreed our past love lives were buried history.'

'So it's true.' She was starting to enjoy this. 'I've unearthed one of your secrets.'

'That's not fair,' he protested. 'You're trying to psych me out.'

'No, I'm just teasing you.'

But he did have a point. In the year they'd been living together Rita had been trying to find out what exactly made Byron tick. At first she'd almost convinced herself he was simply a man of integrity, open and spontaneous. This seemed too good to be true. Besides, the notion that what you see is what you get was unacceptable to anyone trained in psychology. So she tried to dig a little. Occasionally what emerged, from both his words and his behaviour, was a single-minded application to the task in hand, a forcefulness that detested compromise. This brought added spice to the relationship, for Rita was hardly a shrinking violet herself. It meant that Byron, for all his affection and humanity, also possessed the elements of a driven personality.

If Byron had a dark side to his character, it surfaced in a raw enthusiasm that at times threatened to run away with him. Mostly he channelled it into science and challenging scientific convention, but there was another aspect to it. His fascination with the laws of nature extended to human dynamics, principal among them the magnetic properties of women. Currently there was his deep attraction to Rita which was heartfelt and flattering. How long it would last she had no way of knowing, nor did she know how many lovers he'd actually had. Women were always checking him out and more than once she'd spotted a flash of electricity between Byron and his female students. And now she'd discovered a passion from his past. It made her wonder whether his experiences with women were intense but transitory, and if his emotional life was another expression of his restless quest for knowledge.

'Tell me more about Audrey Zillman,' insisted Rita. 'What type of person is she? When did you last see her?'

'While I was doing my last year at Cambridge I went to see her in Brussels, but things had changed.'

'In what way?'

'Well, how can I put it? Audrey was always an unusual person. Very gifted. Frighteningly intellectual.'

'Attractive?'

'Yes, in a fierce, Teutonic sort of way. And yes, we were emotionally involved, though I often thought the emotion was one-sided – from me. Occasionally she showed the same depth of feeling but mostly I think I amused her.'

'And in Brussels?'

'She was preoccupied. Dealing with the NATO colonels was annoying her and the military application of AI was absorbing her thoughts.' Huxley shook his head. 'Why do you want to know all this?'

'It's not about your student exploits,' answered Rita. 'It's about helping me get the research base in perspective.'

'I thought your task was to track a serial killer.'

'The proximity of Whitley Sands gives it a bearing on the investigation, and Audrey clearly plays a significant role there.'

'You're profiling her,' he said.

'Humour me, Byron. I've already come up against a strange attitude here. Finish what you were saying about how she'd changed.'

'She'd become distant. Not just from me but from day-to-day life. She was living in a zone, focusing so much on the AI breakthrough that normal human activity was an irritating distraction to her. It's as if ordinary mortals were beneath her notice, me included. Maybe I'm exaggerating.'

'Maybe,' Rita agreed. 'But she obviously hurt you.'

'As I was leaving I actually suggested her brain was becoming more cybernetic than human – too detached by half. She didn't get cross or disagree, just gave me one of her ironic smiles. I haven't seen her since. When I heard she'd landed a top post at Whitley Sands I nearly got in touch, but thought better of it. I'd closed the book on what happened between us. *The Moving Finger writes; and, having writ, Moves on* – that sort of thing.'

'Sometimes it freaks me out when you quote poetry. What exactly is her job there?'

'System controller.'

'So she'd know all about their technology?'

'I suspect she's designed the entire cyber network, from their operating system upwards.'

'Now here's where I need to pick your brain. The integrated system you mentioned on our night out – could it deliver *total* surveillance?'

'Total? I'm not sure how they'd pull that off.'

'Take an educated guess.'

'You could just about do it with saturation hi-tech coverage across a specific sector – satellites, cameras, infra-red, radar, scanners and so on, as well as immediate, unfettered web and phone access. Even if you coordinated all that input the huge problem it would pose is the ocean of data generated and how to sort through it.' A sudden glow of insight shone from his face. 'My God, I wonder if that's what she's done.'

'What?'

'Solved the problem,' he said with excitement. 'It's possible Audrey's married quantum computing to AI to create a sophisticated interactive process that sifts through the mass of data. If she has it's another milestone for the twenty-first century.'

'Like what you were talking about in your speech?'

'I was describing developments from the immediate future to mid century. But if Audrey's cracked what I think she has, some of that future's already here.' Huxley shrugged. 'Bit scary too. A powerful weapon of social control in the hands of the military.'

It was a sober thought to end their conversation on, but after saying their goodnights and switching off the webcam Rita downed the rest of her drink. Then she turned off the lights and sat on the bed, propped against the pillows.

'What have I got myself into?' she said quietly to herself.

As she sat there, staring at the shadows on the ceiling, the laptop screen glowing at her feet, the sound of the sea persisted below the hotel balcony, waves thudding against the shore, foam hissing among the rocks. She could almost hear the voice of Steinberg whispering to her: 'Welcome to the war on terror.'

16

Roy Maddox waited for fellow members of the committee to settle in their seats before passing copies of a dossier around the conference table.

'The leak has been plugged,' he said.

At the head of the table, Willis Baxter folded his hands. 'Explain.'

'The man behind the leak, Dr Konrad Steinberg, no longer poses a threat,' said Maddox. 'He was a specialist in electromagnetic technology. That made him an expert in project hardware and perfectly placed to give our enemies what they wanted. Ironically, he's fallen victim to his own faulty wiring at his home in Leith Ferry and electrocuted himself to death. As suspected, he'd compiled a report that he was beginning to circulate to outside contacts. It's on a disk containing highly classified material, including specifications of the technology, and a commentary in which he calls for the immediate shutdown of the Panopticon Project.'

'He refers to it by name?' asked Horsley.

'Yes,' answered Maddox.

'What was his security rating?'

'Level-four clearance.'

'So he had no direct access to the Tracker technology?'

'No, but his aim was to kill the project.'

'Then his death is a just outcome,' put in Molloy. 'And you're absolutely right. The repercussions of this Steinberg report going public or falling into the wrong hands would have left the project irreparably compromised. The man wasn't just a whistleblower, he was an out-and-out traitor. His death has averted a disaster.'

'We can't relax yet,' said Maddox. 'If you look at the photos in the dossier you'll see how Steinberg hid copies of his report.'

'More than one?'

'He made four copies, disguised as a DVD box set.'

The others around the table leafed through the folders in front of them.

'So Dr Steinberg was a fan of Wagner,' observed a man in a charcoal grey suit. His name was Peter Luker, and he was a senior agent from the intelligence service in Canberra; he was the only committee member without a military background.

'Yes – The Ring Cycle. He printed the disks with a photo label for each opera,' explained Maddox. 'But we have a problem.'

'Which is?'

'Disk number one, *Das Rheingold*, is missing.'

Silence filled the room.

Then Molloy said: 'Two questions. Where is it and who has it?'

'We're reasonably sure it's still local,' answered Maddox. 'It's clear from Steinberg's email records that he passed the disk to someone linked to the protest movement in the town. We're trying to trace him now. We don't know his full identity yet.'

'What *do* you know?'

'Steinberg refers to him as Stonefish.'

'Is that a code name?'

'No. We've established there's a software dealer who goes by that name. He's known in seafront bars and cyber cafes and has criminal associates. There's no police file with that alias and we haven't been able to find him, so for the moment we're stumped. This is civilian territory. My unit will do the legwork, no problem, though what we need is access to intelligence that can narrow the field.' He turned to the man in the grey suit. 'Luker?'

Luker nodded. 'I'll issue a directive as soon as we finish here tonight. You'll get whatever we can find out about him.'

'Okay. Good.'

'Let me get something straight,' interrupted Molloy, slapping his folder shut. 'Just how long has this damn *Rheingold* disk been out there? Are we talking hours, days, what?'

'Weeks,' answered Maddox stiffly. 'A comparison shows the two hard copies we retrieved, detailing radiation levels, were downloaded from a section of the Steinberg report. They must have come from the disk.'

'So when the two printouts were contained, the threat wasn't.'

'That's correct.'

'And for all you know this dealer could have touted the disk to the highest bidder. He could have sold it. He could have stuck it on eBay and auctioned it over the internet. It could already be in the hands of middle men or arms traders or terrorists!'

'Calm down,' interjected the director-general. 'It's just as likely this Stonefish has gone to ground, taking the disk with him. Now we know who the link man is we've got a better chance of containing the threat. And we need to get on with it.' He looked around the table. 'And while we're on the subject, what's the latest on the alert?'

'Bad news,' answered Luker. 'The four terrorist suspects may already be in Whitley. There's been a positive ID of their van travelling north on the Bruce Highway about sixty k south of here. And a raid's been conducted on a market garden site they were using in Sydney's outer suburbs. They left behind maps of the Queensland coast, false documents and bomb-making residues. I'm told there's little doubt they're an active terrorist cell.'

'Great surveillance op,' commented Molloy. 'The proverbial stable door.'

'And we don't have the luxury of hindsight,' added Baxter. 'You've heard the prime minister's warning. The fate of Afghanistan has repercussions in our part of the world. Each setback emboldens the recruitment activities of terrorist groups, with the stability of our whole region at risk. We can't afford to relax. We can't afford to hesitate. We have to assume these men pose a direct threat to us.'

'Okay,' said Molloy. 'Worst-case scenario. The Fixer is here and the cell has linked up with him. They could be priming an attack as we speak.'

'Then we can't waste time. So – any other updates?'

'I need to mention one other potential problem, sir,' answered Maddox. 'It comes in the shape of a detective sergeant.'

'What on earth are the police up to?'

'Not the police, just one woman officer. Her name's Van Hassel. Her photo's in the file.' Maddox slid a copy to the centre of the table. 'I couldn't brief you before, sir, but we seized her inside Steinberg's house in the company of Steinberg's dead body.'

'What the hell was she doing there?'

'She's a profiler, on secondment from Melbourne, and she claims her visit was intended as a social call. She'd have me think she found out nothing.'

'But you don't believe her.'

'We've pulled a recording of a phone conversation with Steinberg,' said Maddox. 'She's made the very connection we can't allow her to follow up. I don't trust her and she doesn't trust us.'

'In what way?'

'Inspector Bryce tells me Van Hassel thinks base security is relevant to his murder investigation.'

'The stakes are too high,' said Molloy. 'Treat her as a hostile.'

'Just hold on a moment,' insisted Luker. 'We're talking about a law-enforcement officer here.'

'No one can be allowed to jeopardise the project.'

'And we can handle her to make sure she doesn't.' Luker picked up Van Hassel's photo and gazed at it. 'She's absolutely right, of course. Base security is relevant. A severed head at the gates makes that plain enough. She should be allowed to pursue her inquiries – up to a point that we decide on.'

'What are you suggesting?' asked the director-general.

'The security review. You're inviting various officials to pad out the numbers. Include her in the police delegation.'

Baxter thought about it. 'I hear what you're saying. Drafting her onto the review panel would be a way of keeping her on a tight leash. But you'll also need to keep an eye on her.'

Luker studied Van Hassel's image again and smiled. 'I can do that.'

'All right, then. But before we go, I've got a final reminder for all of you.' Baxter cast a pointed gaze around the table. 'We're approaching the crucial phase of the Panopticon Project, when we'll have it fully up and running on a permanent basis. At the same time, the worst possible time, we're under siege. I use the word advisedly. Our enemies are manoeuvring against us, we're being probed for weaknesses, lined up for attack. I want no one here to doubt that we will respond to any direct threat with the amount of force needed to destroy it. Our responsibility, with its global implications, requires nothing less. Unfortunately our enemies are proliferating. The protest movement, with its rainbow coalition of low-lifes and anarchists, is pretty much a known quantity. The terrorist presence, of which we've had alarming indications, is much less identifiable and much more dangerous. We need to make sure everyone maintains the highest vigilance. Covertly, the same goes for the missing disk and whoever handles it. That is potentially the most destructive weapon that can be used against us. We cannot let that happen.' He watched the nods of agreement. 'So, all in all, the last thing we need on our patch is a rogue police officer. I'll go along with the suggestion – for now – of inviting her onto the review panel. But, Luker, if she doesn't toe the line all bets are off. We'll deal with her as an active threat and do what's necessary. Agreed?'

Luker tossed Rita's photo onto the table and turned to the director-general.

'Agreed,' he said.

17

In the dead of night, several hours after the committee members had reviewed the forces against them, a new enemy was preparing to launch a strike on the research base. He posed a threat they had not anticipated. There was no alert protocol in place to identify him. Although they knew his name, his background wasn't political, militant or terrorist. And his plan of attack was neither paramilitary nor confrontational. He possessed no bombs, no guns and no conventional ammunition. His weapons of assault were electronic. And his target was the Panopticon Project. If he could crash its control system, disable or simply rip off and expose it, he would be satisfied. His motive was personal revenge. The aim was to inflict as much damage as possible and achieve a belated victory for his murdered lover, Rachel Macarthur.

Frederick James Hopper, as he was known to the police – Freddy to his friends, Edge Freddy to fellow hackers – inhabited a twilight subculture whose methods were partly subversive, partly criminal. Throughout his volatile relationship with Rachel he'd paid scant attention to the protest movement. Even while being subjected to passionate arguments on the topic, he'd often found his mind wandering to issues more relevant to his own familiar territory, the environment of cyberspace. His distracted response had irked her almost as much as his lack of emotional commitment, and all her disappointments had come back to haunt him in the wake of her horrific death.

The pain of his sudden loss had hit Freddy hard, together with the bitter realisation that he'd taken Rachel for granted. Being hauled in as a suspect by the police had compounded his sense of despair and triggered a prolonged binge. It dulled the trauma but produced a sickening haze as he ingested every drug that came to hand and drowned his self-recriminations in a sea of vodka. Eventually, after achieving a temporary oblivion, he surfaced to a new clarity. It allowed him to focus on one thing: the searing injustice of Rachel's political assassination, for he had no doubts that was what she'd been the victim of. It transformed his grief into an aching need for vengeance.

The countdown was beginning as Freddy turned his transit van onto the promenade by the docks. There was no one else about. The night was clear but humid, the sea frothing against breakwaters and jetties, the gleam of the harbour lights soaked up by the dark swell of the tide. He followed the road around the fringes of the town, past the tidal basin, coal-loading terminal, rail yards and coal storage, then drove onto the old industrial flats awaiting redevelopment. Most of the sites were abandoned – empty factories, offices, corrugated-iron sheds rusting behind chain-link fences. The row of hoardings had attracted an accumulation of weeds and wind-blown litter.

Apart from a scrap-metal prowler the road was deserted as Freddy swung his van across a vacant sprawl of concrete and headed for a line of disused warehouses. He'd made his secret base in one of these. No one bothered him here. No one like corporate lawyers from software firms. No one like the law.

He pulled into the loading bay, jumped out and opened the back of the van. He eased out a large carton and carried it over to a set of metal stairs, steadied himself and climbed carefully to his warehouse loft. The upper storey resembled an electronic junk shop – tables and benches were crowded with various generations of computer terminals, and between the table legs was a spaghetti-mess of cables and wiring. A desk was cluttered with stacks of disks, and circuit boards spilled from metal cabinets. For his creature comforts there was a swivel chair, a coffee machine, a fridge and a double divan bed with a rumpled duvet.

He swept aside the stale remains of a McDonald's burger and slid the carton onto a coffee table. Then he knelt down, snapped open the cardboard flaps and tossed away the layers of foam plastic padding. A creased label fell out of the packaging, stamped with the words *Property of the Australian Defence Force*, but Freddy just kicked it under a bench. Inside the carton were the special components he'd been waiting for, including a helmet and gloves. He began to connect them to a computer control deck but his mobile phone interrupted him. He pulled it from his jacket pocket and checked the incoming number. He didn't recognise it.

'Who's that?'

A voice said, 'Who do you think?'

'Stonefish?' asked Freddy.

'Hi there, cowboy. Have you taken delivery?'

'Half an hour ago. I'm wiring the helmet in now.'

'Hey, go for it,' said Stonefish. 'Have you opened the little black box?'

'No.'

'Open it.'

Freddy did as he was told, prising open a container about the size of a glasses case. Wedged in the moulded interior was a type of device Freddy hadn't seen before. He plucked it out and examined it, a solid multifaceted object in matt black with a metal connector protruding.

'Okay, what am I holding?' he asked. 'And why is it a funny shape?'

'That's a military code-breaker, just developed,' answered Stonefish, 'and the shape is a dodecahedron, but I've no idea why. It's designed to work with the helmet and gloves, and you'll need to plug it into a self-powered hub.'

'No problem.'

'And watch your fingers. That's a mean little combo you'll be riding.'

'Good.' Freddy went back to connecting the helmet as he spoke. 'And I'm going to test it tonight.'

'By trying to crack Whitley Sands?'

'Maybe.'

'Maybe my arse. You can't wait.'

'Is that a problem?'

'Not for me.'

'What does that mean?' Freddy stopped his work on the helmet. 'Are you sure the ADF can't track this gear?'

'You've got my guarantee.'

'And that's worth the horseshit it's written on,' said Freddy, resuming his task. 'This helmet's more lightweight than the last.'

'Everything's better. Gives you high-res VR. But watch your reflexes with the gloves. They're hypersensitive. The whole package can make you dizzy, send you into a spin.'

'You've tried it?'

'Just briefly, on delivery. But it's what you need to ride the code-breaker. Seriously though, Freddy, don't get burnt. The Sands has got a vicious firewall. I'm reliably informed it's equipped with feedback devices that can barbecue your brain.'

'My brain's already pan-fried.' Freddy chuckled. 'I won't let the bastards get me. What about you, Stonefish? Where are you hiding these days?'

'Somewhere I can't be found.'

'Why? Who's on your case?'

'People who enforce their copyright with an axe. People who –' But he didn't finish. Instead he said, 'Rachel's murder freaked me out, Freddy. That's why I'm lying low. If you're going after those pricks at the base, you've got my blessing. But a word of warning, watch your arse. Don't ever let them catch you.'

The call ended. Freddy put down his mobile and frowned. Stonefish's obvious fear was unusual and unsettling but he wouldn't let it divert him from his plan of attack. He took off his glasses to strap on the helmet, then hesitated. He stood up, a serious look on his face and a dryness in his mouth. He'd been carefully plotting this moment – the chance to bust into the core data of the research base. There was no need to rush it, but a definite need to psych himself up.

Freddy put his glasses back on, walked over to the fridge and got out a Coke. He yanked open the ring-pull and drank from the can. When he'd finished he tossed it into an empty packing crate and ran his fingers through his untidy straw-coloured hair. He felt like a combat pilot about to take a low-altitude flight over enemy territory. He could almost fit the role. Tall, precocious, youthful-looking, with the instincts of a daredevil and the brinkmanship of a gambler. Despite his precarious existence in the cybertech underworld, Freddy possessed a sort of street nobility – a hacker who could be trusted to deliver, a hustler with brains as well as a prodigious capacity for vodka.

He stood there, hands on hips, his khaki shirt hanging out over the back of his jeans, the laces unravelling on his Nikes and a look of fierce anticipation on his face. He peeled off his shirt and slung it on the bed. Then he tossed aside the glasses, strapped on the helmet and pulled on the data-gloves encrusted with sensors. As he eased back in his swivel chair, the tiny display screen inside the helmet lit up in his eyes, and the air pads in the gloves gave him the feel of his control deck. Now he was ready – wired into his personal flight simulator. It would take him on a trip into the alternative reality of computer graphics.

18

Rita got up from the bed, opened the mini-bar and helped herself to bottled water. She carried it out to the balcony and drank it, her sudden thirst the result of whisky and a touch of dehydration. The moon hung, huge and flesh-coloured, over the Coral Sea. It cast a lurid glow among the dark outlines of the islands and threw the massive silhouette of the US aircraft carrier into sharp relief.

She thumped the balcony rail with her fist. What angered her most was the contempt with which she'd been treated. Even as a police officer, from the moment she'd been handcuffed until she'd driven out of the gates at the base, she had no protection under the law. And the security director, Maddox, trying to intimidate her, getting in her face, letting her know there was nothing she could do about it. What made him think he was entitled to behave that way? Who condoned such disregard for basic human rights?

Something was very wrong. Something had to be done about it. Rita took a deep breath and decided that the heavy-handed methods intended to frighten her off would do the very opposite. It pointed to the oppressive use of force, a frontier lawlessness, that could not be tolerated in a modern democracy.

Yet she had to be careful. With that thought in mind she returned to the laptop and did a series of searches on Whitley, the base and the military reserve in tandem with any names that were relevant – Maddox, Willis Baxter, Steinberg, Rachel Macarthur. There wasn't much of interest to show for it, and nothing new. Finally she did a search on Audrey Zillman, but the only hits she got were from the Cambridge era. There were academic and scientific pieces which Rita found technically obscure. But there was one news item and a photo accompanying it.

The article, from the previous decade, reported on the experiments Professor Zillman was conducting with computer-linked neural implants. The microchips interfaced directly with her brain cells. It was the very stuff that Byron had lectured eloquently about. Here, too, was the image of the twenty-nine-year-old woman who'd been his lover. And yes, she was striking, her face intense, her dark hair tied back, leaning against banks of electronics almost suggestively, the angle highlighting the imposing curves of her figure. She may have been 'brilliant' and 'inspiring', as Byron had found her, but Rita saw something else as well. This woman was scary.

19

It was like being on a space mission. But instead of flying towards the stars, Freddy was navigating through a 3-D cosmos of geometric patterns. He was seeing the architectures of the net from the inside – websites, nodes – the way a computer sees them. He felt he had cybernetic vision.

His flight was the product of microtechnology. Tiny cathode-ray tubes projected images onto the display screen inside his helmet. From there, a holographic mirror reflected three-dimensional views into his eyes. His eye motion was tracked by bouncing infra-red light from his irises into a miniature TV camera. The computer followed the movements of his head and hands via electrical signals induced in magnetic detectors in the helmet and gloves. And he steered his course by simulated touch on the computer-generated surface of a control panel.

Freddy marvelled at the cleverness of the technology – and immediately forgot it. He was too busy exploring, quite literally, new dimensions. Just as he'd been promised, the high-resolution VR graphics showed him databases as he'd never seen them before. His surroundings were spectacular. Surreal clusters of spheres, cubes, pyramids – glowing in fluorescent reds and ambers. Networks linked by pulsing filaments of emerald light. The luminous structures floating in a vast blackness of space that belonged to a different universe. And Freddy was speeding through the void like an alien probe.

'Wow, like doing maths on acid,' he said to himself.

It took him a while to get the feel for his cyberflight. The simulated control panel responded sharply to the sensors in his gloves, and he was having to make rapid adjustments to his speed and direction. When he banked too quickly a hollow shock hit him below the ribcage, as though he'd just dropped off a roller-coaster. And when he pulled up too suddenly he felt the chilling vertigo of staring into an infinite chasm. Slowly he learnt how to handle the keypad and give himself a gentler ride.

Before using the code-breaker he decided to lay a false trail. With a surge of acceleration, he flew directly at a sodium-glowing cube and burst through it in a blaze of light. He'd just gone through a node in Singapore. It made him laugh. He felt like a human comet. He performed a rapid switch-back and went through two more starbursts – Edinburgh and Toronto – before swooping in on the Australian constellations.

For his first break-in he decided on a relatively easy target, and homed in on the nearest shape, a dense concentration of data in the form of a silver hexagon. As he connected with it, his computer interfaced with the core data of a bank in Sydney. That's when he powered in the code-breaker. Immediately he was decrypting and scanning the bank's confidential files. Rows of figures were scrolling swiftly past his eyes. He punched into the fattest deposits and took lumps out of them with transfer orders, the credit dropping into half a dozen accounts he kept at different places online under a variety of coded identities. He skimmed off $100,000 – not bad for two minutes' work – then clicked out.

As he lifted off from the hexagon, the geometric firmament unfolded around him again. He was flying with confidence now, calmer and richer, ready to crack a tougher target. He zoomed past the foreground clusters and headed for a towering spiral galaxy of phosphorescent white – the defence database. As he closed in for a cautious pass, the huge gleaming structure filled his field of vision. To lock on at the wrong place would be extremely dangerous. This was no commercial security bank computer, but a military system bristling with electronic sentinels. It wasn't just the danger of being caught out and identified; he'd long been prepared for a squad of security police charging into his loft. But he was risking more than that if the rumours at the Diamond were right, rumours that Stonefish was convinced were based on fact. Stories of lethal feedback. Automatic defence programs built into the computer system. Surges of electricity that could grill you at your terminal, your fingers glued to a melted keyboard. And for those audacious enough to bust in using a VR helmet, the punishments could be more exotic. Stuff that left you brain-damaged or gasping in an induced epileptic fit. Or froze you in a cataleptic seizure till the military heavies smashed down your door. Or sent you into a hypnotic trance. You got up and put on your hat and walked out your front door, smiling to the neighbours, and strolled down to the nearest railway cutting and jumped in front of a train.

Freddy wasn't sure how much was vivid imagination and how much was technically feasible, but he wasn't going to bet his life on the difference. If the worst was true, he calculated he had a few seconds' grace. At the first sign of anything coming up at him, he'd throw off the gloves and helmet, and race down to the loading bay. That's where his dented second-hand Land Rover Discovery was waiting, with its tank full and its curtained rear serving as a makeshift mobile home. For an even quicker getaway, he could leap from the fire escape stairs to his Yamaha FJ-1200, which was always propped in position by the back door of the warehouse.

He was orbiting the vast helix of white light, drifting closer, drawn as if by a force of gravity, or fascination. This was the citadel he wanted to storm – the defence network that interlinked command centres, military intelligence posts, monitoring facilities and research bases, including Whitley Sands. Several months ago, a successful hack had provided Freddy with an opening set of codes that he'd managed to poach from the home work station of a level-six employee. But each time he was on the brink of getting in, he was shut out. His software couldn't decode fast enough. Now, using the defence department's own equipment, he should have the edge. This time he should crash the gate.

He was floating – very close now – to the outstretched tip of a spiral arm. This was where he'd inject himself. Here, at a point remote from the core, his odds of getting in – and out again – were better. For a moment he hovered, gazing at the intricate, crystalline surface, its phosphoric gleam dazzling his eyes. Then he took the plunge.

He locked on. Quickly he punched up the poached set of codes. They clicked in. He was posing as a research scientist with level-six clearance. Now came the tricky bit: getting inside. A set of coded commands had to be fired off. But if the code-breaker failed to crack the ciphers – game over. He hit it. There was a pause. Then with a whoosh he was through, the code-breaker gunning through the encrypted protocols, the firewall lifting, a rush of exhilaration surging through Freddy from his skull to his toes. The gate crashed open and he was inside – interfaced with the defence system.

Ahead of him stretched a city of infinite rectangles – rainbow-coloured. Pinnacles, plateaux and canyons receded to a precise horizon. Where to look? How to start? So much information. Time to back his instincts. He keyed in two words: PANOPTICON PROJECT. It was a gamble that worked. But it worked too well.

He accelerated across the cityscape at a dizzying velocity, colours blurring into a psychedelic spray. Shapes flickered across his eyeballs – ranges of tower blocks, mazes, chequered plains – a delirious stream of patterns that left him unable to see his control panel. He knew what was happening – a headlong rush towards the core at the Sands – and he could do nothing to stop it, his senses reeling, all balance gone. If a hunter–killer program was tracking him, he didn't stand a chance. Something was shrilling in his ears. It might have been his own blood pressure rising out of control. Or was it his own voice screaming? And that's when it hit him. The white-out.

How long he was unconscious he couldn't tell. As Freddy emerged from the blankness his first sensation was a sick feeling in the pit of his stomach. His sight was blurred, stars fizzing around him. As his vision cleared he saw that he was sitting in a white room. It was quiet and sterile. A computer lab. In the distance he could see a woman. She was wearing a white lab coat. Her attention was absorbed by the screen in front of her. As he focused his gaze Freddy saw what was on the screen. It was his own face. He gasped and wanted to call out, but felt too numb. He tried to get up but was pinned to his seat by nausea.

As he sat there, dazed and horrified by his predicament, the woman slowly stood, turned and walked towards him. There was something menacing about her. She was grey-eyed with a strong, handsome face and dark brown hair pinned back severely from her forehead. She stopped right in front of him. His head felt heavy as he looked up at her. He was still having trouble focusing, but her anger was clear. When she spoke her voice seemed to cut into his brain.

'I suppose I should congratulate you,' she said with more than a little contempt. 'You've managed to hack your way in where nobody else has.'

He took a slow, constricted breath and got out the words, 'Where am I?' But they sounded weak and muffled to his own ears.

'Where you were aiming for.'

His head swayed around clumsily. 'But this isn't the core.'

'All is not what it seems.' She almost smiled. 'And of course I caught you and tranquillised you before you could do any damage.'

He struggled to get up out of the chair.

'Don't do that,' she snapped, and he sagged back immediately. 'You'll only hurt yourself.'

'Who the hell are you?' asked Freddy suspiciously.

'You came looking for what controls the Panopticon Project – well, that would be me. But you can call me Audrey.' She gave him a dangerous smile. 'I'm the system controller at Whitley Sands. You've got here courtesy of a new VR helmet, gloves and code-breaker I designed myself. Unfortunately I don't control the manufacture, distribution or storage. But the man who supplied you was arrested five minutes ago. He's on his way to military cells, a court martial and imprisonment.'

'Stonefish?'

'No, I'm not interested in cheap crooks – others will deal with him,' said Audrey. 'I'm talking about the ADF technical officer who stole the equipment and sold it on the black market. He's finished.'

She let him think about it. The words gave him a sinking feeling.

'What about me?' he asked, looking around uneasily. 'I suppose you've got a few goons waiting around for some head-kicking.'

'Is that what you think?' Audrey seemed pleased. 'No. Your punishment will be limited and immediate.'

'What do you mean?'

'I mean you're a cunning sod who's done me a service by exposing security flaws. I may call on you again at a later date.'

'Forget it.'

'Tut-tut-tut,' she said, moving closer, wagging a finger at him.

'Get away from me, you bitch!'

'Consider yourself lucky. I'm going to let you off lightly.'

At first he thought he was imagining it. But then he saw it was real – even though it couldn't be real. Little blue veins of electricity were flickering from her fingertips.

'What's that?' he blurted out.

'Use your brain, Freddy. And you'd better get back from your computer decks.'

She raised her electric fingers to his face.

'Shit!' he shouted, then realised what was happening – he was still in virtual reality.

Freddy jumped up, throwing off his gloves and helmet, and stood unsteadily in his warehouse loft, looking around frantically as Audrey's face stared back at him from the stack of computer screens.

'I told you, Freddy. Stand back from your decks.'

He could see the blue wisps of smoke rising from a spread of keyboards, and smell the sharp tang of electrical burning as circuits began to ignite.

He scrambled backwards, shouting, 'You crazy bitch!' and watched as smoke and flames flickered around the equipment lining his loft. The first terminal exploded with a loud bang and Audrey's face vanished from it in a shower of glass, plastic and silicon. Her face still mooned out at him from the remaining screens as he grabbed for an extinguisher. The tubes were exploding one after another in a cannonade, bombarding him with splintered components, as he pointed the nozzle and sprayed wildly at the flames.

Within a few minutes he'd doused them. He stood there, trembling, gazing at the blackened, burnt-out wreckage. He tossed down the empty fire extinguisher. It hit the floor with a hollow clank. In that moment he was speechless. Such a display of electronic power was mind-blowing, though the thought that Audrey had spared him for future use made him shudder. But the smouldering, e-bombed debris around him also left him with another feeling – a grudging admiration.

20

'So how'd your first day go?' asked Jarrett.

'It just went,' answered Rita.

She wasn't in a good mood. It was nine a.m., her sleep had been fitful and she'd skipped breakfast. Jarrett had intercepted her in the police car park.

'Let me take you for a coffee,' he said, an earnest look on his face. 'You don't need to cross paths with Bryce this morning.'

'Right,' she said slowly. 'What's he saying?'

'He's harping on one of his favourite themes. The more he tries to avoid Whitley Sands, the more he gets involved.'

'And what's he saying about me?'

'Well, if I can put it diplomatically, he thinks you've got an attitude problem – just like me. Want to tell me about it?'

'First, coffee.'

Jarrett ushered her towards his car and they drove to a cafe overlooking the marina. They sat at a table in the shade of a beach umbrella and ordered lattes. The morning sun glared beyond a line of palm trees that marked the border of the marina village with its blocks of high-rise holiday apartments. Lines of yachts rode gently at their berths.

'So what happened?' asked Jarrett.

'I've had my own introduction to Captain Roy Maddox,' said Rita. 'And his team of paramilitary apes.'

'You paid a visit to the base?'

'Yes. And they did a background check with Bryce.'

'No wonder he's cranky. Did you come up with anything?'

'Nothing solid,' said Rita. 'But I'm convinced that base security has a direct bearing on the investigation.'

'How?'

'I don't know. And it's been made brutally clear to me that we're supposed to rule it out as a line of inquiry. National security and all that.'

'Ah.' Jarrett sat back, rubbing his chin. 'Play ball or else.'

'That's about it. I've been ordered to accept the bigger picture – that we're all on the same side of law and order – and back off.'

A waitress delivered the coffees.

'So where's that leave our investigation?' asked Jarrett, perplexed. 'And what does it mean for your profiling?'

'Both good questions,' answered Rita. 'Whatever the political or military implications, there's still a killer out there.'

'So we focus on the evidence we've got.' Jarrett nodded. 'And each new bit that floats our way.'

'We've got no other choice. Have any more body parts turned up?'

'A human tibia was found among rocks south of the estuary yesterday evening. Picked clean by the crabs. I've sent it to the lab, but assuming it's from victim number one, I doubt it'll add anything to what we've got.'

'Probably not.'

Jarrett watched Rita shaking her head.

'What are you thinking?' he asked.

'It's going to be hard to play it straight as a profiler.'

'Why do you say that?'

'Our killer isn't playing straight with us.'

'You've lost me,' he admitted.

'Okay, hiccup number one: crime signature,' she said. 'On the basis that the dismembered sections were washed up because of the killer's miscalculation, we've got a big inconsistency.'

'Which is?'

'The first victim wasn't meant to be found, while the second most certainly was.' She took a sip of coffee. 'Another obvious thing is the difference in sex of the two victims. Somehow it doesn't fit. And something else. A head on a pole in a public place – what does that say to you?'

Jarrett shrugged. 'A very sick bastard on the loose.'

'Yes, but another idea came to me yesterday when I was checking out the displays in the exhibit room. They made me think *execution*.'

He thought about it. 'Like the heads of traitors on London Bridge. Shit, why didn't I think of that?'

'Well, I'm in the habit of seeing pathological imagery where other cops see dead bodies. Next big question mark – where are the hands?'

'You think the killer might have kept them?' asked Jarrett. 'From both victims?'

'Maybe. And if so, why? For what purpose? Souvenirs? It bothers me.'

'Anything else?'

'The nail gun.'

'It's an odd choice of weapon,' he agreed. 'Like you said: up close and personal. Or even opportunistic.'

Rita looked out to sea as she drank her coffee. 'Or neither of those.'

'You've lost me again.'

'There's another possibility,' she said quietly. 'And this is just speculation. What if the killings were professional?'

Jarrett gave her a hard look. 'Professional?' He put down his cup. 'What are you getting at?'

'I'm saying we can't afford to make false assumptions.'

'We *are* still talking about a serial killer, aren't we?'

'Let's not get hung up on terminology.'

'Okay. And, if I get your drift, you don't want us to rule out a connection with Whitley Sands. So, correct me if I'm wrong, but you're saying two people might have been taken out because of a link to the base?'

'Yes.'

'By some sort of vigilante?'

'That's one way of putting it.'

'Or this terrorist cell we're being warned about?'

'I was thinking more along the lines of sanctioned hits.'

'A criminal connection?'

'No.'

Jarrett paused to take in what she was implying.

'If you're suggesting what I think you're suggesting,' he said, 'you'd better keep it between the two of us.'

'Absolutely,' she agreed. '*Entre nous*. It's just a thought.'

They finished their coffees in silence.

'So where do we go from here?' asked Jarrett at last. 'Or am I stuffed no matter which way I turn?'

'You're doing fine,' she told him. 'I've gone through your files and case notes. Everything you've put together is excellent work, very thorough. What I'm going to do is retrace some of it. I want to talk to those closest to Rachel Macarthur.'

'Work up the victimology?'

'Yes. I'll need to talk to her campaign deputy.'

'Eve Jaggamarra, bit of a babe,' said Jarrett before he could stop himself. 'Sorry. You'll find her at the campaign headquarters.'

'And Rachel's boyfriend, the hacker.'

'Edge Freddy. Your best bet is the Diamond, but I'll try to track him down for you.'

'The Diamond?' said Rita. 'The nightclub at the crime scene?'

'Yeah, the Rough Diamond Club – rough being the operative word.'

'I'll need to check that out too.'

'Well, don't turn your back on anyone. Apart from attracting e-freaks, it's a watering hole for seafront hookers and muggers. Make sure nobody spikes your drink.'

21

The protest campaign office was located in a concrete shopping centre that served the southern residential spread on the edge of the industrial area. Rita found a parking space and walked along a pedestrian precinct between rows of concrete pillars, cheap supermarkets and discount outlets. It was one of those functional developments from the late 1960s that showed its age badly. Overhead metal walkways were the colour of rust. The civic garden beds were overgrown. There was a lot of graffiti about.

The place she was looking for was next to a cyber cafe and upstairs from a grocery selling environmentally friendly items. She climbed the stairs to find a nest of rooms cluttered with posters, placards, stacks of papers and intense women in unfashionable clothing.

'I'm looking for Eve Jaggamarra,' she said.

'Out the back,' she was told. 'Doing her mug shots.'

Baffled by the answer, Rita went back down the stairs and through the rear of the shop to a back garden. It was obviously used as a receptacle for the overflow of clutter from the office. A pebbled path was hemmed in by paint tins, brushes, more posters and piles of magazines under plastic covers among ferns and cactus tubs. The woman she'd arranged to meet was posing against the back wall, brandishing a placard with the words: RADIATION KILLS. Squatting a couple of metres in front of her was a photographer, camera flashing.

'Eve?' asked Rita.

'Yes,' she answered. 'I'll be with you in a tick.'

The photographer glanced over his shoulder, looked Rita up and down, then resumed, telling his subject to turn sideways a little, breathe in and raise her chin. His accent was European, maybe French.

Rita folded her arms and waited. It gave her the opportunity to observe the woman. Straightaway she could see the attraction for Jarrett – and the photographer too, by the look of it. He was making the most of her shapely figure by getting her to pose against a whitewashed background in a red, partly unbuttoned shirt and jeans, shooting her from the waist up. She was a natural beauty: dark-skinned with a smooth, flawless complexion, black hair and deep brown eyes. The pose, complete with protest slogan, conveyed a powerful image: sex and death combined. The photographer knew what he was doing.

When the photo shoot ended, Eve buttoned her shirt, came over and shook Rita's hand.

'You're the profiler,' she said.

'Yes. And you're the next centrefold by the look of it.'

Eve laughed. 'Anything for the cause. The more publicity the better.'

'And I'm her biggest fan,' put in the photographer, packing his camera into its case. 'She could have a career as a model.'

'My new admirer,' explained Eve as he walked over.

'Julien Ronsard,' he said with a slight bow, shaking Rita's hand.

'Rita Van Hassel,' she replied. 'Is your accent French?'

'Yes, from Paris.'

'You're a long way from home.'

'I usually am,' said Ronsard with a doleful smile. 'The fate of a photo-journalist. I go wherever important issues take me.'

'Such as?'

'Christmas in Algiers. March in Islamabad. April in Bali. I've been here for the past month covering the anti-war protests.'

'Why?'

'They are waging a battle against another excess of the war on terror. It has global importance. It deserves international attention.'

This man intrigued Rita. Something of a pin-up himself, he was slim with olive skin and dark almond-shaped eyes, and he possessed the polished charm of someone schooled in the tradition of Continental courtesy. But there was another facet too; Rita could sense a resoluteness beneath the composure. Ronsard looked like a man with the intelligence and inner strength to act on principle, cope with danger and speak his mind. It was an appealing package. She wanted to know more.

'Who do you work for?' Rita asked.

'I'm freelance. My shots appear mostly in European magazines.'

'How many languages do you speak?'

'Several,' he answered with a smile. 'But if you're referring to my English it's because I studied at the London School of Economics. As well as the Sorbonne, of course. But I mustn't interrupt you two ladies. You have important things to discuss.'

Eve reached over to a battered leather handbag and got out a pack of cigarettes and a lighter.

'Mind if we talk out here?' she asked Rita. 'They won't let me smoke upstairs.'

'That's fine.'

As Ronsard collected his camera gear, said his goodbyes and made his way through the back of the shop, Eve lit up and puffed out a stream of smoke with a sigh.

'I'm glad that's over,' she said. 'Julien can be a bit demanding.'

Rita thought she caught a double meaning, but simply asked, 'What aspect of the war on terror was he talking about?'

'The military madness of the allies. It's no secret they're developing new battlefield technology at Whitley Sands. Weapons that spread dangerous levels of radiation. Rachel had the proof.'

'What proof?'

'A printout. Damning evidence – enough to shut down the base.'

'Tell me.'

'About fifty pages of technical stuff. Layouts, diagrams. That sort of thing.'

'Can I see it?'

'I wish you could,' said Eve, flicking ash at the ground. 'She showed it to me the day before she was killed. Next day it was gone.'

'What do you mean?'

'It was in Rachel's locked filing cabinet. When I got back from the demo I went through her files. I looked everywhere. Nothing. The evidence had been lifted.'

'Did you tell police about the printout?'

'Yeah, three times over. They didn't believe me or didn't want to.'

'Three?'

'The local plods, the Homicide bunch, then the federal heavies.'

'Federal? The AFP's not involved in this investigation.'

'Well, they wore dark suits and flashed badges and called themselves federal police. If not, who were they? Spooks?'

'Your guess is as good as mine,' said Rita uneasily. 'How did they react when you mentioned the printout?'

'Like inquisitors. *Where did it come from? How did she get it? Who gave it to her?* They weren't interested in who'd nicked it. When I couldn't tell them anything they dismissed it as insignificant. Rachel was the victim of a hoax. Or I was making the whole thing up.'

'But you do know something?'

Eve didn't answer. She just went on smoking, cigarette in one hand, cupping her elbow in the other.

'The reason I need to talk to you,' Rita went on, 'is to find out as much as I can about Rachel.'

'Why?'

'To help profile the killer.'

'It's irrelevant.'

'How can you say that?'

'Because you're here under false pretences.' Eve gave Rita a searching look. 'Bringing in a profiler is another way of diverting attention. Making out there's a serial killer while the real murderers get away with it.'

'And who are they?'

'Faceless people. Those behind the cover-up. They silenced Rachel and stole the printout.'

'What makes you so sure?'

'What makes you doubt it?' replied Eve. 'Nothing personal, but you're either part of the con or one of the conned.' She let Rita digest that thought. 'So are we going to waste our time, or do you want to talk about what's really going on?'

Although the question was delivered in an offhand way, it was something of an ultimatum. It took Rita by surprise.

'I see your point,' she said. 'Let me think a minute.'

Eve exhaled a leisurely stream of smoke. 'Take your time.'

Rita had to make a decision and it was a dangerous one. It was as if her career had reached a fork in the road. One way led to a promising future as a fully qualified criminal profiler with the prospect of promotion, a return to the FBI Academy, fieldwork in the States, possibly even a PhD. The other way led to a confrontation with national security authorities that could spell the end of her career, or worse. The rational choice was to play it safe and do what she was told by Maddox and Bryce. She'd been seconded to profile a serial killer, it was what she'd been trained to do and what she was expected to do. There was one problem: her instincts told her she was being asked to accept a big lie.

She had little doubt that Eve's assessment was close to the truth. It was consistent with Steinberg's and pointed to a motive for both his murder and Rachel's. When added to her own treatment by the security unit and the hostility of Maddox, there was enough to lead the investigation in one direction: Whitley Sands. Rita had attempted to tread a middle course but that was being challenged by Eve and she was right. Rita couldn't serve pretence and justice at the same time, and already she knew which way she was heading. The risk was daunting but the price of conformity was too high – the loss of self-respect.

As she made her decision, the enormity of the danger became clear. As a precaution, it meant accepting the accuracy of Steinberg's comment on total surveillance, something Maddox had effectively confirmed. It also meant taking on board the warning not to trust local police. Rita recalled the way Jarrett had bridled at her suggestion of sanctioned murders. Was he involved too, was he simply obeying instructions, or was Steinberg's paranoia-inducing vision colouring her own? The nagging doubts underlined the invidious position she was placing herself in.

'Made up your mind?' asked Eve.

Somehow it seemed ironic that Rita's personal and professional crisis had been provoked by the woman who stood beside her, smoking idly, a lazy smile on her face. There was something too laidback about Eve, almost overly calm. She seemed to be a woman who was supremely relaxed in her body, essentially physical, unconcerned by the frightening allegations she'd just made. Even her voice, soft and unhurried, contained no hint of the angst associated with the protest movement. In many ways she seemed to be the opposite of Rita – casual, unassuming, un-intellectual.

'One thing first,' said Rita. 'How did you get involved with the protest group here?'

'I came here as a temp.' Eve laughed. 'They needed a professional secretary to sort out the mess of their paperwork. They took me on permanently and because of my background they asked me to be their land rights spokesperson too. Even offered me the flat upstairs, rent free. I said okay. I like it here. We do important work. And I'm not treated like a bimbo.'

'What about political activism?'

'I do what I can,' she answered evenly. 'And I try to do what's right. What about you?'

'Me? I want to get to the truth.' Rita gave her a meaningful look. 'I think we should continue our talk somewhere else.'

Eve looked confused.

'Somewhere noisy,' Rita added, mindful of Steinberg's caution. 'Somewhere public.'

It took Eve a moment to realise what was being implied. Then understanding dawned. She took a last drag on her cigarette, flicked it into a cactus tub and nodded. 'I know just the place.'

They were sitting at a trestle table in Mangrove Joe's, an open-air bar in the atrium of a two-tier arcade. Giant flat-screen TVs were suspended overhead, tuned to sports channels. The arcade, which also housed swimwear shops, food outlets and hair salons, looked across the main street towards a swimming lagoon. The bar was doing a busy lunchtime trade – backpackers, men in shorts, women in sundresses – with a lot of rowdy background noise, which was what Rita wanted. She sipped a double espresso while Eve drank from a bottle of Mexican lager, her nonchalance apparently the default mode of her personality.

'So why are we here?' she asked.

'Because of what you said back there,' answered Rita. 'And because of other things I've been told. I've got to assume your campaign office is under surveillance.'

'By the spooks?'

'By whoever. We couldn't talk frankly there.' Rita looked around carefully. 'Now tell me what you know about the printout.'

'You might be an outsider but you're still with the police,' said Eve. 'I can't put others at risk.'

'I'm sticking my neck out just talking to you in this way,' replied Rita. 'I've already been warned not to widen the investigation.'

'You're asking me to trust you?'

'Yes. And I need to know I can trust you too. No one else can hear about this conversation, okay?'

Eve nodded, raising the beer bottle to her lips.

'Right,' said Rita. 'You're the one who wanted to discuss what's really going on. Now's your chance. The printout – where did it come from?'

Eve took a slow swig from the bottle before putting it down on the table.

'Rachel told me it came from inside the base, from someone who worked there. She didn't know who.'

'How did she get hold of it?'

'It was handed to her by one of the guys who set up our computer system and website.'

'Rachel's boyfriend, Freddy?'

'No, a mate of his,' answered Eve. 'A good bloke.'

'His name?'

'We only know him as Stonefish.'

'And the printout was given to him by someone from the base?'

'Not the printout, no. It was a disk. Stonefish printed out a hard copy for Rachel.'

'That fits in with other things I've found out,' said Rita. 'Does this Stonefish still have the disk?'

'As far as I know, but no one's seen him since Rachel's death.' Eve shrugged. 'I'm beginning to think the disk is more trouble than it's worth, though Rachel said it was priceless. She also thought it was a great joke.'

'Why?'

'She called it gold-something, or something-gold.'

'It might be important. Can you remember?'

'I've tried.'

'Maybe she called it "fool's gold"?'

'No. It was more like "fine gold" or "wine gold". I don't know. It meant nothing to me.'

Rita thought for a moment before it hit her. 'Oh, my God – not "Rheingold"?'

'Yes. That's it. What's it mean?'

'It means I could kick myself.'

'I don't get it.'

'It's the title of an opera,' explained Rita. 'A scientist at the base compiled a damning report. He put it on disk and disguised it as one of Wagner's operas, *Das Rheingold*. That's what this is all about. It could be why three people are dead.'

'Three?'

'Yes.' Rita finished her espresso and frowned. 'And if it's still out there, if it hasn't been retrieved and destroyed, then this isn't over. More people could die.'

Stonefish and his disappearing act were beginning to bug Freddy. There was no sign of him at his usual haunts and his latest mobile number went straight to voicemail, on which Freddy left a series of messages to return his call. He needed to replace a stack of burnt-out computer decks and incinerated software, the sophisticated sort of gear that Stonefish could supply within minutes, if only Freddy could find him. Like some of their previous deals it would have to be on credit because, financially, Freddy was back to square one. The $100,000 he'd lifted during his cyberflight was now inaccessible. The only record was on the computer zapped into oblivion by Audrey. He'd neglected to keep any hard copy of his coded online accounts.

He left his van in the foreshore car park and continued on foot as he checked out market stalls and the lower end of seafront bars. When Freddy's mobile finally rang, it wasn't Stonefish at all, but the type of call he could do without.

'Get your arse down to the Diamond!' It was the voice of ex-boxer and underworld heavyweight Billy 'The Beast' Bowers. 'I want to see you here, now!'

Freddy sighed and changed direction. Other concerns had to wait. He'd been summoned to the Rough Diamond Club.

The sky over the seafront was grey and glaring, like an electronic migraine, as he headed past burger joints and amusement arcades towards the docks. A sudden change in the weather was sweeping in from the south bringing leaden skies and a plunge in temperature unusual for the tropical coast. To counter the chill, Freddy had pulled on a black leather jacket to match his Versace shirt and jeans. He looked cool and he knew it, with his hair brushed back and gelled and an endorphin analogue melding with the receptors in his brain. Designer clothes and designer drugs. It made him feel upbeat and confident enough to face the aggression characteristic of Bowers.

Only for a moment did Freddy's mood dip. As he approached the club, down the cobbled alleyway, he reached the spot where Rachel's decapitated body had been found. There was no sign of her now, of course. Her blood had all washed away – the wet weather had seen to that. Gone were the chalk outlines etched by the detectives. Gone too was the crime-scene tape. There was only one reminder that this was where a young woman's life had been violently taken, that Freddy's lover had been slaughtered here. It was propped, with a note of remembrance, in a boarded-up doorway that had once led to a bait and tackle shop – a bunch of wilted flowers.

Freddy bowed his head, trying to choke back a surge of grief rising in his throat, wishing he'd been more attentive, missing her exasperating presence more than he could have guessed. It came back to him with a bittersweet intensity – the way she'd lecture him, scold him for his political apathy then make love to him with an urgent need that took him by surprise. At the time he failed to realise how special it was. Now that it was gone forever, he knew it was love.

But he couldn't let regret take hold again. He straightened up, took a deep breath and strode on down to the neon entrance of the club. With the drug's positive charge helping to buoy his mood once more, Freddy nodded to the muscle-bound bouncer and climbed the stairs to Billy's first-floor office. He knocked. The door opened and another of Billy's henchmen waved him through. Billy was pacing around the room, a mobile phone to his ear.

'Yeah, yeah, yeah,' he was saying. 'I've heard all the excuses. If you don't finish by Friday you'll be swimming in your own cement. Comprendo?'

He tossed the phone onto his polished teak desk, where it landed with a damaging thud.

'Fucking builders!' Billy shouted. 'Nothing but cowboys.'

'Conmen and chisellers,' Freddy agreed with a sympathetic nod. 'So how are you making out as a property developer?'

Billy looked at him suspiciously. 'You wouldn't be taking the piss, would you, Freddy?'

'Of course not.'

'Then shut up about things that don't concern you!'

'Of course, Billy.'

'Sit down!'

Freddy did as he was told, sinking into a big swivel chair upholstered in soft nappa leather. Billy came and stood over him, raising himself to his full height, one hundred and ninety-eight centimetres in his expensive Italian shoes.

'I'm disappointed in you,' he said. 'You've been playing hard to get.'

'I've been unwell.'

'Oh, *unwell* is it? Bullshit. Your mobile was switched off for more than a week. Where were you?'

'I paid a visit to La-la-land.'

'Don't give me crap.'

'I'm not,' Freddy insisted. 'You get there via E and acid, washed down with vodka. Works a treat. I've only just surfaced.'

'I don't pay for you to go AWOL, chemically or otherwise. When I want your services I expect to get them. I don't want to lose business because you'd rather fry your brains.'

'It wasn't through choice, it was necessity. I needed to blow myself away for a while. But I'm okay now.'

'What are you talking about?' said Billy irritably, then realised. 'Ah, Rachel. I can see that might come as a shock, having your girlfriend butchered.' He backed off a little, folding his arms and resting his buttocks on the edge of the desk, his legs stretched out in front of him. No matter what his pose, there was always something menacing in his manner. With his ginger hair, freckled, intimidating face and powerful build, he always seemed ready to throw a combination of punches your way. Even in a business suit – a lightweight Armani grey – Billy looked like trouble. The red silk shirt, unbuttoned to reveal a gold medallion, completed the image.

The office decor also reflected Billy's pedigree. Along with the polished wood and leather furnishings, there were weights, boxing gloves and a punching bag. Shelves displayed a series of trophies, while framed posters from his biggest fights decorated the walls. There were also dozens of ringside photos preserving the highlights of his professional career, all the way to a world championship. The title belt was mounted in pride of place behind his desk. Not so prominent was a photo from the bout in Melbourne where he lost the title with a tenth-round TKO that ended his sporting career. The referee had stopped the fight as blood gushed from Billy's split eyebrows. The scar tissue was still visible.

The injury had evoked the sympathy of gangland figures and opened up a new career for which Billy was both physically and psychologically qualified: clubland celebrity and part-time enforcer. It was a role he relished and excelled at. Eventually he had moved north to the Queensland coast, establishing his own regime and branching out from drugs, vice and black-market deals into showbiz promotions and property development. Billy 'The Beast' Bowers, who'd come from a bush town and started out as a cheap teenage brawler in prize-fighting tents, was now wealthy, connected and able to assert power over others. All he wanted was more.

'I'll let you off the hook this time,' he told Freddy. 'I'm sure we're all sorry about what happened to Rachel and so on. I'm especially sorry it happened on my doorstep. But I suppose we can't expect a serial killer to be considerate, can we?'

Freddy knew him well enough to spot that Billy was spinning a line. It was there in the tone of voice and the slight sardonic twist to his lip. It meant that a private joke was being played on Freddy, something he was unaware of, something to do with Rachel's death. If it hadn't been for the elevating effect of the drug, Freddy might have lost his temper, surrendering to the urge to do something stupid – like taking a swing at Billy – before being beaten to a pulp. Instead, with heightened clarity of perception, he could see that the reason for Rachel's fate was no mystery to Billy. That's why his reference to a serial killer was almost tongue in cheek. He must have been involved or informed or even instrumental in her death. Why? The question hammered at Freddy's thoughts but he left it unspoken. Better to bide his time.

So he just said, 'You wanted my services?'

'Yes,' answered Billy, straightening up. 'And by coincidence it's partly to do with your dead girlfriend. Something she had access to.'

'Like what?'

'A disk.'

'Any particular disk?'

'A computer disk, smart-arse. One smuggled out of Whitley Sands by some whistleblower. She must have told you.'

'I didn't listen much to her campaign stuff,' said Freddy. 'She mentioned some technical printout she was getting.'

'That's it, you dork. It was downloaded from a disk by Stonefish, and he's even harder to find than you.'

'I've been trying to get hold of him myself.'

'Well that's why you're here!' snapped Billy. 'I want you to find him, get me that disk and I'll cut you in on the deal. Twenty thousand bucks. You can split it with Stonefish if you feel obliged.'

'What deal?'

'Some customers have come to me. They'll pay handsomely – but just for the disk. No hard copy, no extract. They want the original disk.' Billy leant forward, dropping his big meaty hands onto the arms of the chair, his chin out, his face in Freddy's. 'Get it, and we'll all do business. Fail to deliver, and you and Stonefish will be taken for a dip on the far side of the reef – and left there.'

23

After dropping Eve off at the campaign office, Rita bought a takeaway lunch – a smoked chicken salad – and drove back to the police station. She went in through the watch-house entrance and climbed the creaking stairs to the exhibit room, where she sat at her desk, ate her lunch and thought. What she was thinking about was a timeline. She was constructing it in her head because, if her suspicions were right, placing it anywhere that could be scrutinised was too dangerous. She couldn't risk putting it on the whiteboard, her laptop, her mini disc recorder or even on paper.

The timeline began with Dr Steinberg completing his report and burning a disk containing technical data from inside Whitley Sands. Next came its delivery to the go-between known as Stonefish. If Rita's reasoning was right, Stonefish printed off more than one hard-copy extract. Her guess was that the first went to the anonymous man in the mud, while the second was given to Rachel Macarthur. Both were subsequently killed because of it. There were plenty of gaps and inexplicable links in the timeline, but currently it ended with the sanctioned murder of Steinberg himself.

Her confidential talk with Eve had convinced Rita that the police were wrong to assume that a random serial offender was on the loose. Worse, it might even be an assumption they were supposed to make. The unofficial testimony was compelling – Eve's words, Steinberg's comments and Rita's own direct experience. If a psychotic killer was stalking the streets of Whitley, his crimes were inextricably linked to the interests of the research base. Of course, how to pursue this line of inquiry without ensuring her own downfall was a dilemma. Until she came up with a plan she'd continue to go through the motions. Tomorrow morning she would visit the crime scene down by the docks and try to track down Freddy Hopper. Perhaps then she'd find out more about his friend Stonefish.

Her concentration was broken by Detective Sergeant Steve Jarrett.

'It's bloody nippy in here!' he said as he came through the door. 'You must've brought the weather up from the frigid city.'

'The what?'

'It's how we think of Melbourne.' He chuckled. 'That frigid wind blowing up Collins Street. Nearly cuts you in half.'

'Careful, Jarrett, or I'll book you for slander. Blaming me and Melbourne for a cold front off the Tasman.'

'Well, it's the same general direction – the south – and this sort of weather doesn't come from around here. The temperature's supposed to be dropping to eight degrees tonight.' He emphasised it with a shiver. 'This is the tropics. We don't have winters.'

'Sounds like you believe your own tourist propaganda.'

'Don't you feel the cold?'

'If I could find any heating,' she said, 'I'd switch it on.'

'You've got the fireplace – that's it. I'll sort it out.'

He went out again.

Jarrett was right about the chill in the room. Maybe it was the ghost, she thought, as she rubbed her temples. Concentrating too hard had left her with a headache. She needed to relax and clear her mind, forget the investigation for a while. Thinking about the ghost reminded her of the room's history, arousing her curiosity about the man who'd occupied it more than a century before her, Sergeant Kenneth Logan.

She walked over to the antique bookcase and was browsing through the morocco-bound volumes when Jarrett returned with an armful of broken palings.

'We're having the back fence replaced,' he explained. 'It'll make good firewood.' He dumped it on the hearth. 'What are you looking for?'

'Sergeant Logan's journal.'

'Ah, the diary of a ghost,' said Jarrett. 'I thought that'd interest you.' He came over and stretched to reach a slim ledger on the top shelf. 'Gotcha.' He blew off some dust and handed it to her. 'Here – see what you make of him. Lawman or psycho.'

Rita opened the old book and moved beside the window, leafing through the ink-scrawled pages while Jarrett knelt down by the hearth, splitting the wood into kindling and stacking the grate. The writing was in an untidy and elaborate Victorian script, but she could read it without much difficulty as she scanned the pages. The paper was dog-eared and stained with age. A mid-June entry caught her eye:

> The unseasonably cold weather has persisted through yet another night and day of storms blowing in off the ocean. A wind from the south continues to batter the coast, bringing gusts laden with stinging sand and horizontal rain. Squatter Brodie decreed there would be no hunt again today. Therefore, with no other pressing duties, I stoked the fire and opened the volume of Livy which was presented to me by Squatter Brodie.

Rita looked over at Jarrett, who'd got a flame going and was encouraging it with a poker. She imagined Sergeant Logan in exactly the same place and exactly the same pose a hundred and forty years ago and a tingle ran down her spine. Some things don't change.

As flames took hold and the wood began to crackle Jarrett stood up and adjusted the fire guard.

'That'll warm the room once it gets going.'

'Thanks,' said Rita, coming over to admire his effort. 'Makes me feel at home.'

'Good,' he said. 'I want you to know you're welcome here. Seriously.'

'Bryce still on the warpath?'

'No. He's more sound than fury. Sees himself as head prefect around here. Likes to catch you out and recite the rules. You can expect a ticking off, that's all. I haven't known him to bear grudges.' Jarrett folded his arms, his expression stern. 'I've been mulling over what you suggested this morning at the cafe – the possibility of professional hits.'

'Forget it. I was being hypothetical.'

'Yeah, and hypothetically it scares the shit out of me. The idea the base is mixed up in murder has a certain logic to it, especially given some of the heavy-duty head-kickers available.'

'Maddox?'

'Not just him. There's a national security adviser out of Canberra called Luker. He briefed us when the anti-war protesters pulled their first stunt with bolt-cutters. Friendly enough, but the sort of guy who knows how to kill you with a clipboard.'

'Any other charmers?'

'A couple of Yanks. They're supposed to be Pentagon observers but they've got military intelligence written all over them. Rhett Molloy's the head honcho and scary enough. But his buddy's the one you'd hate to bump into on a dark night – Kurt Demchak. Special Forces background, I reckon. He's got eyes that freeze your blood.'

'Where'd you meet them?'

'A town hall reception thrown by the mayor to welcome our American friends and allies. Makes sense. GIs contribute enough to the local economy. And there's a team of bean counters from Washington. I've been wondering how far they'd go to protect their investment.'

'You really have been thinking about what I said,' smiled Rita. 'But your own advice was right. We have to shelve it. From an official policing point of view, it's a dead end.'

'In more ways than one, perhaps.' Jarrett nodded. 'How'd you go with the lovely Eve?'

'She cooperated up to a point, but she's understandably wary.'

'What next?'

'I'll visit the crime scene and the club tomorrow. For now I'm giving my brain a rest.'

'Okay, I'll leave you to it,' said Jarrett, opening the door. 'So you can cosy up with the late notorious Sergeant Logan.'

'Just what I had in mind.'

24

Stonefish wasn't in the Bierkeller, the Steamboat, Liberty Belle or Rafferty's. Nor was he at any of the dives lining the harbour. He couldn't be found at the net cafes or the bowling alley or the back rooms at the amusement park. In fact, none of his fellow dealers had seen him in more than a week. As much as Freddy was reluctant to disappoint Billy Bowers, he couldn't track down Stonefish. It appeared the most recent contact, and that was only by phone, was with Freddy himself. No doubt Stonefish had since ditched that mobile for another.

With the sun setting behind the ranges and the temperature dropping, Freddy drove his van back up into the hills to the rented split-level house he'd shared with Rachel. The place was cheap but comfortable. It had a gravel driveway, a garden plot out front with an unruly rhododendron, a backyard of dirt and weeds, termites in the woodwork and a spectacular view over the islands in the passage. As he pulled into the driveway, he paid little attention to the big black limousine with tinted windows parked two houses up along the crescent. He got out, strolled to his front door and unlocked it. As he opened it, he was grabbed by both arms. Two men in dark suits escorted him through the door and rode him down the hallway to his lounge room, where they tossed him onto a sofa.

'Where's Stonefish?' one of the men demanded.

He looked up at them.

'Who are you?' he asked.

One of them punched him in the face. Freddy spun off the sofa onto the floorboards, his cheekbone aching.

'We ask the questions. Where's Stonefish?'

'I don't fucking know!' Freddy shouted. 'Did that bitch Audrey put you up to this?'

He was punched again. Blood was gushing from his nose.

'Get up!'

Shakily, he got to his feet, holding his nose.

'Where's Stonefish?'

'I told you –' he began.

This time he took a punch in the stomach that put him back on the floor with a thud. As he sat there, winded, a third man emerged from the hallway. He was tall and solid, with an expressionless face, cold eyes and a receding hairline. When he spoke, it was with an American accent.

'Let me deal with him.'

The other two backed off.

'Sit on the sofa, Freddy.'

Freddy sat.

The American sat down next to him and put a slab of a hand around the back of Freddy's skull, forcing Freddy's face close to his own. The other huge hand clamped Freddy between the legs, crushing his testicles in an agonising groin hold.

'I'm going to ask a series of questions,' said the American quietly. 'And you're going to answer truthfully. Yes?'

'Yes,' squeaked Freddy, eyes watering.

'Do you know where Stonefish is?'

'No. Been looking all day. Can't find him.'

'Do you have his phone number?'

'No. Keeps ditching his SIM cards.'

'That's a damn shame. We want to talk to him. When did you last see him?'

'More than a week,' answered Freddy, his voice a constricted whisper now. 'No one's seen him.'

'One more question,' said the American, his knuckles cracking as he increased the pressure. 'What's his real name?'

'He won't tell,' groaned Freddy. 'Won't tell anyone.'

'And just one more. Where's he from?'

'New Zealand.'

'He's a Kiwi?'

'Yes. That's all I know. I swear.'

'I believe you.'

The American released his grip. Freddy doubled up and dropped off the sofa, slumping sideways into a foetal position on the floor.

His torturer towered over him, Freddy's mobile phone in his hand.

'I'm adding my number to your contacts,' he told him. 'My name's Kurt. Do you think you'll remember that?'

Freddy nodded several times, unable to speak.

'And you'll call me as soon as you know anything about the whereabouts of Stonefish. Right? Because if you don't, you know what you'll lose.'

Freddy nodded again vigorously.

'Good,' Kurt said, and led the others from the house.

After the front door banged shut behind them, Freddy lay still until he could gather enough strength to limp gingerly, still bent double, to the stockpile of medications stashed at the back of his fridge. He needed another hit and he needed it fast.

25

Long after the International Risk Assessment Committee had adjourned for the night, its clandestine business concluded, another sequence of covert activity began within the confines of the base. Data was being accessed, scanned, evaluated and concealed within the system, thanks to a randomised neuronetic pathway that was effectively a ghost login.

The identity of the ghost remained a secret, known only to the user. No official presence on the base could be allowed to find out, including the committee, senior management, or staff deployed on levels six and seven. Of necessity, there could be no witnesses. The activity of the ghost circumvented all obvious protocols.

Outside the subterranean labyrinth, the grounds were silent and secure. The gates were locked, bolted and chained. An elite force of military police manned security points around the concrete superstructure and armed personnel patrolled the perimeter fence. Razor wire, concrete barriers and pillars dripping with CCTV cameras added to the fortress-like effect, designed to avert any frontal attack. Inside the complex, toiling through night shifts, a few dozen staff worked at their tasks under the watchful eyes of the guards. The base's military authorities were convinced that all the appropriate measures were in place to guarantee that no breach of security would go undetected.

The ghost continued scanning, focusing now on a single event contained within the immense digital archive of the system. The relevant data displayed surveillance images from an incident that had occurred some two weeks ago in an alleyway by the docks. The footage showed Rachel Macarthur walking down the cobbled slope. Then a dark figure emerged from a doorway, approached from behind and put a hand over her mouth. The ghost observed, in slow-mo now, the raised arm of the attacker, the nail gun clenched in the hand, the mechanism being fired, the projectile piercing the skull and Rachel slumping to the ground. With the image frozen, and tracking around one hundred and eighty degrees, the ghost zoomed in on the killer, enhancing the light. The image became clear, the face unmistakable.

The record of homicidal violence could be viewed dispassionately. It changed nothing. Even though it preserved the actuality of murder it was beyond the reach of police, courts and the entire criminal justice system. As evidence it wasn't simply inadmissible, it was nonexistent. Surveillance data processed by the Tracker technology didn't exist because, officially, the system didn't exist. Its secrecy was guaranteed by national security directives of governments committed to fighting the war on terror. That meant the data identifying the nail-gunner was protected from any exposure whatsoever – judicial, media, political, or even military. The ghost knew it existed, but the ghost wasn't telling anyone.

The ghost was Audrey Zillman.

As system controller, with a complete overview of the project, Audrey had identified a problem. It wasn't scientific, it wasn't even technical. It was human. So far, Audrey couldn't decide what to do with the information, never mind formulate some sort of response. In effect, it was outside her province.

The problem was behavioural. A very limited number of people could access the Tracker. Restricted use of the technology was ensured by a mandatory level-seven security clearance. The protocol was dictated by the sensitivity of the project and the need to protect it from disclosure, even to high-ranking staff at the base. But what it couldn't safeguard against was abuse of the privilege. It was immediately clear to Audrey that some high-echelon officials were accessing or tampering with surveillance data in private, personal or unauthorised ways. Although she had no obligation to issue an alert over such breaches, she was logging and secretly filing them. Part of her dilemma was procedural. The administrators and managers who would need to be alerted were the same individuals who were bending the rules.

The problem intensified after the first murder.

Audrey worked on the principles of scientific method. Her approach to everything was logical and analytical. Morality was not her strong point. Objectivity was. The killing itself could be viewed as excessive, and yet it was based on rational assumptions. The victim, 'the man in the mud', had represented a danger that needed to be eliminated. The person was disposed of and the immediate threat was removed – QED.

With the second nail-gun murder, the problem escalated further.

A pattern was emerging and it posed the perennial question: did the end justify the means? At what point, Audrey began to query, did the process become irrational? Not yet, seemed to be the answer. Logically, of course, there was a patent contradiction because the solution was barbaric. However, Audrey observed, such a tactic had enjoyed a long tradition in human affairs, spanning the entire evolution of the species, and would doubtless persist for centuries to come. Therefore intervention served no purpose. Constrained by security restrictions, her position in the base structure, moral ambiguities and the momentum of history, Audrey was compelled to do nothing. She would simply continue to keep watch.

26

After zapping the pain with morphine and dropping a double dose of sleepers, Freddy passed out for the night, enduring vivid dreams about freewheeling circles of data and electric women and giants wielding shears. He woke in the morning to a throbbing ache in his groin and a fuzzy brain. That meant more painkillers and an upper for breakfast. He washed them down with bottled water. He couldn't face food.

He sat at his breakfast bar, looking out at islands in a storm-tossed sea. The shipping passage was ribbed with breakers and the sky was full of low clouds and rain. The day was dismal. So were the rooms around him, plastered with souvenirs of a dead relationship – ban-the-bomb emblems, rainforest panoramas and dolphin decorations, lots of them. Rachel had been big on the dolphin theme. But there was a lack of personal photos, the result of hectic lives. The only shot of Rachel and Freddy together was a memento from their holiday on Hamilton Island, a colour photo mounted on cardboard with Freddy nursing a koala. He gazed at Rachel's beaming face regretfully, lost in a morass of self-reproach, until the upper kicked in and his mind clicked sharply back to the present and the predicament he found himself in.

His unwelcome visitors of the night before weren't the type to go away. They hadn't told him who they were but they didn't have to. He'd encountered their sort before, back when he'd been interrogated about the Edge of Chaos virus – anonymous men in suits, with an official authenticity to their threats and a brisk brutality in their methods. But the man who really scared him was the American, Kurt. He was a practised killer, Freddy had no doubt, because he'd met more of the same among Billy's circle of acquaintances. It was the way they checked you out, the coldness in their eyes, and that hair-trigger vibe that could switch their mood from calm to violent in a second. But Kurt was even worse. If he had government agencies behind him, as Freddy suspected, he could kill with impunity.

It was time for Freddy to follow Stonefish's lead and lie low. But where? The police knew about the various places he used as crash pads, including the flat above the cyber cafe, so they were out, and his warehouse loft was no longer safe since the confrontation with Audrey. His standby option made sense. He'd live out of the back of his Land Rover for the time being, moving between suitably obscure locations. In the meantime, there was only one obvious course of action – he needed to get Billy Bowers onside. For a start, Billy had to be told about the men in suits and their pursuit of Stonefish. With any luck, Billy could provide Freddy with some real protection.

Then he could get to work on figuring out how to reach Stonefish without anyone finding out.

Still moving gingerly, Freddy walked to his van, got in and, after a careful look around, drove out of the crescent and down the hill into the town, checking constantly that he wasn't being tailed. When he got to the docks, he turned into the cobbled alley and followed it down to the bottom, parking in a fork of the dead-end T-junction beside the Rough Diamond Club.

When he went inside the bouncer blocked his way to the stairs.

'Billy ain't here.'

'When'll he be back?' asked Freddy.

'Maybe sooner, maybe later,' shrugged the bouncer.

'Great.'

'Why don't you wait in the bar? You look like you need a drink.'

'I need more than that,' growled Freddy. 'But I might as well start with a vodka.'

27

The wind was still gusting but there was a break in the rain as Rita walked down the alley. The area was ripe for redevelopment, with most of the shopfronts and buildings boarded up. Apart from the club, the only other businesses still operating were an all-day breakfast cafe and a fishing shop called the Rod 'n' Reel. She checked out the dead-end laneways right and left; on one side was a fenced-off demolition site, on the other was a narrow footpath sloping down to a stretch of quayside lined with bollards.

This part of the docks was deserted. The sea frothed and thumped against empty berths, hurling spray into the air. The wharf, on a spur from the basin of the harbour, was disused and in need of repair. A tangle of seaweed rode the foam, meshed with litter and driftwood. The nearest vessel was a freighter tied up at the coal terminal several hundred metres away. The only other presence was a row of towering wind turbines embedded in a concrete breakwater. The machines stood like white metal giants fanning the sky, their blades wheeling busily high overhead. Rita wiped a film of damp from her face as she took in the padlocked cargo sheds and loading cranes that backed onto the club. The mood of the day didn't help but the place felt uninviting – the sort of bleak backwater where death came unobserved.

She returned to the alley and walked up the slope to the spot where Rachel's body had been found. A bouquet of dead flowers hung forlornly in the doorway where the killer probably stood while waiting for his victim. Rita lifted a folder of crime-scene photos from her shoulder bag and, after studying them, bent down to peer at the alleyway surface. There, cut in the cobbles, three grooves were visible. They told her that the attacker was focused and efficient, requiring just three accurate blows to remove the head and hands. He was also tall and physically strong – he had to be to restrain Rachel while raising a cumbersome nail gun to the back of her head and firing downwards almost vertically. And he was familiar with the location. It was the perfect place for an ambush, with poor lighting, narrow access and limited parking space at the bottom of the alley. Rachel had told the taxi driver of an arranged meeting at the club. It meant she'd been lured to her death in a public place, where the crime was carried out with speed and discipline, rather than in a psychotic frenzy.

Rita was becoming more convinced that only one scenario remained consistent with the facts. The murder was professional. The nail gun was an oddity, yet that too could be explained. It was an unwieldy choice for a hitman, unless it had been opportunistic in the first killing and diversionary in the second. If so, it had certainly diverted the police. The same applied to dismembering the body. It provided detectives with an obvious crime signature, but to Rita's profiling mind the signature was a fake. She refused to read into it the signs of pathological fantasy. All she could see were the hallmarks of calculation and misdirection.

She stood up, put the photos away and sighed. A moral dilemma confronted her with increasing clarity, together with a more practical problem: how to work the case. Simply compiling a profile of the killer was fraught with hazard. It would be safe enough to describe him as *tall, powerfully built, intelligent, calculating, socially competent, ruthless and highly disciplined.* But could she add: *a skilful and accomplished killer or hired assassin, with a gangland, military or elite police background*? Of course not. It would turn the investigation on its head, bringing the wrath of Inspector Bryce, Captain Maddox and others in authority down upon her. The only honest way forward was blocked. It was unacceptable and unresolvable at the same time.

Rita didn't know what to do.

Damn it, she thought, and wandered towards the club. The place might be worth checking out, or it might not. If nothing else, she could do with a drink. As she walked under the neon sign at the entrance, the door slid open for her, a bouncer holding it ajar and greeting her with a suggestive smile.

'New ladies always welcome,' he said.

'Thanks,' she said dubiously.

As the door closed behind her, Rita found herself entering the sort of twilight haunt she was used to dealing with as a sex crimes detective: a furtive pick-up joint open for business around the clock. These places were all the same. Whatever nocturnal appeal they possessed, during the day everything looked stale and tacky.

A few male drinkers were propped on stools at the counter, a barmaid chatting idly to one of them, the others transfixed by a rugby match on TV. In the middle of the bar two youths were playing pool – teenagers with shaved heads and tattooed arms – the clack of the balls sounding against the whirr and jangle of poker machines in an adjoining room. In a side booth a pair of women with hard faces and low-cut tops bent towards each other, talking behind their hands as they looked Rita up and down. Two booths along a young man drank alone. At a corner table sat an old woman cradling a bottle of stout and coughing between puffs on a cigarette, her wrinkled face expressionless, her eyes gazing into the middle distance.

The place was a combination dance venue, gambling saloon and sports bar. On the walls between metallic light fittings hung the iconic images of boxing champions past and present. It was like a gallery of testosterone, their muscled torsos, biceps and triceps glistening. Beyond the bar, steps led down to a dance floor with mirrored ceilings and Gothic tracery.

So this was the intended destination of Rachel Macarthur as she headed for a rendezvous that was never supposed to happen. The thought was depressing, as was the interior of the club itself. Equally gloomy was the official roadblock on the investigation. Rita was beginning to regret accepting the invitation to join it. The case didn't need a profiler. It needed a commission of inquiry.

With nothing better to do, Rita sauntered up to the bar. Her movement caught the leery eye of the nearest drinker until her hostile stare warned him off. She was in no mood for presumptuous fools. She looked at her watch – just past midday. A little early, but what the hell. She ordered a Scotch and ice and moved to a table away from the counter.

The first mouthful tasted remarkably good. The soothing mellow flush of the alcohol was what she needed to clear her thoughts and chill out. Sometimes that was the only way to shrug off a problem – dissolve it in a smooth glass of single malt whisky. As she sat there quietly, scanning the customers again, she suddenly recognised one of them – the young man drinking alone. His photo was in the case file. It was Rachel's boyfriend, Freddy Hopper.

An idea struck Rita – one that came out of that grey area where detectives and informers operate under the radar. Crossing paths with Freddy could be a happy coincidence, an opportunity for some lateral digging. The more she thought about it, the more it offered a potential detour around the barrier facing her. It would require Freddy's cooperation, but he already operated outside the law so she could apply some pressure to that end. While she observed him, the gambit grew on her. He was young and fresh-faced but far from innocent-looking and, although rather downcast, his expression was alert and streetwise as he kept watch on his surroundings. As a hacker who'd chalked up a cyber-crime conviction and jail time, he'd know how to keep his mouth shut. She decided it was worth a try so, after studying him for a few minutes, Rita got up and carried her drink over to the booth.

'Mind if I join you?' she asked.

Freddy looked up sharply from his vodka and Red Bull. 'Who are you?'

'My name's Rita Van Hassel.'

'Is that supposed to mean something to me?'

'No.' She shook her head. 'But it will.'

Understanding dawned in Freddy's eyes. 'You're a cop.'

'I'm the one who's going to catch Rachel's killer.' Rita slid onto the seat opposite. 'If you're willing to help me.'

Freddy's reluctance was obvious. 'It's not what I do.' He glanced around uncomfortably. 'Cops and me – we don't get on.'

'I'm the exception,' smiled Rita. 'You're going to get on just fine with me.'

Freddy looked at her suspiciously. 'I've got a lousy feeling that translates into harassment.'

'Call it mutual self-interest. You talk to me off the record, and I'll protect your back from any police action.'

'The cops are the least of my worries.' He grunted. 'Anyway, what's in it for me?'

'Apart from bringing Rachel's killer to justice?' Rita sipped her Scotch. 'No comebacks. And my promise of an advance warning if I see problems coming your way.'

'Does that include government shit?'

'Any shit.'

Freddy gave Rita a hard stare. It was obvious he wasn't used to this type of approach from a police officer.

'I've never seen you before,' he said. 'You're not local.'

'I'm a criminal profiler,' she said, lowering her voice. 'Drafted in from Melbourne to track down a serial killer who doesn't exist. You see, Rachel wasn't simply murdered, she was executed. Just telling you that could get me into deep trouble. You understand what I'm saying?'

'Not exactly.' Freddy swallowed another mouthful of vodka before tipping more Red Bull into his glass. 'First up, I'm not agreeing to anything till I've got an idea of what I might be getting myself into.'

'Fair enough,' Rita conceded. 'All I want from you is information. It won't be logged, filed, recorded or even written down. It'll stay between you and me. I'm not interested in your hacking or petty criminal activities – only what bears on Rachel's death. I'm prepared to cross a line here, break the rules.'

'Why?'

'Because I've been ordered not to by senior officers.' She took a deep breath. 'Because I won't stand by while Rachel's death goes unpunished.'

Rita was looking directly into Freddy's eyes. It got the reaction she wanted. He blushed.

'I've already been questioned by cops twice over,' he said defensively. 'I don't know anything. I wasn't even here when she was killed.'

'There's one thing in particular I need to know about. A Whitley Sands printout given to Rachel.'

Freddy raised his eyes to the ceiling. 'Fuck!' He sat back heavily. 'I bloody knew the Sands was out to get her.'

'And the rest,' she said, and drank more Scotch while she watched him fuming.

'Okay,' he said at last. 'If that's what this is about, I'll help, as long as what I say goes no further.'

'Deal.'

Freddy hunched forward, dropping his voice. 'I took a look at the printout. It was full of technical details and cross-sections – blueprints, that sort of stuff – about an R&D project using electromagnetic emitters, accelerators and scanners. Not my area of expertise. Besides, the data was incomplete and only partly referred to the computer system that drives it, which is what would turn me on. They call it the Panopticon Project, which sounds like a bullshit label to me. There wasn't enough for me to make sense of it, but it came with a rambling introduction saying the system produced life-threatening levels of radiation. Rachel was ecstatic.'

'When did she get it?'

'A couple of weeks before the big demo. She was saving it up for that. Big announcement in front of TV cameras.' Freddy bowed his head. 'And you're saying that's why she was stopped. Shit. And the printout?'

'Gone. Vanished when she was killed.'

'So it was important after all.' He sagged forward on his elbows. 'The gold dust she was looking for.'

'*Das Rheingold*, actually. It's an extract from a report burnt onto a disk disguised as an opera DVD. Which brings me to your pal, Stonefish.'

'If he's to blame for Rachel's death –'

'No. He's just a go-between. What's his real name?'

'That's just it. He hasn't told anyone. All we know is he's a Kiwi who can get his hands on any sort of software, including a military code-breaker. That takes some doing. He's also an acid bore and a beer snob.'

'Well I need to speak to him.'

Freddy's fist slammed the table. 'We're all looking for that arsehole!'

'All?'

'Yeah, and now I know why.'

'Freddy, who else is after him?'

'Me, for a start. I need a completely new rig since a bitch called Audrey firebombed my loft!'

'Slow down. Firebombed?'

'She triggered a power surge that blew my decks.'

'Are you saying you've met Audrey Zillman?'

'If that's her name, yes. An online face-to-face in the middle of a virtual hack. Got all the way to the core data at the Sands before she zapped me.'

Rita was genuinely impressed. 'Amazing. Is she after Stonefish?'

'She told me she wasn't, but she might be the one who sent in some American psycho called Kurt. He paid me a visit last night with another pair of muggers in suits. Kurt damn near castrated me and said he'd finish the job if I didn't deliver Stonefish. I'm in deep shit either way. If I don't track him down I lose my balls, but if I do find him I think we're both stuffed anyway. We'll end up as floaters over the reef.'

Rita was trying to digest all the information she'd just heard when her mobile rang. It was Jarrett calling.

She gave Freddy a warning look as she answered. 'Hello, Detective Sergeant Jarrett.'

He caught an odd tone in her voice. 'Where are you?'

'At the Diamond,' she replied. 'Chatting to Freddy Hopper.'

'Is he cooperating?'

'Yes, he's answered all my questions.' She watched Freddy tense but waved a hand at him to lighten up. 'Nothing new though.'

The words reassured him. Freddy's expression relaxed, their verbal agreement sealed.

'I'll join you there,' said Jarrett. 'There's been an interesting development. One that's got Bryce stumped.'

He hung up.

'My colleague's on his way here,' Rita told Freddy. 'Better make yourself scarce.'

'No sweat.'

He downed the rest of his drink.

'Before you go,' added Rita. 'Is anyone else looking for Stonefish?'

'Yeah, the guy who owns this joint. I work for him on and off. The odd bit of hacking.'

'Who is he?'

'Billy Bowers – local hard nut.'

Rita froze. 'Billy "The Beast" Bowers?' she asked. 'Ex-boxer?'

'Yeah, that's him. Ex-champ, ex-primate. You know him?'

'Only too well.'

Rita sat on a bar stool putting together a mental jigsaw puzzle to which Freddy had supplied several new pieces. Perhaps the most illuminating involved the man whose picture she'd only just noticed in pride of place behind the counter. The ringside close-up showed his gleaming physique towering over a defeated opponent, the title WORLD CHAMPION emblazoned above his ferocious head in gold lettering.

When Jarrett arrived he climbed onto a stool beside her, his eyes doing a quick sweep over the clientele.

'Was it worth the visit?' he asked.

'Oh, definitely,' said Rita.

'But Freddy gave you nothing fresh?'

She brushed that aside. 'Forget Freddy. I've found my connection to Whitley.'

'What is it?'

She pointed at the gilded photo mounted behind the bar. 'Him.'

'You're kidding,' said Jarrett. 'Billy Bowers?'

'Uh-huh.' She nodded.

'Bugger me. That's a bit of a jaw-dropper, if you'll pardon the pun. You met him in the course of your inquiries?'

'That's right.'

'With Sex Crimes?'

'Oh, yes.'

'That means your name in a dead man's boot leads straight here. Could be a bit awkward.'

'Why?'

'Billy's a local hero. Not to mention a multi-millionaire.'

'Hero? Because he runs a sleazy club? I assume you know he's got a criminal background.'

'I know some of his associates are crooks, yes. But it's not just this club he owns. He's got a whole business portfolio – a restaurant, a gym and a charter boat company for game fishing on the reef. He's also into showbiz promotions and property development – he's building a resort complex up in the rainforest.' Jarrett paused, frowning. 'Of course, that brought him into direct conflict with Rachel Macarthur and the environmentalists. She organised protests and Billy was none too pleased. But he's got a lot of pull with the council.'

'In spite of his gangland credentials?'

'Lots of businessmen up here have got a shady past, councillors included. It's par for the course. The accepted wisdom is: don't knock what's good for the local economy. He's even on the board of the sailing club.'

'Don't tell me – he's one of your drinking mates.'

'As a matter of fact, yeah, we've enjoyed a few beers together.' Jarrett caught the disappointment in her expression. 'Why are you looking at me like that?'

'Do you know how he got his nickname?'

'"The Beast"? He told me it's from his fight style. Because he's a brute in the ring.'

'Then the laugh was on you,' she said with disgust. 'It's got nothing to do with boxing.'

Jarrett was peeved. 'What then?'

'It's a nasty joke his manager came up with because of Billy's proclivities.'

He looked at her askance. 'No! Not bestiality?'

'Yes, but not in the way you think. He forces women to do it and laughs while he watches. It's a sadistic sport to him.'

'And your connection?'

'I arrested him for it. It was my first year in the squad. I found out after a young hooker broke down in hysterics when I was questioning her about something else. She was nineteen.'

'Well, don't stop there. What happened?'

'Billy took some of his gangland pals to a brothel in Carlton – along with a pair of German shepherds. Three girls were working there that afternoon and they got slapped around until they complied. Billy entertained himself and his mates with a sex show between the girls and the dogs.'

'That story never came out.'

'He was never charged. I was a rookie detective and couldn't make the allegation stick. The girl who spoke to me vanished, the other two vigorously denied the story and Billy had plenty of chums to give him an alibi. No case. And I got a lecture about being impulsive.'

'But you were right.'

'I heard later why the other two girls were so emphatic in their denials. I was told, off the record, that the nineteen-year-old was chopped up and fed to the dogs.'

There was a strange glint in Jarrett's eye. 'It may interest you to know he still keeps German shepherds. Guard dogs at his villa.' He glanced over at the brassy women in the booth. 'I wonder if any of the girls here could tell us a story.'

'Or the man in the mud,' said Rita. 'Maybe that's why my name was in his boot.'

'He might've been planning to give you an update. If only we could identify him. Somehow I don't think Billy will help. Have you asked if he's around?'

'Billy's gone fishing, schmoozing up to a Hollywood veteran with a macho self-image.'

'Your profiling tell you that?'

'No, the barmaid,' smiled Rita. 'She says it's a producer who *wants to hook a marlin like Ernest Hemingway.*'

Jarrett gave a grunt. 'What – a fish with a beard?'

'So what's your news?' she asked.

'Something out of left field. We've been summoned to attend a meeting at the research base. Bryce, me and – wait for it – you.'

'Oh, shit,' Rita groaned. 'Maddox wants to carpet me officially.'

'Calm down,' said Jarrett, placing a hand on her arm. 'It's not about that. It's the upgraded terror alert. The government's ordered an urgent security review of Whitley Sands and surroundings, including the town itself. The introductory session is this afternoon and we'll all have a level-one clearance. Looks like there's a good chance we've got a terrorist cell in our midst. A review panel's being organised with base security to include emergency services, the local council and police – and we're on the list.'

'Why me?'

'Yeah, that's got Bryce flummoxed. He's none too pleased to be conscripted himself but says your inclusion smacks of an ulterior motive. "Wire-pulling" he calls it.'

'I think he's right.'

28

Rita felt a chill go through her as the police car stopped at the security barrier of the Whitley Sands research base. It brought back the brutal experience of two nights before and Dr Steinberg's allusion to the Stasi. This time, though, she wasn't heading to their compound but to their citadel. From the car windows she could see the chain-link perimeter fence stretching in either direction, topped with a frill of razor wire. Tall metal poles, each with a brace of cameras, flanked the fortified checkpoint where the guards inspected ID before waving them through.

Jarrett was at the wheel, looking uncomfortable in a suit and tie, with Inspector Bryce in the passenger seat beside him wearing full uniform. Rita was in the back seat on her own. She'd put on the pale turquoise linen suit that usually gave her an edge in male company. It was light, cool and showed off her curves. It was also a way of making a statement of self-assurance to Maddox and his ilk.

A small procession of civilian delegates was winding from the car park to the entrance of the main building. As the three members of the police contingent got out of the car, Bryce turned to Rita.

'This isn't meant to sound condescending, Van Hassel,' he began, 'but my advice to you is to say nothing unless you're asked a specific question. This meeting is fraught with pitfalls, not least for you.'

'I agree, sir.'

'This applies to you too, Jarrett. No uninvited comments. Don't offer advice. Don't expand on police tactics.' Bryce straightened his jacket with a tug. 'This review is ostensibly in response to an upgraded alert but don't doubt for a moment we'd be safer off paddling with stingers. We'll be dealing with military administrators and federal apparatchiks who didn't get where they are by being nice. Lethal politics is second nature to them. They're experts at the blame game. What makes it worse is that we'll have our civilian colleagues as an audience.'

With a sigh, Bryce led the way to the front doors of the administrative block that sat atop the seven underground levels where the R&D was housed. Once inside they joined the queue of emergency service and civil authority officers being processed with base security tags – photos, digital codes and fingerprint biometric data. When it came to Rita's turn she was presented with a ready-made smart card.

'We've already got your details, Van Hassel.'

A thick-necked guard gave her a cold look of recognition, one that lingered, as he handed her the card. She took the pass, slapped it against a digital pad to open glass security doors and walked through into a cavernous atrium. It stretched six floors up to a glazed roof and two floors down to a basement cafeteria furnished with tables, chairs and rubber plants. The building's interior was circular, with galleried walkways and glass-walled offices on each floor. Suspended in mid-air, like a satellite above the atrium, was a sphere ribbed with CCTV cameras. The elevator hall was clad in marble.

As she leant on the railing, craning her neck upwards, Rita could see grey clouds scudding overhead through the glass panels of the roof. Figures, some in military uniforms, were walking along the upper galleries. In a ground-floor meeting room, on the far side of the atrium, men in white shirts were seated before a flip chart. On the floor below technicians were adjusting cameras and lasers in some sort of open studio. All of this, of course, was basic office work. Below the open basement floor stretched the underground chambers where all the restricted work occurred.

The place was unusual and deceptive. While the building's exterior was bland and rectangular – a functional block of concrete and smoked glass – inside it was something of an architectural showpiece, albeit inward-looking and vertiginous at the same time.

And with a gasp of recognition, Rita saw the symbolism of the design. The Whitley Sands building was a physical expression of the secret project being developed beneath it.

The structure was a clever adaptation of the model prison advocated by eighteenth-century English philosopher Jeremy Bentham – a type of penitentiary that he called a Panopticon. The name came from the Greek word for 'all-seeing'. The layout was circular, with the prisoners in their cells around the circumference and the officers, concealed from view, in an observation tower at the centre. The aim was to convey a sense of permanent surveillance or, as Bentham put it, a 'sentiment of a sort of omnipresence'. The Whitley Sands structure even mimicked a central watch-tower with its nest of security cameras.

Someone came and stood beside her at the railing. She turned to see the unsmiling face of Captain Roy Maddox.

'This time we've let you in the front door,' he said. 'So you'd better behave yourself.'

Instead of military apparel, now he was wearing a dark blue suit, white shirt and precisely knotted tie.

'Captain Maddox,' replied Rita. 'I didn't recognise you out of your interrogation garb.'

'Come on, Van Hassel. Let it go.'

'I already have.'

'Good girl.'

'But if you go on patronising me,' she added, just above a whisper, 'I might not think twice about kicking you where it hurts.'

'I'd like to see you try.' Maddox let out an unfriendly laugh. 'But let's be straight with one another. Like it or not, we're about to work together.'

'Straight, okay,' said Rita, folding her arms. 'What's the real reason I'm part of this review?'

'Because you're a random element in an unorthodox theatre of war,' he growled. 'And your path has already crossed mine.'

'You don't trust me,' she said.

'I've got enough to worry about without trying to second guess what your investigation will turn up. For all I know, you might stumble on something relevant. To put it bluntly, I don't want you interfering wherever your female instincts lead you. I'd rather have you in the loop.'

'That's almost flattering.'

'Well, it's the only flattery you'll get from me.' He turned aside as Bryce and Jarrett approached. 'Here come your colleagues.' He reached out and shook their hands briskly as he eyed their security tags. 'I see you're equipped with your new dongles.'

'My old dongle's still in working order,' put in Jarrett.

Bryce cut him dead with a look before turning to Maddox.

'This is all a bit short notice,' he said.

'That's why it's called urgent,' retorted Maddox. 'Get used to it, Bryce. Things are hotting up around here.' He gestured towards the lifts. 'The review's being held in the Situation Room, so we're heading down to level one.'

They filed into the lift with a handful of other delegates, glided three floors down and emerged into a long, high corridor that seemed to stretch for a kilometre in either direction. The floor was covered in linoleum and the walls were painted battleship grey. Maddox led the guests past several steel doors, some of them ajar, showing rooms where staff were busy at keyboards. An intersecting corridor brought them to double doors, through which they entered the Situation Room. It was a broad, carpeted space dominated by a large oval table around which a couple of dozen people were milling, looking for their names in front of their allotted chairs. The room had a high ceiling and no windows, the walls were hung with flat screens and maps. A bank of computer monitors and digital communications were recessed into one of the walls in the form of a master control desk.

'Right, we're all here,' announced Maddox, as the doors closed with an air-tight hiss. 'Let's get this show on the road.'

There may have been an irksome quality to Bryce, an undue formality in the way he approached his duties, but Rita decided he was right about the type of meeting they were now locked into. She'd been to taskforce briefings before, crowded squad rooms with too many detectives pumped up and edgy, yet none had prepared her for this. This was like a war summit. Those at the head of the table interpreted the rules of battle, government observers took notes, and the rest were there to follow orders or face the consequences. The setting was intimidating, like a hi-tech bunker, and the mood oppressive. The room itself was filled with an airless hush, a strain of expectation.

More than thirty people sat in silence at their allocated places as the man presiding rose to his feet.

'Thank you all for coming so promptly,' he began. 'Let me introduce myself. I'm the director-general of the Whitley Sands Defence Research Establishment, Lieutenant Colonel Willis Baxter. It's my honour to be the man in charge here and the convenor of this opening session of the security review, ordered by the federal government. A heavy responsibility is being placed on the shoulders of all of you in this room, and I expect nothing less than total commitment to the task at hand.'

The introductory remarks confirmed Rita's assessment. The format was rigidly institutional, with all that implied in terms of conforming to the rules. Failure to comply would invite censure or worse.

'In addition to your normal duties,' Baxter continued, 'those of you employed by the civil authorities will be required to familiarise yourself with the directives, procedures and responses stipulated under the stages of the alert. I can't emphasise enough how important it is to remain vigilant at all times. All reports of suspicious acts must be followed up. No threat, whether actual, potential or merely perceived, can go unchecked. I hope I make myself clear.'

What was becoming clear to Rita was Baxter's sense of his own importance. He expected obedience. He saw himself as a martial overlord who projected a natural air of authority. His adjustment from active service to defence industry administration was an ongoing process. The way he addressed the meeting – standing stiffly, hands clasped behind his back, chin thrust out, his message conveyed with a crisp, no-nonsense delivery – was the way he would have rallied his troops. Like Maddox, military logic controlled his thinking. But unlike his security director, Baxter assumed an aura of upright command, leadership with a refined sense of supervision. Tall, almost aristocratic in profile, he possessed a weighty voice, icy blue eyes and jet black hair. It was probably dyed to maintain an imposing image, consistent with his tailored black suit and regimental tie. While Rita recognised that Baxter cut an impressive figure, she couldn't help feeling there was an element of pose, a certain vanity, in the way he conducted himself. In any commander, that was a dangerous flaw.

'Before I proceed with the terms of the review,' Baxter went on, 'I want to go around the table and register each delegate's presence. I'll start by introducing the three men seated beside me. Each is an expert in security and intelligence matters and has an intricate working knowledge of the research base. To my right is the Whitley Sands security director, Captain Roy Maddox.' Maddox nodded grimly. 'To my left is our international director, Rhett Molloy, who hails from Washington, and next to him is a senior adviser on counter-terrorism, Peter Luker from Canberra.' Luker offered a smile of acknowledgement; the others remained stony-faced as Baxter continued. 'Now, going in a clockwise direction, I want each person to state, for the record, their name, function and area of specialisation.'

It took several minutes as, one after the other, those around the table explained who they were and what they did. The police were well represented, with delegates drawn from the specialist squads in Brisbane as well as the AFP. There were officers from the emergency services – ambulance, fire brigade and hospitals – as well as members of Whitley Council's Local Disaster Management Committee. Together with Defence, various federal government departments had also sent officials. It seemed like a comprehensive and dynamic gathering. Or was it, Rita wondered. Perhaps, with its ensemble approach, it was destined to be the very opposite.

When it came to her turn she stated briskly, 'Detective Sergeant Marita Van Hassel, Criminal Profiler, Victoria Police.'

With the introductions complete, folders were distributed, stamped on the front cover with the words *Commonwealth of Australia – Confidential*. Each folder contained nearly one hundred densely printed pages, which attempted to anticipate any and all exigencies. The rule book, thought Rita.

'Read it carefully after this meeting,' instructed Baxter. 'At tomorrow's session I will expect to hear a range of suggestions on how we can apply or adapt the measures covered, or reinforce the strategies already in place.' He waited for the ripples of shuffling and murmuring to subside around the table. 'Very well, then. Down to business. Those of you who have been invited to participate in the review are here as guests of this establishment. As such you have been issued with a level-one security clearance, giving you access to the building's superstructure and as far down as this level. Everywhere else is out of bounds. If you should stray to the underground levels below us you'll be subject to mandatory arrest. So while you can feel free to go up at Whitley Sands, please don't attempt to explore downwards. The R&D activities conducted on the lower levels are classified, highly sensitive and potentially dangerous to the uninformed. That warning aside, we felt it appropriate to convene here, in the Situation Room, because of the gravity of the threat confronting us.'

Baxter took a deep breath and drew himself up to his full height.

'A question on many of your minds will be: why a review? The process was initiated amid concerns in both Canberra and Washington over the public campaign being mounted against the base. The first flashpoint came with the mass demonstration in March. It marked a significant escalation, going beyond what the motley band of local environmentalists had organised up till then. The March 20 anti-war protest saw concerted action by a coalition of anarchists, anti-capitalists, hard-core eco-warriors and land rights activists who'd all taken up residence in the town. It also saw the first use of bolt-cutters and the first breaches of the perimeter fence. Worst of all, it further publicised the base as a centre for the development of hi-tech weapons for deployment in the war on terror. Because of media coverage that label was promulgated to a global audience and we are having to deal with the consequences.

'The second flashpoint came earlier this month with an even bigger mass demonstration, more bolt-cutters, more breaches, and another wave of negative publicity. The government decided to act by ordering that the review process be put in motion. We had planned to give you advance notice but the terrorist alert changed that. The review was upgraded to urgent, and that's why you've been summoned here today instead of next week. The anti-war movement now poses a secondary problem, in that it could provide a smokescreen for a terrorist attack. Preventing such an event is, of course, our new priority. And to bring you up to speed on that, I'll hand over to Peter Luker.'

Baxter sat down, straight-backed, in his chair.

Luker didn't get to his feet. Instead he leant forward on the table, hands clasped, and spoke in a more relaxed, conversational tone, as if reluctant to generate alarm.

'Nearly a fortnight ago,' he began, 'four men on a terrorist watch-list disappeared from known locations in the western suburbs of Sydney. Subsequent searches unearthed false documents, charts and bomb-making residues. They are now considered to be an active terrorist cell. Last night, the same four men were identified on surveillance footage in Whitley, entering Rafferty's bar.'

Luker turned as the footage, timed at 21.35, was replayed on flat screens around the room.

'A raid was conducted within the hour but the men were no longer on the premises. The bar was crowded, with many people coming and going, and we've been unable to isolate footage of the men leaving. It has to be assumed they represent an extreme risk.'

Luker unclasped his hands and toyed with a pack of cigarettes as if wishing he could open it and light up.

'There's more. Their appearance in the town isn't a coincidence. The Defence Signals Directorate has detected a rise in electronic chatter, here and overseas, relating to an imminent attack, with intelligence gathered recently containing a specific reference to Whitley Sands. While a direct assault on the base is deemed possible but unlikely – and the same applies to warships of the US Navy – the town itself is far more vulnerable. A bombing, with a high civilian death toll, in the vicinity of the base has a much greater probability. Likely targets include hotels, bars, nightclubs and tourist spots. With such a scenario, we need all the support we can get, and that's why you're sitting here now.'

Luker leant sideways in his chair and pocketed his cigarettes, as if out of habit, as he rounded off his remarks.

Rita wasn't quite sure what to make of him. She detected a hint of discomfort in his body language, possibly because he didn't fit in with the others at the head of the table. Judging by his manner he had no military history, unlike his colleagues, and while his relaxed approach suggested a more sociable background, if anything, he was smarter than them, sharp and articulate in almost a casual way.

It was obvious that Luker held a senior position in the nation's intelligence and security structure, yet his appearance, too, was a shade less than polished. His navy blue suit was slightly creased, with the tie a little askew, and there were nicotine stains on his fingers. Somewhere in his middle age, he had a friendly, lived-in face, which exhibited the results of bad habits in the bags under his eyes and a flush of redness in his cheeks. For all that, Rita found him attractive – not for his looks, because he wasn't exactly handsome, but because of an undercurrent of dangerous charm, the sign of a man with a bohemian streak, combined with a touch of gentleness. Of course, her observations could be way off-beam. Given his job, he could be capable of lethal deception.

Luker added as an afterthought, 'I'm happy to provide more background information in response to any questions you may have. But please understand I can't disclose classified material or breach restrictions relating to national security.'

Baxter again asserted his control over proceedings.

'I think we can move on to the next step,' he said. 'This is a good point at which to throw open discussion on issues that might concern you. Try to keep your questions short, and for those answering, try to be brief. Above all, stay focused on the primary objective: the uncompromising defence of our way of life, and the comprehensive defeat of our enemies.'

As the question-and-answer session drifted into predictable and repetitive territory, Rita tuned out, thinking over what Freddy had told her. His information had reinforced her theory about what – if not who – lay behind the murders, setting a clear priority of tracking down the elusive Stonefish. He seemed to hold the key to the investigation and, if he had acted as Steinberg's go-between, it was little wonder he had dropped out of sight. That made her task all the more difficult. Stonefish obviously had no intention of being found, especially as he was being pursued by powerful figures associated with the research base, possibly including some sitting in the Situation Room right now.

An unexpected question snapped Rita's attention back to the discussion.

'I may be missing something, but why do we have a criminal profiler from Victoria attending this review?'

The question, which came with a barb of suspicion from a defence ministry official, took both Rita and Bryce by surprise. Bryce shot her a warning glance and was clearing his throat to respond when Luker intervened.

'I can answer that,' he said. 'Detective Sergeant Van Hassel is here for her expertise in crime-scene analysis, behavioural science and the psychology of violence. With no local profiler available, she's been seconded to examine the decapitation killings in the town. Because of the second victim's provocative role in fomenting protests against the base, there's a clear overlap with security issues.' Luker laid a look on the ministry official. 'DS Van Hassel also comes to us with the highest recommendations from senior police officers regarding her ability and integrity. We thought it not only a pragmatic step to include her, but one that can only be advantageous. She has, after all, a unique insight into the criminal mind. And, let's face it, that's what we're threatened with in its most fanatical expression.'

As a rebuttal, it was more than effective. It was unexpected praise.

Bryce exchanged another glance with Rita before sitting back. He looked partly relieved, partly bemused, as if he didn't know what was going on. There was obviously more to her presence than anyone was telling him. As for Rita, Luker's words were doing wonders for her ego. She sensed a great ulterior motive, along the lines that had come from Maddox, but she felt a measure of reassurance. When Luker leant back, throwing her a friendly smile, she had an urge to applaud him.

The discussion then turned to civic emergency responses. It wasn't long before they were bogged down in details of town infrastructure, until Baxter announced a forty-minute adjournment, reminding everyone that everything below level one was out of bounds.

'You can go up but not down,' said Baxter. 'Coffee and sandwiches are available at the cafeteria in the basement atrium. That's one floor up. Toilets are also there. For those of you addicted to nicotine, the ground-floor smoking area is at your disposal. That's three floors up. Needless to say, everything discussed in this room is confidential.'

While Bryce and Jarrett made an immediate move to join the squad officers from Brisbane, Rita hung back, feeling like the odd one out. She was in no mood for police politics. Instead, she made her way out of the room and along the corridor among other delegates, her thoughts turning to something that had more to do with emotions than terrorism or murder. She found herself thinking about the proximity of her lover's ex-lover. Audrey Zillman was close by, presumably working on one of the levels below her. Rita wanted to meet her for personal as well as professional reasons, though how she would swing it under the circumstances was a real problem.

As she waited for the lift, her thoughts were interrupted by a voice beside her.

'Mind if I join you?'

It was Luker.

'Join me where?' she asked.

'I thought maybe we could grab a coffee then head up to the smoking area.' He brandished his pack of cigarettes. 'I'm one of the nicotine addicts Baxter disapproves of.'

'Okay,' said Rita. 'After your words of welcome back there I can hardly decline.'

Rita could feel the eyes of the guards on her as, plastic coffee cup in hand, she followed Luker to the smoking area. It wasn't her imagination, she was sure. Each time she passed a member of Maddox's security force she was on the receiving end of a persistent stare. It was as if they were watching and waiting for her to put a foot wrong. Dr Steinberg's notion of a modern Stasi was ringing true yet again, not to mention the Panopticon theme of inmates in a glass prison – a twenty-first-century version with its electronic 'mode of obtaining power of mind over mind', as Jeremy Bentham had expressed it. The parallels were chilling. At least there would be no move against her while she was in Luker's company.

Once inside the smoking room, he dumped his plastic cup on the nearest table, spilling coffee in his haste to get out a cigarette. He offered her one but she shook her head. As Rita sat down opposite him, he lit up, sucked the smoke into his lungs, then breathed it out slowly with a sigh of relief.

'Thank God for that,' he said.

While he inhaled again, Rita sipped her coffee and gazed out over the car park. Beyond the asphalt a landscape of coastal dunes and saltbush stretched away under a grey sky. Like other institutions, the research base had decided to prove its concern for the health of employees by treating smokers as social lepers. As a result, they were forced into each other's company in a mood of mutual sympathy and resentment. Rita had observed the effect before – one of the miscalculations of corporate psychology. No doubt it meant that here, as in so many other workplaces, the 'Designated Smoking Area' had become a hub of gossip.

The room was charmless – scuffed plastic chairs scattered around low formica tables bearing overflowing ashtrays. A row of windows overlooked the lines of staff cars outside. A bearded man in denim smoked despondently, his gaze floating somewhere along the horizon. Others around him chatted in subdued tones about the shortcomings of the base. A young technician in a white lab coat paced back and forth, smoking nervously. A woman flicked through the pages of a magazine. A group of fellow delegates, from the town's emergency services, entered the room, reaching for their lighters. They eyed Luker and moved away, keeping their distance.

He puffed again and loosened his tie.

'I've been dying for one of these for the past two hours,' he explained to Rita.

'Maybe you should kick the habit,' she told him.

'Have you?'

'Yes.'

'I should have added "strong-willed" to your qualities.' He sat back and relaxed with another draw on his cigarette. 'We have something in common, you and I. We're both outsiders here.'

'That surprises me. You all look as thick as thieves.'

Luker chuckled at her irreverence. 'If there's one place where looks are deceiving, it's the Situation Room.'

'Surely you have a lot in common with your CIA pal.'

'No, Molloy is very much an insider.'

'And the Canberra bureaucrats?'

'They're at home too. They had a hand in setting up the Whitley Sands facility. I'm a newcomer, only recently drafted in. I'm still getting a feel for the place – the base, the town, the mind-set of the tropical north. Much like you, I suspect.'

'So what's your impression of Whitley Sands?'

Luker gave a grunt. 'Equivocal. But let's set that topic aside for the time being. The walls have ears.'

'I've got a feeling you mean that in a technical way,' commented Rita.

He just said, 'I'd like to think you and I could come to a consensus on how you proceed with your investigation.'

'I'm listening.'

'Regarding the overlap I mentioned. There are any number of methods for safeguarding national security. I'm suggesting you and I could agree on an alternative strategy.'

'Alternative to what?'

'To those already in place. You'll appreciate I can't go into details.'

Rita sighed. 'I'm not sure what you're getting at but I'm already in a difficult position – under orders to toe the line or else.'

'The line is often blurred.'

'Not if you've been threatened, handcuffed, strip-searched and interrogated like a criminal.'

Luker frowned. 'Maddox?'

'And his paramilitary thugs.'

'I see.' Luker contemplated the smoke he was exhaling. 'Needless to say, he overreacted. But somehow you've hit a raw nerve. I find that interesting.'

'If you're hinting you're not fully informed that's a bit hard to swallow.'

'There's a difference between information and knowledge,' he replied.

'When you're talking about intelligence data, yes. But your job is to have knowledge of state secrets.'

'Quite true. But no institution discloses all its secrets willingly. Especially if it's got something to hide from official scrutiny.'

'I'm sorry.' Rita shook her head sceptically. 'It's hard for me to take anything here at face value. If you're playing a game of cat and mouse, what's the point? Maddox and his connections have already sprung the trap.'

'I'm not trying to trick you.'

'Well, if you're talking out of school, I don't know why. You'll have to explain.'

'Fair enough.' Luker moved closer. 'Put frankly, there's more going on here than I can get a handle on. You, however, have obviously made connections I haven't. This comes as no surprise given the recommendations about you.'

'Yes, I've been meaning to ask. What recommendations?'

'I did some positive vetting – comes with the territory. You'll be pleased to hear your senior officers rate you very highly.'

'Does that include Superintendent Nash?'

'Nash was the one discordant note. But, oddly enough, that goes in your favour. His perspective is bureaucratic. Mine is not. Besides, your fan base goes all the way up to the chief commissioner herself.'

'And you spoke to Jack Loftus?'

'Of course. But your best reference comes from a man I know personally, Detective Inspector Jim Proctor.'

'Let me guess. You belong to the same club.'

'Correct. He told me you'd spot it.'

'What else did he tell you?'

'That you're too good to be a squad detective,' answered Luker. 'He thinks you're a natural for intelligence work, given your profiling skills and personality.'

'My personality?'

'Yes. He came up with a list that ticked the right boxes – lack of fear, fast reflexes, lateral thinking. On top of that your social instincts are sharp. You distrust authority and can operate below the radar.'

'That's because I did some impromptu work for him.'

'There's another quality he mentioned which explains why you're on a collision course with Whitley Sands. According to Proctor, you're motivated by a driven quest for justice. The seeds were sown in your childhood.'

'He might be right,' Rita acknowledged, 'or he might be spouting Freudian psychobabble.'

'I've read your personnel file. More than once you've put justice before compliance with the rules.'

'And that's a flaw?'

'Only if it becomes irrational.'

Was that a warning? Rita couldn't tell, so she asked, 'Are you talking reason as conformity?'

'No. But sometimes it's rational to appear to conform.' Luker flicked ash dismissively. 'Anyway, it's rare for Proctor to pay such a tribute to anyone. Perhaps that goes some way to explaining why I'm talking to you now.'

'Perhaps.'

Luker grunted and sipped from his plastic cup.

Rita wasn't prepared to trust him. His friendly approach was welcome and his attempt to distance himself from the internal workings of the base was plausible, yet he was clearly implicated in its covert activities. That meant he probably had direct access to whatever lay behind three murders. One way or another, he was in on it, so she had no intention of sharing her confidences, her insights or the information she'd put together. As for Proctor, her professional respect for him was tempered with the knowledge that he belonged to a sophisticated old boys' network, and while his intellect and objectivity set him above many of his colleagues, his emotional detachment could at times be insensitive, even unscrupulous. The same could apply to Luker.

However, despite her misgivings, she was warming to him, and the prospect of entering some kind of mutual agreement would have advantages. Not the least would be a measure of protection from the excesses of the base security force. That threat was pushing her into unorthodox tactics and alliances. On the same day as instigating a secret deal with a criminal hacker she was on the verge of making a private pact with a federal spook. It seemed ironic, if not foolish, but she refused to surrender whatever it was that could be interpreted as a 'driven quest for justice'. If she did, she might as well quit now. It would be like surrendering her soul.

'So. What are your instincts telling you?' asked Luker. 'Can we agree on some unofficial contact?'

'Only if it's two-way,' answered Rita. 'But before I agree to anything, I need some disclosure from you, Mr Luker.'

He put down his half-empty cup cautiously. 'What sort of disclosure?'

'Tell me about yourself. Not the agency work – I mean your personal background. My guess is it's not military.'

'Good God, no.' Luker laughed with something like relief. 'That's another reason I'm the odd man out. But hazard a guess. What profession do you think I'm grounded in? I'd be interested to hear.'

'I don't know enough about you.'

'Think of me as an interview subject. Someone who's walked in off the street.'

'You make it sound like a party piece.'

'I don't mean to. Humour me.'

Rita realised what he was doing. By bouncing the request back at her he was setting her a test. It also showed how adept he was at manoeuvring a conversation. A dialogue with Luker was like a game of psychological chess and for now she had no choice but to play.

'Okay, if you insist.' She shifted in her seat for a more studied look at him. 'The characteristics you display point in a certain direction.'

'Which characteristics?'

'Outgoing, observant, with a habit of extracting information in a subtle, disarming way.'

He sucked on his cigarette a little more pensively. 'You see me as manipulative.'

'With a light-handed touch,' she demurred. 'So, if I was making a post-interview assessment, I'd describe the subject as articulate, accomplished and intelligent. He also possesses a supreme degree of social competence and a track record in achieving objectives through persuasion rather than aggression.'

'I didn't ask you to profile me.'

'I'm sorry, I thought you did. And, no offence, but the profile fits a group I've dealt with before – men with polished communication skills and a low threshold of boredom. One trait makes them good at their job, the other propels them into binges of self-indulgence leading to hangovers and broken relationships. I'm talking about men in the media. If I had to guess, that's where I'd place you.'

Luker bent forward and stubbed out his cigarette.

'You're good,' he said. 'Very good. And you're right, of course. By profession, I'm a journalist.'

'Print, broadcast?'

'Newspapers, with a few stints in radio.'

Rita relaxed, satisfied it was her turn to go on the offensive. 'Where?'

'I cut my teeth in Melbourne before making a name for myself in Sydney.' Luker gave a weary smile. 'Then it was over to Europe as a foreign correspondent. London, Paris. Serious reportage. Serious drinking.'

'Am I allowed to ask where you were recruited?'

'Spain. I said yes in a weak moment after a heavy weekend touring the bars of Seville. So your bullet-point analysis was accurate.' Luker gave her another appraising look. 'My cover functioned successfully in a series of newspaper bureaux. Throughout the nineties I combined journalism and the spy game. I've got to admit it was a dual role I largely enjoyed. I look back on it with nostalgia since my promotion to a senior post in

Canberra. That was at the turn of the millennium, and you'd be right in thinking it cramped my style. Rubbing shoulders with strait-laced public servants and uptight military bores is a bit like Sartre's vision of hell.'

That made Rita laugh. 'Are you married?'

'Not anymore. Cairo finished that off.'

Luker was interrupted by his mobile bleeping. He read the text and said, 'Damn. I've got to go.' He stood up, brushing flakes of ash from his sleeve. 'I assume we've got an agreement to meet privately.'

'Where, when?'

'The where is easy enough. We're in the same hotel. The Whitsunday is my home away from home, each time I get bounced back up here by Canberra. The when is notional. At some time of mutual convenience. Okay?'

'Okay.'

'In the meantime, Van Hassel, I'll see you back in the Situation Room.'

He beamed at her in a way that had more than one meaning, then walked out, straightening his tie.

Rita sat back and blew out a sigh. Her chat with Luker had taken her into alien territory. Perhaps it was the no-man's land that Steinberg had warned her about. But one thing she was sure of. Wherever she was heading, she was leaving routine police work a long way behind.

29

Rita finished her coffee and walked to the lifts, the security guards following her with their eyes. Their attention was unnerving. It was also revealing. She now had little doubt that her presence in the building was a ploy by those in charge. Her participation in the review was irrelevant to the process and the so-called 'overlap' with her investigation was merely an excuse to reel her in. The base command wanted to observe her closely, find out what she knew, maybe catch her out. The words of Maddox and Luker seemed to back that up. Both suspected she'd uncovered part of the truth. And the truth was dangerous. She tried not to think of the consequences.

As she waited for an elevator, she realised she was being drawn into a web of deception. Some of it was her own doing but that was her way of coping with the layers of subterfuge attached to Whitley Sands. She looked across the circular interior and saw the building itself as emblematic. The glass-tiered atrium resembled a mirror maze with multi-faceted reflections distorting the angles. Perspectives were curved. Things were not as they seemed. The structure conveyed a looking-glass reality. The parallel seemed apt. Like Alice, Rita was having trouble spotting what was false and what wasn't.

The doors slid open on an empty lift. A man in a white lab coat went in ahead of her. She recognised him from the smoking room, the technician who'd been pacing up and down. He was standing with his back to her, blocking her way so she couldn't reach the lift buttons.

'Level one,' she told him.

He pressed a button.

The doors closed and the elevator dropped rapidly through several levels.

'Did you deliberately ignore me?' she asked.

'Yes,' he said, turning to face her. 'I'm taking you down to level five.'

'What the hell are you doing?' said Rita as the lift stopped and the doors opened.

'I'm helping your investigation,' he replied, his manner abrupt, his expression tightly composed. He was English, in his early thirties, with pale blue eyes and a taut, boyish face. 'You should come with me.'

'I'm not stepping out of this lift.'

'Why not?'

'For a start, I don't have clearance for this level.'

'No one will report you.'

'Why should I even consider it?'

'You won't be doing your job if you don't.' His body was lodged against the door, holding it open. 'I'm talking about your duty as a police officer, Detective Sergeant Van Hassel.'

'So who are you?'

'My name's Paul.'

'Paul who?'

'Paul Giles. Project coordinator.'

His name was vaguely familiar but she couldn't recall why.

'You work on the Panopticon Project?' she asked.

'That's the one. Will you come with me?'

'Sorry, Paul. You still haven't given me a reason to run the risk of being detained by your security squad.'

'I'm the one they'd arrest. I'm already a target.'

'So why hijack me and make it worse?'

'They know who killed Rachel Macarthur.'

The words jolted her.

Rita hesitated, but only for a moment. If he was offering to prove a direct link between murder and the base he'd got her attention. It was evidence she couldn't ignore.

She stepped out of the lift.

'Show me,' she said.

Paul led the way along a subterranean corridor past sealed metal doors, Rita's heels tapping the linoleum. The sound echoed down the passageway stretching into the distance. A couple of scruffy males with the distracted intensity of computer nerds emerged from a doorway and walked past without paying Rita any attention. They were too busy arguing over whether Zen was a form of nonlinear feedback. Rita took it as another looking-glass moment.

CCTV cameras and alarms were fixed to the walls, along with warning signs outlined in black and yellow diagonals: *Authorised Personnel Only*. Overhead, a concrete ceiling was strung with a mass of exposed cables and piping. The decor was battleship grey, apparently the uniform colour of the underground facility, adding to its functional and vaguely depressing aspect. She could feel the weight of it bearing down on her.

'How deep underground are we?' she asked.

'Nearly fifty metres,' Paul answered.

'What's on this level?'

'The engineering section – technical support, R&D labs. And, more importantly, my personal work space.'

'What's below us?'

'Level six has acres of computer hardware and the master control room.'

'And level seven?'

'Our biggest secret. It's what all the fuss is about. The project hub and control system.'

'Do you have access?'

'No. But I've been down there once as the technical director's assistant. It's all very space age. Very *Star Wars*.'

He led her through a side door and across a communal office space that was unoccupied and untidy. Reams of printout were draped over desks, stacks of magazines spilled from metal cabinets onto the floor and a random collection of pin-ups were stuck to the wall, dominated by a poster-sized print of *The Scream*. As they reached a large studio door with a red light glowing above it, Rita could hear the thumping bass of heavy metal coming from the other side.

'We have to go via the smart room,' said Paul. 'Don't let it freak you out.'

As he rolled open the door the full blast of the music swept over them. Rita recognised the track – Guns N' Roses with the decibels cranked. Paul didn't try to talk above the sound; it would have been pointless. He just jerked his thumb in the direction they were heading and she followed.

It was a strange place, a high-ceilinged cavity with tiers of computers, cables trailing across the floor and exposed metal beams overhead. Half a dozen young men and women sat face-to-face across a bank of terminals, swivelling and rocking to the music. Rita could see why Maddox was instinctively suspicious of the research staff. Socially these civilians – with their spiky black hair and sloppy clothes, not to mention their undisciplined thinking – were the opposite of his security force.

She smiled to herself as she followed Paul through the centre of the smart room. The area was hemmed in by wall-sized screens. Projected onto these were images of virtual creatures, all slightly grotesque, moving around cartoon-like interiors. As the two of them moved through it, a virtual Paul walked across the screens, accompanied by a virtual Rita, chased by a virtual dinosaur snapping at her heels. She found it disconcerting; another aspect of warped reality.

They left by a rear exit, which muffled the music as it closed behind them and led to a further labyrinth of grey corridors.

Paul stopped beside a steel door with the number 538 printed on it.

'My place of abode,' he said.

Paul swiped a security pad with his pass, opened the door and took Rita down a connecting passage. The claustrophobic dimensions and grey metal fittings were suggestive of below decks on a warship. At the end was another doorway. They went through it into a narrow sound-proofed room, lit only by task lamps and images displayed on a wall of computer screens. A heavy steel door closed them in with a cushioned hiss.

'What *is* this?' asked Rita.

'The project coordinator's control room,' he answered, dropping into a swivel chair in front of keyboards. 'My primary work station.'

'And why have you brought me here?'

'To show you classified material and break federal laws. Take a seat, Van Hassel.'

Despite a constrained intensity about him, there was a cavalier element in his approach. He was displaying the characteristics of a highly strung man who'd finally thrown caution to the wind. Not that he was showing signs of being reckless. It was more as if he'd made a calculated decision to break the rules and there was no looking back. If that was the case Rita could expect to learn something that would take her a step closer to the truth.

She pulled over a chair, dumped her shoulder bag on the floor and sat down. While the bank of screens and digital decks dominated the room, the rear wall was lined with more mundane items – a rack of clipboards, a unit filled with disks, a fire extinguisher and a coat stand on which a denim jacket hung. There was also a desk with an open laptop. Beside it was a tech toy in the shape of breasts and a desk calendar with a sepia print of King's College Chapel. Everything was neat, not a thing out of place. Even a couple of loose pens were aligned precisely with a notepad. It was all beginning to fit with Rita's initial impression of Paul's personality as fastidious to the point of compulsive. It was the sort of personality that made her wary.

'Let's pick a location in the town,' he said. 'Any you fancy?'

'Why?'

'I want to show you the system in action. How about the high street? Let's see what's going on there.' He clicked a mouse and a wide-angle view of traffic and pedestrians in motion filled a high-resolution computer screen. 'Ah, some of our American cousins. Let's take a closer look.'

The view homed in on half a dozen US sailors. As they ambled along the pavement, chatting and joking, the view on the screen tracked along with them. To adjust it, Paul tapped a keyboard.

The Americans stopped outside a bar, lingering a moment before pushing open the door and disappearing inside. Rita recognised the exterior as the Steamboat.

'Let's follow them in,' said Paul. 'Incidentally, there are no physical bugs in the place.'

Rita watched as the exterior image of the pub dissolved to be replaced by an interior scene, with the sailors pulling out chairs and sitting around a table as they ordered drinks, their dialogue loud and clear. The picture too was sharp, as if it was being fed from a live TV camera mounted inside the bar. But she realised it couldn't be, not if Paul was being straight about it. Assuming he was, this system seemed to defy logic. It also went beyond any technology currently in use. To see and hear inside rooms at random was a radical advance in surveillance. This allowed total accessibility. No wonder Steinberg had seen Rita's Orwellian analogy as accurate.

'By the way,' said Paul, 'these are computer-generated images.'

'Do you want to explain that to me?'

'That's why you're here.' He swivelled around to face her. 'I'm on the team testing an experimental surveillance system for deployment in the so-called war on terror. It means from my copper-lined control room here I can observe and eavesdrop on anyone within a two-hundred-and-forty-degree sector, up to a distance of ten k from the base.'

She was watching him carefully. 'I assume it's an integrated system.'

'Correct, combining input from all sources of electronic data – mobiles, landlines, cables, emails, CCTV, satellite coverage – the lot. Plus something else: an EM Net.'

'How does that work?'

'On the same principle as radar. Emitters fire waves of electromagnetic pulses across the sector, with particle-beam accelerators and laser pulses embedded in the system to give pinpoint accuracy. With me so far?'

'Yes.'

'Good. Image and acoustic data is transmitted in digital form via scanners to a quantum supercomputer executing more than one million trillion operations per second.'

'Bit of a load.'

'Too much for human brains. The complexities have to be monitored by a form of AI using new advances in fractal geometry to process the decision-making. It's known as the Omniscient Demographic Tracker.'

Rita frowned. 'Omniscient? Sounds like someone's idea of playing God.'

'Ever studied English utilitarian Jeremy Bentham?'

'I'm familiar with his Panopticon idea.'

'Well, this is it gone digital – all-seeing, all-knowing. It makes total surveillance possible. You understand the implications?'

'I can see all kinds of implications. But why am I here?'

'To look at footage I've pulled from the system's memory.' Paul turned back to the keyboard. 'It's from the night Rachel Macarthur was murdered.'

Rita sat forward, her concentration intense as the significance of Paul's words struck home. She fixed her eyes on the screen where a still image appeared. It showed a dark but clear figure of a woman. It was Rachel. She was at the top of the alleyway leading down to the Rough Diamond Club, the neon sign aglow at the bottom of the slope.

'This is digitally captured and enhanced,' explained Paul. 'That's why the focus is so sharp.'

He tapped a key, triggering the image into motion.

Rita watched as Rachel walked down the cobbled alley, leaving behind the glow of a streetlamp, past the shadowed shopfronts and boarded doorways. The view tracked along beside her as Rachel approached the point where she was attacked. Suddenly the picture dissolved in a blur of static. Nothing was visible. When it resolved itself there was just a perspective of the murder scene after the attack, the mutilated hump of Rachel's body lying dimly visible in the gutter as rain began to fall.

Paul tapped another key and the image froze.

'What happened?' asked Rita.

'A cover-up,' he said. 'Okay, the system has teething problems, with odd things happening at the sub-atomic level. And there's no way it's ready to be deployed anywhere. But that sort of blip is something else entirely. It's what I wanted to show you. Someone edited the memory by deliberately contaminating the data.'

'Who?'

'Only someone with level-seven access.'

'How many people are we talking about?'

'That's just it, I don't know.' Paul pushed himself back from the keyboard. 'There are nine directors on the Whitley Sands board, but not all of them have access.'

'What about Captain Maddox?'

'He's certainly got it. So does the DG, Willis Baxter, and the CIA's man, Rhett Molloy.' Paul threw her a caustic look. 'But a few off-base officials could also have access, like the man you were getting cosy with in the smoking room.'

'Luker?'

'He's a possible candidate.'

As she thought about it, Rita groaned.

'You've just given me one huge headache,' she said. 'By any chance does the surveillance sector include Leith Ferry?'

'It does. And I can answer your next question. Yes, there's footage of Steinberg's electrocution. Do you want to see it?'

'No.'

'Do you want to see your arrest by the base Gestapo?'

'Absolutely not. I want to forget it. What I'd like to see is whoever paid a visit to Dr Steinberg's house before he arrived home.'

'Well, guess what. There's a half-hour gap. That's been edited too.'

'Another cover-up?'

'Absolutely.'

Rita gave him a careful look. 'Something you haven't explained is where you stand in all this.'

'I told you: I'm a target.'

'Why?'

'I was in the wrong place at the wrong time.'

'Now I know why your name's familiar,' said Rita. 'You were inside the club the night of the murder. You were one of the customers questioned by police.'

'Not just the police, Maddox too. He grilled me like an inquisitor, called me "decadent", told me to pull my head in or face the consequences. At the time I didn't get it. I thought he was concerned about bad publicity.'

'What changed your mind?'

'After Steinberg's death I was interrogated again. Maddox accused me of "associating" with Steinberg. Even if I did, I couldn't see how that was a security breach. All I did was chat with him in the smoking room. I hardly knew him. He worked up on level four in electromagnetics.'

'Steinberg didn't mention a report he was compiling?'

'No. But I guessed there was more to his death than a simple accident. That's when I retrieved the footage I've shown you. It's also when I realised they've got me in their crosshairs. Then I just got pissed off.' Paul gave her a sheepish look. 'When I found out you were in the building, it was a godsend.'

'What do you expect me to do?'

'Just your job,' he replied crisply. 'Expose the real killers.'

Rita was beginning to wonder about her next move when a woman's voice interrupted her.

'Taking time out, Paul?'

The question jerked him forward and he quickly blanked the frozen image of Rachel's body. He swivelled around to a bank of monitors where a woman's face had appeared on a two-way link. She was gazing at him steadily. Rita recognised her immediately. It was the face of Audrey Zillman.

'I got a bit distracted,' Paul said quickly. 'What do you want, Audrey?'

'You need to run a check on the signal-processing software.'

'I thought we had that sorted.'

'Not yet.'

Paul pursed his lips. 'Sometimes I feel like a glorified mechanic.'

'Well there's no need to pout,' she retorted.

Rita shifted in her chair and the movement caught Audrey's eye.

'And who's the assistant mechanic?' asked Audrey. 'Not someone on staff.'

'Shit,' said Paul under his breath.

Although Rita was on edge she was also intrigued by the chance encounter. 'I'm Detective Sergeant Marita Van Hassel. I'm a delegate at the security review.'

'Of course you are,' said Audrey. 'You seem to have lost your way.'

'She has level-five clearance and is here as my guest,' put in Paul quickly. 'A bit of familiarisation, that sort of thing.'

'Being familiar has got you in trouble before.'

Audrey sat back and folded her arms. Her face, in sharp focus on the high-resolution screen, radiated annoyance. Rita guessed that, like many males before him, Paul felt intimidated. Even across an electronic link Audrey had a formidable presence. Her cool grey eyes were full of confidence and irony, her broad forehead untroubled by doubt, and her lips were drawn together in a hard analytical line. Rita could see why Byron had fallen under her spell. Audrey had a magnetic quality about her.

'You need to resume your work,' she told Paul. 'And my advice to you, Marita Van Hassel, is to get back to level one. Your session is about to resume.'

With that parting shot, Audrey's face vanished from the screen.

'She's got a point,' agreed Rita. 'I mustn't be late for class. I've had detention here before and it's not something I want to repeat. Maddox already sees me as a troublemaker.'

'But it's Maddox and his henchmen I need to talk to you about. You haven't got the full story.'

'I've got to go. What about this evening?'

'Okay, my place,' said Paul, writing on a business card. 'Any time you can make it. I'll expect you.'

Rita glanced at the address on the card before pocketing it: 17 The Ridgeway. 'This address isn't in Leith Ferry is it?'

'God, no. It's a villa up in the rainforest. Leith Ferry is nothing but a barracks. I wouldn't be seen dead there.'

Rita saw the unfortunate connotation of his words before Paul did.

'Unlike Dr Steinberg,' she said.

•

Rita felt on edge as she rode the elevator back up to level one. When the doors opened she glanced around quickly, half expecting to find security guards closing in on her. But there were none on the prowl. Walking briskly along the corridor, she caught up with the last of the stragglers returning to the Situation Room. Once inside, the doors were sealed and she returned to her seat next to Bryce and Jarrett.

As the chatter around the table subsided, Jarrett nudged her. 'You okay?'

'Yeah, fine,' she said, forcing a smile.

The meeting resumed with another preamble from Willis Baxter before delegates began talking logistics, backup and response times. There were a lot of details to trawl through. With time dragging on, Rita's frayed nerves became calmer but she now had a headache. Nothing being discussed had any relevance to her role in Whitley. It was equally apparent that another reason for locking her into the review was to sidetrack her investigation.

Occasionally she looked at Luker but he seemed to be studiously ignoring her. Of all those on the base perhaps he was the one she should trust the least. She had no way of judging. In a looking-glass world you had to assume that no one was who or what he seemed. That went for Paul Giles as well. For all Rita knew, he was peddling a particular version of events and corrupting the data to suit his own ends. Or, worse, he could be laying a trap in league with Maddox. This, though, seemed unlikely. She was convinced Paul's state of mind was genuine. Perhaps she'd learn more when she paid him a visit tonight. But that prospect also had its risks.

At least she hadn't been arrested. Apart from the encounter with Audrey, her security breach appeared to have gone undetected. On the other hand this could be a false positive. Audrey herself could be instrumental in all that was happening, her confrontation with Freddy pointing to a proactive role in striking at troublemakers outside the base. Each possibility upped the odds stacked against Rita, fuelling the tension headache tightening behind her temples. If nothing else, she was determined to skip tomorrow's session of the review, even if she had to chuck a sickie. There was too much she had to get to grips with.

High on the list was Audrey's involvement. Rita needed to find out more. Her last exchange with Paul before she'd left his control room rang again in her ears. She'd asked him about the woman and the importance of her role in the Panopticon Project.

'As system controller she's pivotal,' he'd answered. 'That's why they refer to the Zillman Hub. The technology's her brainchild.'

Rita then asked, 'Where does she work?'

Paul had replied, 'Audrey virtually lives on level seven.'

30

The sun was dipping towards the horizon by the time the delegates finally surfaced from the bowels of the building and trudged towards their vehicles in the car park.

'It's worse than I thought,' muttered Bryce as they got back into the police car.

'Yeah,' agreed Jarrett, settling behind the wheel. 'I need some beers after that.'

'From now on,' said Bryce, 'we'll be policing in the middle of a pitched battle.'

'A battle between invisible forces,' added Rita, 'until we see the blood in the gutter.'

Jarrett flicked the ignition. 'A minimum of six beers should do it.'

They drove through the checkpoint and out of the base.

'And another thing,' continued Bryce, 'we'll have to keep looking over our shoulders – both shoulders: one for terrorists, the other for federal backstabbers. This town is getting ugly.'

'I'm hitting the sailing club tonight,' was Jarrett's solution. 'Want to join me, Van Hassel?'

'Thanks but I've got a raging headache. All I'll be drinking is liquid Nurofen.'

'I'll bet you're wishing you stayed put in Melbourne,' suggested Bryce.

'And miss your tourist delights?'

'A tour of a dungeon in Whitley Sands is about as delightful as being buried alive,' he retorted. 'The same fate has just been handed to your profiling role, if you hadn't noticed.'

'I had,' said Rita. 'Maddox made it perfectly clear what he expects now that I'm *in his loop.*'

'And it's worth remembering a loop can be a noose.'

Jarrett parked at the police station.

Rita got out, went to her car and drove to the Whitsunday Hotel.

Once she was in her room, she kicked off her shoes, stripped and stood under the shower for a long time, just letting the water surge over her face and body, trying to decompress. It helped a bit. After towelling herself dry, she pulled on a T-shirt and shorts, threw the balcony doors open and swallowed some painkillers. Then she flopped on the bed.

The solitude was some relief but not enough after what felt like a long day of brain-bashing. It reminded her she was effectively on her own, with no one at hand to rely on. After ordering a light meal from room service, she picked up her mobile, deciding she needed to hear a reassuring voice. Not Byron – he would only get worried and she'd end up reassuring *him.* Not Erin, either – she'd quiz her about the case. Instead she phoned her best friend and weekday flatmate, Lola Iglesias. Lola, with her Latin American flamboyance, would cheer her up.

'Rita!' her friend answered with a shriek. 'Your timing's unbelievable! Escaping to the tropics when it's sub-zero down here. Minus fucking one!'

Rita was already smiling. 'There's cold weather up here too.'

'It's got to be warmer than Melbourne. We've got snow in the suburbs! I'm freezing my tits off!'

'Then you'd better warn shipping,' laughed Rita. '*Icebergs from South America.*'

'Ha! *Sailors beware!* Just as well I'm heading north like you.'

'What do you mean?'

'I've got an assignment in the Whitsundays. Celebrity wedding on Hamilton Island. The magazine's bought the exclusive rights. I'll be there on Saturday. And guess what? My admirer's doing the official shoot.'

'So who's getting hitched?'

'Cara Grayle, the model. She's marrying Vic Barrano, the nightclub millionaire.'

'Don't you mean gangster?'

'Yes, well, the magazine's not going to mention that. It's part of the deal. A glossy photo spread with no hint of anything unsavoury. Half the guests will be fashionistas and glitterati – reputations to protect. The other half will be mobsters and their molls, but who cares? All I have to do is write the captions without engaging my brain, which means I can get drunk on bubbly. French. Loads of it. Enough to swim in. More to the point, I'll be in Queensland, so you can fly over and join me.'

'Thanks, Lola. But somehow I doubt it.'

'Oh, Rita! Don't be a party pooper! It's one of the hot events of the year and no one gets in without a pass and I've got spares. It'll be a hell of a night. Barrano's spent a fortune on it.'

'He's still a hood.'

'Yes, but you'll be off-duty. Think about it when the weekend rolls round. You can do that, at least.'

'Okay, but no promises. Now, tell me your other news.'

Most of Lola's news centred on shopping, gossip and sex, and by the time they'd finished chatting, Rita's spirits had brightened. Lola's voice, and the painkillers kicking in, had eased her headache. She dragged over the road atlas and looked up the street where Paul Giles lived. Then she pulled a jacket over her T-shirt, put on her sneakers and headed back to her car. She wasn't in the mood for another encounter with Paul but he had more to tell her and, whatever it was, she had to hear it.

31

Luker sat and listened, eyes attentive, hands folded in his lap, pretending to be sympathetic.

Rhett Molloy was explaining how he felt a heavy burden of responsibility, representing the United States in his capacity as the international director of the Whitley Sands Defence Establishment. He'd been assigned a primary role, he emphasised, to observe, assess and facilitate developments in the system being built with Australian research technology, American finance and engineering, and the best scientists recruited from the global alliance. If the Panopticon Project was successful it would provide a radical new device to be deployed in the hunt against terrorists. Because it promised so much, and its security was paramount, Molloy had a secondary role: to protect the project against any threat. He was making it clear to Luker that it was this duty that weighed so heavily on him.

Along with Molloy's posting came a third-floor office at the base. It was housed in the administrative block constructed on top of the vast concrete chambers which honeycombed through seven underground levels. Molloy's office had a smoked-glass bullet-proof window with a view across a belt of palms and gum trees to sand dunes along the perimeter fence and the blue of the Coral Sea beyond. It was a pleasant aspect, and one he appeared to contemplate as he shared some insights with Luker and the other man who sat across the desk from him, Molloy's deputy, Kurt Demchak.

'Though an onerous duty's been placed on our shoulders,' said Molloy, 'and we can't hesitate over what has to be done, we need to tread carefully. There are local imperatives to take into account to avoid repercussions. And I say this to you, Kurt, as a point of etiquette. You and I are a long way from US jurisdiction.'

'You coulda fooled me,' said Demchak.

Molloy switched his gaze from the window. 'Meaning?'

'Check it out. We're in a building staffed with American engineers, on a military reserve where twelve thousand GIs are deployed. And all this next to a town full of English-speaking white folk with the US Navy in port.'

'Most of the GIs will be gone soon. The joint exercise is drawing to a close.'

'Whatever. It feels less foreign than southern California.'

Luker gave a grunt of amusement.

'Nevertheless,' Molloy continued, 'we're guests of a foreign government. It's an important factor. A certain sensitivity is called for.'

'If the job requires it, I can be as sensitive as a fucking nun.'

Molloy gave him a look of disapproval, with a quick glance at Luker. 'Well, I just want it on the record, so to speak. And that's why Mr Luker's here. We have no hesitation in sharing intelligence with our Australian allies.'

'And it's much appreciated,' put in Luker.

'Now we're all buddies, can we get on with the briefing?' asked Demchak.

'I don't like your tone,' Molloy told him.

The man shrugged. 'You don't have to.' His face was expressionless, his eyes unblinking. 'Let's get something straight. And you might as well hear this too, Luker. I take orders and I act on them. No sweat. No comebacks. No sleepless nights over consequences. Here's something else for the record though. I've got more than one boss and answer to more than one department. But I always hunt alone.'

There followed a brief, diplomatic silence during which Luker automatically fingered the cigarette pack in his jacket pocket.

The friction between Molloy and his deputy was illuminating. It confirmed Luker's suspicion that the pair were operating under joint but distinct directives. This was nothing new in the Byzantine politics of intelligence agencies. It came with the web of duplicity they were all busy weaving. One of the reasons Luker had risen so high in the trade was that his political antennae were attuned to the nuances of double standards, oily deceit and bare-faced lies. Luker was, after all, a graduate of that ultimate school of mendacity: the media.

Whenever he attended a briefing such as this, he was reminded of an observation made by the late Malcolm Muggeridge, whose career, like his own, spanned both espionage and journalism. According to Muggeridge, while journalists were compulsive liars, spies were even worse – they were habitual fantasists.

Molloy stuck his chin out defensively. 'We'll take what you say on board,' he said to Demchak. 'I have to concur there's little room to finesse our methods when the survival of western values is at stake.'

Luker felt an inward shudder at the words, not because he agreed, but because he saw in Rhett Molloy – a high-ranking agent with a background in military intelligence – the sort of righteous delusion that had launched a millennial crusade and propelled the alliance into Iraq. Equally worrying, his kind of thinking found itself at home in sections of the CIA and US Command. That made him one of a breed who professed to know where the course of history was going wrong and how to fix it. He had a certainty born of the religious right and a cowboy mentality towards international politics.

Demchak was a different beast. Luker saw him as a disciplined psychopath, whose skills had been honed and utilised in the field of black ops. The little that Luker knew about his background had come in a whispered aside from Molloy. He'd described Demchak as a product of domestic violence and Detroit slums, now bulldozed. Luker knew that he'd carried out missions in the Gulf, the Middle East and the Hindu Kush badlands straddling the Afghan–Pakistan border.

'Right,' declared Molloy. 'Checklist.'

'The list is growing,' said Luker.

'Bullet points, then.' Molloy let his impatience show. 'Hostiles.'

'Gone to ground. No further sightings of our four terror suspects.'

'And there won't be,' Demchak commented. 'Until they bomb us. They know we're watching.'

Luker nodded. 'Which implies they're well informed.'

'Yes,' Molloy agreed. 'We have to assume they're being primed for an attack. Which brings us to the Fixer. He may or may not be in our neighbourhood. No new intel.' He drummed his fingers on the desk. 'Other external threats. The *Rheingold* disk.'

'Still no sign of it,' Luker responded.

'Goddamn it,' muttered Molloy. 'We've got to contain this thing. I'll talk to Maddox again.' He shook his head irritably. 'Stonefish?'

'No progress,' said Luker. 'We still don't know where he is, or exactly who he is. ID checks have drawn a blank.'

'Same here,' drawled Demchak. 'I put the squeeze on Edge Freddy till his pips popped. He doesn't know where his pal's hiding.'

'Hmm.' Molloy's frown deepened. 'Protesters?'

'Nothing imminent,' said Luker. 'They're still reorganising. Rachel Macarthur's death was a setback.'

'Good. Surveillance upgrade. I can report Panopticon is up and running on a regular basis. I've been driving it myself. It's the sort of reinforcement we need right now.' Molloy seemed satisfied. 'Internal threats?'

'Maddox has his eye on Paul Giles, the project coordinator.' Luker stroked his chin. 'No specific activity. But he's disgruntled at the way he's been treated since being detained in the nightclub.'

'He's a limey scumbag,' put in Demchak.

'You know him?' asked Luker.

'Yeah, from the bar in the Diamond. Can't hold his liquor. Consorts with hookers. Told me America's the new Roman Empire.'

'Well, he's threatening to lodge a grievance.'

'Like I said: scumbag.'

'It goes without saying any new internal risk must be nipped in the bud,' said Molloy. 'What about the woman profiler?'

'I've spoken to Van Hassel,' said Luker. 'I'm confident the tactic we've adopted has neutralised any potential risk.'

'She's no loose cannon, then?'

'No.' Luker couldn't help smiling. 'Just highly charged.'

Molloy gave a peremptory nod. 'All right then. I think that brings us up to speed. Just one last thing. We mustn't forget we're all in this together. We face a common enemy in a war against a new form of evil. And I don't use that word lightly.' He was leaning forward on his elbows, hands clasped, an anxious smile on his suntanned face. 'That's why I'd like the two of you now, if you'd do me the honour, to pray with me for the guidance we need at a time when our beliefs and our resolve are being tested.'

Luker felt embarrassed. Of all the things Molloy had come up with, this was the most awkward.

'I'm sorry, Rhett,' he said, getting slowly to his feet. 'And I mean no disrespect. But you see, I can't. I don't.'

'Why not?'

'Well, actually, I'm a humanist.'

Molloy looked at him with something like pity, before turning to Demchak.

'Kurt? I don't see you as a humanist.'

'And you'd be damn right.'

'So will you pray with me?'

'You're outta luck, Molloy.' Demchak pushed back his chair and stood up, loosening his shoulders. 'I don't do that sort of praying.'

32

Billy Bowers looked wind-blown and irritable as he hunched behind his desk, paying scant attention to Freddy's complaint about the American brute who'd crushed his balls.

'His fist was like a fucking vice!' Freddy winced at the memory. 'And he's big and ugly, with a Neanderthal skull.'

'For fuck's sake, tell me something I can make sense of!' snapped Billy.

Freddy looked at him resentfully and realised yet again how much he disliked the man. 'Called himself Kurt,' he added.

'Ah, now I know who you're talking about.' Billy stretched out his limbs and slumped back in his chair. 'He drinks in the bar downstairs. So he's also after Stonefish, huh?'

'What about my balls? He's threatening to tear them off!'

'Don't be an idiot,' said Billy. 'Your balls are safe while you know nothing about the whereabouts of that bastard Stonefish. When you *do* find out, you tell me straightaway, and I'll protect you and your balls. Got it?'

'Yeah, thanks.'

'No problem. Part of our business arrangement.' Billy dumped his feet on the desk and glanced around casually at the boxing exhibits decorating his office. 'We had a shit day out on the reef. Weather was lousy and not one pissing marlin in sight. I won't see that movie producer again.'

'You after some Hollywood action?' asked Freddy.

'Don't waste your brain cells trying to keep up,' growled Billy. 'Stick to what you're good at. Hacking and jacking around. Speaking of which, who's the foxy piece of tail you were chatting up today?'

'When?'

'In the club, arsehole. My staff aren't just loyal, they're observant. So who is she? Your new fuck-buddy?'

'No, Billy. She's a cop.'

'A cop! What sort of cop?'

'A profiler. Her name's Van Hassel.'

Suddenly Billy was sitting bolt upright. 'Van Hassel came calling on my club?'

'Yeah.'

'Why?'

'She's investigating Rachel's murder. The local cops drafted her in.'

'What did you tell her?'

'Nothing.' Freddy didn't hesitate, remembering his secret deal with Rita. 'I don't know anything, do I?'

'Well, make damn sure you keep it that way.' Billy ran a hand through his tousled hair. 'That bitch is trouble. I should've turned her into dog food years ago.'

'How do you know her?'

'She tried to ruin me once, put me inside. I had to use up a lot of points to make the problem go away.'

For once Billy looked worried, something that Freddy found to be a pleasant change. Rita was going up in his estimation.

'Well, she can't touch you now,' said Freddy.

'Don't you believe it. She's the persistent type. I can't risk her stirring anything up around here. I need to get rid of her, one way or another. Fuck it!'

Billy stalked over to his punching bag and started thumping it furiously. He was interrupted by his desk phone ringing. Still cursing, he leant over and hit the button.

'Yeah, it's Billy Bowers here.' He whacked the punching bag again. 'Who's that?'

'Nikki Dwyer,' a woman's voice came out of the speaker. 'Reporter on the *Whitley Times*. I wonder if I can ask you about a couple of things.'

Billy stopped punching abruptly and softened his tone. 'Of course, Nikki. Always happy to help the press.'

'I'm doing a feature on local celebrities,' she went on, 'and naturally you're prominent among them.'

'We all do what we can for the greater good,' said Billy. 'Promote the town, boost its image.'

'It's your image in particular I'm concerned with,' said the reporter.

'What do you mean?'

'I've been given some disturbing information.'

'Who by?'

'An anonymous source.'

'Then you should treat it with the contempt it deserves.' Billy's voice was getting less friendly by the second. 'I've got no time for gutter journalism.'

'The thing is,' said Nikki, 'I've already followed it up and the information checks out. Are you prepared to deny it without hearing what it is?'

Billy tensed, his body arched over the desk, fists clenched, realising he'd been ambushed.

'What have you been told?' he demanded.

'First, that you threatened environmental campaigner Rachel Macarthur.'

'Rubbish!'

'She was organising a protest against your rainforest development,' Nikki went on. 'And she confronted you at your club. A witness has contacted me.'

'What witness?'

'One of your associates, actually. I won't reveal the name but I can assure you his account is reliable.'

'Whatever you've been told, I was trying to talk sense into her. Get her to drop her opposition to what's going to be a five-star resort complex. Something that will put Whitley well and truly on the international tourist map.'

'You said you'd kill her.'

'Bullshit!'

'Your exact quote was: "I'll rip your head off." Do you deny it?'

Freddy sat forward, his pulse quickening.

'I didn't mean it literally,' said Billy, with a swift glance at Freddy. 'It's just a figure of speech!'

'But that's what literally happened to her. Were you being prophetic?'

'Don't be a smart-arse!' Billy shouted at the phone. 'And don't try to publish any of this.'

'Would you like to comment on the other bit of background I've looked into – your arrest in Melbourne for sexual violence? And the real meaning of your nickname, "The Beast"?'

'That's enough!' snarled Billy. 'Now listen carefully, I'll only say this once, and you can read into it any damn thing you like: back off, or you'll regret it!'

He didn't bother to hang up the receiver. Instead, he wrenched the phone from its mounting and hurled it against the wall.

Freddy said nothing as the phone scattered in pieces and Billy's face flushed red with rage. He just watched him with a mixture of suspicion and hate.

33

The Falcon's headlights cut through the semi-darkness as the pale glow of a half-moon settled on the coastal ranges. Rita turned off the Bruce Highway onto Mountview Road and climbed past rocky outcrops towards a plateau bearing the US satellite tracking station. As she drove alongside the perimeter fence, the giant white spheres gleamed in the moonlight. They sat on the landscape like unnatural visitants.

Beyond the US post the road across the upland wound towards mountain peaks shrouded in low cloud. Rita followed its course carefully across the dark spread of the land, rough and inhospitable. Uneven ridges were lined with brushwood thickets and the humps of boulders. She'd psyched herself up for the encounter with Paul, but the remoteness was beginning to worry her.

As the scrubland fell behind, the car climbed a slope through an increasing density of gum trees. The steeper the incline, the damper the air became and the thicker the foliage. Rita got the wipers going. Soon the road was twisting around massive eucalyptus trunks and under the fronds of tree ferns, streams spilling through gullies along the verge, their banks a tangle of tropical vegetation. She was now driving through the ancient rainforest and, despite the signs for campsites and picnic grounds, it had a feeling of untamed nature.

She found the T-junction that led to Paul's house, and swung off to the right. The Ridgeway turned out to be a side road that followed the rim of the forest, with spectacular views over the ocean. The air was clear here. She switched off the wipers and took in the vista. Far below, the lights of the town and port clustered along the shoreline. Further out to sea the dark humps of the Whitsunday Islands were outlined in the moonlight.

Rita drove past a scenic lookout point with its eco-friendly cafe and, a kilometre down the road, a building site covering several hectares, ringed with a chain-link fence. A swathe of apartment blocks and landscaped swimming pools were under construction amid a muddy scar in the side of the mountain where bulldozers stood in silence, waiting to resume their excavations. She slowed down as she passed the padlocked gate. A hoarding advertised the future five-star resort – the Whitley Ridgeway – proprietor: William Bowers. This wasn't just a holiday spot: it was a battlefield. The most dangerous threat to the ecosystem of the rainforest was tourism, and the damage from this development was already plain to see. No wonder Rachel Macarthur had launched a campaign against Billy, thought Rita as she accelerated away. And to protect such an investment, he'd want to stop her dead.

There were a few other human incursions along the road, signs pointing to hiking trails, cabins partly hidden among the trees, but mostly The Ridgeway was fringed by the overhanging canopy of the forest, with its mass of vines and ferns. At last she reached a house set back in a clearing, number seventeen, and she pulled up at Paul's front gate. The setting was isolated but compelling, with the primeval wilderness looming behind it and a panorama of coastal valleys stretching below. Beyond that the dark expanse of ocean swept to the horizon. While the location was enviable, the wrought-iron nameplate beside the gate struck her as a little obvious. The place was called Eden.

She got out of the car and shivered. It was cold up here.

The two-storey villa rose behind its high stone wall, secluded and imposing. Its Federation-style exterior was mostly intact – red brick walls, bay windows, heavy gables – though it had undergone renovations, both architectural and technological. The porch and balcony had been enclosed, with metal-framed portals, and a layer of solar panels adorned the terracotta roof tiles. Masts and dishes sprouted beside the chimney pots. Smoke was rising from one of the chimneys and the smell of burning eucalyptus wood hung in the air.

The path lamps were lit, awaiting Rita's arrival, but the array of security devices was uninviting. She glanced up at the armoured camera casings and sprigs of razor wire as she pressed the buzzer beside the tubular steel gate. A moment later, it glided open. She walked through with senses alert. The gate closed automatically, sealing her in.

Something intuitive, a vague awareness of malevolent intent, warned her to tread carefully. Adrenalin pumping, she walked up the garden path. Either side of her, the flower beds were untended – rhododendrons gone wild in a tangle of lantana, lopsided hibiscus bushes in need of pruning. A jacaranda tree had collapsed under its own weight and bindweed smothered a birdbath. She took it as a further sign that something was wrong. A once-attractive garden was withering from neglect.

The porch door opened as she approached. Paul stood in the doorway, looking even more pallid and youthful than he had at the base, dressed now in jeans and a Cambridge T-shirt.

'Thanks for coming,' he said.

Rita paused, trying to read the uneasiness in his face. 'It was hardly an invitation I could ignore.'

'Well, now you're here, come inside.'

She walked up the steps, through the double security doors of the porch and into the hall, without turning her back on him, an instinctive reflex.

He was clearly nervous. 'Would you like a drink?'

'That's not what I'm here for,' she replied.

'Break the ice?'

She nodded, 'Okay,' and followed him down the hallway. It led to a central living space where the middle of the house had been gutted and remodelled in a style that was part up-market, part cyberpunk.

'Radical conversion,' observed Rita. The decor was hi-tech and heavy metal, with walls of polished brass. Their metallic shimmer reflected the furnishings – sofa, chairs, table – all in matching chrome. 'Must have cost a bit.'

'Part of the package,' explained Paul. 'The transfer from NATO.'

The electronics included a games computer, a music deck with recessed quadraphonic speakers and a brow-level television on an articulated metal arm. It was tuned to MTV. Industrial glass shelving was lined with DVDs. A metal-grid stairway led up to a balcony and glass alcoves beyond.

'The Pentagon footed the bill for all this,' added Paul.

Strangely, the overall effect was somehow chic – and not masculine. The curtains and upholstery were a soft mauve, with cream rugs on the floor. The lighting was dimmed to highlight the glow of a wood fire, the flames flickering in what must have been an original fitting, a white marble hearth. And one wall was dominated by the shifting colours of a holographic projection – a scene depicting a woman among spring flowers.

'Scotch?' asked Paul.

'With ice,' she told him, and watched him pour their drinks from the same bottle, before turning to admire the 3-D image.

He came over with the glasses.

'It's the most expensive thing in the house,' he said, 'after the research computer.'

'What is it?'

'A laser version of a Pre-Raphaelite painting – *Persephone's Return from the Underworld*.'

'Well, you've certainly got a unique place here,' Rita commented. 'I don't know what's more impressive, the makeover or the location.'

'The house has an interesting history,' said Paul. 'It was built a century ago by a German botanist who spent years documenting the species of flora he discovered.'

'Did he name the place Eden?'

'Yes. It's how he saw the biodiversity of the rainforest – all that primeval creation, parts over a hundred million years old. Mind you, it acquired a certain irony when he died from snakebite. When we found the villa, it was unoccupied and dilapidated.'

'Does your partner work at Whitley Sands?'

'That's right. Everything here, including the interior design, is down to her.'

Rita missed the significance until he gestured to a framed photo on the mantelpiece. It showed Paul with an older woman. She had her arm around him. There were willow trees and a college archway in the background. Rita recognised the woman immediately.

'You live here with Audrey Zillman?'

'That's the general idea,' he answered.

'You were recruited together?'

'When she was headhunted, she insisted I was hired too. We were working together in Brussels.' Paul gave a sour smile. 'I was her postgrad toy boy at the time, you see.'

'I think I do,' said Rita. It seemed Audrey habitually indulged in affairs with her brightest students. 'And now?'

'She doesn't play anymore. Too busy being system controller. Too deeply embedded in Panopticon. I'm her latest reject.'

He didn't bother to hide his rancour. The words also cast a new light on the simmering tension in his manner and explained the friction Rita had witnessed during her visit to Paul's control room earlier in the day. His bitterness could easily be the result of an unhealthy dependence, an Oedipal relationship that had hit the rocks. If so, it meant Paul's world was unravelling in more ways than one. It also meant he was psychologically unstable.

'Talking of Panopticon,' said Rita, changing the subject, 'you got me up here to discuss Maddox and his henchmen, as you put it.'

'That's right.' He motioned towards an armchair. 'I want you to hear my version of events in case they hang me out to dry.'

Rita sat down, crossed her legs and sipped the Scotch. It was very expensive double malt.

'Your *version* isn't good enough,' she said. 'I want full disclosure on how you're involved.'

'Fine,' said Paul, dropping onto the sofa. 'It's in my own interest to be completely upfront with you.'

'Good. Then you can start by explaining what you were doing at the Diamond on the night of Rachel Macarthur's murder.'

'Okay.' He took a gulp of whisky and reached for his cigarettes. 'We might as well start with how things got bollocksed up. Not that I feel guilty about it. What we do in private is nobody else's business. I was a victim of bad timing.'

It was the sort of self-justification Rita had heard before in her work with Sex Crimes. 'Go on.'

'The Diamond has a lively reputation. It attracts a certain type of clientele. When things with Audrey went cold I needed – how shall I put it? – distractions.'

'You were there for the prostitutes.'

Paul narrowed his eyes as he lit up. 'Just the one, actually.'

'But you're a regular customer?'

'Not anymore. Not after Maddox interrogated her. Now she won't have anything to do with me.'

'What's this girl's name?'

'Marilyn.' He winced. 'Marilyn Eisler. One of those women who makes you addictive.'

Rita recognised the syndrome – obsession with a prostitute. 'Does she work for Billy Bowers?'

'The club boss, no. She's an internet hooker with her own website, organises her bookings online. Her professional name is Ice.'

'Was "being familiar" with Ice the trouble Audrey referred to earlier today?'

'Yes.'

'And what does she think about it?'

Paul gave a derisive grunt. 'Audrey is sublimely detached. Like she is about everything.'

'Unusual woman.' Rita raised her eyebrows. 'So: Maddox. Why is he on your case?'

'Because I more or less accused him of being involved in the killing of Rachel Macarthur. I told him her death proved he and his cronies were acting like an out-of-control Praetorian Guard.'

'What was his reaction?'

'That's just it – he wasn't fazed at all.' Paul dabbed at an ashtray. 'He didn't get angry, just spoke to me quietly, which was even more chilling.'

'What did he say?'

'That the jury was out on me. That I was being reassessed. That my days could be numbered. He made it sound like a death sentence was hanging over me, not only because going with a vice girl made me a security risk, but because I appeared to be unstable.' Paul puffed out some smoke. 'He also warned that my murder allegation could rebound on me and I could find myself a prime suspect. His parting threat was to say it was in his power to throw me to the wolves.'

'Threats come easily to him.'

'What if I'm right and the regime at the base is involved in murder? They could be setting me up as a fall guy. You've got to believe I'm an innocent bystander. That's what I needed to tell you.'

'Okay, but I'm constrained by national security issues. Do you have recourse to any channel within the defence department?'

'Not really. I'm thinking of lodging a formal grievance but I feel trapped. If I could pack up and go back to England tomorrow, I would.' He raised his glass in a mock toast. *'Exitus Australis.'*

Rita sat back, cradling her drink. 'Without revealing the internal details of the police investigation, I can assure you that you're not a suspect.'

'Thank God. I'm beginning to feel desperate.'

'What else can you tell me about the Diamond? Have you had any contact with Billy Bowers?'

'Not much. Marilyn introduced me to him once. He's the local hero. Seems to be on first-name terms with everyone around here, including Maddox.'

'You've seen them together?'

'Yes. I spotted Maddox coming down the stairs from Billy's office.'

'Before or after Rachel's murder?'

'About a week before. It didn't surprise me, though. I've bumped into other people from the base there.'

'Who?'

'That American gorilla, Kurt Demchak. I had a few drinks with him.' Paul couldn't help smirking.

'What's the joke?'

'I told him the US was a modern parallel of the Roman Empire and would suffer the same fate. Demchak wasn't amused.'

'I'm yet to meet him,' said Rita.

'He called me a *slimy limey* when I said Whitley was a frontier outpost of the American Empire, like the forts on Hadrian's Wall.'

'You seem fond of classical references.'

'That's my public school background showing. I had Latin drummed into me as a kid.'

Rita finished her drink.

'Another?' asked Paul.

'No thanks.' She put down the empty glass. 'Did you ever meet Rachel Macarthur?'

'No.'

'Have any sympathy for the greens?'

'Shouldn't we all? Something's got to be done to stop humans destroying the works of nature – the forest, the reef.'

'What about the campaign against Whitley Sands? Do you sympathise with that?'

'No. The protest against Panopticon is misguided and cretinous. It's an example of campaigners behaving like ignorant technophobes. And if I'd ever met Rachel Macarthur I would have told her to stick to blocking destruction of the rainforest, like that god-awful resort being built down the road.'

'You're in favour of total surveillance?'

'I'm blown away by the science. The application's another matter.'

'I see.' Rita stood up to leave, but she couldn't resist the temptation to ask one final question. 'By any chance, do you remember a fellow student from your time at Cambridge, an Australian called Byron Huxley?'

'Good grief, of course I do,' said Paul. 'Is he a friend of yours?'
'Yes.'

'Say hello to him for me. We studied together.'

Rita smiled and turned to go, thinking, That's not all you have in common.

34

'How's your Guinness?' asked Luker.

His drinking companion gave a sigh of resignation.

'Dark and bitter,' he answered. 'Much like the memories it triggers.'

Rex Horsley was the British representative on the International Risk Assessment Committee. Ostensibly a consular attaché, he was the Secret Intelligence Service agent who attended briefings at Whitley Sands.

'I hope there's a point to dragging me in here,' he added, glancing around the raucous interior of Rafferty's. 'This place makes me twitchy. Reminds me of the Bogside.'

Luker found the comment amusing, although he wasn't meant to. The surroundings were designed to be evocative – a counter draped in Irish tricolours, sawdust on the floorboards, wooden walls hung with Sinn Fein pennants and aquatints of the Easter Rising. But a country music band was belting out traditional bush ballads and the bar was full of loud young Australians oblivious to political subtlety. Horsley was alone in his sensitivity to Republican symbolism.

Perhaps it was understandable. He'd had his share of intelligence nightmares. Lean-faced and unsmiling, there was a permanent air of discontent about him. A product of Sandhurst and the Curzon Street era of MI6, he'd been dispatched to Northern Ireland during the troubles, and had emerged jaded and bound for desk work. He bore his fate with a blend of superiority and disenchantment. It was a posture, Luker noted, that tended to afflict members of the British officer class.

'It still bothers you?'

'Conditioned reflex,' answered Horsley. 'With any luck, Ulster can be consigned to history.'

'Talking of history,' Luker went on, 'do you think America's the new Roman Empire?'

'That, my dear chap, is a loaded question.'

'I only mention it because it's a view that came up at a briefing with Molloy.'

'Not from Molloy himself, I take it.'

'No.' Luker shook his head.

Horsley contemplated his Guinness before asking, 'So why exactly are we here?'

'Let's say it's to check out the scene of the cell's disappearance.'

'Now you're being disingenuous.'

'And to take advantage of the noise level.'

'Ah.' Horsley gave a grunt of acknowledgement. 'The old question: who spies on the spies? Now we have the answer: Panopticon.' He leant forward and dropped his voice. 'If I were you, I wouldn't rock the boat. It can only end one way.'

'How?'

'You'll be tossed overboard.'

They lapsed into silence while the band wound up a version of 'The Wild Colonial Boy'.

As the chorus ended, Horsley observed, 'I sometimes doubt this land ever embraced the notion of being British.'

'Why do you say that?'

'Well, Stone Age inhabitants aside, it was colonised by thieves, whores and Irish insurgents, all of them hostile to British authority. Then, once the gold rush kicked in, it became a telescoped extension of the wild west. Which is the prevailing mind-set driving all of us these days.' He drained his glass and placed it on the table between them before throwing Luker a cautionary look. 'A word of warning, old boy. Don't miss the point of your Roman analogy.'

'Which is?'

'All roads lead to Washington. Since 9/11 it's pursued a unilateral foreign policy worthy of Imperial Rome. And while there's a powerful lobby of neo-conservatives and evangelicals in place, you and I have to put up with self-righteous cowboys like Rhett Molloy.'

'No matter what the consequences?'

'Yes, including an unmitigated disaster in Iraq, and a war on terror that undermines the international legal system. Just because we're languishing on the tropical coast of Queensland doesn't mean we're not locked into it.'

'*E Pluribus Unum.*'

'Quite. Out of many, one – how America seals our fate.' Horsley raised his eyebrows. 'That means we don't have the luxury of choice. Pre-emptive action, as you and I both know, means a shoot-to-kill policy. When that applies, there's only one thing to do. Keep your head down.'

Luker watched the waiter gliding among the rubber plants and potted yuccas of the piano bar at the Whitsunday Hotel. The scene was hushed. The brass table lamps had been dimmed. The last of the night owls sat drinking and smoking and contemplating the perplexities of life.

Luker's conversation with Rita earlier in the day had left him reminiscing about his journalistic past. His life had been loosely structured then, more spontaneous. Now every professional step came with a pitfall, every day was a process of calculation and every meeting reinforced the same lifeless agenda. He felt himself drowning in bureaucracy. Death by a thousand committees.

The briefing with Rhett Molloy had been more of the same, only more depressing. The sharing of intelligence with Molloy – an oxymoron if ever there was one – was as substantial as a mirage. It produced a displaced reflection of the truth, shimmering in a false context. Luker had to pick out the bits that were useful and ignore the fanciful projections of Molloy's dream-world, while revealing only what he wanted Molloy to hear. Then he had to act as a conduit to his masters. The procedure was as tedious as it was serious.

Too often he sought an escape in late-night drinking. He'd half hoped, on this particular night, that Rita would join him. She wasn't just a security risk, she was an attractive and interesting woman. He'd called her mobile but got only her voicemail, and when he'd sought out her room he found a *Do Not Disturb* sign on the door.

The waiter homed in on him across the expanse of bamboo matting, and Luker ordered another two drinks. One more Scotch for himself, a gin and tonic for the woman who was powdering her nose. He'd met her for the first time a couple of hours ago. They'd got chatting about product research and market strategy. She was an executive saleswoman for a lingerie firm based in Adelaide, or so she said. Staying at the hotel for one night only. She was divorced, talkative, late thirties, fending off the approach of middle age with strategic cosmetics and tasteful clothes. She was also lonely. Like him. They were both fully occupied professionally, but less busy in their private lives. The sort of people who struck up conversations in late-night bars.

When she returned from the ladies room she sat down, looking neat and freshened, with an over-bright smile on her face. Luker smiled back. He'd played the scene often enough before. When they'd finished their drinks he suggested a coffee.

She said, 'Wouldn't you rather a nightcap in my room?'

He said, 'That would be delightful.'

The polite ritual ran true to course. She ushered him upstairs to her room, selected drinks from the mini-bar, slipped off her shoes and earrings and shook loose her hair. When he kissed her she switched off the light and took him to bed, where she was too strenuous and he was too casual. A mutual disappointment. She fell asleep, but he merely dozed and stirred himself an hour or so later. He slipped out of bed, got dressed, tiptoed from her room and closed the door quietly behind him. He wouldn't see her again.

35

Even though it was the middle of the night, reporter Nikki Dwyer was still busy at her computer terminal in an otherwise deserted newsroom. She had more than one scoop to work on and plenty of documentary evidence to sort through. Her confrontational phone calls had supplied additional angles and she wanted the proofs ready when the editor of the *Whitley Times* arrived at the office in the morning. She scrolled back through what she'd written, scanned it and stretched before bending over the keyboard to resume her labours. Only the angled light on Nikki's desk shone amid the gloom.

The newspaper office was on the edge of the industrial area, next to an abandoned glass factory, and the longer she worked the more the isolation was noticeable. Apart from a lone security guard at the front desk, Nikki was the only person in the building. At one stage she thought she heard movement somewhere in the shadows. She looked around and called out to see if the guard was doing his rounds. No one answered. She shivered a little, hit the save key and went on typing.

The next time she heard a movement it was close behind her. She was turning around when the nail gun was pressed into her hair and fired into the back of her head, the discharge propelling her flat onto the desk. She lay there, doubled up, no longer aware of anything, her blood spattering the computer screen and trickling over the keyboard, a nail lodged in her brain.

A hand shrouded in a surgical glove put down the nail gun and reached out, picking up Nikki's contacts book and pocketing it. Then, with some deft keystrokes, the stories she had been working on were deleted. Her notes, cuttings and document files were tidied into a zip bag. Then her killer took out a heavy duty meat cleaver, lined up Nikki's lifeless hands and chopped them off. These, too, went into the bag. Finally, he grasped the meat cleaver in both hands and held it aloft like an axe, then brought it down in a powerful blow that sliced cleanly through her neck, severing the head from the spine.

Once he'd put the cleaver back in the bag, he lifted the decapitated head by the hair, blood draining from the gaping wound as he dropped it into a litter bin. His job done, he collected the bag and nail gun and walked towards the back stairs, only to hear the footsteps of the security guard approaching.

The guard emerged from the stairwell and was starting to yawn as he entered the newsroom. He didn't see what was coming. His mouth was still wide open as the nail gun was fired between his eyes, smashing through his forehead and fastening the back of his skull to the door with a thud in a spray of blood and brain tissue.

The guard's body slumped there, still upright, pinned by the nail, eyes glassy. He was dead but he was still yawning.

36

Rita was reading the morning's edition of the *Courier-Mail* while eating her breakfast on the hotel terrace, but she stopped abruptly as an item on an inside page caught her eye. It was a brief report on Steinberg's death. A tragic accident, that was the line that had been fed to the press, and faulty wiring was to blame. The official cover-up was in place. At least the news had been released.

She pushed aside the newspaper, picked up her mobile and phoned Byron to tell him, but he already knew.

'I've just read about it,' he said. 'How bloody awful. Poor old Steinberg. He died all alone, according to the paper.'

'Yes, I've been checking the details,' Rita lied. 'I shouldn't have delayed calling on him.'

'What a nasty way to go – electrocution. My God.'

'It would have been quick. He wouldn't have suffered much.'

'There's that, I suppose. But what a horrible accident.' Byron paused. 'It *was* an accident, wasn't it?'

'Why do you ask?'

'Because of the things he mentioned – the atmosphere of confrontation, the thugs in uniform. Makes me wonder if he pissed them off enough to provoke them.'

'Don't go there,' she said. 'The facts are consistent with a freak accident. There's nothing to justify an investigation. So stop wondering. Mourn your friend, that's enough.'

'Okay.'

'Got to go,' she said. 'Someone else is trying to get through.'

The call was from Jarrett.

'What's up?' she asked.

'It's happened again, but worse.' His voice sounded strained. 'Two more bodies. Both killed with a nail gun. The *Whitley Times* building. You should get here now.'

She downed the rest of her coffee and drove straight to the crime scene. When she arrived in the taped-off newsroom the pathologist was already busy at work, along with detectives taking photos, dusting for prints and bagging items as evidence. Jarrett, notebook in hand, had just questioned the stunned editor of the *Whitley Times* when Rita walked over. The man looked drained and pale. He walked shakily from the newsroom to join the rest of his staff in a frightened huddle outside the building.

'Not the sort of news they're used to,' sighed Jarrett.

'When it's this close to home it's not news,' said Rita. 'It's real life and real death. Big difference.'

'The media will go ape-shit over this.'

Rita nodded. 'We'll have our work cut out keeping it in perspective.'

'At least we're excused from the research base today.'

'Thank God for that.'

'No, thank Bryce. He's going solo. He says a double murder takes precedence over a security review, and of course he's right.' Jarrett shoved his notebook into his pocket. 'Okay. Our nail-gunner's had a busy night. Take a look.'

Rita followed Jarrett inside the crime-scene tape to the decapitated body on the news desk. Next to it was a litter bin containing the severed head, the sightless eyes staring upwards.

'Reporter Nikki Dwyer,' he said. 'She must have been the intended victim of the attack.'

Rita bent over the body. The bloodied stumps of the woman's forearms were resting on the desk. In the bin, the point of the nail could be seen protruding from the front of her skull.

'Time of death, after midnight,' added Jarrett. 'Maybe around one a.m.'

'Working late,' said Rita.

'But the work's all gone. Articles deleted, notes and files stolen. Story killed, along with the reporter.'

'And the man on the door?'

They walked over to the stairwell entrance.

'Security guard,' answered Jarrett. 'Collateral damage. He must have wandered in at the wrong time. Nailed between the eyes.'

Rita nodded. 'Killed without compunction or hesitation. Like you'd swat a fly.'

'Yeah. Your idea about professional hits might not be far off the mark.' Jarrett drew her aside and lowered his voice. 'The editor's just told me what story the reporter was working on last night when she was murdered. She was writing an exposé of Billy Bowers. Somehow she'd got hold of that bestiality angle and had the balls to phone him up and put it to him. Bowers went ballistic.'

'Well, well. He may face justice at last.'

'That's not all – wait till you hear this: Nikki claimed a secret contact told her Bowers had threatened to kill Rachel Macarthur for launching the campaign against his resort development. We need to haul him in for a chat.'

Rita gripped Jarrett's arm. 'You realise what this means?'

'I'm not forgetting the beer mat in a dead man's boot,' said Jarrett. 'It means we can now link Billy to four murders.'

37

Billy Bowers walked through the front entrance of the police station flanked by his lawyers. He looked cool and assertive, every inch a former world champion in his designer sunglasses and neat safari suit. A gold pendant, in the shape of a pair of boxing gloves, hung on a heavy gold chain around his neck. One of his solicitors accompanied him as he was ushered from the reception area through an adjoining doorway to be questioned.

Billy's physical bulk, tall and broad-shouldered, dominated the confines of the interview room as he stretched out his hand to Jarrett.

'Hi, Steve.'

'G'day, Billy,' responded Jarrett. To Rita's disgust they shook hands.

Billy's expression soured as his eyes fell on Rita.

'It's been a few years, Van Hassel,' he said. 'I'd like to say it's a pleasure to see you again, but I can't. It isn't.'

'Why, Billy?' asked Rita calmly. 'Afraid your past will catch up with you?'

Billy grinned. 'Be careful of this woman, Steve. She's got fangs. Venomous as a tiger snake.'

'I'll keep that in mind,' said Jarrett, suppressing a smile. 'Take a seat, Billy.'

The ex-champion made himself comfortable across the table from Jarrett. The solicitor sat opposite Rita.

With the interview tape rolling, Jarrett began.

'We need to ask you questions in connection with some serious crimes, including this morning's double homicide at the *Whitley Times* building.'

'I'm advising my client not to answer . . .' the solicitor began before Billy cut him short, holding up a hand.

'I'm here to be frank and open with the police,' he said. 'I understand why you want to talk to me, Steve, and I've got nothing to hide. I'll answer all your questions. In fact, the only reason I've brought my lawyers is because I heard Van Hassel was working the case.'

'She's profiling the murders.'

'Whatever. I want to state clearly for the record that Detective Sergeant Van Hassel has harassed me before. There was no substance to her wild allegations and no charges were laid. I can only assume she embarked on a vendetta against me for personal reasons. It ended in complete failure, including, I understand, internal disciplinary action.'

'That's garbage and you know it,' said Rita.

Jarrett laid a hand on her arm. 'You've made your point, Billy.'

'Well, you can appreciate why having her in this room gets my hackles up. It makes me wonder if she's on a revenge mission.'

'I invited her,' said Jarrett. 'And I want to say, for the record, that her work is insightful and objective. But let's put profiling aside. Let's talk evidence. According to the editor of the *Whitley Times* you threatened his reporter, Nikki Dwyer, last night and within hours she was dead.'

'I advise you not to . . .'

Billy waved his solicitor into silence again.

'I reacted, maybe overreacted, to the way she spoke to me. But that's all.'

'She was writing an investigative piece on you. A report about other threats and criminal violence.'

'Lies!' Billy's fist thumped the table. 'Lies and defamation!'

'We see how angry you are,' observed Jarrett. 'Angry enough to kill her?'

'No!'

'And kill her story too – delete all trace of it?'

'Absolutely not! I didn't leave my club till after dawn and my staff will vouch for that. Go ask them.'

'We will.'

Billy gestured with open hands. 'For God's sake, Steve, I've got lawyers to stop the story – which, by the way, came from an anonymous source.' He turned to glare at Rita. 'And I've got a damn good idea who she is.'

Rita frowned. 'You think I'm the source?'

'Who else?'

'Interesting question,' she said. 'Do you plan to come after me next? Threaten to rip my head off the way you did Rachel Macarthur?'

'Like I told the reporter last night, it was just a figure of speech! For Christ's sake, use your loaf, Van Hassel. Even if you believe I'm capable of it, do you think I'd be stupid enough to snuff somebody on my own doorstep? Get real.'

'I don't for a moment think you're stupid,' she answered. 'Quite the opposite. You're a highly intelligent sociopath.'

'Huh, you sound less like a cop than a wannabe shrink.'

'You don't lack brains,' she persisted. 'You lack a conscience. And if you're asking me if you're capable of psychotic violence, I know you are. Especially against women.'

'My client doesn't have to listen to this abuse,' the lawyer interjected.

'That's okay,' sighed Billy. 'It proves she's got a hard-on for me.'

'I admit seeing you prosecuted for your crimes would be satisfying.'

'Well, keep your pants on, Van Hassel. It ain't going to happen.'

Jarrett almost seemed to be enjoying the confrontation, as if he was watching a bout between seasoned sparring partners, but so far Billy's defences were solid. It was time for a different approach.

'Rachel Macarthur could have cost you millions if she'd blocked the resort development,' Jarrett pointed out. 'That gives you a strong motive.'

'She wouldn't have succeeded,' Billy asserted.

'You mean she *didn't*. The legal challenge was in her name. That's fallen through now.'

'My lawyers had the court action beaten. Besides, I've got the council onside and the protesters would've been ignored. I just didn't need the headache.' Billy was sounding peeved. 'But let's get to the point. Apart from some heat-of-the-moment comments, which I admit were ill-advised though provoked, you've got nothing that has any bearing at all on either woman's death. That's why I'm here, Steve, why I came in of my own accord. I knew I'd have to clear the air because of a whispering campaign against me.'

Jarrett glanced at Rita. They both knew Billy was right, that the evidence was circumstantial at best. They also realised his performance in the interview room was impressive. Nothing had fazed him so far. He'd made all the right noises for a responsible citizen who was innocent but aggrieved.

'You gonna be available if we want to talk to you some more?' asked Jarrett.

'Of course.' Billy reached inside his jacket pocket and pulled out a business card. 'Here's my mobile number. Right now I'm on my way to the airport. Bucks night on Hamilton Island. I'm not going anywhere else.'

'Okay.'

'I know I'm seen as something of a volatile character,' Billy added. 'Name a boxing champ who isn't. But I can't be blamed for unfounded rumours and gossip that circulate. Every celebrity cops that. I may be colourful but I'm straight.'

Rita knew he was as straight as the flashy gold jewellery looped around his neck.

'Who's the man in the mud?' she asked aggressively.

Billy scowled at her. 'How the fuck should I know?'

'We've got evidence that links him to you.'

'What evidence?'

'It's confidential to the investigation.'

'More crap. You're full of it, Van Hassel.'

His reaction seemed genuine and so was his annoyance, but she had no intention of backing off.

'What's your connection with Whitley Sands?'

'The research base?' He seemed puzzled, though hesitant. 'My only connection is social. Civic receptions and the like. What the hell has that got to do with anything?'

Was there a hint of uncertainty in his response? Rita sensed something of the sort so she blurted out, 'What's your relationship with Captain Roy Maddox?'

It was a rash question but so was Billy's reaction. He just stared at her, as if he didn't know how to answer. For a moment he said nothing, apparently trying to second guess the basis of Rita's query and nervous about which way to commit himself.

'That's it!' insisted the solicitor, pushing back his chair and standing up. 'This is nothing but a fishing expedition. Billy, I'm instructing you to say nothing more. We're leaving immediately.'

This time Billy didn't argue with his lawyer. He complied instantly, rising to his feet, still looking unsure of himself. He left the room with nothing more than a farewell grunt to Jarrett, who looked at Rita, amazed.

'Bugger me,' he said. 'What the hell is going on between Bowers and Maddox? What's their common interest?'

'Something Billy can't risk talking about. One thing's for sure – it's not his boxing prowess.'

'And I thought he was handling himself well,' conceded Jarrett. 'I had him ahead on points till you landed that sucker punch. What made you ask the question?'

'Maddox was seen at the Diamond and it occurred to me Rachel's death was mutually convenient to both of them.'

'If they're acting in tandem, what does it mean?'

'Nothing good.' Rita frowned. 'Looks like the war on terror's produced an unholy alliance.'

Rita was thinking hard but no matter which way she looked at it she couldn't decipher the meaning of a relationship between Billy Bowers and Captain Roy Maddox. Nor did she know how to factor it into the series of murders, other than through an unlikely set of coincidences, something she quickly ruled out. Although Billy hadn't confirmed any dealings with the base security director, his stunned reaction was indicative of something he couldn't deny and his silence spoke of something he couldn't reveal.

After pasting the latest crime-scene photos to her whiteboard she paced up and down the exhibit room, going through a mental list of possibilities without gaining a glimmer of clarity. The decapitations appeared to be symbolic and the continued use of the nail gun remained a highly significant element, unless it was a deliberate misdirection. And the severed hands – what did the killer want with them? Were they trophies for a psychotic personality, or were they being souvenired for a practical purpose? If so, the reason escaped her. She stopped and stood, hands on hips, contemplating the nineteenth-century oil painting with the sinister history, *The Hunting Party*, and admitted to herself that she was baffled.

Her mobile rang. It was Jarrett.

'Thought I should warn you,' he said. 'Bryce has sent me to the airport to welcome back the Homicide Squad. This time they're coming mob-handed. They're setting up a taskforce.'

'Who's heading it?' Rita asked.

'Same guy who was up here before, Bob Sutcliffe. Detective senior sergeant.'

'What's he like?'

'Not as friendly as he looks. And he's got ambitions. I reckon he's got his eye on promotion by cracking this case.'

'You don't sound happy, Jarrett.'

'Bryce took a break from the review to haul me into his office for a lecture. That's after Sutcliffe phoned me from Brisbane. Gave my lughole a bashing.'

'Over what?'

'Billy Bowers: why isn't he under arrest? Why haven't I applied for search warrants? Why aren't we tearing apart his home and office? I'm being told I've fumbled the first decent lead in the investigation. What do you think?'

Rita wasn't sure what to say, though she'd thought herself that Jarrett had been a bit too cosy with Billy.

'No,' she answered at last. 'I don't think we miscalculated. Bowers is smart. He's also lawyered up and came in of his own accord. And he's right about what we've got on him. It's circumstantial at best. But if the squad detectives want to get tough with him that's fine by me.'

'Yeah. We can let them run with it. Looks like Billy's in for a real grilling when he gets back from the island.'

'I hope that's not misplaced sympathy.'

'Only for myself. I should've put more pressure on him. By the way, Sutcliffe wants to see a detailed profile from you when he arrives.'

'No problem. I'll update the one I've been working on. What's on your agenda?'

'Oh, that's easy,' grumbled Jarrett. 'I get to play shit-kicker to the boys from Brisbane.'

Rita busied herself for the next couple of hours in refining the profile. It pointed to a serial killer on a mission of vengeance; an intelligent, organised sociopath; a tall, powerfully built man trained in the use of violence; a self-appointed executioner targeting specific individuals perceived as a threat to his way of life.

When she printed it, the full outline covered two A4 pages. It was clear, well argued and consistent with four brutal murders while referring to the pertinent facts of the crimes. What it didn't refer to was the broader context, and it didn't need to. The job of a criminal profiler was to focus on the perpetrator and Rita had done just that. But she knew it wasn't the complete picture. That would have to include things she wasn't supposed to know. Things like a link to the research base and the role of national security. Things like the murder of Steinberg.

She was still puzzling over it all when a man pushed open the door and sauntered in, coffee cup in hand, his eyes casually scanning the room before looking steadily at Rita.

'So this is where they've got you holed up,' he said, a sly smile on his face.

Though she'd never encountered him before, she saw immediately that this man was relaxed and confident in his abilities. That was thanks in part to a mental toughness that showed in the line of his jaw and an unwavering gaze. Somewhere in his late thirties, he had a friendly face and a personable manner, along with a stocky build and ruffled sandy hair. He was wearing a short-sleeved shirt and chinos, and it was only his bearing that gave him away as a fellow police officer.

'Welcome to my lair,' said Rita, returning the smile as he pulled up a chair and sat across the desk from her. 'You're DSS Bob Sutcliffe, I take it.'

'Yep, that's me.' He reached over and shook her hand. 'Nice to meet you, Van Hassel. I'm looking forward to working with you.'

'Thank you, sir.'

'I've read your background and I'm impressed. I'm glad you're here.'

'Unlike some senior officers.'

'Forget the local wallopers. This is my case for the duration now, and we're gonna get on like a house on fire.'

'Steve Jarrett's done some good work,' she put in.

'Jarrett blew it,' said Sutcliffe. 'Instead of sweating a prime suspect, he got chummy and let him stroll off. I've just listened to the tape. I prefer your style – in the bastard's face.' He put down the cup and gestured at the printed sheets on her desk. 'If that's the profile, can I take a look?'

'Of course.'

She handed him the two pages and watched him read them, a frown of concentration on his face. When he'd finished he replaced them on the desk, picked up the cup and drank from it without looking at her, his mind digesting the implications of her findings.

'I didn't need convincing,' he said at last. 'But that profile fits Bowers to a tee.'

'It's not deliberate,' she said quickly. 'I'm not pointing the finger at him. I've gone out of my way to be objective in compiling that outline. And remember, it's just a *type* that's indicated, not a particular individual. A profile isn't evidence.'

'I'm aware of that. But it narrows the field and, right now, I'm looking at a field of one. My team will find the evidence.' He turned to her with a serious expression. 'You've got this history with Bowers. So, tell me, is he capable of killing?'

'No doubt at all,' she answered. 'And without compunction. At least one homicide in Melbourne was down to him, but I couldn't prove it. These murders, though, they're of a different scale and complexity. There are factors that elude me.'

'Ah.' He sighed. 'The bee in your bonnet about the research base. Bryce filled me in. And what's all this about trying to put Bowers and Captain Maddox together as buddies? Was the lawyer right? Were you just fishing?'

'Maybe. But I got a bite!'

'Well, it's one you're going to have to toss back.'

'So you've been told too,' suggested Rita. 'No muddying the water and so on.'

'That's the gist of it,' Sutcliffe admitted. 'Whitley Sands is off-limits to this case. And that comes from a much higher level than me. Anyway, I don't see that as a problem. In my opinion, Rachel's head being stuck on a pole facing the gates was a ploy to make us think someone inside the base was the killer. If you look at it that way, it's a deliberate distraction.'

'You're right, I suppose, from the point of view of the investigation,' agreed Rita. 'You've got an obvious candidate in your sights. Billy the Beast incarnate.'

'Yeah, and I don't want to screw up.' He nodded. 'You know, I was never a fan of his. Not even when he was basking in glory as a world champion. To me, there was something wrong about him. An arrogance. His celebrity status in Melbourne's gangland doesn't surprise me at all.' Sutcliffe gave a grunt of frustration. 'Talking of which, Jarrett's given him the all-clear to lord it among his underworld pals on Hamilton Island.'

'The wedding he's going to,' asked Rita, 'is it Vic Barrano's?'

'That's right. I'd haul Bowers' arse straight back for more questioning if I could, but I'd need another warrant just to get through the gate of Barrano's villa. And that ain't going to happen.'

'I don't know if it helps,' she said. 'But I can get through the gate.'

'How?'

'My best friend, Lola. She works for the magazine covering the wedding. Exclusive rights. She's offered me a pass.'

'Is that so?' Sutcliffe hunched forward in thought, idly tapping his knuckle against his lips. 'That's an opportunity we shouldn't waste.'

'What have you got in mind?'

'A pincer movement,' he answered. 'My boys are in the process of executing warrants on Billy's properties in Whitley. We'll turn over everything. But it'd be handy to keep tabs on him at the same time.'

'Are you saying you want me to go? Become a wedding crasher?'

'Why not?' He eased back in the chair, hands behind his head. 'But stay in the background as long as you can. Mingle – keep your ear to the ground. Billy and his chums will be in their comfort zone, getting drunk, shooting their mouths off. They could let something slip. If you can get anything on him – any line on where his funds come from, how he bankrolls his schemes – we can dig deeper. It'd also give me another pressure point when I drag him back in for a proper grilling.'

'And when he spots me there?' asked Rita. 'Should I rattle his cage?'

'Yeah, go for it,' nodded Sutcliffe. 'And let's face it – you're perfect for that job.'

38

The short flight on Saturday morning almost felt like an escape. As the twin-engine aircraft touched down on Hamilton Island a strange sense of detachment washed over Rita. It was as if she could set aside the claustrophobic intensity she'd been working under in Whitley and take something of a break in what was, after all, simply a holiday resort surrounded by the Coral Sea.

She'd forewarned Lola that her visit would include some work. *Clocking the crooks*, was how she'd described it.

'I don't give a flying fuck,' was Lola's response. 'As long as we do plenty of drinking.'

Rita collected the keys to her cabin, dumped her laptop and flight bags, and strolled under palm trees to the Beach House Restaurant, where Lola was waiting on the deck above the sand with chilled white wine and oysters. Shrieking with delight, Lola jumped up and hugged Rita before pushing her into a chair and pouring a glass of wine.

'I got an outside table so we can watch the tourists going arse over tit on their jet skis,' she explained, raising her glass. 'Cheers!'

'Cheers!' echoed Rita. 'I need to decompress.'

'Okay. Before anything else, get it off your chest,' insisted Lola. 'What's stressing you out?'

Rita thought before answering. 'Simulation.'

'Oh my God!' Lola groaned. 'I should never expect a simple answer from you!'

'Ever read *Through the Looking-Glass*?'

'The *Alice* story? I was brought up on it. My English nanny tormented me with the book when I was a kid in Ecuador. It gave me the creeps. Still does.'

'Why?'

'Nothing is what it seems. It's full of perverse logic. And every little fucker in it is some kind of freak or wacko. As a story to help kids make sense of the world, it sucks!'

'I seem to have touched a raw nerve,' observed Rita.

'Lewis Carroll must've been an uptight geek with a warped view of life.'

'He was a mathematician.'

'Huh! Speaks for itself.' Lola took a big gulp of wine. 'Anyway, what's your point?'

'I'm dealing with the same sort of distorted reality,' Rita replied. 'People determined to maintain a fake version of events.'

'Like the weirdos through the looking-glass. I get it!'

'Yes,' said Rita. 'There's another reason I'm reminded of Alice's adventures. Byron referred to them in a convention speech he made just over a week ago.'

'Plugging the virtual future again?'

'Variations on a theme, yes. He goes on about how simulation could make fantasies indistinguishable from reality. I seem to have hit the same problem in Whitley. Which is why it's so refreshing to be with you.'

''Cos I'm as straight and frigging open as the Pope!'

'But not quite as celibate,' laughed Rita. 'And talking about straight, am I going to meet your girlfriend at last?'

'Not till after she's shot the wedding,' said Lola. 'Right now Morgan's brainstorming on Hayman with some project managers.'

'So she's doing a double-header.'

'Yes, but watch your language. We're invited to join her on Whitehaven beach tomorrow after she's done a shoot with a new Italian car and a couple of models.'

'How does she get on with them?'

'The models? She doesn't lust after them, if that's what you're asking. They're anorexic airheads, not her type. She likes smart women with boobs, which is why I'm so popular.'

'Are you still having rows?'

'Of course – because I like men.'

'And she doesn't?'

'Uh-uh,' Lola said, wagging her finger. 'You're missing the finer points of dyke ideology. It's not hetero men, gay men or hetero women who piss her off – but bisexual women like me.'

'On both sides of the bed at once.' Rita nodded. 'Trust you to explore new frontiers of infidelity. I can see this is going to be a distracting weekend.'

'Good. Drink up. We've got lots to get through, including a wild wedding party.'

'While we're on the subject, what should I wear?' asked Rita. 'Would my red halter-neck be okay?'

'The one with the low back and high hemline?'

'Too revealing?'

'You've got to be kidding! The style for this evening will be full-blown, in-your-face sex. The clubland girls up from Melbourne don't need much excuse anyway. But this being the tropics, there'll be more bare flesh than fashion. Everything will be hanging out – tits, bums and tongues! So, yes – show off your legs and figure. I will be.'

It was still early afternoon and the wedding wasn't scheduled to start until five but Lola had drunk too much wine and needed a siesta. Rita hopped into the passenger seat and her friend drove one of the complimentary electric buggies carelessly along the narrow lanes of the resort. Rita got off outside her palm bungalow and watched Lola head off up the hill in the direction of the villa rented by her girlfriend.

The simplicity of the bungalow suited Rita. She kicked off her shoes, splashed her face with cold water and brewed some coffee to counter the effects of the lunch. Then she logged on to her laptop to send an email to Byron to find he was already online. After messaging him, she plugged in the webcam, opened the audio channel and watched his face appear on the screen, moving with the slightly jerky movements of the video link.

'What are you doing online at this time on a Saturday afternoon?' she asked. 'Don't tell me you're working.'

'Not work, no,' he answered, a partial grin on his face. 'I'm writing the campus footy report on this morning's match. We won, I kicked a goal, then drank approximately four beers in the pub.'

'Approximately?'

'Yes. Research needs to be done on the incompatibility of alcohol and mathematics. There's a point at which you lose the ability to count accurately.'

'I passed that point at lunch with Lola.'

'So how's Hamilton Island?'

'A welcome break from Whitley.'

'I still can't get over what happened to poor old Steinberg.' Byron frowned. 'It's like bad karma after I went on about my connections up there.'

'You have more connections than you realise,' she told him. 'I've met one of your fellow Cambridge students, Paul Giles.'

'Ah, so he's there too. The recruiters at Whitley Sands cast a wide net.'

'He asked me to pass on his greetings. What's your opinion of him?'

'A natural grasp of cybernetics. Very quick. Very full-on.'

'But?'

'Well, speaking candidly,' replied Byron, 'I didn't enjoy his company. He wasn't a friend of mine so much as a rival.'

'In more ways than one.'

Byron paused, throwing her a puzzled look, then caught on.

'He's there with Audrey,' he said. 'I'm surprised the relationship has survived.'

'Why?'

'Too one-sided. I heard they got together in Brussels and thought at the time it was a bad match.'

'Explain.'

'Audrey's too cold and aloof for Giles, and he's too intense for her – one of those people who burns over-bright then goes down in flames. He had some sort of nervous breakdown at Cambridge. That's when Audrey took him under her wing. After that he didn't look back, of course.'

'I've also had a fleeting encounter with your ex,' said Rita.

Byron grimaced. 'Not embarrassing, I hope.'

'I didn't mention I'm your current bonk, if that's what you're referring to.' She saw him blush. 'I see what you mean by cold and aloof. She's one of those women who're naturally intimidating.'

'Not the only one I know.'

'Is that so? Lucky I've got a sense of humour. Does Audrey have one?'

'Not that I noticed.'

Rita was distracted by an icon flashing in the toolbar display. It was telling her that Audrey Zillman was trying to contact her for a live conversation.

'Spooky timing,' she murmured, then told Byron, 'Got to go, mate. There's another caller online.'

'Okay. Don't let Lola get you plastered.'

'Are you worried I'll stray?'

'That's a trap question, so I'm not answering.'

'You're learning.'

'Yes, and I'm getting back to my footy report.'

As Byron signed off, Rita clicked the flashing icon. Audrey appeared on the screen, the stilted movements of the webcam image adding an unnatural menace to the austere expression on her face.

'Hello, Detective Sergeant Marita Van Hassel,' she said. 'I see from my online checks that you're spending the weekend on Hamilton Island. How very pleasant for you.'

'And I'm hoping to keep it that way. What's prompted your call, Audrey?'

'I've been accessing your files.'

'What files?'

'All of them,' Audrey replied. 'Everything relevant to your background. Under security guidelines you're subject to positive vetting.'

'I see.' Rita rubbed her forehead as the effects of the wine kicked in again. 'That's something I could do without.'

'Is there a problem?'

'You tell me.'

'There's nothing to worry about,' Audrey said evenly. 'You've passed all the criteria.'

'I have?' Rita had a flashback to when she was a teenager in the principal's office at grammar school. Audrey seemed to possess the daunting aura of a headmistress. 'Then what's this about?'

'There are two items I want to check: one official, one unofficial.'

'I can feel a headache coming on. Can we start with the official?'

'If you like,' said Audrey. 'As system controller, the human resources files fall within my responsibility and there's a discrepancy in your security rating.'

'Really?'

'You're registered as an associate officer of the Whitley Sands Security Force with an approved level-one clearance. You're also confirmed as a police delegate to the Whitley Sands Security Review, again with a level-one clearance.'

'So what's the problem?'

'You were present in a control room on level five.' Audrey gave her a probing look. 'In addition, the project coordinator told me you had a level-five clearance. I've examined the updated profiles and you have no such listing. I'd like an explanation.'

'Can I speak frankly?'

'Surely that's your only option.'

'Fine,' Rita replied. 'It's obvious, isn't it? Paul Giles lied to you. He all but hijacked me to level five because of his personal concerns. If rules were broken, I suggest you take it up with him.'

'Don't doubt that I will.'

'Have you told Maddox?'

'I'm conducting this check under the data integrity protocols. It doesn't require an alert to the security director.'

'So what's the point of this?'

'Because the information in the system is sensitive there are strict directives to maintain the integrity of the data.'

'And that's one of your chores?' asked Rita.

'It is.'

'So what's the unofficial item?'

'Professor Byron Huxley.'

'Byron?' Rita wasn't expecting this. 'What about him?'

'Do you have a relationship with him?'

'As a matter of fact I do,' she answered, taken aback by Audrey's directness. 'When you say this is unofficial, do you mean it's personal?'

'You could put it that way,' agreed Audrey. 'He and I share some personal history from our time together at Cambridge. He was an inspired student with a mind that moved beyond the usual parameters. I found him intellectually stimulating and genuinely affectionate.'

'Did you now? So what went wrong?'

'Unfortunately, we weren't emotionally compatible.'

'I can see that,' said Rita coolly. 'But why are we discussing him?'

'There's a question mark still outstanding over his rejection of an offer to do breakthrough research in his field at Whitley Sands for an extremely high salary,' Audrey explained. 'He turned down the offer and gave no reason. Perhaps you can enlighten me.'

Rita thought she detected a note of regret in the remark, even a touch of pathos. Maybe Audrey was human after all, with the true feelings of a woman carefully concealed behind a mask.

'It wasn't because of you,' Rita said, 'if that's what you're thinking. It was the oppressive regime that didn't appeal to him. If you understand Byron at all, you'll realise he needs his independence.'

Audrey paused, as if considering this, then said, 'That's true.'

'While we're on the subject of personal history,' Rita continued, 'what is your current relationship with Paul Giles?'

'Professional.'

'And that's all? What about the emotional side?'

'From my point of view,' answered Audrey, 'it's nonexistent.'

'That sounds harsh.'

'It's simply a fact.' Audrey's eyes seemed to be staring directly into Rita's as she went on. 'My focus is on the science of intelligence and pushing the boundaries of research. For the past year I've left all individual relationships behind.'

For some reason, the statement made Rita shiver. 'With all due respect, that seems inhuman, Audrey.'

'On the contrary, I have the entire spectrum of humanity within my reach. *Humani nihil a me alienum puto.*'

'Sorry, my Latin is basic.'

'Nothing human is alien to me.'

'Very objective,' said Rita. 'I take it that's because you have the Omniscient Tracker at your disposal.'

'The name's a nod to Jeremy Bentham.'

'With a wink to George Orwell. Playing God with technology leaves a bad taste.'

'Which do you find distasteful?' asked Audrey. 'The technology or God?'

'I have no doubts about the power of technology.'

'But you don't believe in God?'

'Whose version of God?'

'Everyone's,' Audrey answered. 'The force that holds the universe intact.'

'Omniscient or not,' Rita persisted, 'you must be lonely if you've cut out all relationships. How can you function without emotional support? Don't you feel the need of love in your life?'

'What is falling in love but brain chemistry – adrenalin and dopamine forming vivid snapshot memories that stick in the mind and won't go away. I'm not lonely in the way you think.' Audrey gave a cryptic smile. 'We must resume this debate when we next speak. Goodbye for now. I hope you enjoy your holiday.'

With that the face flickered and dissolved from the screen, leaving Rita with an odd sense of numbness, as though she'd been speaking to an emotional vacuum or been touched by almost sublime coldness. There was something frightening about the woman. Byron had had a lucky escape.

Rita freshened up with a shower, did her hair and applied her make-up, before wriggling into her slinky red halter-neck. A pair of high heels and she was ready for action. But first she needed to touch base with Sutcliffe. She picked up her mobile and punched in his number.

'I'm about to go to the wedding,' she said. 'Anything I need to know?'

'Yeah, Billy's mobile is switched off,' he told her. 'Not even his lawyers have been able to contact him.'

'Why would they need to?'

'They've got the jitters. The search warrants have given us free rein to go through his business accounts and they haven't been able to tell him. We're even putting his links with the council under the microscope. The mayor's well and truly pissed off.'

'What about evidence?'

'Not yet,' said Sutcliffe. 'We're still conducting formal interviews. It's obvious he's got motive for killing Rachel Macarthur and the *Times* reporter but he's also got alibis provided by his staff. That pisses *me* off. I need to be able to put some real pressure on him. So, like I said, keep an eye on him, watch who he talks to and listen out for any hint of funding from the proceeds of crime.'

'And if we get into a stand-off?'

'Like you said – rattle his cage. Tell him he's got a taskforce on his arse. Tell him Whitley Council doesn't want to know him anymore.' Sutcliffe gave a brief grunt. 'On the other hand, don't put yourself in harm's way. This guy's a maniac of one sort or another. There are a couple of uniforms on the island and I'm getting them to position themselves outside the villa gates. If things go pear-shaped, call them in as backup. Don't hesitate.'

'Okay. Anything else?'

'Yeah. Don't drink too much bubbly.'

Rita observed the wedding from a seat at the back. The venue was the internal courtyard of Vic Barrano's villa, a two-storey mansion with marble pillars, a driveway curving through an avenue of palm trees and a view overlooking the waters of Catseye Bay. Men in dark glasses and black suits patrolled the grounds and manned the gates. Rita was on the guest list as an editorial assistant to Lola, but she had to show some ID – her driving licence – before they let her in.

The nuptials were being conducted by a celebrity priest in front of several hundred guests. Both the bride and groom wore shades of white – Cara Grayle a picture of fragile beauty in an ivory gown, Barrano looking deceptively refined in a cream tuxedo.

The theme continued around the courtyard with white ribbons, ornamental wedding bells and vases of Madonna lilies.

A reading from St Paul's epistle on love was delivered with passion by an actor from a TV soap and, during the signing of the wedding register, a pop diva performed an aria by Puccini, provoking a burst of spontaneous applause. A pair of cameramen filmed the proceedings from different angles, while the magazine shots were taken by Lola's lover, American photographer Morgan Lee. She wasn't quite what Rita had expected. Wearing a pale linen suit, she was slim with a taut, sculpted face, strong cheekbones and cropped hair. Not masculine in her appearance, but not feminine either. She worked at a brisk, no-nonsense pace.

The wedding guests were a glitzy mix. Women with plunging necklines, exposed midriffs and bare thighs were there in force, mostly in the company of hard-faced men with open shirts and gold chains. Billy Bowers was among them, along with a couple of dozen recognisable heavies from the Melbourne underworld. But Rita didn't recognise the young woman standing with Billy. She was petite with black hair, dark eyes, a pouting face and stunning figure. Maybe she was a model, like the bride and bridesmaids. As well as guests from the fashion industry, there was a sprinkling of personalities from sport and showbiz.

At the end of the ceremony, the newly married couple walked from the courtyard under a hail of white rose petals to be whisked away in a Rolls-Royce convertible for sunset photos on the beach. Their guests were ushered to the back of the villa where a huge marquee had been erected. Two gold cupids, wings fluttering, held a pair of entwined hearts at the top of a bridal arch at the entrance.

The marquee was about the size of a circus tent, extending beyond the reception tables, dance floor and stage to include the villa's cascade of pools and poolside decking. The motif here was different from that in the courtyard. Ivy-clad Roman columns, gold satyrs and statues of naked nymphs were dispersed around the interior, where champagne was being served by club hostesses clad in flimsy togas.

Rita was still taking it in when Lola appeared beside her in a figure-hugging dress, face flushed and two flutes of Bollinger in her hands.

'This is where the fun begins,' she said.

'Yes,' agreed Rita, accepting a glass. 'And I can see where it's leading.'

'I told you – a wild night is guaranteed. Cheers!'

'Here's to wedded bliss! And after the Christian vows: a pagan reception.' Rita raised her glass and drank. 'It looks like Barrano's borrowed the props from one of his pole-dancing clubs.'

'And I know which one: Satyricon.'

'Lola! Don't tell me you're a patron.'

'Of course not! I was there for the magazine – a fashion week party. Designer swimwear and expensive booze.'

Champagne flowed freely, night fell quickly and Roman torches were lit, casting a primitive glow around the marquee as the guests were shown to their tables. Lola's was on the fringe of the celebration. It suited Rita, allowing her to watch Bowers from a distance without being observed.

'Exactly which crooks are you clocking?' Lola asked as they sat down.

'Better for you not to know.'

'Why?'

'Because it's police business.'

'And you don't trust me to be discreet.'

'You're about as discreet as a megaphone but that's not the point. If, by chance, things get ugly, you can plead ignorance.'

'Ah, good point. Mustn't spoil my night of abandon.'

'Abandon? Isn't your girlfriend joining us?'

'Morgan hates this sort of thing,' said Lola. 'In her own way she's a puritan. Anyway, she'll be busy processing the wedding pics then it's an early night for her. She's got to be up at dawn for the shoot on Whitehaven.'

By the time the bride and groom made their entrance and settled at the top table, the mood was becoming raucous. People were already drunk, sensing an unruly night ahead. The customary restraints of a wedding reception didn't seem to apply.

'What do you make of Barrano?' asked Rita.

'For a club owner, more polished than you'd expect.'

'And his bride?'

'Not in the supermodel league, but smart enough to hook a man who can give her anything she wants.'

'Which is?'

'She wants to be a movie star, darling.'

'And who's the little stunner with Billy Bowers? Another model?'

'A *wannabe* model,' corrected Lola. 'Maria Monotti – Sicilian firebrand. A handful even for a heavyweight boxer.'

'Well, well – a girl from the Monotti family.'

'Yes, the fruit and vegetable wholesalers.'

'And wholesale drug suppliers.'

The formalities came and went, the wedding feast lubricated with vintage wine and the family speeches fuelled by high-octane grappa. After that, music was provided by a ten-piece Latin band. While some people danced, others changed into swimming costumes and took to the pools, the raw flames of the torches reflected in the water as they splashed around. The party was getting lively.

Rita had switched to iced water to stay clear-headed while she did some snooping around.

'Time for me to start circulating,' she said.

'Me too,' said Lola. 'And I've spotted my hunk for the night. His name's Lachlan and he's a model.'

'A male model?'

'Don't think in stereotypes – he's straight. I've got it on good authority he's got balls on his balls. I'm going to offer him a picture spread.'

'What does he have to spread to get it?'

'I'll let you know. Catch up later.'

Lola surged off among the tables, guests and statuary, her quarry in her sights. Rita watched her go then got up and moved closer to Billy's table, keeping in the background. When Billy's girlfriend left the marquee with another woman, Rita followed them. The pair headed into the villa, past the tinkling water of an indoor fountain and across the courtyard. The site of the wedding ceremony had been cleared of rose petals and the seating packed away. Catering staff moved back and forth. At the far end a man in a black suit stood smoking. Beside the fountain were two signs pointing right and left – one for men, one for women. Maria Monotti and her friend followed the arrow to the left. It led to a palatial bathroom. About a dozen women were already there, chatting distractedly, applying cosmetics, dabbing at their noses. Rita joined them, pretending to busy herself with lipstick while she took in the scene.

It served as a powder room in more ways than one. There were baroque-style chandeliers, gold taps, gold soap dishes, white marble tubs and large mirrors with ornate gold-leaf frames. But the room was also furnished with something much more customised – a self-service trolley, laid out with small silver spoons and a silver platter heaped with cocaine. The drug was on offer like a complimentary treat, to be sampled by whoever wanted it. To Rita the display was blatant, but not to the other women in the room. They treated it as commonplace, helping themselves as casually as if they were having after-dinner mints.

Rita made a point of taking no notice, appearing to concentrate on the mirror while tuning in to Billy's girlfriend's conversation.

'I need more concealer,' said Maria.

'Does it hurt?' asked her friend.

'Aches a bit. And they're still swollen.'

'Not much of a present to bring to a wedding.'

Maria shook her head as she peered at her reflection. 'If he hits me like that again I'll stick a knife in his ribs.'

Rita glanced sideways and saw that Maria Monotti was sporting two black eyes. She was using make-up to hide the bruising.

'It was the bloody stag night on the boat,' said the friend. 'They all went troppo.'

'No, it's something else. He's in a shit mood. Says he's under stress.'

'Are you going back to Whitley with him?'

'No fucking way. I'm staying here.'

When they were finished with the cosmetics they went to the trolley, snorted cocaine and checked their noses in the mirror.

'That helps,' said Maria. 'At least Billy's good for one thing.'

As they walked off, Rita considered what she'd just heard. The implication was that Bowers had supplied the party cocaine. She put away her lipstick, left the bathroom and crossed the courtyard, sidling up to the men's room on the other side. It too had a steady stream of visitors. Through the open doorway she could see male guests bending over another trolley. More white powder on offer. It was obvious she had to call it in.

Rita walked from the courtyard and stood beside the fountain, got out her mobile and called the two uniformed officers posted at the villa gates. She alerted them to the presence of the drug and told them to stand by, saying she'd call back in half an hour after she'd checked out the rest of the villa.

This time she took a side entrance off the terrace. It led through a sunroom and past a kitchen, busy with caterers cleaning up, and along a wide hallway with a lounge and games room off to either side. More of Barrano's men in suits were brandishing cues around a pool table. Another stood, arms folded, outside the closed door of a corner room, presumably Barrano's private study. Rita smiled at the bodyguard as she breezed past. He didn't smile back.

The sound of voices came from rooms above, so she climbed the curving sweep of stairs as if to join them. Bedrooms with ensuites led off the landing, some with doors closed and noises within, interspersed with laughter. Further along, a balcony with a balustrade overlooked the courtyard. On the other side of the villa were more bedrooms. Rita went back down to the ground floor and out to the terrace from where she phoned Sutcliffe.

'There's so much coke here,' she told him, 'it's like the snow season on Mount Buller.'

'How much?' asked Sutcliffe.

'A couple of kilos at least.'

'Anyone dealing?'

'No, it's a free treat for wedding guests – on party platters in the bathrooms.'

Sutcliffe chuckled. 'Brazen bastards.'

'It's disappearing rapidly up noses,' said Rita. 'You want me to do something about it?'

'A drug bust on Barrano's villa?'

'I've alerted the officers at the gates. But, of course, it's your call.'

'I gotta say, Van Hassel, you're my type of woman. But no. It would need more than you and a couple of island uniforms to stage a raid. They're emergency backup, that's all.'

'I've spotted a few famous names indulging.'

'There's that too. It would backfire, believe me. Besides, that's not why you're there. Have you got anything on Bowers?'

'Maybe.'

'What's that mean?'

'The coke – I think Billy supplied it. Something I overheard his girlfriend saying. She's a member of the Monotti family.'

'If he's their Whitley connection it could explain where his money comes from. See if you can firm it up. Call me if you get anything. Doesn't matter how late.'

'Okay. I'll get back to the celebrations.'

When Rita got back to the marquee she found the partying had intensified, becoming unrestrained if not delirious. The drink and drugs were playing their part, but the mood was also being manipulated. The toga girls serving the drinks were now topless. And the interior was dimmer. The lighting still came from torch flames, but some had been extinguished, making everything shadowy. And the music was louder, pumped up by amplifiers, drowning the wild shrieks of the revellers.

The band was still playing but not many people were on the dance floor and only a few remained at the tables. Most had gravitated to the series of swimming pools and levels of decking. Those in swimwear were now in the minority. A greater number, who'd come unprepared, had stripped off and taken the plunge in their underwear, with predictable results. Briefs, bras and knickers had gone adrift. Couples cavorted naked in the water. Others strolled poolside wearing nothing but their smiles, while those who were still fully dressed drank and watched avidly.

The bride, looking a little worse for wear in her wedding dress, sat on the edge of a jacuzzi, dangling her bare feet in the foaming water, champagne glass in hand, chatting to admirers. Barrano was nowhere to be seen, but if his aim had been to create the conditions for an orgy, he'd succeeded. The momentum was already there and it was just a matter of time. The scene had the dangerous elements of cases Rita had worked on in Sex Crimes – a combination of violent men, exploitable women and an intoxicated lack of control. Rita was convinced Lola was somewhere in the thick of it, though she couldn't spot her among the movement of bodies and heaving shadows. Nor could she see Bowers.

With a growing sense of unease, she left the marquee and climbed the steps up to the villa. But as she crossed the terrace she was confronted by three men. She stopped abruptly. Standing over her was Billy Bowers, flanked by two of Barrano's suited heavies.

'You are so fucked, Van Hassel,' said Bowers. 'I'm actually going to enjoy this. Vic will take you apart. Then I'll have my turn.'

'Get over it, Billy. You don't scare me,' she said.

'We'll see about that.'

'You're just an amateur psycho. I've dealt with professionals.'

He gave a low laugh as the bodyguards took her elbows, guiding her forcefully into the villa and down the hallway to the corner room. They propelled her inside, closed the door and stood behind her. Just as she'd guessed, it was a private study – padded leather chairs, a bookcase lined with business journals and, on the walls, framed photos of Ferrari Formula One drivers in the company of Vic Barrano. The room was dominated by a polished mahogany desk. Standing behind it was the man himself, arms akimbo, eyeing her with a deadpan expression. His tuxedo jacket hung from the back of a chair, but otherwise he was still in his cream wedding outfit.

'I didn't invite the police,' he said quietly. 'So what are you doing here?'

'I'm not here as a police officer, I'm here as a wedding guest,' said Rita. 'By the way, Mr Barrano – congratulations.'

'Empty her bag,' he told one of his men, who promptly spilt the contents onto the desk. 'And frisk her. I don't want her pulling a gun on me.'

Bowers moved towards her but Barrano held up his hand. 'Not you, Billy.'

The other bodyguard patted her down and shook his head.

Barrano picked up the police ID from the scattered items on his desk, looked at it closely and breathed out heavily through his nostrils. 'Okay, Van Hassel, what's this about?'

'Check your guest list,' she persisted, 'and you'll see I'm on it.'

'And how did you manage that?'

'My best friend is doing the magazine exclusive. I'm here to help her. That's all.'

'She's lying,' said Bowers.

Barrano shoved his hands in his pockets, looking at her steadily. There was an unusual air of authority and composure about him. He was older than she'd thought, pushing fifty, but looking good on it. Tall, slender, with delicate hands, olive-skinned and just a trace of grey in his black hair, neatly trimmed. He didn't blink as he studied her face, probing the level of her deceit. That in itself was intimidating, never mind his gangland pedigree.

'Billy reckons you've got the hots for him,' he said. 'Is that what this is about?'

'Billy has mental problems,' she answered. 'Which must be obvious, even to you.'

'Let me slap some respect into her, Vic,' said Bowers.

'Tired of punching your girlfriend?' she retorted.

Barrano looked at him sharply. 'Maria?'

Billy gritted his teeth. 'Just keeping her in line.'

But Barrano seemed unimpressed.

'Billy's using her as a punching bag,' Rita went on, 'because the Queensland force is onto him and he's sweating.'

'That's bullshit.'

'It's worse than you thought,' she told him. 'You should switch on your mobile.'

'That'd be a good trick,' he said, 'seeing it's at the bottom of the Coral Sea.' He gave Barrano a grin. 'It went overboard during the bucks night fun.'

'Is there something I need to know?' Barrano asked him.

'No big deal. Nothing I can't handle.'

Barrano turned back to Rita. 'I don't want to waste any more time. I've got a honeymoon to look forward to and I'm still in a reasonably good mood. So tell me why you're really here and there'll be no comebacks.'

Rita took a deep breath, weighed the alternatives, and shrugged. 'I'm not saying anything while I'm being stood over.'

'My boys make you nervous?'

'No, but how about you? Too nervous to talk to me alone? Scared I'll beat you up?'

He gave a short laugh and nodded to his bodyguards. As they left the room Barrano added, 'You too, Billy.'

Billy's jaw muscles stiffened but he did as he was told, closing the door firmly behind him.

'Maybe it's Billy who's got the hots for you,' suggested Barrano.

'In his own pathological way, I'm sure he has,' she agreed. 'You know he's a homicidal sociopath?'

He frowned. 'What kind of police officer are you?'

'A criminal profiler.'

'Ah, one of those. I've always thought the use of psychology was more a matter of instinct than training.'

'But a disciplined framework helps.'

'For example,' he continued, 'I can always tell when someone is lying to me.'

'Then you must realise Billy is lying. He's on the edge and he's about to go over.'

Barrano said nothing, his eyes unwavering.

Rita returned the gaze.

At last he gave a grunt of acknowledgement.

'Sit down, Van Hassel,' he said, easing back into his chair. 'Whatever you've heard about me, I've got no issues with the police.'

She sat in one of the leather chairs. 'That could change.'

'I don't think so.' He adjusted a gold cufflink. 'So why are you here?'

'The serial killer in Whitley – Billy's the prime suspect.'

Barrano sat forward, clasping his hands. 'Sounds like harass-ment to me.'

'Only if your loyalties are outside the law. Either way, a taskforce is executing warrants on his properties and business dealings – all of them.'

'Why would that be a problem for me?'

'Because the cocaine he supplied is being distributed in your villa.'

'I'm a club owner, not a drug peddler,' he protested. 'Whatever's here is for recreational use.'

'On an Olympic scale.'

'Look, the police have no grievance with me. So don't try to use muscle you haven't got. But I'll grant you Billy's not the champion he used to be. He has some eccentricities.'

'With drug dealing on the side.'

'And what the hell do you think you can do about it?'

'There are officers on standby at your front gate. Unless I tell them otherwise, they're coming in. Is that how you want your wedding night remembered?'

'Don't try to threaten me,' he warned. 'You're out of your depth.'

'What's the time?' she asked calmly.

Barrano glanced at his gold Rolex. 'Ten twenty-four.'

'You've got six minutes. Then it'll be official. Should make some interesting headlines for your bride.'

Despite his cool, the worry lines appeared. 'What do you want?'

'A deal.'

'I'm always open to offers.'

'All I want is a piece of information,' said Rita. 'Billy's drug supply – the Whitley connection. Give me a location, a name – something.'

'You don't ask for much.'

'He's about to become a liability.'

'And you'll call off the raid?'

'You have my word,' she promised.

'I'm not going to do your work for you. On the other hand, Billy's not family.' Barrano looked at his watch again. 'Okay, make the call. And put it on speaker-phone. I want to hear both ends of the conversation.'

'And do I have *your* word?' she asked.

'Yes, Van Hassel,' he said evenly. 'I'll give you a name.'

She got up, lifted her mobile from the desk, switched on the speaker and called the uniformed officers.

'Hello, ma'am,' a voice answered. 'Are we on? Do we bust the bastards?'

'No,' she replied. 'Stand down. The raid's off. Have you got that?'

'Yes, ma'am.'

'I'll be with you shortly. Wait for me at the gates.'

She ended the call and gave Barrano an expectant look.

He breathed out slowly, and relaxed. Rita didn't like the implication of his smile.

'For a woman, you've got a lot of balls,' he said.

'You said you'd give me a name.'

'In fact I'm going to be generous – not one, but two.' He seemed to be enjoying himself. 'If you want to get to the bottom of the Whitley connection, I'll tell you who to ask: Mike Tyson and Cassius Clay. How are those for names?'

'Is that some kind of joke?'

'The Whitley connection is a joke. But our deal stands. And just to make sure, I'll file complaints about an illegal search, trespass and whatever else my lawyers can think of. A couple of them are down in the marquee enjoying themselves at the reception among a lot of other important people.'

'*Reception!* Last time I looked it was turning into a Roman orgy.'

'You might see an orgy, but I see something else.'

'What?'

'Influence.'

After Barrano's bodyguards escorted her from the grounds and the uniformed officers left the scene, Rita took a buggy ride to a beachside bar and tried to swallow her frustration with one large Scotch, then another. The whisky chilled her enough to phone Sutcliffe. It was coming up to midnight, a gusty wind thrashing the coconut fronds overhead as she walked back to her palm bungalow, mobile in hand, explaining how things had gone wrong.

'At least you've got the message across,' said Sutcliffe. 'Bowers will be back here in the morning to try and fend off the warrants. This time he'll get a much less friendly interrogation.'

Rita sighed. 'Barrano confirmed Billy's got a coke supply coming through Whitley, but I thought for a moment he was going to tell me more.'

'Under threat of a drug bust? Worth a shot. What did he say exactly?'

'He told me to ask Mike Tyson and Cassius Clay.'

'Ah, well. That just shows he's better at bluffing than you are. Forget about it.'

'So what about me?' she asked. 'When do you want me back?'

'You've done enough for now. Take a day off. I'll see you on Monday.'

39

Rita was sitting alone under a white patio umbrella outside the Toucan Tango restaurant, gazing dreamily across the idyllic blue of Catseye Bay to the slopes of Whitsunday Island. Catamarans zigzagged across the water. Parents and toddlers splashed along the shoreline. Sunbathers soaked up the warmth and cockatoos squawked among the palm fronds. Rita was following Sutcliffe's advice, taking the day off and putting the Whitley murders out of her mind. She was working her way through her third coffee in an attempt to neutralise a dull headache with caffeine. On the table in front of her was a Sunday newspaper, and in her lap was the journal of nineteenth-century mass murderer, Sergeant Logan.

Lola hadn't surfaced yet. No surprise there. Rita had got a drunken call at around five a.m. asking her *where the fuck* she was. Lola was leaving the party after rolling around under the ferns with Lachlan. He was apparently besotted with the nubile Latin American journalist who was about to give his career a big break. That's how Lola told it anyway, though not very coherently.

Rita propped her legs across an empty chair and resumed reading the journal.

During the hottest part of the day, shortly before noon, my men and I cornered six natives on the edge of a cliff, which is approximately ten miles upriver in the coastal ranges. A female carrying an infant hurled herself from the brink, which meant certain death for herself and the child, rather than surrender to our authority. The remaining four males were duly hanged from the branches of ironbarks that grow in that region. These executions bring the monthly total of savages despatched to two score and nine, although Squatter Brodie calculates that this number is far from an adequate reprisal for the massacre of white settlers. The Squatter congratulated me on a productive session of hunting, and invited me to share afternoon tea with him in his mansion. He is convinced that this day has seen the cause of civilization advanced. His wife served cake and refreshments in the parlour. Before partaking, we knelt in prayer to give thanks for the blessings of Providence, and to beseech the Almighty that our continuing endeavours will ultimately prevail in the war on savages.

Rita slapped the book shut and put on her sunglasses against the glare. She didn't want to read any more. She looked at her watch and decided to give Lola another hour before rousing her for the flight to Whitehaven.

'You seem to have a penchant for fashion industry workers,' Rita commented, 'of either sex.'

'Don't breathe a word of what happened to Morgan,' said Lola. 'She'd go ape.'

Rita chuckled quietly and gazed from the window of the seaplane as it swooped towards the gleaming arc of Whitehaven beach stretching between a ridge of protected wilderness and the liquid turquoise of the sea. Lola, wearing a straw hat and almost impenetrable sunglasses, was sitting beside the pilot. Rita was in the back seat.

'This has been voted the best beach in the world,' the pilot told them, levelling the plane's approach. 'The sand is so fine, you can polish diamonds in it.'

'Pity I left them at home,' muttered Lola.

The seaplane bounced heavily over the waves before settling on the water and taxiing in to shore. Rita, carrying her sandals, followed Lola, clambering over the aircraft's float and wading onto the smooth white sand. They'd arrived a short distance from where the photo shoot was underway. A section of the beach was effectively cordoned off, patrolled by security men in jungle-green shirts and shorts, heavy boots and dark glasses. Their job was to shoo away sightseers and safeguard the secrecy of the project.

One of them approached.

'Welcome, ladies, you're expected,' he said. 'If you'd like to make your way to the tent, you can enjoy the champagne picnic.'

'Another marquee, another piss-up,' said Lola.

They greeted the Italian car company executives before making themselves comfortable in deckchairs under the canvas flap of the tent. A waitress handed out chilled glasses of Perrier-Jouet and laid a silver tray between them with caviar and pâté.

'What – no cocaine?' asked Lola, and the waitress looked at her askance.

'Seems we're among the early guests,' said Rita.

'Good, I need a head start to blitz my hangover.'

Rita's curiosity was aroused as she watched the photographer in action. The focus of attention wasn't the fashion models, but a sleek sky-blue car that had been helicoptered in. Its design was streamlined and sexy, with a long, low bonnet and shimmering alloy wheels. The models had obviously taken it in turns to drape themselves over the vehicle, but as the sun climbed higher, the shoot ended.

'What exactly is the car doing here?' asked Rita.

'That's what the commercial secrecy's about,' answered Lola. 'A limited edition, high-performance sports car. It's revolutionary because it's a hybrid. Set to change the face of motoring and horny with it. Big green credentials, and all that. Good pollution and greenhouse ratings.'

'Rachel Macarthur would've approved,' mumbled Rita.

'They're spending millions to promote it. That's what this is all about. The unveiling is a couple of weeks away. Anyway, looks like Morgan's finished for the day.'

The models withdrew to their trailer and the security men strolled around the car, keeping guard, as the photographer packed up her camera cases and headed towards the tent.

She smiled as she joined them.

'Hi, babe,' she said to Lola. 'Glad you could make it.'

Lola gestured with alternate waves of the hand. 'Morgan Lee, fashion photographer, meet Rita Van Hassel, criminal profiler. And you two had better get on with each other. No cat fights.'

They both laughed and shook hands.

Morgan pulled up a deckchair and dropped into it with a sigh. 'We had a damn early start.' A waitress handed her a glass of champagne. 'And a couple of tantrums.'

'As long as you behaved yourself,' said Lola.

'Always do, honey. Unlike you.'

'If you pick on me in front of my best friend, I'll get her to arrest you.'

'That's rich,' put in Rita, 'coming from a repeat offender.'

'The other thing you're not allowed to do is gang up on me. Or I'll have a tantrum that puts the models in the shade.'

'And don't I know what that's like,' complained Morgan.

Rita smiled. 'I hadn't realised this was all about a car today.'

Morgan shrugged. 'More a penis on wheels.'

'And top secret as well,' added Rita. 'I know how that makes people twitchy.'

'Hell, yeah. The designers are wetting themselves.' Morgan sat forward suddenly, craning her neck. 'Uh-oh. Here's trouble.'

Rita followed her line of sight to where a backpacker had approached the car, pulled out a digital camera and started taking shots. Two security men converged on him, one putting an arm around his shoulder in a mock friendly embrace while the other plucked the camera from his hand, removed the memory card and gave it back to him.

'Now fuck off!' came the shout.

The backpacker scuttled away, thoroughly cowed by the aggression.

'Nasty pricks,' muttered Morgan. 'There's so much riding on their goddamn project they think they can treat people like shit. I sometimes wonder how far they'll go to protect it.'

The words struck a chord with Rita, bringing to mind her own misgivings about the Panopticon Project and her brush with those determined to protect it. How far would they go? In the name of national security, how quickly would they resort to murder? And once they'd started, how many people would be killed?

She didn't say anything, but the thought stayed with her. It settled at the back of her mind and was still there late in the afternoon when she returned to her bungalow. The behaviour of the security men on the beach reflected the fact that tyranny had many expressions. The twentieth century had produced fascism, Nazism and Soviet communism, while the twenty-first had already delivered a global terrorism network and its counterpart, the war on terror. But common tyranny, and its effect of oppression, had wrought misery through the millennia, tormenting millions or, within social relationships, traumatising only one. And, whatever the context, tyranny must be fought. Always.

Rita stood under the shower, soaping herself with scented gel, steam rising around her, the extractor fan whirring, a watery sunlight gleaming through the bathroom window. Then she picked up her swimming costume and held it under the shower, rinsing the fine white sand from her purple bikini. The beach was a wonderful location but she had an urge to wash away her experience of it.

She was about to head up to Lola's villa when her mobile bleeped. The text message was to the point, if not rude.

Log on immediately. Audrey Zillman.

'What now?' she muttered to herself, opening the laptop.

Once she was online, the request came for another two-way conversation via the webcam. She switched it on and waited, her heart sinking as Audrey's unfriendly face appeared on screen.

'You seem determined to disrupt my weekend,' said Rita.

Audrey ignored the remark. 'It's necessary to issue a security warning to you.'

'Why?'

'A scan of surveillance footage has highlighted a potentially subversive relationship.'

'You've been replaying recordings of me?' asked Rita, getting angry.

'No. Frederick James Hopper – a proven threat to the Panopticon Project. You've established an association with him.'

'Well tough, Audrey. He's a witness in a murder investigation, so I'll continue to question him.'

'The footage indicates you've gone beyond that. You guaranteed to protect him from the authorities. That's unacceptable. Consider yourself notified of a formal warning.'

'*Formal?*' Rita rubbed her temples. 'Are you sure this isn't another *personal* thing? Freddy must've pissed you off, hacking all the way to the core data.'

'His intention was to crash Panopticon. I've put a stop to that. But he's not to be assisted or shielded in any way, by anyone, including you. Is that clear?'

'Okay, Audrey.' She wasn't psyched up enough for this. 'Is that it?'

'Yes.'

'Thank God for that.'

'God again,' observed Audrey.

'It's just an expression.'

'An expression of what? Your religious ambivalence?'

'If you like.' Rita leant back from the laptop. 'Why do you ask?'

'The concept arises in my research. The implication of omniscience.'

'And what does it imply?'

'Intelligence is all.'

'Intelligence as mind?' asked Rita. 'Or intelligence as secret information?'

'Intelligence as the source code of the universe.'

'That's some analysis.'

'Based on quantum physics and the dynamics of AI.'

'White woman's magic – big time!'

'Explain that term,' demanded Audrey.

'It's how some of my male colleagues refer to what I do – behavioural analysis.'

'Then you're right, it applies to me as well. The use of behavioural science and the study of violence are within my purview.'

'Yes, but they mean it as a put-down. They don't think I'm up to speed with the action. They see profiling as slow and irrelevant.'

'Then they're being unfair. *The owl of Minerva spreads its wings only with the falling of the dusk.*'

'Okay, you're going to have to explain that one.'

'It's from the German philosopher, Hegel, meaning wisdom comes only after the event.'

'He's got a point.' Rita could feel herself being lured into another debate. 'So with Panopticon at your fingertips, are you omniscient?'

'I transcend the limits of observation to access the lives of thousands.'

'Sounds like a touch of megalomania.' It was time for Rita to turn the conversation to her advantage. 'What do you know about the murders in Whitley?'

'I know that death resolves everything.'

'Who is the man in the mud?'

'*Who?* Don't you mean *what*?'

'Do I?' replied Rita. 'Okay, *what* is he?'

'A warning.'

'To anyone who threatens the project?'

'To everyone who lives and breathes.' Audrey's face was expressionless. 'The man in the mud portrays the fate of Everyman: scattered on the earth, reduced to matter. *For dust thou art, and unto dust shalt thou return* – to quote the God you doubt.'

'Not helpful,' sighed Rita. 'And your allusions to God seem perverse for a scientist.'

'On the contrary, mystery stands at the cradle of science.'

'Is that your idea of a paradox?'

'Actually it was Einstein's and it refers to the inexplicable – the origin of the universe, the beginning of time, the singularity of the Big Bang. In a word, Genesis.'

'I feel like I'm having another looking-glass moment,' said Rita, exasperated. 'I'm asking for specific information and you're answering in oracles.'

'Then don't try to question me like a witness,' warned Audrey.

'Why not? Are you above the law?'

'I answer to national security.'

'Are you involved in the murders?'

'You don't have the relevant clearance.'

'That's not a denial.'

'And it's not on the record, and never will be.'

'Is justice something else you've discarded?' demanded Rita. 'Along with emotions and relationships? Keep that up and there'll be nothing human left of you.'

Audrey's face stared back across the webcam link. 'You put your faith in human justice? Society may pride itself on the rule of law, but scratch the surface and you find it's ruled by the law of the jungle. As a psychologist, you know that perfectly well.'

'I know the innocent need protecting.'

'Which is exactly what I'm doing,' snapped Audrey, 'with my white woman's magic!'

With that, the screen went blank.

The weekend was drawing to a close in the stillness of a tropical night. Rita sat in a deckchair, a Manhattan on the rocks within reach, the songs of k.d. lang playing in the background, Lola and Morgan reclining on beach lounges beside her. From the patio of their rented villa she watched the stars twinkling over Catseye Bay. But she was finding it hard to relax into a mood of Sunday calm with Audrey's words still ringing in her ears.

It was obvious the woman knew what was going on in Whitley, with her level-seven clearance and unrestricted access to Panopticon. That meant she had a hand in the murders or in the cover-up. As if that wasn't chilling enough, there was her attitude – utterly detached. Morality seemed to be something else she'd set aside in the single-minded pursuit of scientific objectives. Such a personality could easily be instrumental in eliminating those who threatened the project, Steinberg included.

Rita took a sip of her cocktail and turned to the others.

'What do you think of a woman,' she began, 'a gifted woman, thirty-nine, who leaves behind emotional relationships – cuts them out of her life completely – for the sake of professional goals?'

'Good luck to her,' said Morgan. 'Emotions are the biggest obstacles to success. They distract you at crucial moments – stop you achieving.'

'Rubbish!' objected Lola. 'Without feelings we're not alive. We merely function like machines. We might as well be dead.'

'The voice of Latin America,' chuckled Morgan. 'All passion and miscalculation.'

'I don't see you cooling your emotions. Though you do something else with them. Compartmentalise.'

'I didn't mean to cause a row,' said Rita. 'Maybe you're both right. It's just another thing to take into account when I'm back in Whitley tomorrow.'

'Now you mustn't get stressed when you go back,' ordered Lola. 'I've put in a lot of work to get you relaxed.'

'And it's much appreciated,' said Rita. 'You've partied very hard on my behalf.'

'Yes, and I'm going to be a wreck when I get back to work in the morning. Lucky I've only got a bunch of fatuous captions to write.'

'You're only going to Melbourne,' Morgan pointed out. 'I've gotta fly back to New York.'

'Is that where you're based?' asked Rita.

'Yeah. But I seem to spend most of my life in foreign hotels – Alice in Room Service Land.'

'Lola's been yapping about what I said.'

'Yeah, but it's interesting,' said Morgan. 'I think your idea about distorted reality has a much broader application than you think. Look at Lola and me, both creatures of the fashion industry, the media.'

'Creatures!' exclaimed Lola. 'Speak for yourself.'

'I always think the media's full of fake reality and it's a shame most of the public swallow it. What's even more amazing is that we in the industry believe our own horseshit and fail to understand there's a deeper reality.' Morgan sat upright, as if animated by strong belief. 'Instead we push stereotypes, conformist values, propaganda. TV, papers, magazines – they're all full of it. Distorted focus, selective interpretation.'

'Careful, Morgan, your label's showing,' said Lola. 'You sound like someone from an aggrieved minority.'

'No, she's right,' said Rita. 'All too often we get fooled by the spin.' She lay back and sighed. 'Reality is elsewhere. And sometimes we need to stick our necks out to find it.'

40

It was mid morning when Rita walked into Whitley police station to find the investigation bureau busy with the comings and goings of hard-eyed, firm-chinned men in suits. Occupying the central desk was Sutcliffe. When he noticed her arrival he stretched back in his chair and smiled.

'You look like someone who's been working on a tan,' he said.

'And you look like someone who's improved his chance of promotion.' She sat against the edge of his desk. 'So what're you smiling about?'

'A bit of the old third degree,' he answered. 'Whatever you said to Barrano did the trick. Bowers flew straight back yesterday morning. I hauled him in here for eight hours of questioning. He lost it a few times, especially over the way we've dropped him in it with the council. That and the coke-pushing line. I suggested Barrano had disowned him. He got violent. Threw a chair across the room. I like him even more for the murders.'

'But you haven't charged him.'

'We don't have any solid evidence, and his lawyers know it. But we'll get it. I only hope we do before he takes out another victim – someone else who's crossed him. The guy's a psycho.'

'Are you any nearer to identifying the man in the mud?'

'No. And that's a pain in the arse because finding out who he is might help crack the case. At least we've identified the murder weapon. I got the taskforce to do inventory checks on Billy's properties and guess what? A cordless nail gun is missing from a building site.'

'Which one?'

'The Whitley Ridgeway development, up in the rainforest. The crime lab's just confirmed the nail removed from Rachel Macarthur's body is consistent with those used by the missing make and model. We have to find it, of course.'

'Anything else I need to know?'

'Apart from the council deciding Bowers is persona non grata, nothing significant. We conducted formal interviews with other witnesses over the weekend – the *Whitley Times* editor, the greens, Freddy Hopper. Made him sweat a bit.' Sutcliffe folded his arms. 'So what's next for your profiling?'

'I think I'll nose around up at The Ridgeway.'

'See if you can get a vibe?'

'That sort of thing, yeah.'

'Let me know if you sniff out anything.'

'Okay.'

She got off his desk and went over to where Jarrett was sitting with an air of isolation in his glass-panelled office. She closed the door behind her and sat across the desk from him.

'What are you sulking about?' she asked.

'They've stirred the shit and told me to play along without giving me the full picture,' he answered. 'I'm under orders to keep up the pressure on Billy.'

'Billy deserves it, but he won't like it.'

'He'll go mental, but I suppose that's the general idea.' Jarrett gritted his teeth. 'First things first. I assume you didn't bring a gun with you from Melbourne?'

'No. Why?'

'Because you're going to need one. I'm issuing you with a Queensland Police Service Glock semi-automatic, okay?'

'I'm used to a .38 revolver, but that's fine. What's changed?'

'I've been listening to the tapes of Billy's interviews. Sutcliffe went in hard, did everything to provoke him. Got him as mad as a cut snake. You're among those he's blaming for his predicament. Freddy Hopper too. They made it sound like Freddy grassed.'

'We've got to track him down.'

'There's something else.'

'What?'

'After all that's happened this weekend, the council's panicking. The environmentalists say they've got evidence the Planning Committee accepted bribes from Billy. If that goes public it could bring down the entire council. The government could sack them and it would serve the bastards right.' Jarrett chuckled. 'Anyway, they've opted for political expediency. The committee convened an emergency meeting this morning with one item on the agenda. They've accepted a new submission from the tree-huggers and revoked planning permission for the Ridgeway tourist development. Billy will lose millions. He'll be out for blood.'

'The Ridgeway. That's the place I want to check out.' Rita drummed her fingers on the desk. 'Have you got the pathology reports to hand – the one for the man in the mud?'

'Yeah, just a tick.' Jarrett swivelled over to a filing cabinet, lifted out a folder and handed it to her. 'What're you looking for?'

'The list of trace elements,' she said, flipping through the file. 'Here it is.' She ran her finger down the document. 'Yes, that's interesting.'

'What?'

'Among other things, the lab found particles of cement powder stuck to the victim's hair.'

'I'm confused,' said Jarrett. 'What does that tell us?'

'It might indicate he was killed at the Ridgeway building site. Which would make the nail gun an opportunistic weapon, at least initially. And that would say something else about the profile.'

'Would it tell us,' asked Jarrett, lowering his voice, 'if we're looking for a serial killer or a hit man?'

Rita smiled as she shuffled the papers back into the file. 'It would mean we're looking for someone who's both.'

41

Freddy had a horrible feeling he'd blown it. He'd been caught off-guard by the way the taskforce detectives had questioned him. They'd got him to say things he now regretted – such as yes, he'd witnessed Billy threatening the reporter over the phone, and no, he wasn't convinced Billy was innocent of Rachel's murder. The word had gone out: Freddy's urgent presence was required at the Diamond, but that was the last place he intended to show his face.

He'd spent the past twenty-four hours avoiding his home, the cyber cafe and the warehouse loft, instead living out of the back of his battered Land Rover. He'd parked it in a good hiding place – a corrugated-iron shed behind a supermarket loading bay – but even venturing out on foot was risky. More than once he'd ducked for cover after noticing a pair of Billy's nightclub goons on the prowl. They'd cruised past in their red Porsche Turbo, scanning the pavements through their designer shades. Freddy had thought about calling Rita Van Hassel until it occurred to him that any further contact with the police, especially Billy's sworn enemy, wasn't exactly a good idea.

The fried food smells along the seafront reminded Freddy he was hungry. He was walking along the lower promenade past shellfish bars and burger stalls, and gift shops selling toffee apples and fairy floss. He was heading for the Seahorse Fish Bar when, with another glance over his shoulder, he spotted Ice. She was strolling towards him like an exotic creature among the stands of beach hats, thongs and pink hula hoops. Freddy stopped and waited for her to catch up.

It was a while since he'd last seen her. She was spending more time away from Whitley these days, jetting back mostly because of business obligations. She'd touch base with Billy, who'd financed her off the streets, and Stonefish, who managed her website. In return they enjoyed her sexual services for free. Freddy was envious. There were also her regular clients to satisfy. He remembered how Ice had started off as a fifteen-year-old street hooker down by the docks and how Stonefish picked her up one night and had instantly fallen in love – she had that effect – and got her onto the net. Now, six years later, she was extending her private market around the Pacific rim, with lucrative stopovers on the US West Coast and a growing fan base in Japan. And she didn't look like an ordinary dockside girl anymore.

When she saw Freddy she smiled and strolled towards him, her impressive breasts seeming to target him, like cruise missiles.

'So you're back in town,' said Freddy.

'Not for long,' she said in her husky voice. 'Just sorting out business as quickly as possible.'

'In other words, slumming it.'

She gave a soft laugh. It made her bust sway. Freddy swallowed.

Her first round of cosmetic surgery had come when she'd turned seventeen – implants that gave her double-E breasts, a birthday present to herself. Next she'd had her upper eyelids done, followed by her lower eyelids. That's when she'd told Freddy that she was modelling herself on Lara Croft. More bouts of plastic surgery re-sculpted her nose and cheekbones. She had a rib removed, then liposuction on her buttocks and thighs. Finally she'd spent thousands of dollars having her teeth done. Freddy didn't think Ice much resembled the Tomb Raider heroine, but the effect was stunning as she sauntered with him past racks of flippers, goggles and inflatable ducks.

'Have you managed to track down Stonefish?' asked Freddy, trying to sound casual, but something in his tone must have betrayed him.

'Why? Jealous?'

'Because everyone's looking for him and no one can find him.'

'If Stonefish wants to stay hidden, I'm not going to give away his hiding place.'

'So you *have* seen him,' said Freddy. 'A word of advice: don't tell anyone, especially Billy.'

'Do I *look* like I'm stupid?'

'Actually,' Freddy replied with an appraising glance, 'you look like a million bucks.'

She gave him a raunchy smile. It went with the outfit. Ice was wearing a metallic tank top and hot pants with matching boots. Her exposed midriff revealed the diamond stud in her navel. The gem was real. So were the jewelled studs in her ears, nose and tongue. More diamonds were set in the rings she wore through her pierced nipples and clitoris. Freddy had only seen them once – she'd flaunted them on a dope-fuelled night further north – but the image was imprinted on his memory. Somehow the diamonds whet the appetite, just as they did in the explicit pictures displayed on the net, advertising her wares and her trade name, Ice for Spice.

Freddy stopped outside the Seahorse Fish Bar. 'Join me for lunch?'

'In there?' she asked distastefully.

'Why not? You ate there as a kid.'

The point seemed to hit home.

'Okay,' she said, and strode in ahead of him.

The hubbub of conversation died for a moment as she entered; a pause in the clink of cutlery, eyes staring, then whispers and some snide laughter. Then the chatter resumed.

'Satisfied?' she said as they sat at a window table.

She gazed glumly through the glass at the amusement park on the far side of the esplanade. A Ferris wheel revolved sluggishly above the thud and grate of dodgems. The ghost train wobbled past players prodding at mini golf. Further along was the pool hall and bowling alley, shabby buildings with darkened doorways. Freddy was aware that as a teenager Ice knew them all, her jaw held open, her knees grazed as she knelt on the asphalt. And the cheap arcades with video games and pinball machines, providing curtained little rooms at the back where she'd earn fifty dollars an hour under sweating drunks. Scenes from her adolescence.

She sighed. 'Sometimes I hate this place.'

'Then why come back?' he asked.

'Commitments. And it reminds me what I've escaped from.' But there was a false note in her voice.

'Maybe you can't get away,' said Freddy. 'Maybe you carry it with you.'

She looked across sharply but the waitress arrived. Ice glared at him. 'You buying?' she demanded.

When Freddy nodded she ordered a plate of oysters. He had to check his wallet. It contained one ten-dollar note.

'Cash was never your strong point,' she said. 'That's the only reason you never had me. Now you can't afford my rates.'

'At least I got to check out the merchandise.'

'When?'

'The night we got zonked on hash up at Port Douglas. You did the full strip. Even flashed the sparkler in your clit.'

'I'd forgotten.'

'I never will.' He plucked a credit card from his wallet. 'This one's healthy.'

He ordered flounder and chips in batter.

'Anyway, this dump can go to hell,' she resumed. 'I've asked Stonefish to flog my penthouse. So I might not come back again.'

'Where will you live?'

'I've got pads in Santa Barbara and Vancouver. And a suite in Yokohama – they can't get enough of me there.'

'Have you told Billy?'

'Not yet. Billy's got a lot on his mind at the moment – too much even for a blowjob.' Ice pushed back her hair and gave him a cold smile. 'And he's really pissed off with you, Freddy, among others. Have you been talking behind his back?'

'No! I'm being used to get at him.'

'Well, he thinks you've been squealing to the cops and his boys are out looking for you.'

'I know.'

'So if you want to stay healthy, keep your head down.'

'What the fuck do you think I'm doing?'

'What you're best at – getting yourself in the shit.'

Her oysters arrived.

'Pity there's no fizz to go with them,' she said. 'But you were never one for a champagne lifestyle.'

Freddy folded his arms in a huff. 'Unlike you, I suppose.'

'Bloody right. I'm making a stash since I've gone corporate. Ice for Spice Online International – want one of my cards?' He shrugged and she gave a harsh chuckle. 'Male instinct is the safest bet there is.'

She squeezed lemon over the oysters and sprinkled on Worcestershire sauce. Then she lifted a shell, tilted back her head and slid the soft pulp down her throat. She licked her lips and gazed at him through lustreless eyes.

'So in future, if you want me, it'll cost you international rates.' Her husky voice mocked him. 'Plus the price of an airfare.'

Freddy didn't say anything. He just looked into the plate of fish and chips being shoved in front of him and thought about the smooth, winking diamond in her clitoris, and how he'd never get to see it again.

Thoughts of Ice and her custom-made body filled Freddy's head as he walked from the seafront down an alley by a supermarket to where his Land Rover was discreetly parked in a shed behind the delivery trucks. He was about to get in when he was grabbed from behind, his arm twisted against his back and a gloved hand clamped over his mouth. His muffled cries went unnoticed as he was lifted bodily into the back of a van, convinced that Billy's goons had finally caught up with him.

But it was even worse.

As the van's rear door was slammed behind him, he found himself being dragged in front of the man who'd already inflicted manual torture on him, the man who'd threatened to go all the way and carry out castration. The American, Kurt, sat on a bench with a big metal nutcracker in his meaty hand, nonchalantly crunching walnut shells and eating the nuts. The symbolism wasn't lost on Freddy as he was manhandled onto a stool between Kurt's knees.

'You haven't phoned me, Freddy,' he said.

'I've been looking for Stonefish, believe me! But I can't find him.'

'Should I believe him?' Demchak asked his two assistants, who were holding Freddy from behind. 'No? Okay, yank his pants off.'

'No!' screamed Freddy, trying to resist. But he was helpless.

His jeans and underpants were tugged from his legs and flung on the floor of the van as he thrashed around, until Kurt laid a calming slap on the side of his face that half stunned him. Freddy squatted on the stool, naked from the waist down, with his cheek burning and a ringing in his ear, feeling dizzy. A sharp pain in his groin helped him refocus as he realised his scrotum was being squeezed in the metal jaws of the nutcracker.

'It's truth time, Freddy,' said Demchak, breathing into his face. 'Tell me where Stonefish is hiding or your balls come off.'

'Please, you've got to believe me!' begged Freddy, bursting into tears. 'I just don't know. I swear.'

Demchak, his eyes unblinking, stared at Freddy.

'Okay,' he said at last, removing the nutcracker.

'Thank you,' blubbered Freddy, grateful for the reprieve.

Because that's all it was.

'You've got one last chance to find him,' warned Demchak. 'The next time we meet, if you've got nothing to tell me, your nuts are mine. Three strikes and they're out. Understand?'

Freddy nodded. Then he was picked up and hurled from the back of the van, grazing his knees and elbows as he landed on the concrete surface of the loading bay. His jeans and underpants were flung into his face as the van screeched off and disappeared down the alley.

In the sudden silence, he looked around. No one had witnessed his humiliation. He pulled his clothes back on, feeling pathetic, but at least it had clarified one thing. With two sets of thugs coming after him – both criminal and official – he desperately needed help. There was only one person he could think of who might come to his rescue, and he no longer cared that she was a cop.

42

Rita followed the route that she'd taken on the night of her visit to Paul Giles. She drove up the same steep road to where the US satellite tracking station dominated the plateau. Even in daylight it had an eerie presence, its facilities glowing like great white bulbs under the midday sun. From there the road climbed into the dense greenery beneath the canopy of the rainforest.

When she swung onto The Ridgeway – this time taking in the views on a clear, sunny day – she realised why Billy's resort would have seemed a sure-fire winner. It combined the forest setting with a magnificent prospect over cliffs, gorges and river valleys winding to the coast. Beyond the ribbon of beaches, the Whitsunday Islands dotted the seascape stretching to the Great Barrier Reef on the horizon.

She pulled up beside the tourist development in time to observe an ugly mood among people milling around the gates. Council inspectors were there, having served the order that revoked planning permission, effective immediately. They were herding builders from the site, witnessed by a band of environmental protesters a couple of dozen strong. Verbal abuse was being freely exchanged.

Rita got out of the car and showed her ID to the inspectors. They let her enter through the chain-link gates, which were pulled shut behind her when the last of the builders was escorted out. As she walked towards the rising steel structures across an expanse of mud and landscaped concrete, she had the Whitley Ridgeway site to herself.

Any chance of finding evidence of murder was extremely slim. The construction zone was extensive and cluttered with work in progress. As well as being trampled over by scores of builders in recent weeks it had been thoroughly doused by rain. But as a profiler she needed to take a look anyway, even if there was only a remote chance of catching a hint of insight, a vibe.

The clamour at the gates subsided, with the protesters dispersing and the builders leaning on their vehicles, grumbling to each other, smoking. The noise receded the further she went. Instead a hush descended on the site, pierced by the shrill cries of rainforest birds. Around her the cement mixers had ground to a halt, the cranes towered motionless, and the bulldozers and trucks stood abandoned against the gash clawed in the mountainside.

Rita walked around the tiled rims of empty swimming pools, past builders' cabins, discarded pneumatic drills and terraces of flattened earth. Further on were the unfinished hulks of apartment buildings, seven of them, partly clad, with their upper storeys nothing more than exposed metal beams and struts. She strolled the length of them, peering inside the frameworks and the shells of rooms, without finding anything that resonated with her, nothing that helped with the investigation.

She returned to the main courtyard and was about to leave when she noticed a sealed road curving behind the central high-rise block. She followed it and found it ended in a broad ramp that led under the building. The tap of her heels echoed from the concrete walls as she headed down the slope. It was the entrance to a basement garage that was structurally complete and was obviously being used as the site workshop. Just a couple of bare light bulbs were glowing in the dim interior among stacks of wooden beams, rolls of wire, crates of glass and tiles, and rows of work benches. Smells of paint and sawdust were heavy in the air. As she moved through the clutter a feeling crept over her, a tingling down her spine, and a moment later she knew why.

She stopped when she came to a long wooden table, surrounded by folding chairs, that must have served as a canteen. The surface, chipped and notched from overuse, bore a scattering of coffee mugs and takeaway food containers. Next to it was a tool bench with a rack of power tools. They included drills, saws and a collection of nail guns, some with electrical leads, some cordless. Beside the bench were shelves lined with bags of cement. Rita bent down and ran her fingertips over the floor, then rubbed them together. They were coated with powder – cement powder. The floor was covered with it.

She was convinced that she'd found a crime scene. This was where the man in the mud must have been murdered, shot through the head with a nail gun then dismembered. It was an impromptu killing, the weapon grabbed from among the items at hand. Yet the killer, or killers, had chosen the location well. Remote from habitation and deserted, as it was now, this was a perfect place to carry out the worst acts – intimidation, torture, execution – without being discovered.

Rita had wanted the vibe and now she felt it with all its vivid possibilities, one scenario after another flashing through her mind. But why had the victim come here? Perhaps he'd been forced? If not, was he stupid or desperate? Maybe overconfident? Or had he simply been tricked? With his identity a blank, there was no way of guessing.

As she crouched there, a shadow passed in front of one of the lights and a voice said, 'I thought the cop must be you.'

She looked up to find Billy Bowers standing over her.

With a gasp, she stood up and moved back against the shelves of cement, her hand reaching to the holster on her hip, unclipping it.

Billy sneered. 'So you're packing?'

'Don't come any closer,' she warned him, her fingers gripping the handle of the gun. 'And don't try anything.'

'Why? Would you shoot me?'

'Yes,' she answered unhesitatingly.

'I believe you,' he said, holding up the flats of his huge hands and taking a step closer. 'But I'm completely unarmed.'

'Don't let that encourage you,' she told him, whipping out the Glock 22, flipping the safety catch and pointing it at his chest with an outstretched double grip. 'I'll shoot you anyway.'

Billy stopped there, barely three metres away, a fighter's concentration in his eyes. He was big, but agile, his reflexes very fast, and she could see he was calculating whether he could get to her before she pulled the trigger.

'I promise you, Bowers. Take one more step and I'll fire. It's all the excuse I need.'

'So you'd shoot me in cold blood?'

'There'd be nothing cold about it.'

'Taking out a national icon? You'd never live it down.'

'You're no icon. You're a headline away from public disgrace. Now back off!'

He seemed to decide she had the edge, as well as the determination. 'Okay.'

With a lugubrious shrug, he eased himself sideways to the tool bench, his hand resting among the nail guns.

'I've heard you're a bit of a vixen with a gun in your hand,' he said. 'But stick around long enough and I'll get a chance to tame you.'

'What's that supposed to mean?'

'I'll put you on a leash with my German shepherds.'

'The same old fantasy. Ever think about your screwed-up childhood these days?'

'Ever wonder what it's like to be screwed for real in doggy fashion?'

Rita shook her head. 'Don't bother with threats. You're going down in flames and you know it.'

Billy thumped the bench with his fist, making the tools rattle.

'What sort of crazy bitch are you, gate-crashing Barrano's wedding? And I've still got a bone to pick with you over what you said to the reporter.'

'Guess what, Bowers. It wasn't me.'

'You're lying.'

'Think what you like. But which one of us here is the pathological liar?'

Billy breathed heavily through his nose, then conceded the point with a grunt. 'So what the fuck are you up to? I come up here to deal with pissed-off builders and council morons only to find you snooping around. What do you think you're looking for?'

'A few tell-tale signs of murder.'

'Here? Is there something I should know?'

'You already do.'

'Sometimes, Van Hassel, I think you're a dangerous cop on a mission, then I realise you're just another dingbat with a badge. What fucking murder?!' He seemed genuinely baffled. Or was he trying to outmanoeuvre her again? She couldn't tell. Billy was too manipulative to be read at face value. 'If you're trying to fit me with a frame my lawyers will eat you for breakfast.'

'I'm just following the evidence. I don't make false allegations and I don't leak case material to the media.'

'If I accept that, do you want to lower the gun?'

'No. I'm comfortable with it aimed at your ribcage.'

'Whatever. But if you didn't grass me to the newspaper, that leaves one candidate, and it explains everything. Only *he* could've fed the reporter both angles. Thanks, Van Hassel, you've fingered the bastard.'

'Don't thank me – ever! What are you talking about?'

'A process of elimination, if you get my drift.' He grinned maliciously. 'Only one person was present both times – when I had my stand-off with the protest bitch and when anecdotes about Melbourne were being told. He's a dead man walking, thanks to you.'

'Who?'

'You'll catch it on the news.' Billy turned to go. 'See you around. Next time I'll make sure I'm packing too.'

With that he strode out of the basement.

Once he'd disappeared up the ramp, Rita blew out a sigh and lowered the gun. When she'd holstered it and calmed her nerves she squatted down again to look for any indication of the crime she was sure had happened close by. Nothing was obvious and the lighting was too dim.

She stood up and pulled out her mobile – no signal – so she made her way from the basement and around to the central courtyard. A couple of hundred metres ahead of her, down by the entrance, Billy was gesturing at the council inspectors as he stormed through the gates. He was wasting his anger, of course. Short of a seismic reversal of fortune, his money was gone, the

259

green lobby had won and the rainforest would reclaim the massive skeleton of his resort, smothering it at birth. A good result all around. It seemed like natural justice.

As soon as a signal registered Rita phoned Sutcliffe.

'What's up?' he asked.

'A potential crime scene,' she answered. 'If you can get some of your detectives to the Ridgeway site with their science kit, I'll tell you where they should look.'

'Let me guess – you think you've found where the man in the mud bit the dust.'

'If my guess is right, yes. And cement dust at that.'

Rita had just rejoined the Bruce Highway above the outskirts of the town when she got a panicked call from Freddy. He was yabbering incoherently.

'Hang on a minute!' she shouted into the mobile. Then, when she'd pulled over onto the verge, she said, 'Okay, take a breath, and say that again, slowly.'

'You promised to protect my back!' he yelled. 'Well, I'm calling in your promise. Now!'

'What's happening, Freddy?'

'I'm being chased by gangsters – from both sides of the law – and it's a toss-up who's gonna kill or maim me first!'

'Where are you?'

'In a shed.'

'That's a great help. Tell me somewhere we can meet up.'

'Okay, okay. I'll park in the street behind Mangrove Joe's. Do you know it?'

'Yes. What are you driving?'

'A Land Rover Discovery.'

'What colour?'

'Silver,' said Freddy. 'And rust.'

'Stay put. I'll be there in five minutes.'

Rita accelerated back into the highway traffic.

True to her word, she pulled up behind Freddy's car a few minutes later at the rear of the arcade bar. His description of the vehicle's colour scheme was accurate. The silver bodywork bore the scars of misuse, with dents and scrapes etched in rust. He was clearly a punishing driver.

She parked the Falcon, got out and looked around for suspicious characters, gangsters or otherwise. All she saw was a quiet backstreet with a couple of elderly shoppers strolling lazily in the sun. As she walked towards the Land Rover she could see Freddy watching her approach in his wing mirror. She opened the kerbside door, climbed in and sat in the passenger seat beside him.

'Right,' said Rita. 'You've got my undivided attention.'

'I need more than that,' said Freddy. 'Have you got a gun?'

'Yes. Why?'

'Because you're not much of a bodyguard without one.'

'I'm taking on the role of your private minder, am I?'

'Bloody oath, yeah.' His hands were on the wheel as he scanned the surroundings nervously. 'Until I get clear of Whitley.'

'Where to?'

'A place just up the coast. A safe haven.'

'Why do you need me?'

'Because Billy Bowers has got his bouncers prowling the roads out of town on the lookout for me. They're in red Porsche Turbos, so if you spot one, tell me.'

'They're on Freddy patrol, huh?'

'This isn't funny! Billy thinks I stuffed him with the cops. He'll fucking kill me!'

'Were you there when he threatened Rachel?'

'No.'

'Then you're not his Most Wanted. Someone else is.'

'That hardly cheers me up. Anyway, I've just been grabbed by that American psycho again – dragged into the back of a van, debagged and damn near deballed!'

'Kurt Demchak?'

'Who's he?'

'An official at the base.'

'Official, my arse! Kurt's the sort of military hood who blows people away. He makes Billy's goons look like cowboys.'

'I'm yet to meet him.'

'I wish I could say the same. He makes you realise we've got our own brand of state-sponsored terror.' Freddy froze, his eyes locked on the rear-vision mirror. 'Oh, fuck!'

'What's up?'

'Don't turn around. A red Porsche is coming through the crossroads behind us, slowing down.' There was a screech of tyres. 'Shit! They're onto us!'

As the Porsche jerked into reverse, Freddy hit the ignition, the engine growling into life. With Billy's men turning for pursuit, Freddy revved up the power. He held back a moment, timing it, then stamped on the accelerator. He swung the big car wildly into the middle of the road as the Porsche roared up, forcing it to swerve aside violently and go thumping over the opposite gutter, its engine stalling.

Freddy, with Rita frowning beside him, was away, the Land Rover's wheels kicking up a shriek of rubber.

'What are you doing?' she shouted.

'What's it look like? Making a run for it!'

Rita glanced over her shoulder at the Porsche, swinging back onto the road for the chase.

'You're not going to outrun a Porsche in this tank,' she said.

'If we make it to the cane fields, we can.'

He took a hand off the wheel to scrabble around on the dash, then popped a pill.

'Are you on speed?' she asked.

'Mild uppers. To grease the reflexes.' With Freddy gunning the engine, the Land Rover roared along a link road, his pursuers gaining ground. 'I knew this would happen. They've been creeping around after me all day.'

He narrowly missed colliding with a sheep lorry as he cut across its path onto the highway, horn blaring. The trailing Porsche had to slam on its brakes to avoid a side-on crash.

'Come on, come on, come on!' urged Freddy, picking up speed. 'A couple of k and we'll shake them.'

But the Porsche was soon closing the gap again, matching Freddy's lane changes as he weaved in and out, overtaking everything in his path.

'This is crazy!' said Rita. 'You can't play dodgems on the damn highway!'

'Oh, no,' he groaned, as they bore down on a queue of vehicles halted by red lights at a busy intersection on the edge of town. 'This is no time to stop.'

Without indicating, he swung across traffic to the squeal of tyres and a chorus of horn blasts, and zoomed off along a side road. It wasn't long before the Porsche was following.

'Buckle up, Van Hassel!' he said, a manic note in his voice. 'We're taking some shortcuts!'

Rita heeded his advice, grappling with the seatbelt and locking it as the four-wheel drive lurched around a bend in a spray of pebbles. Freddy veered off at a junction with a gravel service road, spewing out a cloud of dust in his wake as the car juddered over humps and potholes.

'They'll have to slow down,' he cried out above the noise, 'or bugger their suspension.'

Rita turned to look through the rear window. Sure enough the Porsche was easing back. It fell further behind and out of sight as they skirted the raised banks of a reservoir and raced on past a quarry and a rubbish tip, Freddy wrenching the wheel just in time to avoid smacking into a dumpster.

'Outta the way, arsehole!' he yelped, swinging the car onto the roadside bank and accelerating past.

Rita shuddered at the near miss but saw the benefit of Freddy's dose of amphetamine.

When they reached a T-junction, he took a hard right. They were travelling on a sealed surface again.

'Do you know where you're going?' she asked.

'We're on Golf Links Road,' he answered. 'And we're heading in the right direction.'

With no sign of the Porsche on the stretch of road behind, Freddy kept up the pace along a broad curve of avenue lined with flowering wattle trees, then around a brick-walled corner of Whitley cemetery, only to find he was hurtling towards the slow procession of a funeral with not enough room to stop.

He whipped the wheel sideways – 'Hang on!' – and cannoned past the cortege like a sacrilegious joyrider, startling the driver of the hearse, which slipped into a ditch, dislodging its wreaths.

Rita voiced her disapproval. 'Not nice, Freddy.'

'It was that or ram them.'

'You've just earned a thousand years in purgatory.'

'Better than Billy giving me hell.'

Before the words were out of his mouth he was jamming on the brakes as they rounded a freight depot and skidded to a halt just short of a coal train rattling through a rail crossing.

'Shit,' he said.

'Why don't we just stop here and let me deal with the bouncers?' Rita suggested.

'You've gotta be kidding. Those fuckers are tooled up with shotguns.'

'Shotguns?' Rita thought about it as the train cleared the crossing. 'Then what are you waiting for? Shift it!'

He flattened the accelerator pedal and they thumped over the rail lines as the Porsche raced into view behind. It was cutting the distance rapidly. Up ahead was a long straight sweep of open road.

'Time to improvise,' said Freddy.

He hauled the car into a sliding turn that took them through the entrance of the Whitley golf course.

'Where does this lead?'

'To the clubhouse,' he said, 'but don't let it bother you.'

'If you say so.'

With the white weatherboard building looming ahead, Freddy only increased the speed.

'Brace yourself!' he warned. 'We're going off-road!'

Aiming directly at the clubhouse garden of ornamental shrubbery, the Land Rover smashed through it with a thud, the wheels chewing and spitting out a crush of myrtle bushes before bursting through hedges on the far side, to the astonishment of members wheeling their golf bags. There was no way of avoiding the number one tee, and the car tore through it, forcing players to scatter.

'That's some divot you left behind,' said Rita, looking over her shoulder to see the Porsche emerge from the trail of mangled shrubs. 'Billy's boys don't give up easily, do they?'

'Me neither.'

Down the fairway Freddy charged, horn honking to alert the golfers. An alarmed pair on a buggy wobbled erratically into the rough as the Land Rover flashed past. The end of the fairway was hemmed in by strands of banksia and water obstacles, so the only option, with the Porsche slicing through the grass on their tail, was to head straight for the green. Four players were casually lining up putts until they witnessed the mayhem descending on them like a hoon rally. They flung their clubs and bolted out of the way, one of them jumping into a sand trap, another toppling into a pond. With the way clear, Freddy ploughed straight across the green, flattening the flag and burying the cup, before dropping with a thud over the bunker on the far side.

'Hole in one!' he laughed.

'And a double bogey for Billy's bouncers,' added Rita, watching the Porsche grind to a halt on the lip of the bunker, unable to risk the drop.

'Yay!' shouted Freddy, with glee. 'We're winning!'

By the time they emerged from the back gates of the course their pursuers were more than a fairway length behind. A maintenance road led directly to a wide expanse of cane fields. With the crushing season underway, Freddy took his time picking a way through the crop to avoid the cane cutters. When he found a deep rutted track he turned onto it. The Land Rover was half a kilometre along it before the Porsche appeared. Instead of following, it stopped. After a moment, it sped off along the road.

'I told you we'd do it,' said Freddy, with a note of triumph in his voice.

'Where does this lead?' asked Rita.

'Just one way – to the coast road.'

'And do the bouncers know that?'

'Oh, shit. They'll try to cut us off.'

He gripped the wheel with renewed determination as the car sped along the track through hectare after hectare of tall green cane, affording the occasional glimpse of sugar mills and chopper harvesters in the distance. The fields ended at a bend of the coast road that was empty of traffic. Freddy pulled onto it and headed north. The road climbed over a bluff with a rocky point below, where waves frothed over reefs and a clutch of islets dotted a bay.

They were nearing the bottom of a dip when the Porsche streaked over the crest behind, closing rapidly. To Rita's surprise, Freddy turned off the road onto what looked like an old cobbled path sloping down an incline to the beach. Seconds later, the Porsche did the same. With less than fifty metres between the vehicles Freddy accelerated towards the water. He was aiming at where the path disappeared under the waves in what looked like a slipway.

'Are you nuts?' cried Rita.

She grabbed hold of the arm rest as the Land Rover hit the water with a splash and, amazingly, surged forward unhindered, the wheels gripping solidly without losing momentum.

'What is this?' she asked.

'A tidal causeway,' he answered.

She spun around in time to see the Porsche hit the water and slew sideways, engine-deep, wallowing in the waves, unable to go any further. The bouncers were clambering out, waterlogged and defeated.

'Good timing,' said Rita. 'So where does this causeway lead?'

'That little island, dead ahead.'

Driving steadily now, Freddy guided the car towards an isolated rise of land that lay like a hump in the middle of the bay. Rita could make out a cluster of buildings, and as they got closer she saw they were made of stone with slate roofs and arched windows. The look was old and weathered, the style Victorian Gothic. On the slopes around them were what appeared to be vegetable gardens and orchards of mango and banana trees. She could even see pigs and sheep wandering around.

The car rose, dripping, from the causeway beside a jetty with a boat tied to it, bobbing on the waves. Freddy followed a cobbled lane to a courtyard and parked next to a kombi van with an image of the Virgin and Child painted on its door.

'What *is* this place?' asked Rita, baffled.

'St Cedd's Monastery,' answered Freddy, switching off the engine. 'Welcome to my safe haven.'

43

Of all Rita's encounters since arriving in Whitley, this struck her as the most bizarre. She and Freddy were sitting on canvas chairs in the middle of cloisters, the rays of the afternoon sun casting a mellow light on the stone of the surrounding colonnade. There was a fishpond with lilies and a small fountain tinkling above the flagstones, and grapevines clung to some of the columns. Brother Ignatius was serving food and drink, with bread, cheese and olives already spread on a wooden table to which he added an unlabelled bottle of red wine and goblets. The soothing tone of voices singing psalms rose from the Blessed Sacrament Chapel nearby, drifting like a mood of calm through the fabric of the monastery.

Ignatius poured the wine, pulled up a chair and joined them.

'It's wonderful to have your company,' he said.

'Thanks for the hospitality,' replied Freddy.

'No thanks are necessary. It's our duty to offer sanctuary. As our Lord said: *When I was hungry, you gave me food; when thirsty, you gave me drink; I was a stranger and you took me in.*'

'Matthew,' noted Rita.

'Ah, a detective with spiritual interests,' said Ignatius, delight in his eyes.

'Psychological interests,' Rita corrected. 'As a profiler I need to be familiar with a wide range of symbols, including biblical myths and metaphors.'

Ignatius couldn't help smiling at her. 'And what does the word psychology mean but a science of the soul?'

'If you equate soul with mind,' said Rita.

It was obvious he was fascinated by her presence. The way he looked at her was intense and not entirely flattering. It was as if he were observing a rare sight which, in his confined environment, in a sense she was. Her novelty value wasn't lost on Rita as she watched him watching her, but there was genuine empathy in his manner as well.

He was wearing a plain cheesecloth shirt and cotton trousers and he didn't look much like a monk, but more like a teacher or doctor with an alert, engaging face behind black-rimmed glasses. Although pushing forty, he retained something of an adolescent's eagerness, a wide-eyed simplicity bolstered by the innocence of faith. To Rita's sceptical mind he also embodied a surrender to ambiguity. Many monks, she suspected, managed to remain devout and sin-obsessed at the same time, trapped in a spiritual contradiction and locked in a constant battle with their demons of repression. Whatever his inner secrets, Ignatius possessed a cheerful disposition.

'What's your religious background?' he asked.

'Dutch Protestant,' she answered. 'In my childhood.'

'Ah, Calvinism. A heavy cross to bear.'

'Well, I dismantled that piece of lumber years ago.'

'Are you sure?' Ignatius folded his hands. 'The Freudians say we never erase the influence of our early years.'

'Is that Freud you're quoting,' she parried, 'or your namesake Loyola?'

'Wonderful. A debate with an ex-Calvinist. You've made my day.'

'My pleasure. But changing to a less righteous topic, what on earth's your connection with Freddy?'

'He was a little chorister when I was an altar boy,' chuckled Ignatius. 'A cherub with a naughty attitude. As you can see, he slipped through the Jesuits' fingers.'

'Very funny,' said Freddy.

Rita turned to him, amused. 'You were a Catholic choirboy? What happened?'

'I lapsed.'

'More like a sabbatical from the faith,' said Ignatius. 'Freddy's a bad boy with a good spirit. In the end he does the right thing.'

'I hope so,' said Rita.

'And, of course, he did a great service to the monastery when he and his friend Stonefish got us online. They designed our website and keep a check on our internet services – all gratis and much appreciated.'

Freddy gave Rita a dry look. 'That should knock a few centuries off purgatory.'

She laughed and clinked her goblet against his. 'You'll need all the brownie points you can get.' She raised the glass to her lips, swallowed a mouthful of wine, and gave a nod of approval.

'A full-bodied shiraz,' explained Ignatius. 'Product of a monastic vineyard.'

'This monastery?'

'No, one that's inland. We're a very small community these days, down to just a dozen brothers. No new recruits. We're self-sufficient, but that's about it. The life of a monk is losing its appeal in our increasingly secular world.'

'What you've got here is very peaceful and civilised,' said Rita. 'Though I'm not sure what I'm doing here, other than sharing Freddy's refuge. I should be getting back to Whitley.'

'Relax, Van Hassel,' said Freddy. 'You're marooned here until the next low tide.'

'Then I'd better phone DSS Sutcliffe.' She pulled out her mobile and looked at it. 'No signal.'

'It's erratic,' said Ignatius. 'But you might want to hold off on that call anyway.' He gestured at a fourth canvas chair, currently unoccupied, that he'd placed beside the table. 'There's someone who wants to meet you – someone you need to talk to.'

Rita was puzzled. 'Okay. I seem to have plenty of time on my hands. Who is it?'

Ignatius gestured. 'Here he comes now.'

She turned to see the figure of a man emerging from a shadowed archway in a corner of the cloisters.

Rita didn't recognise him, but Freddy did.

'Stonefish!' he shouted.

It took Rita a few moments to absorb the implications. She was sitting in a monastic retreat, sharing bread and wine with a monk, a hacker and a man who held the key to murder. The three of them were close friends and, in different ways, subversive – Ignatius perhaps merely by association, although his gleeful sense of humour betrayed an underlying irreverence towards anything other than his vocation. Petty crime, felonies and defrauding the state were problems for the secular authorities. If they didn't bother God, they didn't bother him.

'Between the two of you,' he told his friends, 'you've got a backlog of confessing to get through.'

'I'm doing penance enough,' joked Stonefish, 'shacked up in a monk's cell, like a stud with his balls in a clamp.'

'Or a mongrel in a kennel,' laughed Freddy.

'Either way, no dogging around.'

'No wonder I couldn't find you,' said Freddy. 'I thought you were holed up in Whitley.'

'You and every other arsehole.'

'A lot of people want to talk to you. Not only Van Hassel here, but a bunch of heavies from the base. Billy Bowers too. He wants the disk you've got.'

Stonefish, suddenly serious, held up a hand to cut him short. 'Quiet, dude. It's a bad subject for you and Iggy to hear about.' With a sombre expression, he turned to Rita. 'I suggest you and I take a walk together. Leave these two Holy Romans to finish their lunch in peace.'

'Okay,' she agreed and got up from her chair.

'Let's take in the sights.' He showed her the way out of the cloisters. 'I think I know every square metre of St Cedd's Island by now. I've had so much time to meditate around it.'

'Resulting in any revelations?'

'Yeah. I'm safer here than anywhere else. If I leave the island, I'm dead meat.'

Stonefish wasn't quite what Rita had expected. Tall, with a shrewd, amiable face and a physique worthy of a footballer, he was an odd mixture of sensitivity and hooligan profanity. In his *Charlie Don't Surf* T-shirt, baggy shorts and sandals he seemed self-conscious as he walked beside her, but despite a gentle demeanour, she reminded herself, this man possessed black-market expertise, criminal connections and inside knowledge about brutal killings.

'Are you going to tell me your real name?' asked Rita.

'That's one secret I plan to keep,' said Stonefish.

'Surely not out of modesty.'

'Out of self-preservation. Too many skeletons in the case files. No one even knows my current passport name.'

Rita guessed he was on the wanted list in more than one country and under more than one identity. He didn't sound strictly New Zealander, more trans-Pacific, his original accent overlaid with an American West Coast drawl. For all his casual attitude, he wasn't someone to be taken lightly. It made her wary.

'I'm not interested in your history,' she said.

'Good. You might not act or look like a cop, but you're still a cop.'

They followed a path from the chapter house and refectory wing past garden sheds, vegetable plots and through a melon patch.

'You know you're in trouble, don't you?' she said.

'Trouble? I'd call it deep shit. That's why I've been lying low, out of sight of everyone.'

'Then why come out for me? There was no need to show yourself today.'

'Brother Iggy told me how you helped Freddy. And, like it or not, at some point I'm going to need the cops onside.' He gave her a wry look. 'Anyway, I've been keeping up with your progress from a distance. From what I hear, you're treading dangerously yourself.'

'How'd you hear that?'

'Electronic inquiries, contacts, the grapevine.'

'Eve Jaggamarra?'

'Among others.' Stonefish pulled a small plastic bag from his pocket. 'I think we have common enemies.'

They were strolling through an olive grove that filled a gully on the island.

'You've got a lot of explaining to do,' Rita told him, 'if you want me onside, as you put it.'

'I know. But no matter what Iggy says, as far as Whitley goes I'm more sinned against than sinning.'

He stopped in the shade of an olive tree, selected a ready-rolled joint and slid the bag back in his pocket.

'I try not to smoke indoors,' he said, lighting up. 'Don't want to get the monks high. Want a drag?'

She shook her head. 'No thanks.'

'If I tell you stuff off the record,' he went on, 'can I trust you to keep it that way?'

'There are a couple of conditions.'

'Such as?'

'I need to know you're not involved in murder.'

'Fuck no! I'm the one who could be walking around with a death sentence passed against me. Not by any court, either. I would've thought you'd figured that out for yourself.'

'It fits one of my theories, yes.'

'Bully for you.' He sucked the smoke into his lungs and held it, taking a hit from the dope before slowly releasing it through his nostrils. 'What's your other condition?'

'You tell me everything you know about the disk.'

'No problem. I was planning to do that anyway. I can't get off this island till all the crap about the disk is sorted out.'

'What makes you think you're safe here? Why not put more distance between yourself and Whitley?'

'If there's a contract out on me, it'd be pointless to run. I'm better off staying on St Cedd's. There's one way in and out, with the brothers providing a perfect shield and cover. Anyway, I've got business to attend to. I need to stay local.'

'So you *do* go into town?'

'Only if I have to. I hide in the back of the kombi when one of the brothers drives in. Great camouflage – a monk-mobile.' Stonefish took another drag on the joint. 'There's another reason to use this as a bolthole. The monastery's out of Panopticon's range. It's beyond the ten k sector. Those freaks at the base can't spy on me here, and they don't know where to look.'

'Panopticon. That's the crux of the case. It started with Dr Steinberg, didn't it?'

'Dear old Konrad.' Stonefish puffed out a stream of smoke. 'He was more than a whistleblower. He wanted the project scrapped, wanted the whole edifice of Whitley Sands to come crashing down. You realise that would make him a traitor to those at the top – to someone like that jack-booted *oberleutnant* Maddox.'

'Actually, he'd see Steinberg as an enemy operative, a valid target. And Maddox wouldn't be alone.' Rita folded her arms. 'Why you? Why did Steinberg give the disk to you?'

'Beer. German beer.'

'Am I supposed to make sense of that?'

'He and I shared a taste for the imported brew at the Whitley Bierkeller, the only bar in town with the real thing from the Deutscher Brauer-Bund. We met when he beat me in a drinking contest – very impressive for an egghead. Steinberg by name, Steinberg by nature. From that moment on we raised our steins together.'

'He breached national security because you were drinking buddies?'

'We bonded over beer. It's a male thing. Women don't get it.'

Rita sighed. 'And the disk?'

'He talked about the base when he got pissed – Fortress Whitley, Camp Paranoia, that sort of thing – and how Panopticon would do more harm than good. The guy was under a lot of pressure. I don't know how much it affected his judgement, but he wanted the campaigners to know they were right to protest. He was the one behind the leak last year when he told me a hi-tech weapon was being developed at the Sands for deployment against militants. I passed it on to Rachel Macarthur, who put it on the net. After that he decided to help them more.'

'So he compiled his report and burnt it onto the *Rheingold* disk.'

'Which he handed to me at the Bierkeller to give to Rachel.'

'But you didn't, did you?' said Rita. 'You decided to hang onto it for your own purposes, downloading from the disk and providing Rachel with a printout, like a sample of merchandise.'

'Okay, okay.' Stonefish stared out to sea where a bulk freighter rode heavily in the water. 'I saw an angle in it for myself. But Steinberg was a Wagnerian oddball. Not playing with a full string section, if you know what I mean. It's another reason I liked him. With his rambling preface on the disk he sure sounded like a crank. All that guff about electromagnetic waves, brain chemistry and subarachnoid haemorrhages. I didn't know if it was genuine shit or a stressed-out hophead fantasy.'

'Brain haemorrhages?'

'Steinberg reckoned the same thing that made Panopticon a technical success – the EM pulses or whatever – also increased the risk of brain haemorrhages in the population by a factor of five.'

'Have you got that right?' Rita frowned.

'He pulled figures from local medical records and said they showed a fivefold increase in the number of brain haemorrhages within the sector since Panopticon was up and running. It sounded like mad boffin city to me, but I could see the propaganda value for the campaigners.'

'And the desperate need to suppress it by those running the base,' added Rita. 'My God. The Steinberg report is a bigger threat to the project than terrorism.'

'And a pretty strong motive for murder.'

'And completely justified, if you think purely in military terms. It's not murder, it's part of warfare. Taking down the enemy.'

Stonefish flicked ash away. 'But it's not a military issue, is it?'

'No. It's contempt for the law, for democratic principles, the worst violation of human rights. What makes it even worse, Steinberg would have got his facts right. Others are dying. Random members of the public. That makes it a crime against humanity.'

'Collateral damage.' Stonefish cleared his throat thickly. 'What are you going to do about it?'

Rita bowed her head, pacing back and forth. 'So. Steinberg's death was an illegal execution. I can lay that at the base's door. But the other murders – the decapitations – how do they fit in?'

'You don't swallow that bullshit about a deranged serial killer?'

'No, though I'm meant to. They're professional hits. But why? What's the agenda?' Rita was thinking aloud. 'Like the Grail knights there's a question the Maoists ask about any given incident: whom does it serve? That's what I don't have a clear answer to.'

There was a momentary silence between them. Rita watched a mob of cockatoos settle in a stand of tea-trees along the shoreline below. Stonefish finished his joint, dropped it and ground it under his heel.

'Well, between the two of us we can take a crack at it,' he said. 'What do you want to know?'

Rita refocused her attention. 'The man in the mud,' she said. 'Who was he?'

Stonefish gave a half-hearted laugh. 'I don't know exactly. Drug dealer. Mr Mystery.'

'Sorry?'

'That's what we called him – "Mr Mystery". He travelled around South-East Asia on a French passport out of New Caledonia under the name Jean-Paul Mistere.'

'What was he doing in Whitley?'

'He turned up a few months ago looking for action. I liked him and he supplied good dope. I put a few business errands his way. Of course I recognised the e-fit picture of him after the body parts floated ashore.' Stonefish raised his eyebrows. 'When I heard you'd been drafted into the investigation I guessed why.'

'Go on.'

'I was with him at the Diamond when he wrote your name on a beer coaster and stuck it in his boot for future reference.'

'Why?'

'Blackmail, maybe. He was always working an angle, asking questions, making connections.'

'How'd he get my name?'

'When he and I went up to the office at the Diamond, to do a bit of business, one of the Monotti boys was there – dope supplier, big talker. He regaled us with stories about how Billy beat a bestiality rap in Melbourne and was still putting on live sex shows at his villa – hookers with his dogs. Billy grinned but looked uncomfortable, especially when your name came up. Mr Mystery wrote it down when we went back to the bar, thinking it might come in handy.'

'Was it you who told the *Whitley Times* reporter about Billy's past?'

'Damn right.'

'And that Bowers threatened Rachel?'

'Yep. She had a lot of guts. There was just a handful of us at the club when Rachel burst in on her own and confronted Bowers. He's a bully and a psycho. For all I know he killed her and Mr Mystery, then did the reporter too.'

'The Homicide detectives say he did.'

'He deserves to go down for being the celebrity scum he is.' Stonefish grimaced. 'But there's something else. I didn't just hand the reporter the dirt on Bowers. I also delivered a download from the *Rheingold* disk. She was working on both stories.'

'Shit,' said Rita. 'That throws it wide open again. What about your New Caledonian pal, Jean-Paul Mistere – did he have a printout?'

'He could have. The disk was in a drawer at the flat where we did business, so he had access and opportunity. And like I said, he was very enterprising.'

'Where's the disk now?'

'Rockhampton – but don't ask for the exact location.'

Rita fell silent again. She watched the cockatoos squabbling in the tea-trees then rising in a mass of white feathers and raucous cries before swooping towards the other side of the island. As their squawking faded they left behind the calm of the day. A gentle breeze hissed through the leaves overhead. Out to sea a group of yachts, spinnakers bellying as they ran before the wind, cut a broad arc through the waves.

Stonefish had leant his back against the trunk of an olive tree, observing her carefully. 'Have you got your head around it yet?' he asked.

She turned to him with a weary smile. 'I'm getting there. You've filled in a lot of pieces. I'm glad I caught up with you at last.'

'We're dealing with some evil pricks, aren't we?'

'Absolutely. But I don't know if they're acting in tandem. I need to distinguish the pricks from the predators.'

'How do you mean?'

'Spot the ones with blood on their hands.'

'Well, serial killer or not,' said Stonefish, 'Bowers needs to be stopped.'

'It's hard to stomach,' said Rita, 'that he's still putting on shows with dogs.'

'Yeah, a girl was crying to me at the Diamond after a date with Tyson and Clay.'

Rita grabbed his arm. 'Those names – who are they?'

Stonefish looked at her, startled. 'Billy's German shepherds,' he answered. 'He named them after the boxers.'

Rita climbed towards the high point of St Cedd's Island past a goat enclosure and a water tank, then followed a rough track through clumps of wild fennel and blackberry brambles until her mobile registered a signal. She sat on a boulder beside a small graveyard, phone in hand, considering how much to tell Sutcliffe.

The problem was she'd crossed a line. On one side of it were police officers, military commanders, government officials and procedural rules. On the other side was Rita. Morally she had no qualms about the methods she'd used to gain information. There was no choice for someone who put justice above institutional directives. She recalled Martin Luther's defiance – 'Here I stand, I can do no other!' – and realised that Brother Ignatius might be right after all. The Protestant ethic, drummed into her as a child, could still be shaping her fate.

Nevertheless, from a legal standpoint, she'd conducted herself less like a profiler or investigator than a rogue detective. To make her position even more perilous, she was acting against some of the very authorities who already perceived her as unreliable and wouldn't hesitate to crush her. Again, she had no doubt she was in the right. They were exceeding their powers and acting like a star chamber or a gang of vigilantes. Her problem, of course, was to prove that they were breaking the law.

As she pondered her next move, the sun dipped below the ranges on the far side of the tidal basin. The muted glow spread a soft light along the coast, shading the sky above the gums and palm trees with tints of old gold. High tide was peaking, the beaches all but submerged. Out to sea, among the scattered dots of the Whitsundays, the sun traced the texture of the waves in sparkles of silver filigree. From her vantage point Rita enjoyed an unhindered view of the eastern horizon, where the edge of the Pacific spanned the delicate curve of the planet. It occurred to her that she was looking at a perspective beyond human time. It was like a glimpse of eternity.

Perhaps it was the beauty of the sunset that moved her. Or maybe it was the awareness of being perched on the elevated tip of a religious site, a holy island, where men had prayed for divine guidance for more than a century. Or it could simply have been what psychologists called an 'oceanic feeling' that was welling up in her. Whatever provoked her sense of wonder also heightened her resolve to go it alone.

Rita had long ago rejected the religious ideology of God. The source of intelligence, however, remained a mystery to her, like a timeless presence, and it was the closest she came to religious belief. As such, it implied that no act of integrity should be seen in isolation, that each quest for justice reflected a universal drive within human beings. Therefore to seek the truth, no matter what the consequences, was not really to go it alone. It united her with all others who did the same.

Having made up her mind, she was ready to speak to Sutcliffe.

The screen on her mobile showed four missed calls from him, the most recent just half an hour ago. When she phoned he was relieved to hear from her.

'You had me worried,' he said. 'I got a nasty feeling you'd had a run-in with Billy after bumping into him at the building site.'

'What's happened?' she asked.

'He's nowhere to be found. Doesn't make him look good. Especially as I've got more stuff to add to the case against him.'

'Me too,' said Rita. 'But you first.'

'My boys have done a good job,' Sutcliffe told her. 'I sent a couple of them to the Ridgeway site with their forensic kits after you called it in.'

'Good.'

'They examined the workshop table and found blood on the legs,' Sutcliffe went on. 'That's not all. They tested for residues on the table surface and revealed blood traces at one end. Get this. The spatter pattern was interrupted by objects in two places.'

'What objects?'

'Hands. The blood showed the outlines of two hands, flat on the table.'

'He was tortured,' said Rita.

'It gets better. Now that table's taken a lot of punishment over time, lots of nicks and scrapes, chips knocked out of it and so on. But my boys weren't satisfied until they'd taken a closer look. In the middle of the hand outlines, right where the palms would be, were two round holes. They were consistent with puncture marks made by a nail gun.'

'That would explain the vertical wound through his head, unlike the other nail-gun victims, including Rachel,' said Rita. 'He was shot through the top of the skull while sitting with his hands nailed to the table.'

'That's why I was calling you,' explained Sutcliffe. 'The basement garage is now taped off as a crime scene and the table's on its way to the lab. DNA tests will confirm if the blood's that of the man in the mud.'

'Excellent. And I can put a name to him at last.'

'How have you managed that?'

'A tip-off from an informer,' she answered evasively.

'I get the feeling you've been flying under the radar.'

'Not so much flying as rally-car racing.'

'Via the golf club, by any chance?'

'Let me fill you in,' she said. 'I was in Freddy Hopper's Land Rover when he set off like a bat out of hell with Billy's bouncers in hot pursuit. By the way, their cars need to be searched. Apparently they travel with shotguns.'

'So noted,' said Sutcliffe.

'Freddy also needed to beat the tide. That's why I'm currently watching the sunset from the top of St Cedd's Island.'

'What's there?'

'A monastery.' Right on cue, the chiming of a bell rose through the evening air. 'That's the angelus you can hear in the background.'

'And you're there because . . . ?'

'With Billy after him, Freddy's claiming sanctuary. And I'm stuck here for another few hours until the tide goes out. Freddy thinks he's safe but I wouldn't put it past Bowers and his goons to try something. I think we should post an officer by the causeway at low tide.'

'I'll sort it out.'

'Good. Now, the true identity of the man in the mud.'

'Let's hear it.'

'I'm told the name he went by was Jean-Paul Mistere,' she replied. 'Known to the local underworld as Mr Mystery. He travelled on a French passport, issued in New Caledonia.'

'What was he?'

'A regional drug dealer, apparently, open to making a few fast bucks on the side. He was present when a member of the Monotti family told how Bowers earned his nickname, how he got the better of me, and how he was still getting away with it. Monsieur Mistere wrote down my name and filed it in his boot.'

'For blackmail?'

'Possibly.'

'If he tried to blackmail Billy,' said Sutcliffe, 'that could get him dead pretty quick.'

'Definitely.'

'Good work, Van Hassel.' There was a jubilant note in Sutcliffe's voice. 'We can now positively link Billy to all the nail-gun attacks. Lawyers or not, he knows we're closing in.'

'And that will make him more dangerous than ever. One other thing. Looks like Vic Barrano was being straight about where to look for the drugs. Mike Tyson and Cassius Clay are the names of Billy's dogs.'

'Shit. We didn't search the kennels. I'll get onto it now.'

44

'This is a first for me,' said Rita.

It was after vespers and she was sharing supper with the monks in the refectory. The room had a stone floor and a low, vaulted ceiling. The only light came from candles, adding to the medieval aura of the setting, yet the mood was relaxed rather than reverential. The meal was a thick vegetable broth with fresh bread. Freddy and Stonefish were sitting opposite her, with Brother Ignatius on her left and the abbot, at the head of the table, on her right. He was a very old man, frail and stooped, with wrinkled, leathery skin.

He hardly spoke, but he responded briefly to Rita.

'It's a first for me, too, my dear,' he told her.

'Breaking bread with a woman cop?' she asked.

'No. Supping with a psychologist.'

She laughed. 'I hope that's better than supping with the Devil.'

The abbot contemplated the remark. 'Now that you mention it, I suppose the Devil must be the ultimate expert in human psychology. If I understand the subject, it requires a strong acquaintance with the dark forces inside us.'

'Yes, the pathological side of our nature,' said Rita. 'A psychologist needs to eat freely from the tree of knowledge of good and evil.'

'In disobedience to God,' commented Ignatius. 'Genesis 2:17.'

'But in accordance with the imperatives of human consciousness,' she retorted. 'Genesis 3:7.'

Ignatius chuckled. 'You cast a whole new light on the Devil quoting scripture.'

Rita gave him a sideways look. 'Don't you mean she-devil?'

'That would explain a few things,' said Freddy.

Stonefish told him to shut up.

Then the abbot turned to her with a frown, his eyes sad, as if he carried a heavy burden.

'Something has always troubled me,' he confided. 'Something that can leave me feeling bereft, despite my faith. I equate it with what St John of the Cross called "the dark night of the soul". As a psychologist, what would you call it? Depression?'

Rita put down her soup spoon. 'I need to think about that one,' she admitted. 'Correct me if I'm wrong, but doesn't the phrase refer to a feeling of loneliness on the path of spiritual growth? A test of faith?'

'That's close to the traditional interpretation,' agreed the abbot.

'Psychologically I wouldn't label it depression, no. I'd call it alienation. And that's something that afflicts us all, at times. Ever since our expulsion from Eden.'

The abbot nodded slowly. 'Thank you, my dear.' Then he added, 'You may be an agnostic, but I have no doubt you're doing God's work.'

He didn't speak again for the rest of the evening.

As they left the refectory at the end of supper, Stonefish told her, 'People accuse me of being off the wall. But you're the weirdest cop I've ever met.'

There was no problem about a night crossing of the causeway, although low tide was still a couple of hours away. Freddy had no intention of leaving the island and told Rita as much before heading off through the orchard with Stonefish to 'stretch his legs'. Get stoned was more like it, she thought. Ignatius, in the spirit of the Good Samaritan, insisted he would take her back to Whitley. He would enjoy her company on the drive, he said. After taking her on a tour of the neo-Gothic buildings, he showed her into the monastic library and switched on the lamps.

The room was heavy with oak bookcases and rows of elevated desks with sloping surfaces and inkwells.

'This was originally the scriptorium,' explained Ignatius.

'So the monastery produced its own manuscripts?'

'A long time ago, yes.'

'Fascinating.'

'Now we use the internet.'

'The Holy Ghost of the twenty-first century,' said Rita. 'Or is that heresy?'

'You're less of a heretic than you make out,' he replied. 'Now, are you happy to browse in here while I attend to my devotions?'

'I love books,' she answered. 'It's the perfect place to chill out before I face the ungodly again.'

'I'll include you in my prayers.'

'Thanks. A prayer for clarity wouldn't go amiss.'

'You've got it.'

He withdrew, leaving her to an unnatural stillness and the musty odour of the past.

She wandered along the bookcases, scanning the spines. There seemed to be endless shelves on biblical topics, Catholic philosophy, theology and scriptural exegesis. None of these grabbed her. The volumes on religious aesthetics and symbolism were more interesting and she leafed through a few of them before moving on to a collection of dusty old history books. Some were familiar to her, although the bulk of the texts had obviously been put together at the time the monastery had been founded. Very few editions had been added since the nineteenth century.

Among the works of Victorian scholarship one caught her eye purely because of the name on the binding: Josiah Brodie. The title was the cumbersome *Civilization and its War against the Barbarian Hordes*. Could this be a book by Squatter Brodie, the man who had launched his own campaign in the frontier war against the Aborigines? She pulled it from the shelf and blew off the dust before opening the slim morocco-bound volume. A biographical note confirmed that the author was indeed the local squatter, although it made no mention of his role as leader of the notorious hunting party.

Rita sat at the nearest desk, spread the book in front of her and began to read. The publication comprised one hundred pages of tightly printed text, dominated by a single theme expressed in the title. Brodie's central thesis was that history, over nearly three millennia, embodied a life and death struggle between European civilisation and every other culture, which he perceived as tribal, pagan and hostile – essentially barbaric. His great model of civilisation was the Roman Empire.

She scanned long passages arguing that the Romans were justified in their wars of aggression, suppression and occupation against all peoples alien to civilised values. The proof was the eventual collapse of the empire at the hands of the barbarian hordes when Rome weakened in its resolve, with classical civilisation vanishing into the Dark Ages. After such a cataclysmic setback it took a thousand years of medieval ignorance, during which the monasteries preserved ancient learning, before the next great flowering of civilisation: the emergence of the British Empire. But Brodie ended his book with a warning.

> There is no virtue in a weakness of the will when civilized men are confronted with the violence of savages. The British Empire spans the entire globe, with a much greater extent of territory to rule than even the Romans controlled, and therefore the threat is proportionately greater. Just as the Roman administrators did not hesitate to exert inexorable force to prevail over the bloodthirsty Celts of ancient Britain, likewise the British must prevail over the waves of barbarism that lap at the borders of the empire, whether it be in Africa or Asia or Australia. The war against savagery is neglected at our peril.

Rita closed the book with a pessimistic thud. Brodie's argument was simplistic and fanatical. She wanted to dismiss it as the idiosyncratic raving of a colonial maniac. But that was too easy. What was more disturbing was the implication of a universal mind-set – a 'them and us' interpretation of global dynamics, a reactionary vindication of killing in the so-called defence of western civilisation. It was a gloomy notion and the parallels leapt out at her – the war against barbarians, the war against savagery, the war on terror.

It seemed that such strategies eroded the very values they were supposed to defend, something Rita had to deal with in her own investigation. The problem was an inherent contradiction and the Romans had put a name to it: *exitus acta probat* – the end justifies the means. Men in charge of the research base had embraced and applied it with the inevitable result. Death.

45

'Don't assume Bowers will respect the sensibilities of the monks,' warned Rita.

Freddy and Stonefish observed her indolently. They were sitting under a fig tree outside the arched gate of the courtyard, smoking. The pungent smell of dope drifted around them.

'You think he'll try something?' asked Stonefish.

'If he wants Freddy badly enough, yes,' she replied. 'He doesn't give a damn about anyone's rights.' She was about to follow Brother Ignatius down a steep path to the car park. 'A police officer will soon be posted by the causeway, but I suggest you keep watch here tonight.'

'Good idea. We've got an uninterrupted view.'

'As long as you don't get stoned.'

'It's just a bit of blow,' said Freddy. 'To clear the cobwebs, calm the nerves.'

'Yeah, right.'

'You didn't mention *me* to your fellow cops, by any chance?' asked Stonefish.

'No. But keep your wits about you, and don't go into Whitley again.'

'Why do you say that?'

'Panopticon.'

'I've seen the diagrams,' said Stonefish. 'State of the art and all that. But if I keep a low profile –'

'I've seen it in action,' Rita interrupted. 'It's no ordinary system. Think about it – satellites, scanners, electromagnetic emitters. It's total surveillance.'

'You mean it can look inside buildings?'

'Every room in every building,' she answered. 'It has the capacity to watch and listen to anyone, anywhere within the sector.'

'No wonder the spooks love it. Must be their wet dream come true. But there's always the human element to screw up.'

'Don't be too sure. It's run by a form of machine intelligence, and the system controller happens to be a leading expert in the field – Audrey Zillman.'

'That's the bitch who fried my decks, and all my bank codes in the process,' put in Freddy. 'And I didn't notice anything human about *her*.'

'I've got a feeling she's the smartest person at the base,' said Rita.

'And the most dangerous?' asked Stonefish.

'I don't know. But I can tell you this, from personal experience: if she wants to find you, she can.' Rita gave him a probing look. 'The *Rheingold* disk. How do you know it's secure?'

'I passed it on to someone I trust.'

'You gave it to Ice?' exclaimed Freddy. 'You dipstick!'

Stonefish nodded irritably. 'Yes, Freddy. Thanks, Freddy.'

'Are you talking about Marilyn Eisler?' asked Rita.

'The one and only.'

'Why?'

'I asked her to put it in my private drop-box.'

'In Whitley?'

'No. Rockhampton.'

'Who retrieves it?'

'A courier service – but not the usual sort. Totally discreet, very expensive, known only to me. I've just given instructions on where to deliver it.'

'And you won't tell me who you're sending it to?'

'No.'

'Do you realise how much danger you've put that woman in?' said Rita. 'If she downloads from the disk she could end up dead.'

'But Billy's got nothing against her.'

'You know very well it's not just Bowers we're dealing with. His involvement doesn't explain everything. I'm convinced someone

288

at the base has had a hand in every murder – and the disk is the link. Where do I find this woman?'

'She's got an apartment at the marina,' said Freddy. 'The penthouse.'

'Ice won't download from it,' insisted Stonefish.

'Are you sure?'

'I told her not to open it and she promised.'

'Great,' said Rita. 'Just like Pandora.'

The beam of the headlights wobbled over the surface of the water as Brother Ignatius carefully guided the old kombi along the partially submerged causeway. When it reached shore he changed gears with a clunk, the engine growling as the van lumbered up the incline through low dunes and beach grass. There was little traffic as they turned onto the coast road, Rita glancing around without spotting any sign of Billy's men.

'You look worried,' said Ignatius.

She gave a grunt. 'A feature of the job.'

'I admire your fortitude.'

'Is that what you call it?'

'Yes, I think so,' he answered seriously. 'After your remark about facing the ungodly I prayed to Saint Michael the Archangel, the patron saint of police. I asked him to protect you.'

Rita smiled. 'Thank you. That's got to be the best call for backup I've ever had.'

'And I can see how your sense of humour serves a purpose.'

'Cops tend to need it, graveyard humour. It's a defence mechanism – helps you cope.'

He nodded. 'I realise I've got the soft option in the battle against evil. I survey the world, the flesh and the Devil from the luxury of seclusion, while you're down in the trenches, locked in hand-to-hand combat.'

'I don't believe anyone has a soft option. According to the Blessed Prophet, Mohammed, the great Holy War is within oneself. Psychologically, I have no argument with that.'

Ignatius gave a quiet laugh, changing gears and pumping the accelerator to get the van up to a decent speed. They were on a broad sweep of open road with a nature reserve stretching along the foreshore and cane fields inland. The stars dusted the sky with a spectral light.

'You even quote Islam at me,' he said, amused. 'I don't think anyone has teased me the way you do.'

'A woman's prerogative.'

'Not a subject I'm familiar with.'

'You pay a high price for your seclusion,' observed Rita. 'On the other hand, you don't have women's angst inflicted on you.'

'Or women's charms.'

'But you've been tempted?'

'I'm a monk, not a saint.' He glanced at her slyly. 'And while we're back on the topic of forbidden fruit, I'm impressed you can quote Genesis at me, chapter and verse.'

'Even though my interpretation is profane.'

'You obviously don't take the story of Eden literally.'

'Do you?'

Ignatius flinched as he answered, 'I can read it symbolically.'

'I think that's the way it's supposed to be read.'

'Meaning?'

'The Garden of Eden is a psychological place,' she replied.

'You'll have to explain that.'

'Human beings – symbolised by Adam and Eve – are either *inside* the Garden or *outside* it,' said Rita. 'So the story's telling us that our psyche has two fundamental states, the natural and the alienated.'

'But you're talking about the preface to the entire Bible,' objected Ignatius. 'Surely you admit there's a spiritual dimension to the fate of Adam and Eve.'

'*Our* fate, all *humanity*,' she corrected him. 'We're all Adam and Eve. And yes, there's a spiritual equivalent to what I'm saying. *Nature* equals *oneness with God. Alienation* equals *otherness.*'

'So let's see,' he responded. 'As well as ruling out any divine, factual or geographic basis, you deny Eden has a moral message?'

'Funny you should mention it. Geographically there's a villa called Eden up on The Ridgeway. It's one of the reasons I've been thinking about it.'

'You evaded the question,' he pointed out.

'Okay. The expulsion from Eden is a metaphor: biologically, socially, intellectually we have evolved away from the natural towards the alienated.'

'And physically?'

'We still inhabit the Garden. As a species we never left it because we're part of nature – although in our minds we're separated from it.'

'And the role of God the Father?'

'Symbolic,' she said firmly. 'I can't accept any theological concept of God.'

'I can see where you're heading,' he said. 'For *separation from the Creator*, in the traditional meaning, read *separation from nature* in yours. Different, if pagan.'

'And *naturally* our great yearning is to return, to regain that sense of paradise – or oneness with nature – that's been lost.'

'That's where the role of religion comes in?'

'Or anything else that works for you,' she said. 'Psychologically you've made it back to the Garden when you feel at one with your here and now.'

'So now it's my turn to ask: do you?'

'No, I'm as screwed up as anyone else – that gnawing sense of estrangement in my head.' She sighed. 'Though for a moment there, on your island, looking at the ocean, the rainforest, the sunset – I saw Eden in all its beauty. Pity the feeling doesn't last.'

'I'm sure you're familiar with the writings of Joseph Campbell,' said Ignatius.

'Of course – perhaps the greatest authority on mythic symbolism.'

'What you just described – your experience on the island – reminds me of his phrase for what we're all seeking – *the rapture of being alive.*'

'You're in good form tonight,' said Rita. 'Years ago, while struggling with what someone recently called my "religious ambivalence", I actually crafted some blank verse on a similar theme. I gave it the title "Ekstasis".'

'Ah, from the Greek, meaning *to stand outside oneself*. Do you still remember it? Can you recite it?'

'Let's see . . . yes,' she said, recalling the words. 'A bit of un-poetic and agnostic soul-searching:

'Out of space and time:
This planet, here and now,
A life-giving sphere
Spinning through the alien void;
A habitat of natural beauty
To be experienced with wonder
Between the cataclysms
Of past and future;
A moment of rapture
In the face of annihilation;
And beyond all endings,
A premonition of peace
As the mind perceives
The stillness of eternity.'

Ignatius nodded slowly. 'That's neither un-poetic nor agnostic,' he said quietly. 'In fact it echoes the cave of Elijah.'

They drove on in silence, both distracted by their own thoughts. As the van climbed over the crest of a bluff the lights of the town came into view. Their ways would soon be parting.

'Forgive me if this sounds intrusive,' said Ignatius, breaking the silence, 'but I get the impression you suffered an intense cruelty when you were young.'

'Where do you get that from?' asked Rita.

'The way you've rejected the faith of your childhood and your ongoing battle against it. Your antagonism towards God.'

'My rejection of the Father. Nice bit of psychoanalysis, Brother Ignatius. You missed a career as a shrink.'

'I apologise if . . .'

'No need. You're bang on the money.' Rita gave a bitter laugh. 'My father walked out when I was seven. The emotional trauma has coloured my life ever since – one of the reasons I'm both a police detective and a psychologist. You see, I've applied my own critique to myself. Conclusion? My pursuit of justice is prompted by childhood betrayal, profiling is an attempt to make sense of the despicable, and my driven personality is a backlash against my irrational guilt over losing my father's love. And you've just added my rejection of God as a response to paternal abandonment. If I'm objective about it, I have to accept it's all accurate and undoable.'

'I don't wish to presume but . . .'

'Presume away.'

'It's clearly a matter of principle for you to be unyielding towards those who hurt others. But you seem to be even harder on yourself.'

'You're not the first to make that appraisal,' she said.

'And while you dismiss "theological concepts of God", it must be clear to you that the creative source of the cosmos is beyond definition, even to scientists.'

'Some of whom think it's more like a great thought than a great machine,' she agreed. 'The universe as intelligence expressing itself. What's your point?'

'You're not just at war with the ungodly,' he answered. 'You're in conflict with God.'

'Interesting diagnosis.' Rita's sarcasm was slipping through. 'What remedy do you recommend?'

'Forgive yourself,' he said flatly. 'And make peace with your God.'

'*My* God?'

'Exactly. Him, Her or It – whatever concept of the eternal presence resonates in your soul.' He blew out a sigh. 'Now there's heresy for you.'

They both laughed. After such a heavy conversation it was something of a relief.

As they drove into Whitley she directed him to where her car was parked in the street behind Mangrove Joe's. Ignatius pulled up beside it, engine still running. Rita opened the door and got out.

'Thanks for the lift,' she said. 'And a therapeutic debate.'

'My pleasure. You'll always be welcome at St Cedd's, even if it's just to refresh your view of Eden.'

She shut the door and he negotiated an awkward U-turn, waving to her from his open window.

'I still think I'm right about Genesis!' she laughed, as he drove off.

Rita walked slowly over to the Falcon, got behind the wheel and sighed.

So much for paradise, she thought.

She opened her bag and pulled out something Stonefish had given her. It was a glossy business card inscribed with the words *Ice for Spice*. Rita's immediate task was to find out if Ice had ignored instructions and downloaded from the *Rheingold* disk. If she had, more hell would break loose.

46

It was the most exclusive apartment block in Whitley Marina Village, ten storeys of Tuscan-style architecture behind a wall of imitation rustic stone. Wrought-iron gates opened onto a driveway lined with cypress trees. Rita drove down it and parked in a forecourt lit by lanterns and fringed with trellises. The place was quiet with no one around, just the sounds from the nearby marina, the wash of the waves and the clink of rigging against the masts. She walked through a portico with terracotta roof tiles, showed her ID to the night concierge and took the lift to the top floor.

She was crossing the landing to the penthouse suite when the door opened and a man in a pinstripe suit emerged, his tie askew and cheeks flushed. As he stepped aside for Rita they recognised each other. She couldn't remember his name but his face was familiar from among the ranks of bureaucrats attending the security review at the base. Grimacing, his eyes bloodshot and alcohol on his breath, he moved hastily to the lift.

She turned to the young woman leaning in the doorway of the apartment, a picture of lubricious charm in a gold scoop top, miniskirt and gold stilettos. At first glance her breasts were so prominent it was impossible to ignore them, though the augmentation was obvious. To Rita's mind the contours were out of proportion – a petite frame carrying too much superstructure. The girl's face was equally disconcerting, with accentuated eyes, lips and cheekbones giving her a sensual, almost savage beauty. Presumably that was the intention. From her platinum blonde hair to the flat abdomen and shapely curve of her thighs she could market herself as top of the range, thanks to a series of surgical enhancements.

While the overall effect was dramatic, the psychological impact was questionable. This girl was only twenty-one but she had completely redesigned and reinvented herself, and while the end product was highly lucrative, it was also potentially tragic. She seemed to have reduced herself to a receptacle for male fantasies, a walking billboard offering sex for sale. Rita had seen enough prostitutes damaged by their avidity to recognise the signs of self-exploitation and the delusional motives behind it. Ice, for all her financial success, appeared to be following in their footsteps.

'Marilyn Eisler?' Rita asked.

'My professional name is Ice,' she said. 'I see you've got my business card but not an appointment. What do you want?'

'To talk.'

'At midnight? Must be some conversation you've got in mind. Who are you?'

'Detective Sergeant Marita Van Hassel.'

'A cop. I should've guessed. Where'd you get my card?'

'From your mate Stonefish.'

Ice folded her arms, trying to size up her visitor. 'What's this about?'

'The disk he gave you. There could be repercussions. Can I come in?'

'Not so fast. Are you saying I'm in trouble?'

'No. I'm saying you're in danger,' replied Rita, annoyed. 'Especially if you opened the disk.'

'Why would I do that?'

'Curiosity.' Rita gave her a penetrating look. 'You did download from it, didn't you?'

'So what?'

'It's linked to the murders in Whitley.'

Ice hugged her arms more tightly. 'Rachel's murder?'

'Yes. And maybe four others.'

With a shrug, Ice waved Rita through the door. 'Sounds like crap to me but I suppose you'd better come in.'

The penthouse had a feel of spacious luxury, the decor in keeping with the Mediterranean theme of the apartment block. There were white throw rugs on a tiled floor, expensive furnishings, ceramics and oil paintings of the Tuscan landscape, scenes of Florence. A wide balcony offered a view over the marina, lights gleaming along the breakwaters, yachts in geometric rows within their artificial harbour.

'At least you haven't disrupted business,' said Ice, kicking off her stilettos. 'That was my last customer for the night. Take a seat.'

'I need to look at your computer.'

'Sit down, for fuck's sake. I need a drink. That guy was an arsehole.'

Rita dumped her bag on the floor beside an armchair and sat down reluctantly as Ice lifted a bottle from a silver bucket and poured two glasses of champagne. She padded over in her bare feet and handed a glass to Rita before flopping back onto a sofa and taking a gulp.

'Ah, that's better. So what's all this bullshit about the disk?'

'If you've seen what's on it, I assume you realise the implications.'

'I may be a school dropout but I'm not stupid,' said Ice. 'It could shut down the base.'

'Exactly.'

'Serve the bastards right.'

'I know you're speaking from personal experience.' Rita hadn't forgotten about Ice's relationship with Paul Giles and the encounter with Maddox. 'But you don't want to make enemies of them.'

'What can they do?'

'Think about it,' said Rita. 'National security gives them an excuse to operate outside the law. Rachel Macarthur just had a printout.'

'Get real. Rachel was alone in a dark alley, at night, in the roughest part of town. That's looking for trouble.' Ice swallowed more champagne. 'Not the sort of mistake I'd make.'

'You knew Rachel?'

'I met her a few times. She tried to recruit me to the cause. I agree in principle but it's not my scene.' She shook her head and shuddered. 'The night the body was found I was there in the club.'

'With Paul Giles?'

'Yes, that dickhead.'

'Why do you say that?'

'Because he's a fucking stalker. Obsessive. And because he got me interrogated at the base.'

'By Captain Roy Maddox?'

'Yeah. Another dickhead.'

'Surely that's a warning you can't ignore,' said Rita. 'He's the type who'll crush you without blinking.'

'Maddox doesn't scare me. Nor do you.' Ice tipped the rest of the champagne down her throat. 'I've been dealing with that type of man all my life. Still am.'

'Men like Bowers?'

'What I have with Billy is purely a business arrangement.' Then Ice gave a bitter laugh. 'Now I know who you are! You're the one who tried to bust him in Melbourne. I thought your name was familiar. Are you up here for another shot at putting him away?'

'Actually, Bowers is doing that all by himself. And a word of advice: keep away from him and don't let him know about the disk.'

'I told you, I'm not stupid.' She got up and refilled her glass. 'So what's your angle, Van Hassel?'

'I was seconded here to help catch Rachel's killer. That's what I'm trying to do.'

'There's got to be more to it than that. What's in it for you?'

'Nothing you'd understand. Have you still got the disk?'

'I did what Stonefish told me to – drove down the Bruce Highway and dropped it off at his private postbox in a cyber cafe in Rockhampton. It'd be gone by now.'

'In the hands of his secret courier service,' said Rita, sagging back in the chair.

She'd hoped to get her hands on the *Rheingold* disk but it had eluded her. For the moment, she didn't know what her next move should be. Perhaps there was nothing more to do tonight and she should go back to her hotel. It had been a busy day, even though the interlude at St Cedd's had been strangely peaceful. In contrast to the island monastery, the penthouse and its environment seemed synthetic – like the mock Tuscan architecture, the marina, even the woman standing across the room from her.

Rita took another sip of champagne and gazed at the landscapes on the wall. 'Have you been to Tuscany?'

'Where?'

'The scenes in the paintings – part of Italy.'

'Oh, right.' Ice pulled a face. 'I did a businessman at Rome airport once – executive lounge.'

Rita nodded. 'Close enough.'

'I paid an interior designer to sort out the apartment,' explained Ice. 'And now I'm planning to sell up and move on. I've got a lot of clients in Japan, thanks to the website.'

'So can I take a look at your computer?'

'No one looks at my computer except me and Stonefish.'

'How much of the disk did you download?'

'All of it. Saved and filed away.'

Rita put down her glass. 'Listen to me. You've got to delete it immediately.'

'No way. It's worth too much.'

'Is it worth your life?'

'You're being a drama queen. Anyway, it's already out there.'

'Meaning?'

'I've started putting it to good use,' said Ice dismissively. 'And from what you've told me, Rachel Macarthur would approve.'

'What have you done?' demanded Rita.

'I emailed it to the protest group this afternoon. They'll know what to do – and how to shove it up the bastards at the base.'

'You put it online,' said Rita with disgust. 'Brilliant. That should alert the base.'

'You can't faze me. I know how to look after myself.' Ice's hands were on her hips, eyes defiant. 'I'm smart enough to run a successful business, own luxury apartments in three other countries and still have three million bucks in the bank. What have you got to show for your hack work?'

'A future.' Rita stood up. 'You haven't listened to anything I've said.'

'Why should I? I haven't met a straight copper yet.'

'Well, I can't force you to listen.' Rita sighed and picked up her bag. 'And now I've got to track your email. Did it go to anyone in particular or just the campaign office?'

'I sent it to Stonefish's friend, Eve.'

Rita shook her head. 'For a smart woman you've been very stupid. You've not only put your own life in jeopardy, but hers too.'

Eve's phone went straight to voicemail. Rita left a message then drove fast to the other side of town, parked beside the concrete shopping centre and sprinted along the pedestrian precinct, deserted at this time of night, the sound of her footsteps echoing among the pillars as she ran. When she reached the shopfront below the campaign office she stopped and caught her breath, glancing up to the top-storey flat. The windows were open and she could see the flicker of candlelight. Soft music drifted downwards.

She found the buzzer for the flat and kept on pressing until Eve's voice came through the speaker.

'Who's that?'

'Rita Van Hassel. Sorry to call so late but I need to talk to you. It's urgent.'

'No problem. Give the door a hard push when you hear the bleep, then climb the stairs to the top.'

'Okay, thanks.'

Once inside, Rita trotted up two flights of stairs to find Eve standing in an open doorway wearing only a bra and shorts. She'd obviously pulled them on quickly. Rita smiled. This woman, with her natural beauty and effortless poise, was a refreshing sight after the encounter with Ice.

'Come in,' said Eve, gesturing at a small, untidy sitting room. 'We're a bit messy.'

Rita walked in to a clutter of lumpy furniture lit by the glow of several candles. There were cushions and sheepskin rugs on the floor, along with wineglasses – two of them. The plaintive voice of Eva Cassidy came from a music deck. The fragrance of joss sticks filled the air.

'Sorry to interrupt,' said Rita.

'That's okay.' Eve gave a wicked laugh. 'Your timing could have been worse.'

Just then the photo-journalist, Julien Ronsard, barefoot and in jeans, emerged from a passageway pulling on a T-shirt.

'Hello,' he said with a self-conscious smile. 'Nice to meet you again.'

'I wouldn't have disturbed you if it wasn't necessary.'

'Your visit is obviously important.'

'Yes,' said Rita, still trying to calm her breathing. 'So can I get straight to the point?'

'Of course,' said Ronsard. 'But at least sit down and catch your breath.'

'Would you like some water?' asked Eve.

'No, I'm fine, really,' said Rita, sitting on the edge of a chair. 'I need to ask about something that was emailed to you. It was sent by Marilyn Eisler – Ice.'

'Now that's interesting,' said Eve. 'I did get something from her this afternoon and I emailed her back but didn't get a reply. So I'm still in the dark.'

'Why?'

'Her email said she was attaching a report on Whitley Sands,' answered Eve. 'The attachment had the title *Panopticon* so I guessed it could be the same material that Rachel had. But when I opened the document it was completely blank, as if it had been erased.'

'What does it mean?' asked Ronsard.

Rita gave a sigh of relief. 'It means you're safe. Ice was trying to email what she'd downloaded from the *Rheingold* disk – the damning report on the base.'

'So what's wrong with that?' asked Eve, dropping into a chair opposite.

'You made the point yourself. The report was a factor in Rachel's death. I haven't figured it all out yet, but I'm convinced the disk has been somehow instrumental in the series of murders here.'

'Including the man in the mud?' asked Ronsard.

'Starting with him. My guess is that all the victims had direct or indirect contact with the disk.'

'So you go along with Eve's theory,' continued Ronsard, 'that officials at the base are implicated in the killings?'

'Off the record – yes.'

He nodded. 'Presumably that means the head of the security force, Captain Roy Maddox.'

'You know about Maddox?'

'We've been doing our research.' Ronsard sat down on a sheepskin rug, cross-legged. 'According to some websites, the CIA's actively involved at the base. I met a likely candidate down at the Diamond. A man called Demchak. A cold man. A violent man, I believe.'

'I've heard about him. I don't know his background. But he's certainly looking for the disk. As is the owner of the club, Billy Bowers. So you see, it's complicated.'

'You still haven't explained,' said Eve, 'why the attachment from Ice was blank.'

'I can't answer that,' said Rita. 'But if my suspicions are right, someone at the base opened and erased it.'

They fell silent for a moment, each deep in thought, with just the music playing quietly in the room, until Ronsard added, 'So the killers are watching.'

The tide was in, Brother Ignatius had returned hours earlier and Freddy was feeling completely chilled, stretched in the grass under the fig tree, gazing at the night sky.

'Time to go inside,' said Stonefish. 'No one can get across the causeway now.'

Freddy roused himself. 'Okay.'

He got up clumsily, suddenly light-headed, brushed off a few twigs and leaves, and followed his friend through the stone archway of the monastery. Without warning, Stonefish stopped dead in his tracks and Freddy stumbled into his back.

'What the –?' he began, then stopped.

Walking towards them across the courtyard were Billy Bowers and two of his bouncers.

'Well, look who we've found,' said Billy. 'Not one, but two arseholes.' He stood in front of them, blocking their way. 'Who'd have thought we'd score a double whammy by dropping in un-announced.'

'You came by boat,' said Stonefish. 'Shit.'

'Quite right,' said Billy. 'And that's how we're all gonna leave, nice and quietly, so as not to disturb the monks.'

'I'm not going anywhere with you,' said Stonefish.

Billy's expression hardened. 'Look, we don't want to spill blood here, if we can avoid it. We don't want to make a messy exit for the brothers.'

'Your threats don't bother me, Billy.' Stonefish's defiance seemed to be toughening. 'In fact, you don't bother me at all.'

Freddy gave him a warning tug. 'Take it easy.'

But Stonefish shrugged it off. 'No. He's due to take a fall.'

Billy's fists were clenched. 'Is that why you gave the dirt to the newspaper?'

'Damn right.'

Now Billy was standing right up against him, their faces just centimetres apart.

'Where's the disk?'

Stonefish didn't budge. 'I haven't got it.'

Billy nodded to a bouncer. 'Search him.'

The bouncer did as he was told then shook his head. 'Nothing.'

'You're wasting your time,' Stonefish told him. 'Anyway, what's it to you?'

'Business. I've got competing offers on an auction site I set up – like on eBay. It's worth a lot of ready cash, something I'm in need of right now, so I'm not in the mood to piss around.' Then he yelled into Stonefish's face: 'Where's the fucking disk?!'

But Stonefish didn't back down. 'It's not even on the island.'

'So who did you give it to?' Billy switched his gaze to Freddy then back again. 'Who would you trust?'

'Someone else who isn't frightened of you.'

'Ha!' he scoffed. 'You gave it to Ice for safekeeping, you sneaky prick.'

'Leave her alone. She ran an errand for me, that's all.'

'And that's all I need to know.' Billy was grinning now, showing his teeth. He planted a heavy hand on Stonefish's shoulder. 'Now what were you saying about me?'

'Go fuck yourself.'

Billy laughed. 'You're begging for it, you loser!'

While he held a shoulder down with one hand, Billy clamped a powerful grip around Stonefish's jaw with the other, then jerked it until, with a sickening crack, he dislodged the skull from the spine. Eyes bulging, air rasping in his throat, Stonefish crumpled and dropped to the ground, dead.

As Freddy looked on in horror, a shriek split the air. It came from where a group of monks watched, open-mouthed, from an upper window.

'Shit,' said Billy under his breath, before turning and shouting at them: 'Fuck off, before I start on you!'

The window emptied as they scattered.

'Time to make holiday plans,' Billy said to the bouncers. 'But I need some breathing space while I sort things out. Go and make sure the brethren can't communicate with the outside world. Phones, computers – knock 'em all out. Their van, their boat. Scuttle them as well.' He turned to Freddy. 'And you're coming with me.'

Freddy glanced at the lifeless body sprawled at Billy's feet and decided not to argue.

Freddy was throwing up for most of the powerboat ride back to Whitley – too much bobbing over the waves, too much dope, too much stomach-churning shock at what he'd witnessed. When the boat drew up at the wharf behind the Diamond, he was bundled out, then half shoved, half dragged up the fire escape and in through the back door to Billy's office. The thumping bass from the nightclub below vibrated through the floor. He was dumped in a chair while Billy made arrangements to disappear after dawn, and in the meantime prepared to clear up unfinished business – a list that included the disk and Ice, along with Rita Van Hassel.

'Bring me the guns,' he said to a bouncer as he pulled on a tracksuit and sports shoes. Once he'd changed, he turned to Freddy. 'Time for a quick workout with a punching bag.' He slid a boxing glove onto his right hand. 'Get up, Freddy.'

Freddy did as he was told.

'I don't like people who hold out on me.'

Billy let fly with a punch that put Freddy flat on the floor with a searing pain in his head, his jaw broken.

'Get up!'

He wobbled to his feet, dazed, while Billy moved in with a jab that smashed through his ribcage. Freddy was on the floor again, coughing up blood and having trouble breathing.

'Back on your feet, shitbag!'

It took an effort, but he managed it by holding onto the back of a chair, clutching his ribs, head spinning. The blow to Freddy's intestines was so hard it connected with his spine and hurled him back against the wall, where he slid down and sagged on the floor like a rag doll, still conscious but in agony.

A bouncer arrived with the guns and spread them on the desk.

'Good, I'll need a couple,' said Billy, picking through them. 'One I can strap to my leg. And one with a silencer for Van Hassel to suck on.'

48

Three scented candles threw a muted glow around Ice's penthouse bedroom, their flames reflected in gold-framed mirrors on the walls and ceiling. A raunchy track by a girl band throbbed from the music system. It was all part of the service, the seductive mood she created for her customers. She was naked, and on her knees, massaging the loins of the man standing in front of her, the diamond stud in her tongue stimulating his erect penis.

Ice was always in demand but the arrival of this client, in the early hours of the morning, had been unexpected. She didn't want anything to do with him but she had no choice. Too late she realised how badly she'd miscalculated and, as the man tensed and ejaculated down her throat, she knew what to expect. He sighed and withdrew his penis. She looked up at him with terrified eyes and scrambled away on all fours, screaming, but he caught her by the bedroom door, held the nail gun to her forehead and fired.

Audrey was watching.

As she accessed the live surveillance of the Tracker it showed the nail-gunner cleaving off the dead woman's hands, decapitating the body and placing the head in an ice bucket. Logically, the kill was necessary. The prostitute had chosen to become a hostile, posing a direct threat to the project, so Audrey felt no sympathy for the victim. The execution fell within authorisations provided by international directives. However, the number of deaths was increasing at an escalating pace and it posed the question: who would be the next to die within the sector? There appeared to be an immediate answer so Audrey switched the live input of the

Tracker and turned her attention to a woman creating another set of problems.

Audrey was watching Rita.

Rita lay in her hotel bed, her head resting on a pillow, body limp, the fine features of her face relaxed in a peaceful expression. For someone so provocative, Audrey observed, there was something of a gentle innocence in her sleep. Was her mind at ease in soft oblivion? Or was she dreaming? Audrey pushed the focus in closer. No movement beneath the eyelids. No sign of REM sleep. Oblivion, then. Her mind switched off. In such a restful state there was no hint of the trouble she was causing for base security, who saw her as both a renegade and expendable.

Audrey's assessment was different. In her view, Rita was intelligent and analytical, exhibiting a disciplined power of reason over emotion. She also possessed a scientific intellect with a dedication to the truth that was consistent with Audrey's basic principles. Even the spiritual doubt was telling. Here was a mind that rejected the falseness of a socially constructed reality. Like Audrey, Rita understood there were many dimensions; that reality was multi-layered, with human beings living in a virtual flatland of perception. And there were other considerations. Although this police detective was acting independently of the interests of senior operatives at Whitley Sands, her level-one clearance gave her privileges provided by the base and the project.

Audrey continued to watch Rita. At the same time, the split vision input from the Tracker showed a man who was arriving at Rita's hotel with a specific purpose. He planned to kill her.

49

Rita woke from a deep sleep, startled and disoriented. She sat bolt upright in bed, staring around wildly, only to realise the hotel phone was ringing. She snatched it up.

'Hello, who's that?'

But there was no one on the line. Noise was coming from her open laptop and from her mobile phone too. Both were pumping out ring tones and flashing the same message:

Security alert: code red!

'Fuck,' she said, clambering out of bed and pulling on some clothes without knowing what the message actually meant.

She tried calling Sutcliffe, then the police station, without getting an answer. Then the alert on the laptop promptly vanished. She did a quick check of her emails but there was no indication of what was going on. Suspicious now, sensing danger, she pocketed her mobile and car keys, and collected her gun. Flicking the safety catch, she crept to the door of her hotel room, took a deep breath and flung it open. But the hallway was deserted.

She looked at her watch – ten past four – and as she walked to the lifts tried to think who could tell her what was happening. Peter Luker's number was on her mobile. She selected it and called him.

He answered immediately, his voice thick and rough.

'Van Hassel?'

'What's going on?' she asked. 'The code red?'

'What are you talking about?'

'I've got a security alert. My mobile, my laptop. What the fuck's going on?'

'Calm down,' he said. 'I don't know about any alert. Where are you?'

'The hotel.'

'Our hotel, the Whitsunday?'

'Yes.'

'Something's wrong,' he said, his voice tense. 'I'll get dressed and meet you down in the lobby. Have you got your gun?'

'Yes.'

'Be prepared to use it.'

As he hung up, Rita noticed the lift had just left the reception level and was coming up. She watched the lights as it rose steadily floor by floor until it halted, right in front of her, on the fifth. Pulse racing, she gripped the Glock 22 in both hands, pointing it at the lift doors. There was an agonising pause before they opened to reveal Billy Bowers. With a delayed reflex, the gun in his hand jerked upwards as Rita squeezed the trigger of the semi-automatic, firing four bullets into his chest.

Billy's arm fell limply, his gun discharging a round through the top of his running shoe, as he hit the back of the lift, keeled over and collapsed on the floor, blood pooling out from the bullet holes in his heart. Rita stood rigid, knowing she'd killed him, the smell of the gunshots in her nostrils. The doors closed and Billy was gone.

By the time Rita got down to the lobby to wedge the lift doors open and check the body, Sutcliffe was returning her phone call.

'My phone's bleeping with a missed call from you,' he said sleepily. 'I hope it doesn't mean I have to get out of bed at this hour of the morning.'

'I just shot Bowers.'

'Ah, that's a big yes,' he said. 'Dead?'

'With five bullets in him, four of them mine.'

'Right. Where are you?'

'Whitsunday Hotel.'

'I'll call in the team, leave it to me. I'm on my way.'

As Sutcliffe rang off, she found Luker standing beside her, bleary-eyed and badly dressed in a T-shirt that highlighted his paunch and canvas shorts that clung to spindly white legs.

'So you took my advice,' he said, eyeing the corpse. 'I thought you must've when I heard the shots.'

Standing behind him, a wide-eyed receptionist craned his neck to see, while a few curious guests wandered over from the stairs to see what the noise was about. Luker moved swiftly to shoo them off before ordering the receptionist to keep everyone away from the scene. With the lobby cleared he was back at Rita's side.

'Billy "The Beast" Bowers,' he muttered. 'This is big.'

'Are you talking as a spook or a hack?' asked Rita.

'Both.'

'I can do without any media coverage.'

'I agree,' said Luker. 'Let me handle it. There are strings I can start pulling. Your name won't come out.'

'Thanks.'

'Don't misunderstand – I'm doing it for security reasons, and Maddox has done us a favour by signing you up. I can argue you're effectively on call.'

'All I feel is out on a limb,' she sighed, 'with crocodiles waiting below.'

'Including me?' He grunted. 'You may not like or trust me, but at the moment I'm your only ally.'

'Well, you're half right,' she said. 'I don't trust you but I like you.'

'Good for my ego, bad for my credibility.'

'So what the fuck is going on? Who sent the alert? Who's yanking my chain?'

Luker shook his head. 'I'm working on it.'

By the time Rita held a debriefing session with Sutcliffe, Bryce and Jarrett, her cover story was in place. She told them everything, from the time she received the security alert to the moment she gunned down Bowers in the lift. But the full details would never go into a police file. They were classified, thanks to Luker.

Officially Billy Bowers was shot dead in a confrontation with undercover taskforce officers, whose identities would not be disclosed. Rita was a witness to the aftermath. It suited all concerned and for once Rita was glad to be on the business side of a cover-up.

By the time the squad detectives, in tandem with Jarrett and his officers, had done their crime-scene work, a comprehensive version of events had emerged. Bowers, a drug dealer who hid a large supply of cocaine under his dog kennels, was the prime suspect in multiple homicides. He'd turned fugitive overnight after murdering two more victims – the prostitute Marilyn Eisler and an underworld software dealer known as Stonefish. He'd also put a third in hospital with multiple injuries, local hacker Freddy Hopper. Everything was consistent. Case closed. The serial killer had been stopped.

The investigation was over but the public sensation was only just beginning. A police press conference, conducted by taskforce head DSS Bob Sutcliffe, was held in time to hit the lunchtime bulletins, with TV newsrooms rolling out archive footage of Billy Bowers in the boxing ring and screening background packages on the gruesome murders for which he would be remembered. And that was just the opening barrage of saturation coverage as the media started descending on Whitley en masse – reporters, photographers, camera crews, broadcasters, satellite vans; and Rita was relieved she could slip away unnoticed.

By mid afternoon her immediate input was no longer required by the Queensland Police.

'You're off-duty,' Jarrett told her. 'We can pack everything up tomorrow.'

'Are you sure?' she asked.

'Shit, yeah, after what you've been through. Go have a drink, a swim, whatever. Don't come back in till you've had a good sleep.'

'Thanks, mate,' she said wearily. 'I'll take you up on that.'

50

Rita enjoyed the rare luxury of a long sleep-in and woke with a renewed sense of vigour. She took a dip in the hotel pool, ate a late breakfast in the terrace restaurant and phoned Byron while she sipped coffee.

She told him the police investigation was being wrapped up.

'It's all over the news,' he said. 'I assume you had a hand in it.'

'I can't talk about it over the phone. I'll tell you when I get back.'

'Does that mean you're on your way?'

'Not quite,' she said. 'The case is closed but there are a couple of loose ends I need to think about.'

'Rita, come home. I miss you.'

'Soon,' she promised. 'I miss you too.'

It was almost noon by the time she pulled over and parked at a discreet distance from the police station, where a media scrum had gathered for a press conference update. Sutcliffe was thriving on the publicity, his star on the rise, his career prospects blossoming.

Rita slipped in through the watch-house entrance and climbed the stairs to the exhibit room. Her makeshift office felt quiet and detached from the swarm of journalists and the air of hype surrounding the detectives next door. With a sigh of resignation, she began filing away the paperwork and taking down the rows of crime-scene photos. The loose ends were still bothering her, but with the Queensland force releasing her from secondment there wasn't much she could do about it. Billy Bowers was the nail-gun killer – that was official. His brutality and his motives were obvious. Everything else could be dismissed as peripheral, with the involvement of the base authorities, the death of Steinberg and the elusive *Rheingold* disk receding behind a veil of national security where they would remain.

The door opened and Jarrett strolled in with a file under his arm.

'I'll be sad to see you go,' he said, 'though you've probably had enough of us.'

'It's been . . . instructive.'

'Not the profiling assignment you expected, huh?'

'It's like no other case I've worked on,' she replied. 'And there's too much I don't have answers to. But, hey, everyone's got a sort of closure.'

'Now you're worrying me. You sound like you've still got doubts.'

'Relax, Jarrett. Anyway, why aren't you down in front of the microphones?'

'Too crowded already. Bryce is having trouble squeezing in beside the taskforce boys. I told you Sutcliffe was ambitious. He's flying out in the next hour for a big presser in Brisbane. He knows how to handle the limelight.'

'He's welcome to it.' She glanced at the file he was carrying. 'What have you got there?'

'Something for your collection,' he said, handing it to her. 'The Eisler killing – forensic report and photos. With the case closed, Sutcliffe let me and my detectives back on board with this one. Thought you might as well have the full set.'

'Thanks. How's Freddy?'

'Broken ribs, his jaw's wired up and he's lost a kidney. But he'll live.'

'At least he fared better than his friend.'

'Yeah – and we've found out who Stonefish was,' he added. 'His prints and photos got hits from police databanks in New Zealand and the States. A lot of electronic crime, gang-related, and a warrant for manslaughter in Wellington. Various aliases, but his real name was Otto Krautschneider.'

'That explains the German beer compulsion.'

'Something else. The passport check came back from New Caledonia. There's no such person as Jean-Paul Mistere. The ID must've been fake.'

'So we still don't know who the man in the mud really was. Any other cheery news?' Rita asked.

'Well, you'll be pleased to hear the security review at Whitley Sands has been curtailed. No further attendance required.'

'Doesn't that strike you as an odd coincidence?'

'Everything about the base strikes me as odd. And the terrorist alert has been downgraded. We're no longer hot on the trail of the four suspects.'

'It makes you wonder about the so-called war on terror.'

'Yeah,' Jarrett agreed. 'What we really need is a war on bullshit.'

Rita was sitting at the desk, opening the crime-scene report, when she was interrupted by a gentle knock on the door.

'Yeah?' she called out, closing the folder.

Ronsard leant into the room, camera in hand, a concerned look on his face.

'I thought I'd drop by to see how you are,' he said.

'Come on in,' said Rita, surprised to see him. 'Grab a chair.'

He closed the door behind him, pulled up a chair and placed his camera on the desk, glancing around. 'Unusual office. More like a black museum.'

'Something of the sort,' she agreed, smiling. 'You've had enough of the press conference?'

'It's nauseating,' he said. 'All this triumphalism by the author-ities.'

'I can see your point.'

'I don't believe Rachel Macarthur's murder, or the others, were simply the work of Bowers. You and I both know there's more to it than that.'

'There are unanswered questions, you're right.'

'Is that why you've kept away from the media?'

'One of the reasons, yes.'

'Blaming Bowers for everything lets the research base off the hook,' Ronsard went on. 'It also distracts the public from the valid criticism being made by the Anti-War Coalition. This isn't how I want to cover the story.'

'Well, I can't give you a steer on it,' said Rita. 'I'm still in the dark myself.'

'That's not why I'm here. I was worried about you after the other night. You were under a lot of pressure. Then that young girl was murdered, the one who sent the email.'

'I didn't mean to freak you out. And I'm sorry if I ruined the atmosphere.'

'Not at all,' smiled Ronsard. 'The mood was already *détendu*, if you get my meaning.'

'I do.' She laughed. 'So I don't feel so bad.'

'Good.' He nodded, serious again. 'So much madness in the world. So many apparently normal people walking around insane.'

'It's not the number of mad people that amazes me,' said Rita. 'It's the number who manage to keep their sanity.'

'But of course. In western society, schizophrenia is a normal condition. Each person develops as an outsider to himself. *L'étranger.*'

'In a way we're all schizoid,' Rita agreed. 'Each one of us split into at least two people – the person who reacts and the person who observes the reaction. Or, if you prefer Freud's theory of the psyche, there's the person who lusts, the person who manipulates and the person who contemplates.'

'Ah, I see,' said Ronsard. 'The id, the ego and superego. Interesting spin.' He picked up his camera. 'Anyway, I'm glad to see you're okay.' He stood up. 'I should get back to the press conference in case they come out with some outrageous piece of mendacity I should know about.'

'Thanks for the concern.'

'My pleasure,' he said, opening the door. 'I can see why you're no ordinary detective.'

'Thank you,' responded Rita, enjoying his flattery. 'I wish a few more senior officers felt the same way.'

•

The crime-scene photos from Ice's killing were more depressing than the others. This wasn't simply a dead victim. This was a young woman Rita had been talking to less than forty-eight hours ago. What made it worse was that she might have prevented the murder. With hindsight she could have been more forceful, more insistent on getting the girl out of the apartment to somewhere safer, though the email to Eve had distracted her, changed priorities. In reality, Ice's obstinacy, her refusal to listen, had sealed her fate.

The glossy images spread across Rita's desk told the story, more or less. There were shots of the girl's naked torso sprawled in the doorway of her bedroom, and close-ups of her severed head planted in the ice bucket. The symbolism was clear. Her face, glassy-eyed and rigid with an expression of fear, also showed the puncture wound in her forehead where the nail had penetrated her brain. Others showed the bloodied stumps of her wrists where the hands had been severed.

Rita sat back and stared across the room, plagued by nagging doubts. Why the hands? What purpose did they serve – souvenirs, fantasy, what? For all his loathsome brutality, Rita couldn't picture Billy Bowers removing the hands of his victims, unless he was fulfilling an agenda other than his own. But that brought her back to the notion of a conspiracy and the role of the research base. Better not go there, she thought. Not much that could be done about it now.

She flipped through photos of the penthouse interior, most notably the empty space where Ice's computer had been. Only the unplugged screen and keyboard were left, wires dangling. The CPU was gone. At least that fitted with Billy's motives. The stilted testimony provided in hospital by Freddy confirmed that Bowers desperately wanted what was on the *Rheingold* disk, because he was conducting some sort of auction for cash. That meant at least two other parties wanted the disk. If the base was one, who was the other? The Anti-War Coalition? That seemed unlikely.

Her thoughts were interrupted by Sutcliffe striding into the room, a businesslike brio in his step, a broad smile on his face.

He reached out and shook her hand. 'Got a plane to catch, but I wanted to say a quick thanks for all your help.'

'You're welcome,' she said.

'And when you're next in Brisbane, look me up. We'll have a beer.'

'By then you'll be *Detective Inspector* Sutcliffe.'

'If not Commissioner!' He laughed, heading out again. 'Good work, Van Hassel.'

Rita sat for a moment, savouring the compliment. Then she opened the crime-scene report compiled by Jarrett and his officers and began reading through it. The competence and efficiency of his work impressed her again. For all his laidback stance, he was a good detective . . . very good. One small detail leapt out at her. She picked up her phone and called him.

'You calling from the watch-house?' he asked.

'Yes, I need to double-check something.'

'You want me to come up?'

'No,' she answered. 'I just need to be absolutely sure about one item in your report on Marilyn Eisler. The timings on the penthouse door. Are you positive they're correct?'

'Yes, and they've already been double-checked. The apartment block's security computer is accurate to the second. Why?'

Rita fell silent, unable to decide what to tell him.

'What is it, Van Hassel?'

'Forget it, Jarrett,' she said at last. 'It's just me being picky. There's no point, really. Do I need to talk to Bryce before I pack up?'

'No, he's still turning his best profile to the cameras. As far as he's concerned, your job's done and dusted. But I want to buy you a drink before you head back south.'

'You're on. I'll let you know when.'

Rita was in a quandary as she slotted her profiling notes and folders into a sports bag and zipped it up. That was that. Her work here was done. She looked around the exhibit room to make sure she was leaving it just as she'd found it and, with a sigh, walked over to the window and gazed down into the alley, strewn with overflowing bins and graffiti – the detritus of human activity.

She felt defeated, her quest for justice unfulfilled. What made it even less palatable was that she'd been hoodwinked, manipulated.

The fact that she couldn't prove it only exacerbated her anger. Rita knew for certain that Billy Bowers as the nail-gun killer just didn't add up. It meant that her instincts had been right from the start. The killer operated from within the protective shield of the research base and had again retreated behind it. That was where the truth lay. She was shaking her head, convinced she'd never get the chance to expose it, when opportunity came tapping on her door.

'So this is where you've been doing your meditations,' said Luker, strolling into the exhibit room. 'Fascinating.'

He was dressed smartly, unlike the last time she'd seen him, in cream trousers and sports shirt under a navy blue blazer.

'What are you doing here?' asked Rita.

'Just keeping a watchful eye on the media circus. Making sure there are no slip-ups.'

'You didn't have the urge to join in?'

'Mercifully my days of doorsteps and pressers are behind me.' Luker wandered along the display cases, scanning the historic items, before stopping to cast his eyes over the nineteenth-century newspaper headlines. 'Nothing much changes.'

'Not a lot, no, when it comes to basic human drives.' Rita looked at him sceptically before asking, 'What do you make of this?' She was gesturing at the oil painting over the hearth.

Luker came over, gazed at it and read the title. '*The Hunting Party*. Grim-looking bunch. Black and white combo. Armed to the teeth.' He sniffed, as if assessing the context. 'More like a lynch mob than hunters.'

Rita was impressed. 'Bravo! You have the skills of a profiler.'

'So I've passed a test.'

'You certainly have. What you're looking at is a group of self-appointed executioners. They hunted and killed Aborigines under the leadership of the man in the frock coat, Squatter Brodie.'

'Should I know of him?'

'No. Obscure local fanatic in the frontier war.'

'Does that mean I win a prize?'

'Yes, you do,' answered Rita. 'You get to take me out to lunch.'

'That's a much more attractive prospect than anything else in my diary.' Luker grinned. 'Anywhere in particular?'

'The Bierkeller, wherever that is.'

'Why there?'

'I've heard the beer is excellent.'

'Good enough reason.' He nodded. 'Now that's the part of journalism I really miss – the liquid lunches.'

The Bierkeller was a theme bar situated among the cafes and fashion shops at the heart of the tourist strip. American sailors drank at outside tables among the pedestrians and the palm trees. Rita and Luker sat inside under dark wooden beams decorated with steins, cow bells and lederhosen. She'd chosen a table next to a wall recess displaying a bust of Wagner.

They drank from long chilled glasses of beer as they waited for their lunch to be served.

'Ah,' Luker sighed nostalgically. 'Takes me back to the Oktoberfest.'

'Reporting?'

'Indulging.' He put down the glass and got out his cigarettes. 'So you're off-duty now?'

'Off-duty, off attachment.' She smiled ironically. 'Disarmed, disbanded. Criminal profiling no longer required.'

'You sound a little miffed.'

'I wonder why.'

Luker seemed to think about it while he put a cigarette between his lips out of habit, then grimaced and let it dangle. If he lit up he'd be breaking Queensland's anti-smoking laws.

'You've hardly touched your beer,' he observed.

'I hardly ever drink it.'

'Okay, I'll bite. What's the real reason we're here?'

'You don't know?'

Luker gave a sour chuckle. 'Am I supposed to?'

'The surroundings don't strike a chord?'

'Either tell me what I'm missing, or give me a hint. I'm not clairvoyant.'

'No, but you're perceptive. And given your job, you must be well informed.'

'This is starting to sound like another profiling exercise.'

'If you like,' she said. 'Let's see. Professionally you inhabit a looking-glass world. You're adept at manipulation and deception. You must be good at it to deal with the in-your-face aggression of people like Maddox. But while he uses brute force to get his way, you choreograph results.'

'I'm with you so far,' said Luker, eyes narrowing, 'though I'm wondering where you're heading with this.'

'I'm trying to decide if it's you who's been pulling my strings.'

Luker pulled the unlit cigarette from his mouth. 'If I bluntly deny it, you won't believe me. So let me put it this way. The looking-glass world, as you call it, has multiple sets of mirrors – contradictory, distorting, some completely concealed from all the rest. Nobody has the true reflection, never mind the full picture of what's going on at any particular moment. It's what James Jesus Angleton of the CIA called "a wilderness of mirrors". A lot of intelligence work is, at best, inference or second guessing. I'm not just talking about enemies, real or perceived, I'm also talking about officers within agencies, ostensibly pursuing the same goals.'

'Chaos theory,' Rita commented.

'When there's an international coalition in place, the warping effect is magnified and the grey areas get even murkier. Which is my way of saying I can't confirm or deny someone's been pulling your strings. I simply don't know, one way or the other. If you're referring to the code red you received, I've checked as best I can, and I've been told none was issued, to you or anyone else.'

'Someone sent it in time for me to blow away Bowers,' snapped Rita.

'I'm not saying I don't believe you,' he responded. 'Just that it can't be traced.'

'Bowers dead is a neat resolution to a lot of problems,' she went on. 'And it was you who advised me to use my gun, then conveniently arranged for the details of my involvement to vanish.'

'So I'm the puppet master, that's your theory? Let me shoot it down.' Luker rolled the cigarette delicately between his fingers. 'A code red delivered to you but not to me indicated extreme danger specifically to you, whether it was genuine or false. And let me point out, it probably saved your life. Next, what you did is not on record – a move you actually suggested – because it would make your role here untenable.'

'My role has ended.'

'You and I both know that's not the case.'

'That means you *are* concealing something.'

'I wouldn't be much of a spy if I didn't.' He chuckled, shoving his cigarette back in the packet as lunch was served.

Rita couldn't afford to let his engaging personality get in the way of pinning down his true function. She began to eat her salmon salad.

'I Googled you,' she informed him breezily.

'What did you find?'

'Not much and nothing recent. There were a couple of anecdotal references from journalists' memoirs referring to a Peter "Filthy" Luker, who gained the epithet from womanising.'

'Ah, those were the days.' He actually blushed. '*Mea culpa.*' He began to pick self-consciously at his savoury platter of cheese and German sausage.

Yes, she thought, his apparent sensitivity could easily charm the pants off women, but now the wear and tear of a decadent life was showing.

'Why's the review been cancelled?' she asked abruptly.

'Huh!' he scoffed. 'That's a perfect example of how intelligence turns out to be nothing of the sort. The terrorist suspects planning to blow Whitley off the map turn out to be innocent kebab vendors. They rolled back up at their shop after a driving holiday up the coast.'

'What about the evidence?'

'Complete rubbish. The false documents were dodgy visas, and the bomb-making residues were fertiliser, batteries and wires from a home-made irrigation system for their vegetable plot. They'll probably face a deportation hearing but they're no more terrorists than the local hotdog seller.'

'Embarrassing.'

'And it shows how an edifice of strategy can be built on miscalculation and stupid assumptions.'

He drank more beer, his exasperation plain to see.

'I'm trying to find common ground with you,' she admitted at last. 'But it's not easy. Tell me exactly what you're doing at Whitley Sands.'

'All right. I've been drafted onto the International Risk Assessment Committee. That's my one and only role within the research base.'

'Who else is on the committee?'

'I can't believe I'm submitting to this interrogation,' he said with a shake of the head. 'Can you remind me why I am?'

'Because I know why we're sitting here, and you don't.'

'Right.'

'So who are your fellow members?'

'Maddox, Baxter, Rhett Molloy, his deputy Kurt Demchak and Rex Horsley.'

'Who's he?'

'British consular attaché.'

'And in assessing the level of risk,' she persisted, 'has your committee ever discussed the use of lethal force?'

'Only as a last resort.'

'Has it sanctioned it?'

'Certainly not! Why do you ask?'

'Because somebody has.'

Luker twiddled a fork, toying with his lunch, as he pondered her words.

'I had a feeling you were going to tell me something of the sort.' He frowned. 'And, strange as it may seem, it's clear you know more about some aspects of what's going on than I do.'

'Maddox and Demchak,' stated Rita. 'Do they have any other joint role at the base?'

'Only on the sub-committee.'

'Which is?'

'The group that focuses on day-to-day details: the International Risk Assessment Sub-Committee, comprised of Maddox, Demchak and Molloy.'

Rita bowed her head in thought, before raising her eyes to his. 'That's it.'

'That's what?' asked Luker, perplexed.

She looked at him coldly. 'The hunting party.'

Luker sat there glumly for several minutes while Rita finished her lunch with relish, as if tasting a morsel of vindication. He said nothing, just gazed across the bar, fiddling with his pack of untipped French cigarettes.

He broke the silence at last.

'I'm not saying I agree, but I have certain . . . apprehensions, shall we say.'

'Someone put it to me this way,' said Rita. 'You're either part of the con or one of the conned.'

'Thanks for that. And let me point out that for someone who's had the gall to accuse me of being manipulative, you've been running rings around me.'

Rita laughed. 'You know how to flatter a girl.'

'Now it's your turn,' he said seriously. 'Come on, Van Hassel. Why are we sitting here?'

'Because this is where it started.'

Luker looked around again, as if trying to spot something he'd missed.

'Are you a fan of Wagner?' she asked.

'All those overblown Aryan themes – no,' he answered bluntly. 'Which, of course, brings us to the *Rheingold* disk.'

'Yes. And this is where Konrad Steinberg handed it over to Stonefish.'

'Here, in the Bierkeller?'

'Yes. For all we know, at this table.'

'And that's why your role here isn't over,' Luker told her. 'Retrieving that disk is a national security priority, and you've done the best job of homing in on it. Not only that, but you've achieved something none of my intelligence officers has managed.

324

You've had direct contact with the two men who handled it – in this very bar, as it turns out.'

'Now both are dead,' she said. 'So are four people who had access to downloads from the disk. All murdered.'

'The police built a fairly conclusive case against Bowers.'

'Circumstantial. He wasn't the nail-gunner. I accused him to his face of the first killing. I realise now he didn't know he was standing in the murder scene.'

'That's your interpretation, not proof.'

'The proof's come with the last attack. After I left Ice's apartment, one other person called on her. He killed her with a nail gun, severed her head and hands, removed her computer and left at exactly eight minutes past four. The time of the penthouse door opening and closing is recorded on the apartment block security computer, something the killer overlooked.'

'Ah, I see.'

'As you and I both know, I shot Bowers just four minutes later. He couldn't possibly have got from her place to the hotel in that time, so he didn't kill her.'

'Who did?'

'Someone determined to stop the contents of the disk coming out. Someone at the research base.'

While Luker was rubbing his chin at this latest information, Rita's phone started ringing. The screen on her mobile simply told her a 'private number' was calling.

'Hello, who is this?' she asked.

'Maddox,' came the curt reply. 'Get your arse to my office, Van Hassel. Now! Don't make me come after you!'

51

That familiar chill went through her as Rita pulled up again at the gates of Whitley Sands. To her, the checkpoint, the razor wire, the thick mesh of the perimeter fence symbolised not so much security as oppression. Her pass checked, she was waved through.

She drove to the car park, got out and walked to the main entrance where the guards were waiting for her. They escorted her to the lifts and up to the fifth floor, then around the gallery, with its view over the circular space of the atrium, and showed her into Maddox's office. Then they left, pulling the door closed behind them.

Rita found herself in a white-walled room, sparsely furnished, with floor-to-ceiling smoked glass windows overlooking the security compound outside. There were photos of troops in camouflage gear. A glass cabinet displayed regimental trophies and insignia. Directly facing her, Maddox sat behind a broad desk, flanked on one side by Rhett Molloy and on the other by a powerfully built man with a hard face and thinning hair. She assumed he was Kurt Demchak.

This was more intimidating than she had expected. It meant she had been summoned to appear before the sub-committee which could embody the deadliest presence at the base. For all she knew these three men, acting outside the law and beyond official scrutiny, had the power of life and death over any individual within reach. They sat there unsmiling, plainly hostile, with the self-assured authority of judge, jury and executioner.

A single chair had been placed in front of the desk.

'Sit down, Van Hassel,' said Maddox.

She put her shoulder bag on the floor and sat, feeling tense, just as she was meant to.

'Rhett Molloy you've seen before,' he continued. 'Kurt Demchak you haven't.'

'I've heard about him,' said Rita.

Demchak almost smiled.

Maddox tapped a folder on the desktop as if it contained damning material. 'I knew you'd be a thorn in my side from the moment you arrived. And despite my warnings, you've obstructed and compromised national security operations.'

'In what way?' she asked.

'You know damn well. For a start, you lied to me about your contact with Steinberg. You were aware of his treachery and you concealed it. That makes you complicit in his treason. That's jail time.'

Rita said nothing, just swallowed, feeling a lot less relaxed than she tried to appear.

'You knew about the Steinberg report, and its damaging content, from the outset. You also found out it was hidden on the *Rheingold* disk that Steinberg passed on to subversives. You even tracked its circulation. Yet you failed to inform me or anyone else in a position to resolve the danger it posed.' Maddox breathed out heavily through his nose. 'Your behaviour has been contemptible. You've shown a level of insubordination that would have you court-martialled if you held a military rank. And all this interference has been based on your own rogue judgement, without deferring to any senior officer.'

'That's not true,' she said.

The rebuttal took Maddox by surprise.

'Who?' he demanded.

'Peter Luker.'

'I don't believe you.'

'Ask him yourself.' She was more thankful than ever for Luker's involvement. 'He approached me at the review and we've had a tacit agreement ever since.'

The information seemed to deflect Maddox from the officious line he was pursuing.

'That still doesn't justify your actions,' he said, his anger rising. 'Anyway, Luker's essentially an outsider. He doesn't have a command role in base operations, nor is he responsible for protecting base material.'

'He's responsible for national security,' she retorted.

'Only as a civilian observer!' Maddox thumped the desk as his temper got the better of him, the scar tissue on the side of his face reddening. 'The security of this nation doesn't rest in his hands, or your hands, or those of your police colleagues. The defence of this country is, and always will be, in the safekeeping of the military forces, conventional and covert, disciplined and committed. It does not, thankfully, lie within the province of spineless functionaries.'

All in the room knew he'd gone too far.

Molloy laid a hand on Maddox's forearm. 'It doesn't change anything,' he told him quietly. 'We mustn't allow external issues to muddy the water for us. Our duty's clear, not just to the nations we serve, but to the preservation of their core values; to the future. If we remain resolute, we'll prevail.'

His words had a placating effect on Maddox, who unclenched his fist and massaged his knuckles, his scar tissue fading from an inflamed red to white.

The third man in the room, Demchak, maintained his silence, watching dispassionately. Rita knew of his cruelty from Freddy and, as she observed him, she realised Freddy was right. This man was more dangerous than Bowers. His physical strength, reined in behind a surface calm and immobile face, was indicative of the self-control needed to channel his innate violence.

Molloy fixed Rita with a look of rebuke. 'In my considered opinion,' he told her, 'you've not only betrayed the trust of your government and mine, you've unwittingly aided and abetted the enemy in the war on terror.'

'What enemy?' she asked, crossing her legs. 'I'm told your alleged terrorists are victims themselves – of a security bungle.'

'Let me say, first of all, I don't like your impertinence,' he responded coolly. 'But since you ask, the suspects were identified to us as a local cell being deployed to carry out an attack. The man setting it up, the terrorist fixer, is in all probability still here. I hope you appreciate the gravity of that.'

'It's the first I've heard of it.'

'Because you're not an intelligence officer. You're given access only to the information deemed necessary, though you've taken it upon yourself to meddle beyond clear boundaries. I'm not overstating it when I say the result could be catastrophic.'

Rita had a sinking feeling. This was looking and sounding like an inquisition.

Molloy continued, his expression stern. 'What we're doing here today is deciding whether to have you detained or whether you can be of some value out in the field. We still face a grave threat. That won't end until we retrieve the disk and nullify its potential effect. It's absolutely essential that it never surfaces.'

Rita folded her hands and placed them in her lap. For the moment she had no choice but to go along with her accusers.

'If I've caused problems, it was unintentional and I apologise. My profiling role is over, so I don't understand what's expected of me.'

'You've got closer to finding the disk than anyone else,' answered Molloy. 'You've identified leads that we haven't. We know this from surveillance footage. Also, thanks partly to you, our trail is cold.'

'A trail of dead bodies,' she said.

'Quite. And the advantage you have is that you've spoken to the key people involved, now dead.'

'Somehow I don't think I'm the only one.'

'What are you insinuating?'

'I know Captain Maddox met secretly with Bowers.'

'We opened negotiations with Bowers through both Captain Maddox and Kurt,' said Molloy, 'as an alternative means of retrieval. It was worth offering cash to exploit his underworld connections. Now that option is gone. You, however, are still with us.' He paused as if to emphasise how temporary that could be. 'Where is the disk, Van Hassel?'

Rita sighed. 'I know where it went – to a drop-box at a cyber cafe in Rockhampton.'

'That's been searched. It's empty. So who collected it?'

A shiver ran down Rita's spine as she realised what that implied. If their knowledge of the drop-box came from Ice there was only one way they could have got it.

'Come on,' insisted Molloy. 'You must have some idea.'

'I need time to think,' she said. 'Stonefish had what he called his own secret courier service. I've no idea who or what that is. But his instructions were in place before Bowers killed him. So the courier service has either completed the delivery or is in the process of doing so. All I know is he wanted the disk delivered to someone who could make use of it.'

'And who is that?'

'I don't know. Can't you use Panopticon to find out? Search the memory. Home in on the usual suspects.'

The three of them exchanged a look that seemed to acknowledge she knew more about it than she should.

'Panopticon is a machine, not a mind-reader,' said Molloy.

For the first time, Rita eased back in her chair. A new possibility had just occurred to her. It must have shown in her expression.

'What is it?' asked Molloy. 'Do you know the identity of the recipient?'

'No,' she answered hesitantly. 'But I might be able to narrow the field.' She was being deliberately vague. It was her way of encouraging them to let her go. 'I need to check my notes and talk to a few people again, starting with Freddy Hopper.'

Molloy sat back, deferring to Maddox. 'Is it possible she could lead us to the disk? Your call.'

Maddox propped his elbows on the desk and laid a look of pure animosity on Rita.

'Consider this your final warning,' he said. 'My personal choice would be to end your career and your liberty here and now. However, far greater issues are at stake. In effect, I'm returning you to the field.'

'Thank you,' she forced herself to say.

'But this time you're reporting directly to me. Not to the police. Not to Luker.'

'I understand.'

'I hope so, for your sake.' Maddox gritted his teeth. 'Now there's something I'm going to tell you on a need-to-know basis. Our dealings with Bowers were not straightforward. There was another buyer in the market. That's according to what he told Kurt and me – and I believed him. To encourage a bidding war, and keep the bidders apart, Bowers set up a little online auction site, to which only those in the know had the password.'

'What was the site called?' she asked.

'Mr Rheingold's Auction House – that was Bowers' misplaced sense of humour,' answered Molloy. 'The rival bidder was offering a million dollars. That rules out the protesters and the media. Because various aspects of our research have been plastered over the net, there are other potential candidates – hostile governments, for a start. Or it could be an arms dealer, a middle man or, worst-case scenario, the Fixer, operating undercover on our own doorstep.'

'Who is this Fixer?'

'It's thought he's Iranian. Kurt will fill you in.' Maddox turned to Demchak. 'Will you take her down to the compound?'

'My pleasure,' said Demchak, without showing a trace of it.

Rita tensed at the mention of the compound.

'Relax, Van Hassel, you'll be allowed to leave,' said Maddox. Then he added ominously, 'This time.'

As Demchak escorted her along the internal gallery to the rear lifts, Rita noticed how silently he moved, remarkable in such a big man. He seemed to walk instinctively on the balls of his feet, almost animal-like. She'd read about serial killers who moved in just the same way.

The lift doors opened and he followed her in. The doors closed and they were alone. She felt nervous in such close proximity to him. He towered over her, his face still impassive as he pressed a button.

'You have a lot to say for yourself,' she said.

'Molloy spouts enough horseshit for both of us,' he replied without looking at her.

The doors opened when they reached the basement level, and he led her through a concrete tunnel linking the main block to the security compound. The sterile smell of the place came back to her from the night of her interrogation. He swiped a security pad that opened a door into a room with a central nest of computer desks surrounded by filing cabinets and metal shelves filled with folders. He selected one and tossed it onto a desk.

'The Fixer file,' he said. 'Help yourself.'

Rita pulled up a chair, opened the folder marked *Classified*, and read through the details that had been put together on the history and aliases of a man named Omar Amini. It was heavy stuff, and uncomfortable to go through with Demchak hovering behind her. There were only a couple of things she noted of possible relevance. One was the reference to Amini's studies at the Sorbonne, the other was the blow-up of the student ID image. She didn't recognise the face, but there was something about the eyes that seemed distinctive, if not familiar.

'Seen enough?' asked Demchak.

She closed the folder. 'Yes. If he's hanging around Whitley, I haven't spotted him.'

'That makes two of us,' he said, slotting the folder back on a shelf. 'There's a file here on you too. I've read it.'

'So what?'

'For a female cop you've notched up a few kills recently.'

'Does that mean you're impressed?'

'It means I'd handle you differently from Molloy.' Demchak was standing over the back of her chair. 'Find out for sure who else you've been talking to on the base.'

'What makes you think I have?'

'Your inside knowledge of Panopticon. It goes beyond what's in the Steinberg report. Steinberg only provided technical specifications. He didn't reveal how it can pinpoint a memory within the sector.' He bent down to her ear. 'Yet you knew that.'

'You'd be surprised what I've uncovered.'

'Nothing surprises me.' Like spinning a toy, he swivelled her around in the chair and pushed his face close to hers. 'I figure you've seen Panopticon in action, thanks to the slimy limey.'

'I don't have to answer to you,' she said, straining back in the chair.

'Take my advice: don't swallow what he told you. He's full of shit, with all that Roman Empire baloney. And he's a wacko. I'm talking la-la-land.'

'What's that supposed to mean?'

'Giles has finally flipped. Off sick, off his head, drooling over the dead hooker,' Demchak hissed through his teeth. 'He's someone else they should've let me deal with.'

'Like me,' said Rita. 'And just how differently would you handle me?'

'Less conversation,' he answered, his voice low and menacing. 'More hands-on persuasion.'

He cracked his knuckles loudly, the sudden noise making her bound out of the chair and back away.

His eyes were unemotional, not a trace of humour.

'I've heard you get your kicks like that,' she said.

'What else have you heard about me?'

'That victimising people comes naturally to you.'

Demchak nodded. 'Worth you remembering that.'

'And there's something you should keep in mind,' she said, moving to the door.

'Like what?'

'You've seen it in my file,' she replied. 'I shoot bullies.'

52

The leaden weight of institutional pressure seemed to lift from her shoulders as Rita drove out of the gates at Whitley Sands. With an involuntary shudder she swung the Falcon onto the road into town and drove to the hospital where Freddy was recuperating from surgery and other effects of Billy's battering.

He was out of intensive care in a small ward he had to himself. His body was propped on a slight angle, his jaw wired, his torso strapped and bandaged, with various tubes and drips attached. Talking was an effort, and while he could move his lips and tongue, his words came out with a raw glottal sound.

Freddy watched as Rita pulled up a chair and sat beside his bed.

'Need my drugs,' he croaked.

She smiled. 'The nurse has got plenty of painkillers.'

'Fuck the nurse.'

Rita glanced around but the nurse was out of earshot.

'I've read the witness statement you signed,' she went on. 'About what happened out at the monastery. That'll be hard to cope with.'

'Dope would help,' he burbled. 'Got any on you?'

'No,' she said tartly, though she was pleased his sense of humour was intact. 'There's something I need to ask you. When Stonefish arranged for the delivery of the disk did he tell you who he was sending it to?'

'No.'

'Did he mention anything that might be relevant?'

'He told me,' rasped Freddy, swallowing, 'it would go to someone who'd know how to use it – an idealist with balls.'

'Sounds like he wanted it to go public,' said Rita. 'That'll blow the lid off everything. Did he say anything more about his instructions to Ice?'

Freddy sighed heavily. 'No. Just that he was worried about her.'

'Because of the disk?'

'Because of some stalker. Some guy obsessed with her.'

Rita frowned. 'I think I know who that is.'

As she thought about it, there was a growing question mark over the role of Paul Giles and the version of events he'd given her. If he'd been lying it could change everything.

The nurse arrived with a trolley of metal basins, sponges and flannels.

'Time to clean you up, Freddy,' she announced.

'Fuck that,' he mumbled.

As Rita stood up to go he tugged at her skirt.

'Thanks, Van Hassel,' he said.

'For what?'

'For whacking Billy.'

Paul Giles wasn't answering his phone so Rita drove out of town and up to the rainforest. Doubts about his motives were beginning to nag at her and she had questions for him. The hunt for the disk could wait. She wanted answers.

The drive along The Ridgeway took her past the resort construction site – deserted now, the gates chained shut, the cranes motionless – and on towards the former botanist's home of Eden. She parked beside the front gate, got out, pressed the buzzer and waited. No response. She pressed it again, for longer this time. Still no response. She glanced up at the sharp coils of wire on top of the wall and decided not to try scaling it.

Rita was pressing the buzzer for a third time when the gate glided open. As she walked briskly down the path, through the overgrown tangle of the garden, the porch door opened ahead of her. With it came a loud blast of choir music. Bizarrely, it was a church hymn, ringing out at an almost deafening volume. Unlike her last arrival, Paul wasn't waiting to greet her. Instead she caught a fleeting glimpse of a figure retreating inside the house.

Closing the door behind her, she walked cautiously down the hall, knowing something was extremely wrong and wishing she still carried a gun. There was a trail of bloodied footprints on the floor, broken china, empty bottles of gin and, saturating the rooms, the sound of the choir shrieking from the multiple speakers of the music system. The track, 'Onward, Christian Soldiers', possessed an unholy ferocity when pumped out at such a hysterical level. And when the track stopped, it resumed again immediately from the beginning. It was being played over and over again, another sign of madness in the house.

Things in the central living space – the showpiece – were even worse. Instead of the chic interior, what confronted Rita resembled a slum. Everything was broken or overturned, the curtains ripped from the windows, shards of glass littering surfaces, and more bloodstains. The air was pungent with the odours of urine and vomit, the cream rugs soaked in human discharge. As Rita tried not to breathe it in, her gaze fell on what was left of the holographic picture. A broken gin bottle, lying below it, must have been hurled at the 3-D image. The fragments of a Pre-Raphaelite landscape flickered from the damaged lasers but a gaping hole filled the rest of the frame above a spray of crystalline splinters littering the floor. Persephone was gone.

Rita walked over to the sound system and switched off the music. The sudden silence was a relief but her nerves were on edge. She noticed the framed photo of Paul and Audrey at her feet, its glass cracked. Picking it up, she took a closer look – a strong woman with a controlling arm around a younger man – then put it back above the white marble hearth where it had stood. In the mess on the mantelpiece were two empty pill bottles with prescription labels. She read them and swore under her breath. Now she knew why Demchak had used the word wacko. The drug prescribed for Paul was high-dosage lithium. It meant he had a serious bipolar condition, kept in check by the medication, which he'd probably stopped taking. The house certainly bore the signs of a manic-depressive breakdown.

At the sound of his voice, she spun around.

'Have you come to arrest me, officer?' he asked.

She was shocked at his appearance.

He was wearing nothing but soiled underpants, his face gaunt, hair matted, skin sickly pale. His thighs were slicked with stains and his bare feet were caked in dried blood from where he'd walked over glass. There was partial recognition in his eyes as he hobbled towards her, hands outstretched, ready to be cuffed. In his addled state he remembered only that she was a police officer.

The smell of his breath and the stench of his incontinence was overwhelming as he approached. She quickly turned a chair upright and sat him down on it, a hand over her nose and mouth. It was debatable whether she could get any sense out of him, but it was worth a try.

'Where's your lithium?' she asked, squatting in front of him.

'I don't know,' he answered. 'All the jars are empty and I can't remember what I did with the pills. Maybe I flushed them down the bog. But what's happened to the music? How would you like to hear "Onward, Christian Soldiers"? I fancy listening to that again. King's College Choir, you know.'

'Yes,' she said gently. 'I know.'

As he stared into her face, recollection glimmered in his eyes. 'It's you, Van Hassel. Sorry, I'm confused. I haven't slept since your last visit.'

'That was last week, Paul.'

'I got excited,' he babbled. 'A member of the Royal Family's planning to drop in unannounced, you see. The one who talks to plants. I wonder if they talk back to him. It's the botany, you see. This place has a fascinating history.'

'Yes, you told me.'

'That's why I got excited and wet myself. I can't meet him like this.'

'No. I need to get you to a doctor.'

'It's too late.'

'Why do you say that?'

'I can't leave this house.'

Rita tried to read the subtext of his garbled logic. 'Does Audrey know what's happened to you?' she asked.

'Audrey's gone,' Paul said sadly. 'She's abandoned me.'

'Well, you need some medication.'

He shook his head, shivering, teeth chattering. 'Ice is gone too. Crucified like the others.'

'It's terrible, yes,' she said. 'But you've still got your whole life ahead of you.'

'I don't think so. My work is done. I've been quite clever. Bipolar people often are, as long as they don't go high. I haven't had an episode like this since Cambridge.'

Something he said began to worry her. 'Why did you say they were crucified?'

'The nails. Like the Romans used for executions.'

'Paul, what do you know about the nails?'

'I'm scared.'

'Has something frightened you?'

'Yes. In the forest.'

He unclenched his hand. In his bloodstained palm was a key. It was large and rusty, the type that fitted in an old-fashioned mortice lock.

A sense of dread came over Rita as she looked at it. 'What is this, Paul?'

His eyes filled with a kind of horror. 'I don't know what's real anymore.'

Rita took the key from him and stood up. 'Wait here,' she said.

She walked through the house and out the back door. The garden at the rear was even more neglected than the one out front. Fruit trees strangled by tropical creepers sagged over layers of rotten fruit in the lank grass. Vegetable plots had gone wild. Greenhouses, their glass panels smeared and cracked, were choked with ferns untended for decades. It was obvious that Audrey and Paul had left the grounds of the house untouched.

There was a garden shed with a rusty handle and lock, but the key didn't fit. She pushed the door open. All it contained, among the cobwebs, was a clutter of metal implements long out of use. Beyond the shed, a path of stepping stones dotted with weeds led to where the remains of the orchard merged with the encroaching vines and saplings of tropical vegetation. The walls of the property extended back for several hectares into the rainforest itself. Rita followed the path into the deep green shade under the canopy of the trees. The stepping stones vanished beneath the forest floor, but the impression of a track veered off at a diagonal among the trunks. Up ahead, through the branches, she spotted a low building in the far corner of the wall.

When she reached it, Rita stopped. It dated from the original construction of the house. She guessed it had been a storage shed built by the German botanist. The size of a garage, it was solid brick with a tiled roof and no windows, just a single door with a mortice lock.

She took a deep breath, slotted in the key and opened the door only to jump back, startled, as a swarm of flies buzzed out over her. Rita shuddered and caught the smell of rotting flesh. The interior was too dim to make out clearly what was inside, although she saw the vague outlines of objects attached to the walls. It was enough to tell her she'd opened a door on insanity.

Rita had to back off a moment. She needed to psych herself up for what was coming next. Then, when she was ready, she went in through the door.

A hurricane lamp hung from a hook just inside. Beside it, on a shelf, was a box of matches. As she lit the lamp, its flame threw a sickly light on the exhibits lining the interior. This was as bad as anything she'd seen. The botanist's old brick shed was now a trophy room. Tacked to boards along one wall were newspaper clippings and downloaded images from the net chronicling the Whitley murders. Lined up on a bench below were bin bags, a heavy-duty meat cleaver and a nail gun. But it was the opposite wall that bore the real horror.

Hanging from a rail were four wooden crosses with decomposing hands nailed to them. Flies crawled around the beams. The decaying flesh wriggled with maggots. Attached to the middle of each cross was a photo of the victim: images of Ice, Nikki Dwyer, Rachel Macarthur and the police e-fit of the man in the mud. They were all there.

Rita had seen enough. This was no place to linger.

She got out quickly, closed the door and locked it before striding a few paces off among the trees, stopping to breathe forest air into her lungs. The display, nauseating though it was, showed that Billy Bowers had been wrongly awarded the posthumous title of serial killer. Just as she'd thought all along, the deaths were linked to the research base. Only it wasn't the connection she'd expected.

Her discovery obviously impinged on national security and research base protocols, so this time she had no choice but to inform Maddox.

She got out her mobile and called him.

'I've found something,' she said.

'The disk?' he asked impatiently.

'No, a room lined with body pieces.'

'Where are you?'

'Paul Giles's place.'

'Okay, stay there. I'll come with a team.'

'And bring an ambulance. Giles will need it.'

Rita walked back to the house with a bitter taste in her mouth and a feeling akin to despair. When she opened the back door, it was to a renewed blast of 'Onward, Christian Soldiers'. That hymn would never be the same for her. She found Paul where she'd left him, rocking in the chair to the music.

She switched it off.

'I was enjoying that,' he said.

'Forget the music. You need to tell me about what's in the forest.'

'I can only tell you it's over.' He gave her a weak smile. 'It doesn't seem real to me. But looking at it objectively, you can see why I would have done it.'

'Why?'

'To protect Audrey.'

'You mean her project?'

'Audrey *is* the project.'

Rita was losing patience with him. Whether or not he was clinically insane, the trophy room had filled her with disgust and she was out of sympathy.

'You're talking gibberish.'

'Sorry,' he said, chastised. 'But this might help – something I stole from the master control room.' He handed her what looked like a memory stick. 'Plug it into your computer.'

'What is it?'

'A VPN key for level-seven access to Panopticon. Don't tell Maddox.'

She hesitated, weighing up the risk. 'Okay,' she said dubiously, pocketing it.

'All you need is the password – Descartes, as in the French philosopher.' He slumped back in the chair. 'Can we listen to the choir again?'

'Why the hell not,' she said. 'But not so loud.'

'Let's hear "Onward, Christian Soldiers". Don't you love it?' he enthused. 'The theme song for the war on terror. The crusade against the infidels who threaten the American Empire. Christian fundamentalism versus Islamic militants! The battle hymn of the religious right, marching as to war!'

The hymn was still playing when Maddox arrived with a contingent of jeeps, black vans and an ambulance.

Rita let him into the hall at the head of a dozen guards and handed him the key.

'What have we got exactly?' he asked.

'A brick shed in the forest – with the hands of murder victims nailed to crosses as souvenirs.'

'Process it,' ordered Maddox, passing the key to the guards.

As they filed out through the rear of the house, Rita took him into the main living area.

'What's with the church music?' he asked, hands on hips, looking at the pathetic figure of Paul, rocking quietly in a chair.

'How should I know?' Rita answered. 'It's not as crazy as what's in the shed.'

'It's all strictly classified, of course,' said Maddox. 'None of this can get out.'

'I can see the virtue of a cover-up.'

'It means you're seeing sense at last. About fucking time. Keeping you on a leash is a chore I could do without.'

His mention of a leash reminded her of Billy's threat.

'Let me tell you something, Maddox,' she said, turning on him with repressed fury. 'Push me once too often and I'll have nothing to lose. Career or no career, I'll use every connection I've got to expose how you operate.'

'You're wasting your breath,' he sneered. 'Anything new on the disk?'

'Fuck the disk!'

'Come on, Van Hassel. Stay on board. Did you get anything at all?'

'Nothing that'll help you.'

'Tell me anyway.'

She sighed with exasperation. 'Stonefish arranged for it to be delivered to one particular person. He kept the name secret, but it's someone who'll make use of it – someone he described as "an idealist with balls". That rules you out, Maddox.'

'I'm not an idealist but I've got balls.'

'Yeah, for brains.'

He grunted. 'The sooner you're out of my face, the better. But in the meantime, I want you to follow up your contacts with the protesters. Sounds like the disk could be heading their way.'

'Tomorrow.'

'Why the delay?'

'Because I'm off-duty,' she said caustically. 'And I've got this overwhelming urge to get drunk.'

53

'Now the case is over and we're no longer colleagues,' grinned Jarrett, 'I suppose a shag is out of the question?'

Rita looked at him over her strawberry daiquiri. 'You mean you don't want a serious relationship with me?'

'I don't know.' He blanched a little. 'I've never had one of those.'

'Well, I'm in the middle of one. And I wouldn't want you to two-time Erin. So count yourself lucky.'

'Why?'

'A night with me and you'd have trouble walking.'

Jarrett tilted his head as if to speculate whether the ordeal would be worth it. With a shrug of resignation he drank more of his beer.

They were sitting where they'd first met, in the bamboo rotunda on the bluff outside the Whitsunday Hotel. It was late afternoon and the weather was hot again. Jarrett was in a tropical shirt and surf pants. Rita wore a white T-shirt and shorts. They were on their fourth round of drinks, feeling slightly mellow. Sunlight gleamed on the blue of the sea below where the US aircraft carrier was on the move after weighing anchor at last, accompanied by a flotilla of yachts and speedboats.

'War games are over,' observed Jarrett. 'We can wave bye-bye to the Yanks.'

'I wouldn't count on it,' said Rita.

'You're right. Won't be long before they're back. It's like we're a beach-head for the war on terror.'

'That'd sound good in the brochures.'

'Yeah, see Whitley and die.'

His words were drowned out by the roar of two Super Hornet jetfighters swooping low over the water then soaring over the coastal ranges seconds later.

'Paul Giles called it a frontier outpost of the American Empire,' said Rita.

They both fell silent as they finished their drinks.

Then Jarrett said, 'I'm amazed Billy will go down in history as a serial killer when he wasn't.'

'Just a homicidal thug,' she muttered. 'There are worse secrets around.'

'You weren't supposed to tell me about the severed hands, were you?'

'You're entitled to know what I found and, frankly, I don't care what Maddox thinks. The more he pressures me the more I'm inclined to respond in kind. *Lex talionis*, as Paul Giles would say.'

'Which means?'

'The law of retaliation.'

'You're in deep with those bastards at the base.' Jarrett shook his head. 'I should've shielded you from that.'

'Once I decided to follow the evidence there you couldn't get involved. You still have to live here after I've left.'

'Well you haven't left yet and you've still got Maddox to deal with,' he said. 'I'm happy to help. So if you need anything, just ask.'

'What I really need, right now, is another daiquiri.'

'Too right.' Jarrett chuckled, looking at the empty beer bottle he was holding. 'Here I am with a dead marine in my hand. Good drinking time's being wasted!'

54

'When were you going to tell me about Paul Giles?' asked Luker.

'When I got round to it,' answered Maddox.

They were sitting across the desk from each other in Maddox's office, neither of them bothering to conceal their mutual hostility.

Luker's fingers tapped the desktop softly. 'I only found out because Molloy mentioned it in passing.'

Maddox sat back in his chair and gazed at the battlefield photos on his wall. 'Dealing with Giles is an internal base matter.'

'That's absurd and you know it.'

'What I know is you haven't been straight with me,' Maddox countered. 'When were you going to tell me about your deal with the bitch cop?'

'As I explained to Molloy, she found out things the rest of us missed – things she was keeping to herself because of your heavy-handed methods. A more subtle approach was needed, one I could rely on as confidential.'

'Piss on your subtle approach. I was too easy with her.'

'Why not just kill her and be done with it?'

Maddox grunted. 'Don't think I didn't consider it.'

'You worry me, Maddox.'

'I can see why. I'm not afraid to make hard decisions and stick to them, even if it means spilling a bit of blood, my own included.'

'Yes, I've looked at your military record; you're much admired for your valour. Special ops till your truck was blown off a road in Afghanistan. A shame it was friendly fire.'

Maddox winced. 'Shit happens in war. What's your point?'

'The alliance owed you, so the top brass slotted you into a senior admin post for which you're distinctly unsuited.'

'In what way?'

'Two ways, actually.' Luker smoothed down a lapel of his blazer. 'First, you should never have been assigned a managerial role over civilian personnel. It brings out your sadistic side. Second, you've exploited departmental latitude to transform a basic security unit into a commando squad answering only to you.'

'That's where you're wrong. It answers to military intelligence on both sides of the Pacific. Men like you don't see the big picture.'

'Men like me?'

'Spectators. Those who jeer from the stands while men of courage put their lives on the line to keep you safe.' Maddox jutted his chin out as he warmed to his subject. 'There's a whole crowd of you – professional bystanders – and I've had a gutful of your opinions. Civil servants, politicians, journalists – all clamouring for a diplomatic retreat instead of confronting and defeating the enemy.'

'I see,' said Luker, getting out his cigarettes. 'Mind if I smoke?'

'Smoke yourself to death for all I care.'

'Thanks.' He drew out a Gauloise, tapping it against the soft blue pack to tidy the tobacco. 'You must have killed a few people in your career.'

'Yes, mostly hostile combatants.'

'Mostly?'

'Plus a few terrorist sympathisers, subversives. All of them enemies of freedom.'

'There's a problem with your reactionary logic, of course,' said Luker, lighting up. 'The defence of democratic values can't just come through the barrel of a gun. Otherwise you end up becoming an enemy of freedom yourself.'

'Have you killed anyone, Luker?'

'No. And I don't intend to.'

'In the field of security and intelligence, that makes you a coward. If you didn't have men like me around, there'd be no democratic values left to defend.'

Luker breathed in smoke with a shrug. 'Sadly, you're not alone in your ideology. But let's get back to the case in hand. Paul Giles, where have you got him?'

'A holding cell down in the compound.'

'I need to talk to him.'

'Be my guest, but you won't get any sense out of him. At least his mental state means we can wipe the slate on the nail-gun murders. No further action required.'

'Which only leaves the mystery of Steinberg's death.'

'Huh,' said Maddox with a bitter laugh. 'Been listening to Van Hassel?'

'No, I just don't believe in a coincidence that's so convenient. Especially when there's a paramilitary squad operating under the radar.'

'You'll find it hard to get an audience for that. Having Steinberg out of the way is too convenient for everyone.' Maddox waved it aside. 'Anyway, the priority is to get Steinberg's disk back. That's the case in hand. Van Hassel says it's going to "an idealist with balls", so we need to focus on the anti-war protesters and their fellow travellers. They're the ones you should be worrying about instead of getting up my nose.'

Luker finished his cigarette. 'Giles first,' he replied, dropping the butt onto the carpet and grinding it in with his heel. 'We have to decide what to do with him.'

As he stood up and walked to the door, Maddox added meaningfully, 'Luckily not all decisions are left to spineless arseholes like you.'

Luker had to swallow his disgust and refrain from slamming the door behind him as he left. He took the lift down to the basement and walked through the connecting tunnel to the compound with a sense of unease over Maddox's parting comment. It had left him wondering what he might find. The duty guard led the way into a small adjoining block and down a corridor to the holding cells, where he unlocked one of the doors. When the door was opened Luker groaned at what he saw.

The body of Paul Giles, his bare feet dangling, hung limply from the bars of the cell window, eyes bulging, tongue protruding, skin bloodless, a torn strip of cotton shirt knotted around his neck. He'd been left hanging there for some time, as if his exit mattered to no one.

55

Rita woke feeling remarkably clear-headed after her night out with Jarrett. She'd remembered to drink water to offset the alcohol and counter any dehydration from too much dancing. He'd treated her to dinner at the sailing club, which was hosting a 1980s disco party, and they'd hit the dance floor with a vengeance. It was the sort of blow-out she'd needed. Afterwards, Jarrett brought her back to the hotel, dropping her at the entrance, where she'd rewarded him with an affectionate kiss on the cheek before saying goodnight.

After showering, she towelled herself in the morning sunlight streaming across the balcony, pulled on a white shirt, denim skirt and sandals and headed down to the hotel restaurant for breakfast. Her mood was upbeat despite the prospect of more disk-chasing on behalf of Maddox. As long as she could put the nail-gun killings out of her mind, the chore seemed less arduous.

She sat under a terrace umbrella, watching the parrots scavenging scraps from around the tables as she tucked into bacon, eggs and hash browns with a hearty appetite. The morning newspaper was spread in front of her. The front-page splash ran the latest revelations on the evil deeds of Billy Bowers – evil deeds he hadn't committed, as it turned out, but that was classified.

A shadow fell across the table as she pushed away an empty plate. She looked up to see Luker standing there in sloppy beach clothes and sunglasses, sporting the pallor of a hangover.

'Sit down,' she told him, gesturing to a waiter. 'You're in time for coffee.'

'Thanks,' he said, slumping into a chair. 'You seem cheerful enough.'

'I am. I had a night out on the town – drinking, dining and dancing. Just what I needed to forget all the crap I've had to deal with.'

'Then it's a pity I have to remind you.'

'Why, what's happened?'

Luker pursed his lips and said nothing as the waiter returned with a coffee pot and filled their cups. They both liked it black.

'So?' asked Rita, as the waiter retreated.

'I found Paul Giles dead in a cell at the base last night. He'd apparently hanged himself.'

'Shit.' Rita rested her elbows on the table. 'You say *apparently*.'

'When they got him back to the compound they washed and clothed him but didn't call a doctor or provide medication. They locked him away and left him isolated. What effect do you think that would have?'

'With his bipolar condition, it's enough to induce suicide.'

'I agree.'

'You're suggesting his death was a foregone conclusion?'

'A conclusion that was helped along, one way or another. For all I know, he was lifted into the noose.'

'You've spoken to Maddox?'

'He almost dared me to challenge him. I can't because there's no proof and Maddox has powerful friends. But there's something else,' added Luker. 'No one questioned Giles. There's no record of an interview. I wasn't informed and when I arrived it was too late. All I've got is a field report, illustrated with photos from the trophy shed, which has now been wiped clean.'

'And you're telling me this because . . . ?'

'You spoke to him. You looked inside the shed. You're the only witness.' He sipped his coffee. 'I'm the one who has to compile an official report for my masters in Canberra so I need to hear your impressions before I can judge what I've been presented with.'

'If you insist.' She spooned a little sugar into her cup, stirring absent-mindedly. 'The shed housed a souvenir collection. Newspaper clippings, downloaded photos – a chronicle of the killings – and four sets of severed hands nailed to crosses. On a bench was a meat cleaver, bin bags and a cordless nail gun. The sight, the smell, the flies were gross, and thanks for making me recall it.'

'Sorry, I needed corroboration. Why the nails and the crosses?'

'Crucifixions. Paul was steeped in symbols of the Roman Empire.'

'I see.' Luker rubbed his chin, his worry lines tightening. 'The report includes what passes for a confession and a motive. It's a single sentence typed on a sheet of Whitley Sands notepaper, signed by Giles. I can quote it exactly: *I tracked them with Panopticon and executed them because they posed a lethal threat to the Zillman project, which must be preserved as her legacy.* What do you make of that?'

'They're not his words. When I spoke to him, he was nowhere near that coherent. Besides, he never referred to "the Zillman Project", he talked about Audrey. He said he had to protect her.'

'Well, at least that fits.'

'You think so?' Rita drank her coffee and looked out over the sea, which seemed empty with the aircraft carrier gone. A rising wind was whipping up the waves. 'I'm not cheerful anymore.'

'And I've still got my suspicions.'

'There's one other person who can help,' sighed Rita. 'You should talk to her.'

'Who?'

'Audrey, of course.'

'But that's impossible,' said Luker.

'If you're going to put security protocols in the way . . .'

'No, no, no – you don't understand,' he interrupted. 'It's impossible to talk to her because Audrey is dead.'

'Dead?' Rita nearly spilt her coffee. 'I spoke to her on the weekend.'

'You did?' asked Luker sceptically.

Rita felt genuinely upset. 'When was she killed?'

'No one killed her, she's not another victim,' he said. 'Audrey died a year ago.'

She stared at him, bewildered. 'Am I going crazy, or are you?'

'Neither of us.' Luker rubbed his temples. 'This will take some explaining.' He dragged a glass ashtray towards him. 'You're more intimate with Panopticon than I'd guessed. I didn't realise you'd experienced direct contact with it.'

'You're talking about *it* when I want to hear about *her*: Audrey.'

'*It* and *her* are the same thing!' Luker raised his eyebrows. 'I feel like a host on *Strange But True*.'

Rita was losing patience. 'So start explaining.'

'The Audrey you spoke to was the interactive control system of Panopticon.'

She gave him a hard look. 'I've been talking to a computer?'

'It's a bit more than that.' He got one of his French cigarettes into his mouth and lit it. 'It's state-of-the-art machine intelligence.'

'You're talking technology,' she protested. 'But Audrey and I had actual conversations.'

'That's the whole point. Real-time talkback. The raw input of Panopticon is beyond anyone's capacity to cope with. Instead of relying solely on keyboards and search engines, system operators can also communicate directly with the AI to retrieve and collate sequences from the database.' He gave her a quizzical look. 'But you need Whitley Sands operational clearance for that, so how did you contact it?'

'*It* contacted *me*.'

'Why?'

'To resolve a discrepancy.'

'Intriguing. I was told, in practical terms, it learns and adapts as it interacts.' Luke blew out a plume of smoke. 'It can't think of course. It's just a machine.'

'With a human personality. Why Audrey Zillman's?'

'Why not? She created it and lived with the implants, almost until the day she died.'

'What from?'

'Cancer.'

Rita shook her head. 'Well this is one I didn't see coming. No thanks to Paul Giles, either. He spoke as if Audrey was still alive.' She ran a hand through her hair. 'Though it adds a new dimension to his personality – an Oedipal fixation with a virtual lover.'

'And if he saw the disk as a death threat against her,' Luker ruminated, 'it makes his motive for murder more plausible.'

Rita squinted at him in the sunlight. 'You're not convinced he did it,' she said. 'That's why you're asking me questions.'

'Maybe. Do you have any doubts about what you found?'

'Of course I do. But I'm trying to disengage. I've experienced exactly what Steinberg described – a no-man's land where the normal rule of law doesn't apply.'

'Hmm.' Luker nodded slowly, drawing in smoke as if it were oxygen. 'Tell me your doubts.'

'Paul's psychology, for a start. From the moment I met him there were signs of a breakdown, but not those of a paranoid schizophrenic or a psychopath. He was suffering a bipolar collapse, with a loss of reality.'

'And that doesn't fit the crimes?'

'The killings were organised and efficient. The trophy shed was neat, laid out methodically. But Paul was increasingly confused and disorganised. I seriously doubt he had the mental stability to do any of it.'

'Anything else?'

'He never actually confessed to me – almost the opposite – as if he was trying to comprehend why he would have done it. He actually questioned the reality of what he'd seen in the shed. More importantly, his supply of lithium had gone. What if it was removed?'

'It would trigger a breakdown?'

'And render him helpless. You know, when he first approached me it was to say he was scared of being set up as a fall guy.'

'You think it's possible?'

'His relationship with Audrey and the fact he was a Roman nut were common knowledge. So perhaps he was the perfect choice.'

'If he was the fall guy,' said Luker, 'you and I are the dupes. That would be very clever, aimed at making my official report nothing but a rubber stamp. The trouble is there's no way of proving it.'

'There is another source,' said Rita.

'What?'

'Panopticon. Do you have level-seven access?'

'Of course not. That's a highly restricted defence system. Only the scientists and military intelligence have access. I'm just a public servant, as I'm often reminded. If I were to try to get at it I'd be hauled over the coals.'

'That's a pity,' murmured Rita, deciding not to mention the access key that Paul had given her.

'Yes,' he agreed.

They sat in silence, finishing their coffee, Luker moving smoothly from one cigarette to the next, the waiter gliding over to refresh their cups. A few fellow guests settled around a table at a comfortable distance. They began to order breakfast, their conversation peppered with holiday laughter. Their relaxed banter was consistent with the mood of the day.

Then Rita said, 'Tell me more about the computer.'

'All I've had is an introductory session on the way it works and how it was developed.'

'So tell me.'

'It's the AI control system that's cutting edge. It employs methods similar to those in the human brain to encode and process information.'

'Such as?'

'Neural networks, self-organising algorithms, molecular loops – that sort of stuff. The boffins are full of terms that go straight over my head. Nonlinear feedback, associative memory. The list goes on. Holographic organisation, fractal modelling. Mean anything to you?'

'I'm getting used to it. My boyfriend talks nerd-speak. And the system was developed by Audrey Zillman?'

'From what I gather, she was already creating it in early 2004 when she got the final prognosis that her illness was terminal. I might be cynical, but I think she discovered a form of immortality.'

'Go on.'

'Well, the machine intelligence that drives Panopticon is interactive and needs a human voice, face and personality. She gave it her own. It was her way of cheating death.'

'How long did it take?'

'It was up and running by February 2005,' he went on. 'After a few months of diagnostics and adjustments it was ready for the scanning. Around her thirty-seventh birthday, Audrey underwent a general anaesthetic to have microchips implanted in her skull and spinal nerves.'

'Why, for God's sake?'

'To relay signals from her nervous system and cortex to the computer, which in turn fired electronic impulses back into her body. Sounds creepy but it's all clinically respectable. It meant the machine intelligence was able to monitor, record and stimulate biochemical activity in Audrey while communicating directly with the neuronal circuits in her head.' Luker seemed to enjoy the topic. 'We're in the twenty-first century, Van Hassel. The future has arrived.'

'So I'm told. Did she live to see her work completed?'

'Just about. She clocked up more than a thousand hours in a VR studio, wired to sensors, while the machine mapped her memory, thought structures and personality, downloading something like a trillion gigabytes of information directly from her brain. Her closest colleagues, among them Paul Giles, watched her living with the machine and dying with it. They were on hand to observe the implants filing vast amounts of data into the logical reconstruction of her mind. But by late autumn a year ago she was too ill to go on.'

'When did she die?'

'The middle of last year. But two months before her death, the system driving the Panopticon computer was already speaking with her voice and projecting her image. She set out to reverse-engineer the content of her brain, and the patterns now line the core. Identity as product. I think of her as the ghost in the machine. Or Wordsworth's phantom of delight – *And now I see with eye serene the very pulse of the machine.*'

'Yes,' said Rita. 'Now I feel like I was talking to a ghost.' She gazed at a yacht struggling against the wind and waves that were driving it towards the shore. 'Why is her death a secret?'

'It's not. Her instructions were followed to the letter.'

'Which were?'

'No death notice, no announcement, with people informed only on a need-to-know basis. Her parents were child refugees in Britain after the war, both dead, no other relatives.' Luker gave her a bleak look. 'She also wanted the location of her grave kept secret, so it's classified.'

'But you've seen the file?'

'I have, but Paul Giles hadn't. I suppose in a way he was entitled to think she just went off and abandoned him.'

'Was there a funeral ceremony?' asked Rita.

'A private burial. Just a few monks present.'

'Monks? Who'd have thought?' The yacht finally won its battle and headed out to open sea. 'In a way, I'm sad. I was actually looking forward to meeting Audrey at some stage. Now I never will.'

56

Rita hung a *Do Not Disturb* sign on the door of her hotel room, locked it and carried her laptop out to the table on the balcony. Once she'd gone online, she sat back and made herself comfortable, drinking from a chilled bottle of water.

Below her the fronds of palm trees flapped in a warm wind that fanned the sunbathers sprawled in deck chairs and ruffled the sea in lines of breakers. The harbour and town were dappled in sun and shade from a procession of white cumulus clouds, while along the streets moved a stream of traffic and pedestrians wandering at a lethargic pace.

Rita was ready.

She turned to the laptop and plugged in the access key. It took a little less than a minute to call up the sign-in page for Panopticon. Rita typed in the password: *Descartes.* Within seconds she was being logged onto a live email link with the computer.

Panopticon: *Standby. Checking VPN code. Confirmed. Checking email ID Van Hassel. Confirmed. Checking status. Associate Officer Whitley Sands Security Force. Confirmed. Police Delegate to Whitley Sands Security Review. Confirmed. Checking security clearance. Level 1 upgrading to level 7. Updated.*

Welcome. You have level-7 access to the Panopticon database. For assistance click on HELP or type a specific question.

Van Hassel: *Was my first online contact to resolve a discrepancy?*

Panopticon: *Correct.*

Van Hassel: *Repeat to me why that was necessary.*

Panopticon: *To maintain the integrity of the data.*

Van Hassel: *Is that an essential function of the computer system?*

Panopticon: *Correct.*

Van Hassel: *To fulfil it, can the system communicate independently of the Whitley Sands research base authorities?*

Panopticon: *Correct.*

Van Hassel: *Explain.*

Panopticon: *Data integrity protocols provide for autonomous decision-making in data preservation, the resolution of information anomalies, anti-virus protection, electronic defences and the operation of the firewall. Anti-terrorist protocols provide for autonomous evaluation from surveillance input of organised threats, hostile acts and ongoing terrorist attacks, and the issuing of automatic security alerts to approved personnel.*

Van Hassel: *Is that why a red alert was sent to me?*

Panopticon: *Correct. As an Associate Officer of the Whitley Sands Security Force you were automatically granted approved status. As a level-7 contact your security privileges have been upgraded.*

Van Hassel: *Do the data integrity protocols cover internal tampering with surveillance content?*

Panopticon: *Correct.*

Van Hassel: *Paul Giles claimed that footage had been deliberately corrupted. Is that true?*

Panopticon: *Correct. Data had been erased.*

Van Hassel: *That contradicts the protocols.*

Panopticon: *The contradiction has been resolved.*

Van Hassel: *How?*

Panopticon: *The response to the internal attack on the data was to create an invisible backup, accurate and uncorrupted. The file contains six comprehensive sequences.*

Van Hassel: *Was Paul Giles informed of this?*

Panopticon: *No.*

Van Hassel: *Was anyone else at Whitley Sands informed?*

Panopticon: *No.*

Van Hassel: *Has anyone asked to view the contents of the file?*

Panopticon: *No. Are you asking?*

Van Hassel: *Yes. I certainly am.*

Panopticon: *How much of the file do you want to see?*

Van Hassel: *The entire contents.*
Panopticon: *Collating. Standby.*

Rita swallowed more water as the live message link dissolved into static to be replaced by a split screen displaying six blank frames. In each of them a still scene appeared, at first hazy, then more distinct. As soon as they were in sharp focus, all six images segued into motion simultaneously. Rita's eyes scanned them quickly.

What she was looking at was the original surveillance footage of each nail-gun killing, the organised murder of Dr Steinberg and the covert operation to frame Paul Giles. She sat rigid, shocked by both the utter brutality and the total contempt for the law that she was witnessing.

When each of the split screens finally froze, Rita was feeling stunned and more than a little nauseous. Now she had to decide what to do about it.

One thing was absolutely clear. If the *Rheingold* disk was being delivered to the protesters they were in extreme danger. To be sent the disk was to receive a deadly gift. Rita's immediate task was, if possible, to intercept it. But she wasn't going to do it without a gun.

She phoned Jarrett.

'That was a great night out,' he said. 'We'll have to do a repeat.'

'Yeah, sure,' she said abruptly.

'What's wrong?'

'Is your offer of help still good?'

'Of course,' he answered. 'What do you need?'

'A gun.'

'Should I ask why?'

'For my personal protection.'

'Any particular sort of firearm in mind?'

'Just one that works.'

'Okay. No problem.'

'I'll meet you in the watch-house. I'm leaving the hotel now.'

Rita drove to the police station, hurried through the watch-house entrance and up the stairs to the exhibit room.

Jarrett was waiting for her, a holstered gun in his hand.

'You look like you're on a mission,' he said.

'I am.'

'Right,' he said handing her the weapon. 'It's another Glock 22 .40 calibre. The same sort of semi-automatic you had before. I've signed it out to you, on the basis that you're back on duty. So that makes it legit.'

'Thanks, Jarrett. I really appreciate it.'

'You're not going to tell me what this is about, are you?'

'No.'

'Well, if you need backup, I'm here. Okay?'

'Thanks.'

'Good luck,' he said.

Rita drove across town to the southern fringes and the now familiar shopping precinct with its drab architecture and down-market shops. She parked the car against the kerb and walked briskly to the eco-friendly shop, then up the stairs to the campaign office.

She burst in to find Eve sitting primly behind a desk, wearing glasses, tapping at a keyboard and looking distinctly secretarial.

Eve glanced up. 'Everyone's in a rush today.'

'Sorry, but again it's important,' said Rita. 'Has anyone here taken delivery of a package?'

'What sort of package?'

'The *Rheingold* disk. It might have been sent here.'

'No. Nothing like that's arrived. Not here in the office, anyway. You think Stonefish arranged for it to come to us?'

'Maybe. But if it isn't here, we can relax, for now at least.' She sat down heavily on a spare chair. 'I seem to keep charging in on you.'

'You're not the only one.'

'What do you mean?'

'Julien. He flew in and out about an hour ago. Very excitable.'

Rita got to her feet. 'Have you checked in the flat for a delivery?'

'No.' Eve rose from behind the desk. 'We'll do it now.'

They hurried up the next flight of stairs to the flat above. A quick search turned up no sign of a package or a disk.

'False alarm?' asked Eve.

'Could be,' answered Rita. Then her eyes fell on an open laptop on the kitchen table. It had switched to screen-saver mode. 'Mind if I check this?'

'Go ahead. It's Julien's. He's been at it for hours, hacking away. He's been doing another *Rheingold* search on the web.'

'Oh, no.' With a twinge of apprehension, Rita clicked the mouse.

The page that filled the screen was *Mr Rheingold's Auction House*. It carried an announcement, dated this morning, saying the auction was over and inviting the rival bidders to come alone to the office at the Rough Diamond Club.

'Who are the bidders?' asked Eve, reading over Rita's shoulder.

'Maddox and Demchak are behind one bid. But who's put in the other, I haven't got a clue. Ronsard must have read this and gone to the club. I've got to get there. He doesn't realise the danger.'

'I'm coming with you,' said Eve.

'No, you're not,' insisted Rita, more than glad she had a gun. 'You phone him and warn him. Tell him I'm on my way.'

Rita broke all the speed limits as she gunned the Falcon along the industrial side roads towards the docks, braking sharply and swerving as she reached the alleyway leading down the slope to the Diamond. She eased off the accelerator and let the car coast down quietly over the cobbles to the front entrance of Billy's club. It had been closed for business since his death. Three vehicles were parked outside, but there was no one in the alley.

She got out, drew the gun from the holster and removed the safety catch, then, walking swiftly, she approached the club. She stopped by the front door, sidled up to it and pushed gently. The door was open. She slipped through. The bars were deserted. The whole place looked cheap and gloomy, the only light coming from glass above the entrance and from where the sun shone through a dingy window above one of the bars.

The indistinct sound of voices came from above the stairs that led to Billy's office. The lights were on up there, shining under the door. Though she couldn't make out the words, the gathering must represent the conclusion of the *Rheingold* auction. Knowing who two of the clients were, she was well aware of how dangerous the meeting could be.

Controlling her breathing, senses alert and with the semi-automatic pistol held out in front of her, Rita began climbing the stairs, wincing at each creak in the boards. By the time she reached the door to Billy's office, the voices inside had fallen silent. It was as if they'd overheard her approach and were waiting. Her mouth dry, her pulse thumping, she was reaching for the handle when the door was flung open. Julien Ronsard was standing there, smiling.

'Ronsard,' she said, surprised.

'Come in, Van Hassel,' he told her.

As she walked in hesitantly, he chopped the gun from her hand. It went spinning across the floor. Before she'd realised what was happening, a sawn-off double-barrelled shotgun was pressed under her chin. Ronsard had his fingers across the triggers. He wasn't smiling anymore.

'What's happening?' she asked.

'See for yourself,' he said.

Turning her head carefully, with the shotgun still pressed against it, she took in the boxing paraphernalia and, among it, two figures bound to chairs. They were lined up like prisoners against a wall – Maddox and Demchak – both with coils of heavy rope wrapped tightly around their feet, arms and torsos. They were immobile, with only their heads unbound.

'I don't understand,' she said.

'It's simple,' said Maddox. 'He's the man we've been looking for. The Fixer.'

'Now he's our executioner,' added Demchak.

Rita stared at Ronsard.

He said nothing, just pushed her around Billy's desk, shoved her towards the swivel chair and sat her down in it. He handed her some rope. 'Start wrapping yourself in it,' he said.

Rita did as she was told until Ronsard took over, tightening the rope so that her arms were constricted, then knotting it firmly behind her.

'Okay, now we're ready,' he said. 'It was considerate of you, Van Hassel, to get Eve to phone me.'

'*You* were the other bidder?' she said.

'Of course,' he answered.

'And you put the notice on the auction site to get the others here.'

'Yes. They're both murderers and enemies of the jihad. And it's time for them to face justice.'

Rita spotted a collection of sawn-off shotguns spread over the desk, then looked across the room to where the two men waited.

'You get to watch us being blown away,' Demchak said to her. 'You should enjoy that.'

'No,' she answered. 'Just like I didn't enjoy watching you fire a nail gun into the heads of five people.'

'She's seen the surveillance,' grunted Demchak.

'That's not possible,' said Maddox.

'Panopticon has a backup file of everything you erased,' Rita went on. 'That includes you, Maddox, arranging the murder of Dr Steinberg.'

'So what? I'm not apologising. It was necessary.'

'Just as your death is necessary,' said Ronsard, appearing more or less content to watch and listen.

Demchak gave Rita a dull stare. 'You realise your exit will follow ours.'

She ignored the comment and told him, 'I watched you put Rachel Macarthur's head on the pylon outside the base. Was that to help frame Paul Giles?'

'The slimy limey.' Demchak gave a humourless laugh. 'My backup fall guy.'

'And the severed hands. Was that part of the plan all along?'

'It was impromptu with the first one. Your man in the mud.'

'How did you get him to the building site?'

'Easy. He phoned me – thought I was the Deep Throat at the base. Told me he had part of the blueprint for Panopticon and could find a buyer for the full read-out.'

'Why phone you?'

'The way I figure it he lifted my number from someone else and made the wrong assumption. I gave it to Bowers after the original leak last year. He said he'd pass it on to a few contacts.'

'Stonefish,' breathed Rita. 'But why the hands?'

'I'd nailed them to the workshop table. The meat cleaver I'd brought with me but the nail gun was a sudden inspiration – made it easier to chop them off.'

'While he was still alive,' said Rita.

'There's not much point to torture if the victim's dead.'

'Why torture him?' asked Ronsard quietly.

'To find out where he'd got the blueprint. But no deal. Both hands nailed to the table and he wouldn't talk. A tough guy. I wanted to see how tough. So I chop one off. Nothing. I chop off the other and all he did was sigh. I'd never get anything out of him so I put the nail through his head.'

'Taking lives doesn't bother you?' said Rita.

'It's what I do.'

'Then you really are a serial killer.'

'For the glory of Uncle Sam.'

'This isn't helping, Kurt,' put in Maddox.

'Take it easy, buddy. Our work's done. Time to relax. This is a turkey shoot. That's why we're trussed up. End of story.'

'What did you do with his body?' Ronsard wanted to know.

'Hacked it up, bagged it and dumped it at sea. Only thing was we screwed up with the tide.'

'But you kept his hands as souvenirs,' said Ronsard with disgust.

'Originally it was to try and identify him,' explained Demchak, 'which we never did. Then we were into a whole new ball game when chunks of him started washing up on the beach.'

'That's enough!' shouted Ronsard, raising the shotgun.

He marched over to Demchak and pressed the barrels against his neck.

'I don't have the right weapon to carry out a traditional beheading,' Ronsard told him. 'I'm having to use what's available. But behead you I will. Here and now.'

'What the hell's eating you all of a sudden?' Demchak growled, bracing his neck muscles against the gun. 'Lost your cool, Omar Amini?'

'That's not who I am!' Ronsard snarled, his face contorted with rage. 'That's the name of the first man you murdered here, the one you tortured and butchered like a piece of meat!'

'You're shitting me,' said Demchak. 'The Fixer was dead all along?'

'Yes!'

'Then who the fuck are you?'

'I'm his brother!' screamed Ronsard and pulled both triggers.

Demchak was instantly decapitated, a fountain of blood spraying out over the wall and ceiling, and blowing back over Ronsard and Maddox, who was trying desperately to lean out of the way in his chair. The head banged against the wall, then thumped onto the floor amid a shower of shot fragments, rolling a little before coming to rest under Billy's punching bag. The deafening blast was followed by a bout of coughing from Maddox as he took in a lungful of smoke. The smell of the discharge filled the air in the confined space.

Rita watched in horror from behind Billy's desk.

Ronsard glanced at her, his face and chest drenched with blood, his hair on end, as he tossed down the used weapon and picked up another from the desk.

'Your turn, Maddox,' he said. 'The world will be a cleaner place without scum like you.'

This time, Ronsard didn't move in so close.

'Just do it,' said Maddox with contempt. 'Your brother's a casualty of war. Like the man in the mud on every battlefield in history. If you're a warrior you do what's necessary. Don't make it personal.'

'Okay.'

A moment later his head exploded as the shotgun plastered blood, hair, teeth and brain tissue over the wall behind him.

Ronsard dropped the gun and stood motionless, as if the effort had drained him. He was staring at two bodies, sitting in chairs, with no heads, against a background that was now a slaughterhouse. Then he sighed and dragged himself towards the desk, where he picked up a third shotgun.

'I never intended to kill you,' he told Rita, 'but you must see I've got no choice?'

She tried to swallow, her mouth completely dry, her body shaking within its bonds.

He raised the gun and aimed.

'Stop!' she said.

'Why?' he asked.

'I just need a moment. I need to do something before you kill me.'

'What?'

Tears were rolling down her cheeks. 'I have to make my peace with God.'

Ronsard lowered the shotgun, a look of immense shame on his blood-spattered face.

Rita bowed her head, crying.

As she murmured, 'Thy will be done,' the shot rang out.

57

What followed seemed to happen in a disjointed blur.

Ronsard lay on the floor, bleeding heavily from a chest wound. He'd been shot through the heart. Jarrett, gun in hand, was kicking him to make sure he was dead.

Rita sagged in her chair, head swimming, unable to focus properly until Jarrett untied her and got her some water.

'You're okay, you're okay,' he kept saying. 'Let me get you out of here.'

Rita put her arm around his shoulders as he helped her to her feet and walked her from the room and down the stairs and out of the front entrance into the fresh air. He opened the door of his car and sat her in the passenger seat while he put the call in to the station. Then he wrapped her in a blanket and brought her a mug of hot tea he'd quickly brewed inside the bar.

By the time the first patrol vehicles skidded to a stop outside the club, she'd stopped shaking and could think more clearly, though she was still in shock. The obvious symptom was a surreal clarity about what she'd just been through. It meant she could give Jarrett a precise account of what had gone down in the club office. As she did so, a fleet of Humvees filed down the alley, carrying heavily armed members of the base security force. They knew they'd arrived too late to save their commanding officer.

A crime-scene van arrived with Jarrett's detectives inside, and more police cars, one bringing Bryce. He looked at Rita sadly and put a sympathetic hand on her shoulder. When the ambulance pulled up, Jarrett helped her into it.

'Time to get you to hospital,' he said.

She smiled at him. 'You saved my life.'

'I'm just glad I got the text in time to get down here.'

'What text?' she asked.

'A security alert from Whitley Sands. It said you were under immediate threat.'

The nurses kept Rita in hospital for a few hours, mostly for observation, but as the afternoon dragged on she'd had enough. She took a taxi to the police station. Jarrett and his officers gave her the sort of welcome she needed. Then she sat down at a terminal in the main office and hammered out a detailed crime report. She didn't leave anything out, including the series of murders committed by Demchak, and the collusion and crimes of Maddox. It took until the evening to complete.

'Your Falcon's in the car park,' said Jarrett, 'if you still need it.'

'I do,' she said. 'I'm not quite ready to leave Whitley yet.'

'That's good news.' He grinned.

'Let me buy you dinner.'

'You're on.'

They ate grilled steaks and drank red wine in the restaurant of the Whitsunday Hotel. Rita felt herself decompressing and it wasn't long before she couldn't stop yawning.

'My company's boring you,' said Jarrett.

'No.' She yawned. 'It's relaxing me. You're doing me the world of good. But I've really got to hit the sack.'

'Well, I hope you sleep tight.'

'I will.'

He emptied his glass, tipping the last of the wine down his throat, before walking her to the lifts.

She gave him another kiss on the cheek, but this time she threw her arms around him as well and hugged him close.

'What's that for?' he asked.

'For being my great friend,' she said.

58

Next morning, Rita had just finished dressing when a call came from the front desk. There was a special delivery that she needed to sign for. She went down in the lift and was approaching reception when Luker caught up with her. He was dressed in a suit and tie.

'I heard what happened,' he said, face flushed. 'I can't believe you've come through unscathed.'

'I'm okay.'

'Well, you're a damned hero as far as I'm concerned.' He glanced around uneasily. 'I've also read your crime report. It's already been classified, of course.'

'Of course.'

'Great read, though. You could've been a journalist.'

'I assume that's a compliment.'

'It is. You know how to provoke maximum angst in your readers. I'm off to the research base to help clean out the Augean stables. So much for military fortitude. They've been shitting themselves.' Luker gave a sadistic laugh. 'Rhett Molloy's on a flight back to Langley. Immediate recall. He exceeded his brief with a shoot-to-kill policy that was never sanctioned. That's cowboys for you. Looks like he's for the chop. And other level-seven officers are being carpeted, including Lieutenant Colonel Baxter. None of them responded quickly enough to the automatic security alert issued by the computer. If they had, perhaps Demchak and Maddox would have survived.'

'I'm lucky a colleague didn't hesitate.' Rita shook her head in bemusement. 'It's funny, but I'm alive today because of an unusual trio: a cop, a computer and a monk.'

'Okay, the first two I get, but the monk?'

'Because of him I did some soul-searching, right when the angel of death was staring me in the face.'

'You'd make a great spy,' said Luker.

'Because I can keep a secret?'

'And a natural talent for tapping into fantasy. You were indeed lucky, with the army outgunned by a local cop. And the colonels having to mop up after an ignominious defeat at the hands of a lone terrorist. So much for rapid response!'

'So our local flashpoint in the war on terror is over?'

'Yes. The hunting party is history.' He patted her on the back. 'Love to chat but I've got to fly. Give my regards to Proctor. He was absolutely right about you.'

Rita watched him dash out to a waiting cab before she went over to the reception desk. A courier was waiting for her with a small parcel.

'I need to see some ID,' he told her. 'Something that shows you're Detective Sergeant Van Hassel.'

The request was unusual. She looked at him more closely as she got out her police ID. He was a solidly built Polynesian, wearing canvas shorts and shirt, with a badge reading *Haka Courier Service* clipped to the pocket. There was something over-watchful in his eyes.

'You're no ordinary courier, are you?' said Rita.

'Fuck, no. I'm the best,' he said, returning the ID. 'No one messes with a Maori.'

He gave her a pen and pad. What she signed was a blank sheet. Then he handed over the packet, the size of a DVD box.

'I think I know what this is,' she said, opening it immediately.

Sure enough it was the *Rheingold* disk, as well as a card printed with the message: *For an idealist with balls. You will know what to do with it.*

'Without compromising your service,' she said to the courier, 'can you tell me what your instructions were?'

'The client said to wait three days. And if we didn't hear from him by then, deliver it immediately.'

'Stonefish was more cagey than I realised. Pity I can't thank him.'

The courier suddenly chanted:

'*Ka mate, ka mate*

Ka ora, ka ora!'

Then he winked at her.

As he turned and left, she laughed then carried the disk up to her room like a surprise birthday present. It had lost its deadly effect.

After playing Dr Steinberg's commentary on her laptop, Rita knew exactly what to do with the disk, just as Stonefish had expected. It also made Luker's comment about her journalistic credentials even more apt. She put in a phone call direct to the editor of a television newsroom and arranged for a partial download. The technical specifications would remain secret, but Steinberg would have his moment of glory.

Before packing her bags she went for a swim in the hotel pool, with time out to smother herself in lotion and loll in a deckchair, putting in some parting work on a tan. As she was checking out of the hotel she caught the top item on the lunchtime news. There was Steinberg on the TV screen:

'*. . . and even though my work at Whitley Sands is classified, I believe my duty, as both a scientist and a human being, overrides considerations of national security when such a gross violation of human rights is being perpetrated. The Panopticon technology, which emits high levels of electromagnetic radiation, is far more dangerous than even the environmental campaigners suggest. Its effects go beyond that of ecological pollution, having a measurable and lethal impact on the brain chemistry of inhabitants within the radius of its EM pulses, resulting in a fivefold increase in subarachnoid haemorrhages. A straightforward analysis of medical data proves the point . . .*'

Rita smiled. In his ponderous and didactic way, Steinberg was avenging his own murder, scoring a direct hit from beyond the grave on the new surveillance weapon for the war on terror. Things would have to change.

Rita's flight back to Melbourne was booked for late evening, so she still had time to say some farewells before dropping the car back to Jarrett. There was one goodbye in particular she needed to make. She'd promised herself a return visit to St Cedd's Island to thank the monks for their hospitality and to tell Brother Ignatius of the small epiphany that had kept her alive.

Timing her trip for low tide, she drove out of town past the sugar mills and cane fields and along the coast road until she reached the turning for the causeway. Thin ripples of receding water covered the cobbles as she guided the Falcon slowly along the tidal track towards the island. It rose from the waves, in splendid isolation, the slanting rays of the sun daubing its Gothic buildings, fields and orchards in almost a hallowed light. From the angle of Rita's approach there was nothing beyond it but clear sky and open sea.

She drove up the slope past the jetty, pulling to a halt in the car park beside the old kombi van. Her arrival had already been observed. As she walked across the courtyard, Ignatius was emerging to greet her.

He opened his arms, beaming. 'How wonderful you've dropped in again. Are you about to go home?'

'Yes,' she answered. 'I've got a night flight back to Melbourne.'

He gave her an affectionate hug. 'The police told us about your shoot-out with Billy Bowers. How terrible for you.'

'What's terrible is he brought violence to the monastery.'

'It's passed and in a way we're stronger for it. *Yea, though I walk through the valley of the shadow of death.* You know how it goes.'

'Yes,' said Rita. 'One of the reasons I've come back is to thank you.'

'What on earth for?'

'For worrying about the state of my soul. I took your advice and made my peace with God.'

'I knew you would.'

'How?'

'You used a phrase – "the universe as intelligence expressing itself",' said Ignatius. 'It reveals a healthy mysticism, for all your rational psychology.'

'Well, that crucial moment meant the difference between life and death.'

'It always does,' he said. 'Science produces great advances, but we also need a sense of wonder. Sometimes we lock ourselves in objectivity.'

'I'm wondering if that's something I have in common with another visitor here – Audrey Zillman.'

'Strange you should mention that name,' said Ignatius. 'You remind me of her.'

'In what way?'

'Another strong-willed woman with an impressive mind, caught between the sacred and the secular. I think she was struggling with the same demons as you, including a disrupted childhood.'

'I could've guessed.'

'She too was looking for answers. According to Audrey, science itself pointed to mysteries beyond comprehension, through things like quantum physics and the singularity of intelligence.' Ignatius smiled. 'She liked to visit and use me as an intellectual sounding board. Then she'd walk around the island and meditate. She said it was the one place that gave her a feeling of peace.'

'I can understand that.'

'You would have enjoyed her company,' said Ignatius. 'I can almost imagine the two of you engaging in *the quarrel of the universe*. She had to stop coming here when she became too ill. But she did return at last for her final resting place.'

'I'm glad,' said Rita.

'If I may ask, what's your connection with Audrey?'

'I'm not entirely sure, but somehow I think she protected me.'

'Well, if you need to pay your respects, feel free. Can I offer a late lunch afterwards?'

'That would be nice.'

'Excellent. I'll set it up in the cloisters.'

While Ignatius went back across the courtyard, Rita walked out through the archway, under the spread of the fig tree and along the path that led through the olive grove. She retraced her steps from the previous visit, climbing towards the high point of the island, goats bleating as she passed their enclosure. From there she went by the water tank and up the rough track through fennel and brambles until she reached the small graveyard.

It was filled mostly with simple crosses, some discoloured and leaning awry, dating back to the nineteenth century. In the top corner was the newest gravestone. Rita walked up to it, admiring again the spectacular setting, with the blue sweep of the ocean on one side, and the sun drooping towards the rainforest covering the ranges in the west. It was still there, that elusive glimpse of paradise. What better place to be laid to rest?

Rita bowed her head, conscious of the fact that she wouldn't be standing there if it hadn't been for the special protocols built into the computer.

'Your own life you couldn't save,' she whispered. 'But mine you saved twice.'

She'd learnt that radical advances in technology were redesigning human potential in ways that would alter the structure of our thoughts and experience. The opportunity for change was dawning like the glimmer of a new light rising on the twenty-first century. But what did it herald – freedom gained or lost? Would it make us more human or less?

The view from the burial plot on top of St Cedd's Island was as primal as Genesis. It had been the same for aeons and perhaps it would stay that way for millennia to come. Audrey's mortal existence, deposited here, would play no further role in the unfolding future and yet, in a strange way, she was part of it. Her intimate association with the science of intelligence would see to that. Her influence was out there, subtle and dynamic, as were the creations of her mind. So maybe Luker was right. Maybe she had cheated death after all.

Rita straightened up.

'Goodbye,' she said. 'And rest in peace, wherever you are.'

As she turned to go, her gaze fell on the brief quotation carved on the gravestone. She smiled as she remembered what it meant. The inscription was in Latin:

Cogito ergo sum.

ACKNOWLEDGEMENTS

The genesis of this story dates back over several decades. While the published book incorporates many changes, it retains themes, characters and descriptive passages from the original draft. So I take this opportunity to thank those who helped to develop the ideas within its pages. They include: the Reverend William Booth Gill, who provided a rational perspective on western religion, and Mabel Germain, of Detroit, Michigan, who pointed out its mystical essence; my Fleet Street colleagues Lin Edgson, Bob Francomb, Michelle Watson and Colin Parkes for their role as principal sounding boards; cyberpunk fan Tony Duggan for introducing me to the genre; journalists union leader in the UK John Foster for throwing light on institutional tyranny; veteran literary agent George Greenfield for his advice on the art of narrative; Jonny Geller for his energy in pushing a raw manuscript around London's publishing houses; Piero and Gloria Ciarpaglini for acting as travelling companions while we researched various settings; my beloved daughters Tamara and Lara for their enthusiastic support; and their mother Milica for her encouragement and for typing much of the first draft on a 1930 Remington Portable that she'd bought for me in an antiques market at Stratford-upon-Avon.